THE BARLY FIELDS

The Barly Fields

A COLLECTION OF FIVE NOVELS BY
ROBERT NATHAN

WITH AN INTRODUCTION BY
STEPHEN VINCENT BENÉT

THE LITERARY GUILD OF AMERICA, INC.

1938   NEW YORK

TO MY FATHER

STEPHEN VINCENT BENÉT

THE WORLD OF
ROBERT NATHAN

EVERY WRITER worth his salt makes a world of his own, and, in spite of the excellent adage — " Write about what you know about " — the world that he makes is not always the world directly in front of his eyes. For realism, as realism, only goes so far. Otherwise, you could assemble a novel as you assemble a Ford car — and that has been done, as well, and we know those novels. They are admirable books, full of fresh, contemporary problems and temporary life. They deal, in a clear-eyed way, with marriage and divorce, they describe the problems of the dried-fish industry in unflinching detail, they do everything in the world but interest you ten years later. It does not matter, for there are always more of them. And, meanwhile, some small work of the imagination lives forever.

Perhaps it is as good a test of Mr. Nathan's abilities as any that the five short novels collected in this omnibus-volume should show so little age. I wonder of how many contemporary novelists that might be said. It even seems a little unfair, at times. For, while novel after novel that was gripping and devastating and searched the American scene has walked with firm steps and electrically-lighted eyes, wired for sound, direct from its publisher's announcements into oblivion, Mr. Aristotle and Papa Jonas, Mrs. Heavenstreet and the dog Musket have remained very much as they were — living creatures, with foolish hearts and the breath of life. They never pretended to be more, and the life within them has remained. The streets around the Square have altered their look somewhat but the afternoon light still falls in yellow, dusty bars and Mr. Aristotle's tragedy is still a tragedy though it is played by a puppet. The great cock-fight between Bartholomew and the Malay cross is as good as ever it was and the seasons in Barly have not changed. That is something to have done — it is so that work lasts out its year and takes on another life.

It is curious to look back at the beginnings. The required project for young novelists of the Twenties was a school-and-college novel — it changes with each generation. There were a number of them by various hands — through Yale, Harvard, Princeton, Chicago and other leading American universities, the hero took his way, full of irony and pity and very much bothered by life. Among them was one called " Peter Kindred." It was not a successful book, though it had two things which distinguished it among its fellows — a grave sobriety of style and a remarkable paucity of big adjectives. But, as far as plot was concerned, it followed the accepted pattern of adolescence, college and first love. It was easy to see how the author was going to turn out.

He had been born and brought up in New York City — obviously, his next book would be a serious, realistic study of Manhattan and the younger generation. Eventually he might branch out into the other boroughs — perhaps even as far as Long Island. But it didn't happen like that. The next published book was a pastoral called " Autumn," concerned with a country schoolmaster and bearing about as much relation to the literary movements and fashions of its time as Blake's " Songs of Innocence " bore to the movements and fashions of his. There was only one thing about it. A good many other people could have written most of our second novels. But nobody but Robert Nathan could have written " Autumn " — or could write it still.

For here was a kind of writing of which there is never much in any one time — a style at once delicate, economical and unobtrusively firm, sharp enough to cut but without rancor, and clear as water or air. And with it went an airy mockery, and the imagination of the heart. With it also went a sensitive love of life and a deep hatred of all those who would maim and distort it for any end, which, perhaps, have not been sufficiently assessed by Mr. Nathan's critics. For, while Mr. Nathan writes well, he does not write with a sugar-stick, and Metabel's horror in the church is a true horror.

Then there is the melancholy — not an inky cloak but the shadow of a summer cloud — and the humor that illuminates without destroying. The angel, in " The Bishop's Wife," has a difficult time on earth, Mr. Lewis-Levy, in " There Is Another Heaven," an equally difficult one in the Protestant Heaven to which he has been consigned. Even Musket, the dog, does not find all things arranged to his taste, in spite of his artistic reputation. Nevertheless, they live, with enthusiasm mixed with surprise — they are apt to fall down but they are apt to get up again. Let me quote once to give you a taste of the quality. " The love of man and woman is a different thing entirely. It is full of pain, and human hunger; in the unending desert of eternity, it is an illusion of comfort, it is a mirage of consolation. It is also, in addition, an irresistible impulse of a purely animal nature. I know nothing about it myself, but I have studied the poets."

That is George Herman Wutheridge, Professor of Semitic Languages, speaking, in "The Bishop's Wife." It is very easy to read — it is very hard to write, in its sly balance. For you did not expect exactly what you have received, and, by the last sentence, you are gently let down a step that you did not know was there. That is part of Mr. Nathan's method — if you can call good writing a method.

It is this mingling of imagination and reality — of reality seen in the mirror of imagination — that gives Mr Nathan his unique position in our letters. For, even when his tales are most frankly fables, they never lose touch with humanity. Witness the extraordinary depictions of children, from Amy May Holly in "The Puppet Master" to the two little boys known merely as Potter and Johnson in "The Bishop's Wife." They are real children, with all the small barbarisms and touching grace of childhood. They are ruthless, self-absorbed and perfectly enchanting. They live in their own world, and partly in ours. No one has done them better, in our time. Here is one brief incident at a Christmas party.

"Juliet's face quivered. She approached her mother with her head bent and put her arms about her knees. ' I haven't any clown.' she said in a trembling voice ' I love a clown. You gave my clown to Potter. It's my tree. It's my party. You gave him my lovely clown.'

"She began to weep. 'I haven't any party suit.' she sobbed ' I haven't any nice new party suit.'

"Potter paid no attention to her. 'Here I go jumping,' he remarked, throwing the doll into the air, 'and here I fall down, bang.'"

Those are only a few sentences, but, with them, the ghosts of a thousand children's parties rise. Nor is Mr. Nathan any the less accurate, when he is touching a deeper problem — when Mr. Cohen, the millionaire, gives Michael, the archangel-deacon, his own reasons for remaining a Jew.

"No, my friend; if I do not turn Christian, like so many others, it is not because of the religious practises. It is because I do not want my grandchildren to hate the Jews. There is too much hate in the world as it is; in this country it flourishes like the weed. Here even the poets hate one another. Very well, I stay a Jew, I do not go over on the side of the haters. I do not buy my way up, so that I too, can spit down on my people. Do you think I love the Jews so much? How can I tell, when I am one? But I am sick of those who hate them, because I am sick of hate. What we need is more politeness in the world. Let people shake hands and say, Come in.

"Do you think it is a pleasure to be kept out of everything? . . ."

That was written in 1928 — it is part of Mr. Nathan's curious timelessness that it should be so applicable today. But what does make these books so timeless? I wish I knew. Of the five books collected here, two are laid in a country village, two in the city of New York and one in Heaven. The chief characters include a dog, an angel, a famous actress, a bishop, a rooster, a little green man and a woodcutter. They deal with happy love and unhappy, with the small and greater sorrows of the flesh and spirit, with youth and age and the deceptions of Time. They do not inform you, except about human nature, and they are neither pretentious nor obscure. Moreover, they are written with loveliness.

Yet, in spite of these grave defects, one reads and keeps on reading, remembers and turns back to quote. It may be the fiddler of Barly who has just been rebuked for idleness by the Reverend Dr. Flood.

" Left to himself, the fiddler gazed after the retreating figure of Dr. Flood with a smile.

" ' Come ' he said to himself ' there is always the host and the guest, wherever you go. Some people do not like to be the guests; they are only happy if they are hosts. They want to be at home, and make the arrangements. Well, well, my dear fellow, come in; here is a harp and a crown. When you were alive, you never gave me any trouble. Now I will do as much for you. There is no wine here, and the women have wings, but no legs. You have nothing to do but be happy and enjoy yourself in a nice way.' "

It may be Mr. Lewis-Levy, meditating to himself in the strange spic-and-span Heaven of the Gentiles.

" ' Not a soul here ' he said, with a groan ' not a soul to make me welcome, not a grandmother, not a grandfather, not an aunt or a cousin or even something distant — nothing, nobody. I might have known it but I never stopped to think. Naturally the Levys and the Weinsteins are all together somewhere. And mama says: Where is our Sammy: and papa says: What do you expect, he got himself baptized.

" Mama . . . you should know . . . your Sammy is lonesome . . .

" I've never been in a place like this before, where I didn't know anybody. There was always some member of the family around, to be given a cigar, or some advice, or something. When I needed anything, my cousin Becky would do it for me. Once a year I had her for dinner, with her husband. And every Christmas and Thanksgiving, I ate with the family at my sister's . . . she set a good table, poor Minna.

" Now I'll never see her again. She's at home with Abraham, Isaac and Jacob, and great-grandfather Weinstein. And I'm here, and I haven't got so much as a roof over my head."

It may be Bartholomew, the rooster, before his fight. " He opened his eyes again because, after all, that was more manly. But the first things he saw were his own spurs, of shining steel, thin and sharp, curved like a scimitar. There is death, he said to himself, and held them up, one by one to look at."

But whatever it is — from young lovers straying the grass of a summer meadow to a man perplexed on the banks of Jordan — a dog or a cricket — an angel or creatures less divine — it is life that has touched us, with true fantasy, lightly as the touch of a leaf, but memorably. A humorous and wise observer has been at our side. He cannot command every instrument — that is true enough. But the note of his own is true, unforced and searching — you will not find many like it — and it lingers in the mind.

It is not the province of this foreword to discuss Mr. Nathan's poetry, though I could wish that it were. But he was a poet, I think, before he was a prose-writer, and the discipline of poetry shows in his work. As for his literary ancestors — perhaps there was Anatole France, at the beginning; but I should put him nearer Hans Christian Andersen on one side and Nathaniel Hawthorne on the other. The Puritan horror of Hawthorne is absent from his work and the spirit is gentler and more gently mocking. But it is hard to find any other American work but the work of the Hawthorne of " Twice Told Tales " with which this work may be compared. And, as I say, I know of no contemporary work that is like it at all.

For it is work of complete integrity that has finally won its way to a wide public, not by fulfilling one set of fashionable requirements or another, but because the writer wrote with skill, beauty and understanding, and wrote as he chose, of the things that pleased him best. To see such work succeed is heartening — it is more important than movements and groups and trends. We can always have those, and they are very entertaining, but we cannot always have the clean line drawn and the true thing said. And when it is said with wit, imagination and sensitive reality, we may count ourselves lucky.

I have kept you from the books long enough — they are here to be read, and it is always better to read books than to talk about them. It is a number of years now since I first met Jane Demonstration and heard Amy May Holly say " Hold the truth." In that time, a good many things have gone in and out of fashion but it has not mattered to them. The fiddler still plays in Barly, Mrs. Sebold is still kind, Metabel makes her sacrifice and Mr. Lewis-Levy braves the chill waters of Jordan. I expect to find them just so a good many years from now — I doubt if the passage of the years will have bothered them at all. And I envy anybody who is meeting them here for the first time.

STEPHEN VINCENT BENÉT

ᔔ A NOTE
to the Younger Generation

It has not very often happened in the past that a writer, looking back at his own books (written ten years before), could truthfully say: The world has changed since then. But in these times, ten years is an epoch. We have seen too much happen all about us; history is being made too fast, it is hard for the writer to keep up with it.

The literature of the twenties is already a legend. I am even a little surprised now and then to find some of its young men still alive. They belong to a vanished age: they wrote about people who have disappeared like the Sumerians and the Socialists. Yet in their time they were realists: they wrote with fire and truth about what seemed most real to them.

The truth is that what we call real changes every time the world breathes.

My critics complain that I do not write about the real world. To discuss the loves and disappointments of little girls and old men, of mice and roosters, seems preposterous to the young realists of today. Yet what is more real than the hopes and griefs of children? Is a labor union more actual than a doll? Each signifies something in the human heart; neither one seems any more, or any less, significant.

That is not as absurd as it sounds. If little girls did not care to play with dolls any more, the world would be very different. It does not take genius to make such a remark, there is nothing new about it, but it is comforting, because it is true.

One of the most agreeable discussions of realism occurred recently, at luncheon. My step-daughter, aged four, who was eating her spinach, looked up suddenly, and remarked in a dreamy voice,

"I know a little boy who turned into a flower."

That, of course, was fantasy. Her brother, aged six, is the realist of the family. He exclaimed with energy, "That's silly. You have to say what he ate that made him turn into a flower."

I like the young writers of today. I like the hard, clear quality of their prose. But I do not believe that what they talk about is any more real than Little Red Riding Hood. It is good and pleasant to be manly and strong, to have broad shoulders and a shaggy chest; but it is inside the chest that the heart beats and the blood moves.

I know that falsehood and meanness, brutality and

arrogance have increased in the world during these last ten years. Still, there is no reason to make a cult of them. They cannot continue to increase forever, since long before that they will have had to swallow one another like the snakes in the fable. Merely to be muscular and violent proves nothing; unless the bones of the dinosaur can be said to prove anything.

Perhaps it is not necessary to prove anything. Perhaps it is enough to say: We lived; and these were our hopes and our worries, our joys and our fears. This is the way we spoke, if not altogether with our tongues, at least with our hearts.

R. N.

New York, December 1937

CONTENTS

To HENRY L. CALMAN

The Fiddler
in Barly

Chapter I

THE CHOIR stood up to sing. There were four in the choir, yet their voices filled the little church whose steeple disputed with the pines and maples of the valley. As they sang they looked up, for they felt, like the trees, that heaven was above them.

> " Oh, may " — they sang — " this bounteous God
> Through all our life be near us,
> With ever joyful hearts
> And blessed peace to cheer us.
> And keep us in His grace,
> And guide us when perplexed,
> And free us from all ills,
> In this world and the next."

Outside, in the branches brown with autumn, the birds also sang, songs of joy in the mild weather. " Look at me," they sang; " I am doing very well." Soon the wild geese would fly over; then they, too, would fly south, without regret.

" O Lord," prayed the preacher, " look down upon us here, and shed the blessings of Thy bounty upon us."

" Thy bounty," sang the birds, " upon us."

The organ played, and dust swam gently, in a fall of sun, down from the red and blue windows. In the quiet light the men and women of Barly looked around at one

3

another. They saw noses, eyes, bits of cotton and calico: all that made a man or a woman. They saw acres of land, barns, cows, jars of preserve, wash on the line. But Mr. Shrub, the postmaster, saw something else: he saw the letters which came to them, now and then, from other places. A letter from far away did a queer thing to a man; it gave him a secret. Mr. Shrub saw the hills around Barly, and beyond that, other hills — hills, plains, rivers, all the way across the world. It made his heart beat to think of so many places where he'd be a stranger. Not wishing to think about such things in church, he bowed his head, and thought about heaven instead. He was more at home there; there was nothing strange about heaven.

Tiny Flood, the preacher's son, let go the bellows of the organ, and peeked over the choir rail at the congregation; he saw the heads of his elders bowed in prayer, asking for blessings. Whatever was there left for them to ask for? There was Mrs. Sebold, who ran the general store; she had everything in the world, but there she was, praying away fit to break her heart — for what, he wondered? And there was his sister, Edna Flood, looking so solemn. But Edna was in love with Julius Penny, the organist; so maybe she had reason to look solemn. And all the while the soft light came stealing down from the windows, dim and quiet like light in a hayloft, light to be loved for itself, light to be played in, dusty old light to be alone in.

His glance fell upon the red face of little Lemuel Watson, sitting hot but meek in the pew between his father and mother. Lemuel looked back at him with gentle joy. Caught on either side by his family, he could only pull out one ear like an elastic. Then, his eyes straying to the book in his mother's hand, he read:

4

" Dearly Beloved . . ."

Overcome with mirth, he stuck out his long red tongue in the direction of the choir loft.

Behind him Edna Flood sat dreaming, her young, slim hands folded in her lap. From time to time she, too, glanced up at the loft, where Julius Penny sat bowed in front of the organ. She thought about Julius, and she thought about God. God was sweet, but He was severe; she loved His severity. It was a joy for her to have someone to obey like that. When she thought of disobeying God, she sucked in her breath with a little shiver.

Julius was sweet, too, but not severe; her father had more of the stern glory of God about him. The Reverend Flood scattered God's glory around over his congregation, and Julius helped him on the organ. She'd have to take care of Julius, he needed taking care of. He needed the love of a good woman, which was, she thought happily, just what he'd get.

The Reverend Flood was in the middle of his sermon. His tall, gaunt body stood up before Barly; his hands gripped each other with enthusiasm, and his sparkling eyes looked around at the congregation. He was saying that it was the duty of every man to improve himself. " A man is like a parcel of land," he declared; " some of it bears grain, and some is stony." As he spoke he looked sternly at the most no-account man in Barly, Ezra Adams, who sat quietly in the rear of the church with his little daughter Metabel, baptised Mehitable. Mr. Adams looked back at the preacher with a timid air; he seemed to say, " Well, I don't amount to much, but I feel friendly."

Metabel Adams did not see the gloomy looks the preacher cast at her father. She kept her eyes closed, because she was thinking about God. God was the King

5

of Glory like the choir sang; He was behind the hills the way the sky was. He was behind the sky, even, making shadows to run across the fields, making colors in the sunset, so beautiful, so beautiful, making His stars, silver against the green . . . He was in the rain in April, in the clear, yellow light of June, in the cold, fresh mist of evening in the fall . . . always in what was strange and lovely, making her want to dance, making her want to cry . . .

Her young heart, under the patched dress, beat with a sweet emotion; she would have liked to kiss God. She put her hand out, and patted her father's sleeve. " Oh," she sighed, " I love Sundays, Pa."

" Yes, my friends," said the Reverend Flood, " we are like land, some of it good, and some of it bad. The stones are our lusts, lusts of the eyes, lusts of the devil. We need to get those stones out. We need to plough and harrow our land with godly living. Then we'll have a crop for heaven that will pass right in through the pearly gates."

The choir stood up to sing again. Tiny Flood had forgotten his duties; seized by the ear, he returned to the bellows in time to give praise, a little late, a little weak, but in the right key. . . .

". . . Whose lands we hold
By Thy divine decree."

After the services were over, the men and women went slowly out of the church, with low voices and rustling clothes. They were in no hurry to get home and be alone again. The women stood on the steps and gossiped together; they watched little Metabel Adams, going home with her pa. She held his hand, and now and then she gave a little skip. When they passed anybody, Mr.

6

Adams looked shyly at the ground, but Metabel smiled and said how do you do. They thought she might have been a little more dismal, without any harm.

"Look at that," said Mrs. Watson; "it's not godly for a child to be so light on her feet. Not on a Sunday. No."

The men drew off together, and agreed that it had been an edifying sermon. "A man's what he makes himself. Yes, sir, that's what I've always said." They were satisfied with themselves, with what they had done in the world, satisfied with their chances of salvation. The women, however, pursed their lips and gave each other dry or gloomy glances. It might be so; they looked at their husbands, and changed the subject.

Edna Flood and Julius Penny walked home together in the warm bright weather. When the road's turn hid them from the gossips, they took hands. Their young hearts beat with joy, in a quiet way. The sun lay so yellow over the fields, the sky was so blue, the hills stood there so peacefully, shutting in their little world from all outside . . . haying and ploughing, church on Sunday, work on Monday . . .

"Mrs. Watson was saying something about piano lessons for her Lem," said Julius. "But I don't know. What do you think, Edna? I'd have time, I suppose now that the fruit's in, and your father's garden is mostly done."

"You could use our piano, Jule." She looked at him fondly: she loved it when he came to her like that, to ask her things; she felt so able to manage him. It made her heart hum, to feel so able and fond, all together. As for Julius, his plain, shy, serious face glowed with eagerness. He felt swollen with love, and with all that he meant to do in the world.

"What were you thinking of in church, Edna? You looked so solemn."

She wanted to say, " I was thinking of us." But instead she said, " Oh, nothing. I was just thinking."

" Did you hear the organ squeak? That was Tiny; he forgot all about it."

"Oh, Tiny . . . Isn't he just too dreadful? "

But he loved even Tiny on such a fine day. " Well," he said, "that old organ . . ." They were old foes, organ and organist; the strong, young, clumsy fingers fell upon the yellow keys in never-ending quarrels.

Mr. Shrub, the postmaster, walking home behind them, smiled thoughtfully. There were two lovers in front of him; he had a nose for it. Love was a mystery, like letters from another place; it gave a person something you couldn't see; it gave a person a secret. He trembled happily at the secretness of life.

Chapter II

ALL summer long the valleys around Barly are green as the sea. But in autumn they are like yellow pools; over them the clouds swim slowly in the sun, trailing their cold blue shadows across the hills. Goldenrod climbs the slopes, the maples are just turning. How far away the hills look now, touched by the gentle haze of fall, faint, acrid, sweet, like the smoke of a leaf.

It is the time of quiet, the time of crickets and drowsy bees; their voices, faint and sleepy, mingle with the rustle of leaves dying on the branches. Even the blue seems to deepen in the sky, to shine again, as in spring, with other light. It is as though someone were going away; already he is a little absent, making his farewells, smiling with infinite sweetness . . . Good-bye, good-bye . . . let us see you again.

The tassels on the corn were black; the yellow squash, the green cucumbers ripened on the ground. In the window of Mrs. Sebold's General Store, the muslin dresses and straw hats were taken down, and corduroys and woolens put out instead. But the bicycle, hard candy, and pocket knives remained as they were.

Everything in the world was to be found in the General Store. In the first place, there was the bicycle, shin-

ing with paint, and with nickeled handlebars. Tiny Flood
and Lemuel Watson wondered what there was left for
Mrs. Sebold to pray for when she went to church on Sunday. They could hardly believe that Mrs. Sebold did not
admire her own store window as much as they did. But it
was true: Mrs. Sebold wanted something of God besides
bicycles. He was, she thought, a gentle old man who kept
her from being too lonely. He stood at her shoulder in
the evening on the kitchen steps when she fed her hens.
" Look," He said, " what a beautiful sunset." But when
she went in to supper, He was gone. So she used to put
off going in as long as possible. She would have liked to
pray, " Come to supper, God." But who ever heard of
such a prayer? Instead, on Sundays, in church, she intoned with the rest of the congregation:

" Who is the King of Glory? It is the Lord strong and
mighty, even the Lord, mighty in battle."

Was that the Lord, she wondered, who fed her chickens
with her?

She stood on the kitchen steps, and called, and her hens
came running. Cluck, cluck . . . anxious to be second
rather than first, they rushed ahead of one another, only
to wait for the others to catch up again.

She had a queer way with birds, as though she knew
them. They never feared her, not even the wild birds,
the shy singers, with voices like tiny flutes. They came
and sang in her garden, built their nests under her eaves,
watched her with bright, untroubled eyes. She had friends
of her own among them: there was a robin she had tended
since the day she found him, young, perplexed, fallen from
his nest, with a broken wing. He slept in her room at
night, and ate out of her hand.

She treated her birds seriously. " Don't be silly," she

said to them. She expected them to be sensible, but she made allowances. When her robin's head drooped, she fed him castor oil, and rubbed his stomach. "You don't take care of yourself," she told him; "you eat anything. That is not a sensible life."

Mrs. Sebold's idea of a sensible life was this: to be healthy, to be happy, and to let other people alone to do as they pleased. But that did not keep her from speaking her mind when there was an occasion for it. In Barly they said she was bold, because she was not afraid to say what she liked to anybody. To say what you liked, right off, without waiting to hear what other people said, was as good a way as any, they thought, of being wrong. And in Barly folks wanted to be right: that was what they had a preacher for, that was what they went to church for. But Mrs. Sebold never seemed to trouble her head about it, and acted right whether she was right or wrong. It bothered the good people of Barly, who were only right if everyone agreed with them, to see Mrs. Sebold so airy by herself.

Still, she had a good nose for business; everyone had to admit that. She knew what to buy, and what to sell. Twice a year she went to town, to look over the shops, and add to her stock; when she came home, she told the farmers' wives what to wear, or she brought home a new-fangled pot for the stove. They came after it like her own hens, as fast as they could; but no one wanted to be first. The first always went home shaking her head; she felt too daring, and it made her gloomy.

"Yes, sir," said Mrs. Sebold, pointing to her chickens, "they're just like people, always wanting to be second. I have to laugh to look at them."

She was talking to the preacher, who had stopped to

see her on his way home. But the Reverend Flood believed in prudence. " Fools rush in," he said, " where angels, Mrs. Sebold . . ."

She wanted to know if that was in the Bible.

" No," he said. " However, it is a very pious thought."

" I've never liked it," she said. She flung the last handful of corn in a semicircle on the ground. " It makes the fools out better than the angels," she declared.

The preacher held up his hands in gentle reproof. "That is not what I meant, Mrs. Sebold," he said. " What I meant was that some of us go head-first into evil things, in our hurry to be the first one there."

" The early bird gets the worm," she replied, and gazed triumphantly around.

" Cluck," sang the hens.

The Reverend Flood went home with a sober step. He respected Mrs. Sebold more for the vigor of her opinions than for the strange charity of her heart. He was a man who believed in godliness and improvement. He felt that it was his duty to train his flock toward heaven, like polebeans. " The church," he often said, " is a rock of salvation." It was his idea that a rock stands up straight and tall for other things to climb on.

He knew what he would find when he got home; Edna in the kitchen getting supper ready, and Julius Penny improving himself at the piano. Mr. Penny's attempt to improve himself did not seem to the Reverend Flood anything to be thankful for. He sighed, and trudged along. Do re mi fa sol . . . doremifasol . . . Better to think about God. God had made the world, and then written the Bible. God was very real to the Reverend Flood; and so was the devil. On one side everything godly; on the other, all the sins, large and small. A little verse kept creeping into his mind, for all he tried to keep it out —

12

Sugar and spice,
And everything nice . . .

That left the devil with the puppy-dogs' tails. It vexed
him to be obliged to think of such things.

On the steps of her kitchen, Mrs. Sebold looked up at
the sky. It might rain during the night; in that case she'd
go out in the morning and see if there were any birds
come down in the storm. Not that she'd find any this time
of year, but she liked to look. She'd found a robin once,
and she always hoped there'd be another. She thought,
if she were lucky, to find a wife for the robin she had. Or
was it a wife he wanted? She didn't quite know. Well,
a wife or a husband, it wasn't her affair. God, who saw
the sparrows fall, would know; all she could do was
gather up what dropped, and take it home.

Chapter III

SHE didn't find a wife for her robin, not that year. Instead, she found a hired man for herself. Barly never made out, exactly, why she took him; there wasn't enough work around her house to keep even a neighbor busy odd moments, let alone an able-bodied man with nothing else to do but look after her little garden, split some logs, run a few errands . . . They figured she must have found something queer in him, the way she found in birds, to take him in. Not that it was hard to find the queer in him; it stood out all over him, from his thin straw-colored hair and his long square nose, to the fiddle he carried, and the little dog who went along with him. He was pushing a sort of ashcan on wheels when he came to Barly, the kind of barrow street-cleaners use in the city. It was full of earth, and had a purple aster and some carrots growing in it; it was a heavy thing to push up and down the countryside. She was out where the road ran by her barn when she spied him; it was evening, and cool; the sun was down, but the sky was light. He stopped in front of her barn a moment, to pass the time of day, and maybe ask for his supper.

"What on earth's that?" she said, pointing.

He looked at it too, as if he wanted to see what it was, himself.

"It's a barrow," he said; "a street-cleaner's barrow."

"I can see as much," she answered. "But what's in it."

"Food," he said, "and flowers." And he added, patiently: "Dirt should have things growing in it."

Mrs. Sebold opened her eyes at him. She looked at the dog and the fiddle; then she stared at the ashcan with its drooping flower. "What's the fiddle for?" she asked. "Are you a fiddler?"

"It is my profession," he replied. "However, last year I was a street-cleaner. This is my little dog Musket, who dances when I play, and takes my cap in his mouth to collect coins. It is very hard to make a living that way in winter."

And he added hopefully, "I should like to be a farmer."

"You've your own farm, mister," said Mrs. Sebold, smiling and pointing to the barrow.

The fiddler shook his head. "It is too small," he said, "and besides, my flower is dying. Soon it will be too late for dancing; it will be time to gather pumpkins and to sit in front of a fire. Last year I shoveled snow in the streets, and warmed my fingers over a gas jet. That is nothing for a fiddler. But one cannot live by art alone."

Mrs. Sebold looked at him uncertainly. "I've no pumpkins," she said at last.

"Squash will do," replied the fiddler. And he looked at her bravely, as though to say, Do not be unhappy because you have no pumpkins . . .

"I've never had a man on the place," said Mrs. Sebold thoughtfully: "for one thing, there's nothing for him to do. And a fiddler — what would I want with a fiddler, mister? Tell me that. I've no ear for music."

The fiddler replied earnestly, "An ear for music is

nothing, if you have a heart for it. When I played my fiddle in the spring, the flowers danced for joy, and bulls forgot to butt one another. A fiddle in winter makes the fire burn brighter; it helps the hens to lay. Cheer, madam, is what we need in the world, whether we are hens or people."

"Don't I know it?" said Mrs. Sebold.

The fiddler put his fiddle to his chin. "Wait a minute," he said: "Do you like to dance?" And he began to play a lively tune. At once the little dog got up on his hind legs: one, two, one, two, three . . . "Well, now," said Mrs. Sebold, "that's really comical."

The hens looked up from their food, the robin hopped out of the barn and stared at them. Night gathered in the hills, under the pale first stars. The tune rose like a bird's song into the lonely air over the darkening fields.

It was the hour when God and Mrs. Sebold fed the Sebold hens. She saw the hills she knew against the sky, she saw the little dog dancing, one, two, one, two, three . . . And all at once she felt like dancing too.

"Well," she said —

"Come to supper, mister."

And she led the way back to the house, smiling to herself. The fiddler followed her, with his little dog. "Ma'am," he said when he came in, "this is a real kitchen. It gives me an appetite just to look around. There's a good smell in it, a sweet smell, a smell of good food."

"It won't take me but a moment," said Mrs. Sebold.

For supper there were eggs, bacon, potatoes, beans, bread, coffee, and apple pie. "Eat hearty," she told him; "there's plenty more where this comes from."

"I mean to," said the fiddler.

He took a great bite of bread, washing it down with

coffee, which he poured into his saucer, to cool it, and also because he believed it tasted better.

"I always eat hearty," he said, "when I can. I sleep very hearty, too. I believe that a man should do every-thing with enthusiasm."

So saying, he held out his plate for another helping. While they were eating, the robin came in, and hopped up onto the table. For a while he preened his feathers, while he looked about him out of his bright eyes like beads. All at once he skipped across the table and took a peck out of Mrs. Sebold's plate. Then he looked down at Musket with a sly air.

The little dog's heart was heavy. He also liked to eat hearty; but he was obliged to wait until someone gave him something. "If I did that," he thought, "I'd get such a crack . . ."

And he gazed humbly and sadly at his master.

After supper the fiddler told Mrs. Sebold about him-self; he sat back in his chair, and stretched out his feet with a sigh. Then the lamplight glowed upon his homely face, shone in his eyes blue as old stones, on his thin, straw-colored hair. He told her how he went from village to village, helping in the fields, when the farmer needed a hand, playing for village dances in dusty, sweet-smelling barns, or in halls decorated with flowers. He told her how he played in the evening, on a hillside, the village people spread about him, sitting together in the dusk, quiet and dreamy, singing with voices low and uncertain the songs they remembered . . .

Stars of a summer night . . .

Singing together in the dewy grass, under the thin thread of music, silver as the moon, floating as the wind . . .

Ask thy soul if we should part.

Then he explained how he went around with his cap, while Musket danced to the jingle of coins falling one on another.

"As a matter of fact," he said, "we do not starve . . . very much."

Then he added, "That is not a bad life for a fiddler. But now the winter is coming, and I shall have to warm my hands over a gas jet again."

Mrs. Sebold looked at him for a while without speaking; she seemed to be making up her mind to something. At last she got up, and took down a lantern from the wall. "What's your name, fiddler?" she asked.

"My name," said the fiddler slowly, "is Lindeman." He looked a little surprised, himself, to hear it. "When one lives alone," he remarked apologetically, "one doesn't hear one's name so often."

"Well, then, Lindeman," said Mrs. Sebold briskly, "I'll put you to sleep in the barn. There's a bed there, and I'll bring in a wash bowl. Be careful with the lamp. I wouldn't be surprised but what we'd get along all right."

That night, in his tiny room which smelled of hay and harness, the fiddler said to his little dog Musket:

"Musket, this year we shall have a country winter. You will enjoy it, it will be good for both of us. In the evenings we will amuse the neighbors: I will play, and you will dance. That is where art should be, in congenial company, around a fire, with something to eat and drink. If one is not a genius, then one should at least try to be comfortable."

In the kitchen, Mrs. Sebold started to put the dishes away. But before she was done she caught herself smiling again. "A fiddle at evening," she said to herself, "to help the hens to lay." Or was it to keep the bulls from butting one another? She didn't rightly remember. Night had closed in, but she didn't mind it. She went to the back door and stood for a moment looking out across the yard at the barn, black as ink in the darkness. All was still; the tree frogs sang, and in the sky the stars burned like little silver fires, winking in the cold.

Chapter IV

METABEL ADAMS' gold-brown hair hung down her back in two long braids tied with a piece of shoe-string. When she bent over, the braids fell forward on her shoulders; then she pushed them back with an impatient gesture. She did not admire her hair, in which copper lights came and went, or her small thin face with its gray eyes which looked out so happily at the world. She was not vain; and she had no illusions about her own poverty. But she loved what she had: the cold, bare shack where she lived with her father on public land beyond the village, a few plates and pots, her one dress, a book of fairy tales, and a piece of bright blue cloth with which she used to dance when no one was looking.

She was nine; she took care of the house and looked after her father, who spent his time sitting in the sun, scratching his head, and dreaming. Sometimes he took on an odd job or two, helping to lay a roof, cutting hay or shocking corn, but never for long, and then no more than what was needful. He was no-account, that was the truth of it; and he knew it. It didn't vex him any; his tobacco tasted all the sweeter for sitting still.

It didn't vex Metabel, either. She did her chores cheerfully, cooked, cleaned what she could, drew water, and begged eggs of her neighbors. She always had an excuse for him when they asked: sometimes he had a misery, sometimes he was just busy figuring things out. What it was he figured, she never told them, and there was, they felt, no need of asking. "He's figuring on how to sit stiller than he sits," said Mr. Watson to his wife, a remark which made Mrs. Watson laugh, and that was rare enough.

She loved to dance; she'd go off alone in the fields above Barly, and dance to herself: hop, skip, hop, skip, and jump. Sometimes she was the wind, sometimes she was a rabbit; but it all looked alike, her pigtails flying out behind her, and her thin arms waving. Or she'd walk seriously down to the general store, not to buy, just to look. The cool shadowy store with its shelves of goods, its counters of hardware, the great sacks of grain and cereals piled on the floor, seemed to her the best place in the world to tell herself stories. Mrs. Sebold was never out of patience with her; when she fell over her behind a barrel of dried prunes, or bumped into her behind a rack of gingham dresses, the widow only smiled and shook her head.

The stories she told herself were all the same: there was a little girl who had to draw water, cook, and sweep for her father; until one day the king saw her, and took her home with him, and gave her a yellow dress to wear. Well, that changed everything, it made her out so elegant; and that was the end of the story, the-lived-happily-ever-after.

A yellow dress . . .

It made her out so grand . . . as grand as Edna Flood, the preacher's daughter. Edna had a yellow dress; and she was the most beautiful person in the world. She was so cool and brown-and-gold; she looked so gentle; and Metabel loved her. When she was grown up she was

21

going to be like that, too: like something you couldn't hurt, or muss, with such quiet tones in her voice and such a dreamy way of looking.

But no matter how she meant to turn out, Barly saw nothing to admire in Metabel Adams. It wasn't her being poor troubled people; the Bible spoke of charity, and so did the preacher. It was her being happy vexed them. "It's not," said Mrs. Watson, "that I grudge her an egg now and then to keep the life in her body. But you'd think she'd take it modestly, instead of dancing around like she owned it."

Mrs. Sebold sighed. "What's an egg, Josephine?" she asked mildly.

When the Reverend Flood spoke about the Adamses, his face grew very gloomy. He did not expect to find people like that in heaven; and to find them on earth, right under his nose, seemed to him a good deal of a trial. The worst of it was that Pa Adams never missed a Sunday, and for all he knew, might yet be saved and bask in glory. But how to save him, or why, in fact, to save him at all, was more than the Reverend Flood could see. At least in Metabel's case the problem was clearer; there was her dancing. To dance at a church sociable was one thing; but to dance alone, on a hill, with motions like a little goat or an awkward bird, was quite another. He wondered if it didn't have the appearance of evil.

"After all," he said to his daughter, "I do not object to innocent joy. But that is not the way your mother acted when she was a child; and your mother was both innocent and joyous."

Yes, to be innocent and to be joyous was possible, but only in the truly godly. And what was there godly about Metabel? Indeed, what was there godly about any little children? how could one know that godliness was there?

22

Only by their modesty, which kept them out of sight; only by their meekness, their way of looking down when grown-ups spoke to them, only by their lowered eyes and embarrassed glances. There was nothing godly about Metabel.

" Pa," she said to her father as she stood over the sink, rinsing her brown, scorched pudding dish with tender care, " Pa . . . there's the hole come back in my shoe again. Look." And she raised her foot for her father to see. Standing there, on one leg, with her head bent and her hands in soapy water, she looked like a little heron, awkward and anxious.

Pa Adams bent down to examine the hole. " The gum's fallen out," he said; " you've lost your gum, Metabel."

She turned her head around and they looked at it together. " I was afraid of that," said Pa; " yes, sir, I feared it from the start. I expect we'll have to put some pitch in that gum. You get me a little mite of pitch down to the store, Metabel, and a speck of gum, and we'll fix up that old shoe again so's it'll hold good."

Metabel went back to her pudding dish. But after a while her hands began to trail up and down in the soapy water as though that was all they had to do in it. And she stood there dreaming, first on one foot and then on the other. Her dreams were sweet and cloudy; she was happy . . . the dreams of a child, dreams of glory no more meaty than a butterfly.

When her work was done, the dishes dried and put away, she went to the old wooden trunk in which she kept her belongings, and took out her precious piece of blue cloth. Wrapping it around her shoulders like a shawl, she started soberly for the village, in search of some pitch and a piece of gum.

As she walked, her face grew thoughtful, her chin went up, she looked about her with an expression of repose. She was being Edna Flood. " How do you do," she said to a little dog who came out of a yard to look at her. And she gave him a sweet smile.

The little dog looked at her without speaking. Then he turned around, and went back in again.

" There's Metabel Adams," said Tiny Flood to his friend Lemuel Watson; " just look at that, the way she walks." And he stuck out his chest, and made a few struts with his feet.

" She got a loaf of bread off my ma yesterday," said Lemuel, " and my ma says the next time she comes around, she's going down to the cellar and make believe she's not home. So my pa says he'd ask old Mr. Adams would he help him shuck our corn, only he'd likely as not fall right into the silo and never be found again. So my ma says the next time . . ."

" How do you do," said Metabel, going by as elegant as she could, clutching her piece of blue cloth.

But that only sent Tiny and Lemuel into a series of titters. " How do you do," said Tiny to Lemuel, and " How do you do," said Lemuel to Tiny; and both fell with mirth upon the ground.

" How do you do. Oh, my goodness . . ."

Metabel went on; she clutched her shawl a little tighter. She was still Edna Flood, but only just, and with nothing left to spare.

Chapter V

As MRS. SEBOLD's new hired man worked in the garden, turning over the earth in which there were weeds and vegetables gone to seed, he said to his little dog,

"Musket, are you happy? Well, then, do not sit and look at me so anxiously. One would think that you had never seen me with a spading fork in my hands before."

And he regarded with relish the clean, sharp bars of the fork before he pressed it down in the ground with his foot.

"Very well, then," he said, "think what you like. However, you have often seen me with a broom and dustpan, so your anxiety is uncalled for."

When he had turned over the ground where the beans had been, he went to gather armfuls of squash and cabbage. He was happy; the sun was bright and hot, there was a sweet autumn smell in the air, of grapes, of earth and dead leaves. Wasps were busy among the apples, the caw of some crows rose from far away in the fields. He began to sing to himself in a voice full of energy.

> "Now does the spider's house,
> Hang gray upon the wall.
> The carcass of a louse
> Adorns it most of all.

25

"On dry stalks of clover,
    Or under sunny stones,
October will uncover
    The fly's white bones."

Mr. Shrub, the postmaster, who was going by, stopped and leaned against the fence to hear him. When the song was finished, he called out, " Hey, over there."

The fiddler stood up with his arms full of yellow squash. " Yes," he said: " what can I do for you? "

Mr. Shrub scratched his head. Finally he remarked, " You're Mrs. Sebold's new man? "

" Yes," said the fiddler.

" You're a fiddler," said Mr. Shrub, without believing it.

" I am," said the fiddler.

" Well," said Mr. Shrub. And he added politely, " I'm pleased to meet you."

" Thank you," said the fiddler. He stood waiting to hear what the postmaster would have to say.

But Mr. Shrub had nothing more to say. He had heard that Mrs. Sebold had hired a fiddler to do her chores; but he hadn't rightly believed it. What a strange thing. He had a nose for what was strange, so he came over to see. Well, there it was, and no mistake. He spat shyly in the road, and went home in a dazzled way.

Left to himself, Lindeman sat down with a sigh at the edge of the garden. Leaning back in the grass, he said to his little dog, " You are such a sensible creature. You dance in order to eat, not because of art, or anything like that. You ask of music only that it should inspire you to live. Nevertheless, I believe that you like to exhibit yourself.

" Musket, you are a humbug."

At his feet a little bull cricket sounded his bell; and coming upon a lady cricket in the grass, approached her in an irresistible manner. The fiddler bent down with a smile. "See," he said, "how all the world behaves in this clear autumn weather. Like the spring, it is a time for love. Now, when crickets go roving in the grass, I should be playing merry or sweet tunes on my fiddle. But my fiddle is in the barn; and there is all this earth to be turned over."

And with a sigh, he got to his feet again.

Musket, with his nose on his paws, regarded the two crickets with friendly interest. "You," he said to the black bull cricket, "did you know the lady before? Or are you, like me, a stranger here, and was this simply a fortunate accident for both of you?"

Presently the two crickets disengaged themselves. "Well," said the male in a hearty manner to the female, "how do you do?" The lady did not reply; irritated but drowsy, she hopped away in the grass. Her lover gazed after her without regret. "There," he said to Musket, "one would think that I had offended her. When as a matter of fact, it was quite the other way around.

"What do you make of it?"

To this question Musket made no reply. He was not clever, although he had learned to dance, and was of a thoughtful nature. His master had told him the truth about himself; he was a humbug, but he was practical, and his thoughts concerned themselves with reality.

"Is it love," he asked, "which causes you to act in so impulsive a manner? Because I have never seen anything like it."

The cricket nodded his head. "Yes," he said, "it is

love." And he added stoutly a moment later, " I believe in love. But I do not believe in talking about it a great deal. No: with me it is jump first, and then conversation.

" However, there is no question about it, it is love which makes me jump."

At that moment an unmistakable clamor arose from behind the barn where Bartholomew, Mrs. Sebold's Plymouth rooster had come upon another and smaller cock belonging to one of the neighbors. Without waiting a moment, and also in order to defend his wives from flirtation, Bartholomew rushed at the stranger, determined to give him a good peck or at least to discourage him. The smaller bird, unable to flee due to the geography, was obliged to stand his ground, which he did with a certain audacity, enough, in fact, to cause Bartholomew to become discouraged, and to retreat out of the way of harm. Then they scolded each other. The fiddler dropped his fork, and hurried in the direction of the squabble.

" It's a fight," he cried gleefully to Mrs. Sebold, who had come out on the back porch to see what it was all about. And he rushed around the corner of the barn, to encourage the roosters.

" Go on," he said to Bartholomew; " bite him."

Mrs. Sebold went thoughtfully back into the house and forward to the store where Mrs. Watson was waiting to buy a paper of pins.

" Men," she said to Mrs. Watson: " well . . .

" They're all alike."

" They are indeed," said Mrs. Watson.

" They do nothing but fight," said Mrs. Sebold.

" They do for sure," said Mrs. Watson. " I declare, it's sickening." She bent her head hopefully forward. " Who's been at it now? " she asked.

"Nobody," said Mrs. Sebold calmly; "I was just thinking."

"Tst," said Mrs. Watson. And she went home with her paper of pins, looking very much vexed. "She might have told me," she thought, "at that."

Chapter VI

THE HENS in Mrs. Sebold's barnyard were stout and hearty. In the evening they received their corn, and during the day they scratched in the gravel for insects, which they swallowed without hesitation or pity. Although they regretted nothing, they did not seem to enjoy anything. It was always the next insect which attracted them; as for the one they were eating, they did not even bother to taste it. The rooster Bartholomew followed them about the barnyard with an air of disapproval. When he came too near, they fled from him with modest squawks. But one could see that they respected him, and that they were attracted to him.

"Women are all alike," he said to Musket; "they enjoy being pecked." He gazed around him with a gloomy air. "You must not be too considerate of women," he said, "or they will take advantage of it."

And he told Musket a story about a canary who used to hang in a little cage outside a window in Hillsboro, across the valley.

"This canary," he said, "wanted to be a great singer. She had a good voice, but she did not know very much about music. Well, do you know what happened? She fell in love with a mocking bird."

"Ah," said Musket.

30

"He was not a professional singer," the rooster continued, "but he had a very wheedling way. He taught her all he knew . . . la, la, la. She used to be let out of her cage every day; and then they would fly into a tree and sing together. We used to hear them in the bright, warm weather. I can tell you, it was lovely; it made me think of all kinds of pleasant things.

"He wanted her to fly away with him. As a matter of fact, she had promised to marry him. But she was afraid to leave her cage, where she had a piece of dried apple and a porcelain bathtub. 'I must think of my art,' she said. 'For one thing, I want you to be proud of me.' And she said other things of that sort. What nonsense. A woman makes up reasons in order not to be obliged to do what she does not want to do.

"All summer long they sang together in the branches . . . la, la, la. Listen to this, she would say; and she would let out a trill. Then he would show her how it ought to be done. But when he asked me for my opinion, I gave it to him. My friend, I said, she will never marry you. And as a matter of fact, I was right; it turned out just as I expected. At the last minute, the canary found it impossible to leave her bathtub, her apple, and her art. So he had to go home alone, after all. Well, do you know what he did? He let himself be eaten by hawks on the way. When I told the canary this, she exclaimed, 'See what would have happened to me, if I had married him.'"

And he added angrily, "I have no patience with that sort of thing. I do not consider it manly."

"That is a very sad story," said Musket, "and it goes to show that you must never expect too much from other people. However in a measure I can sympathize with the canary, because I am also, in a manner of speaking, an artist."

" I hear that you dance," said Bartholomew; "perhaps you will favor us with a few steps?"

But Musket shook his head. " Some other time," he said; " at present I should like to forget my professional life."

" What is the good of that?" said the rooster. " Be a little obliging. There is nothing goes on here, it is dull as ditch water. Perhaps it is a change for you, but it is nothing for me . . . When I think of all the places you have been, I grow very gloomy."

" I assure you," replied Musket soothingly, " one place is very much like another. And people are the same all over."

The rooster put his head to one side; then he began to scratch in the gravel. Finally he addressed the little dog with a sly air.

" I suppose you have had a number of adventures," he said. And with that he glanced at one of the hens in a manner which made her heart beat. " Oh, my," she thought, " he looked at me." And when her sister came to see what she was eating, she cried angrily:

" You are always in the way."

Then she gave her a sharp peck with her beak.

Musket smiled a little to himself, because he knew what was expected of him. " Well," he said, " as to that . . . you know how it is. An artist, a dancer . . . there are certain opportunities . . ."

The rooster nodded his head. " That's it," he agreed; " if one is something like that, one has everything. A good husband gets nowhere in the world. But a fighting cock — what a life he leads. Or as you say, an artist."

The little dog replied hastily, " An artist's life is not without disadvantages. I suppose it is exciting to flirt with strangers; one learns a good deal about life that way.

Kiss and good-bye . . . how do you do, and a kiss again.
But to fall in love with a friend is much better. Yes, that
is the loveliest thing in the world."

"It is impossible," said the rooster.

Musket continued more earnestly: "Come, how would
you like to be me? Suppose that in the afternoon I have
had a little adventure. What of it — in a moment it begins, and pretty soon it is over. I do not get anything to
keep, and after a while I am not even able to remember
it. I may have been very lively, but just the same, at night
I go to sleep all alone. There is nothing to do but forget
it. But you — if you have had some triumphs, you can enjoy them all over again. They are made doubly sweet to
you because you have someone to confess them to. Do
you know what it is like to be alone? After a while nothing has a taste any more. My home is under the fiddler's
bed; when I creep in there, I am by myself. If I brought
anyone along with me, we would both be thrown out.
Well, you don't realize how one longs for a home sometimes. You look out at the world from the windows of a
hen coop, and you dream of all sorts of things; but as you
fall asleep, the last thing you see is the outline of your
wife against the dark.

"No, I am very practical about these matters, I have
no illusions. I assure you, one is often very lonely in the
midst of glory."

And he went off to attend to something by a tree.

When he returned, the rooster was busily digging with
his sharp claws in the earth. But he stopped long enough
to regard the little dog for a moment. "My friend," he
said to him, "let me tell you something. In the midst of
all this, I am lonelier than you are."

So saying, he went back to his digging again.

Chapter VII

LEMUEL WATSON sat at the Reverend Flood's piano, learning to play scales. One, two, three, and the thumb goes under. Lemuel was bored with it. Where was the glory after the thumb went under? What he wanted to do was to make a lot of sound on the organ, and have Tiny to blow up the bellows for him. One, two, three, and the thumb goes under, but it might just as well not, for all of him.

Julius Penny sighed. Things were much grander when he talked about them than they ever turned out to be. Life had a way of growing smaller the closer he got to it. Look at teaching; it sounded like something when he talked to Edna about it. But what did it amount to really? Little Lemuel Watson trying to make his thumb go under . . .

"One, two, three . . . look, like this . . ."

"What does it go like that for, Jule?"

Everything came to a small end in Barly. Spring came down over the hills and was ploughed into vegetables; autumn glowed for a while in the fields, and was split into kindlings. Nothing ever carried its promise over; nothing got the better of things like fingers.

When the lesson was done, Lemuel ran outside with the devil at his heels. When he saw Tiny swinging up and down on the gate in front of the house, he stopped and began to examine his hands. He wanted Tiny to believe that music was not as easy as it looked. "You got to do some pretty queer things with your thumb," he said.

Julius found Edna at the postoffice, talking to Mr. Shrub. The postmaster stood back of his window underneath a map of the country done in green and orange. All around him were other maps, posters of travel, pictures of trains and ships; there was such a smell of geography in the postoffice, it was like a railroad station, though the nearest trains were at Milford Junction five miles south. And in the midst of all this bustle on the walls, Mr. Shrub sold his stamps and penny postals with a sort of solemn joy, as though they were tickets to somewhere.

Now, leaning his elbows on the counter, he was talking to Edna about the Milford fair in November. "I suppose you're going," he said. And he peered at her hopefully out of his small, shy eyes.

"I expect so," she answered. As a matter of fact, nothing could have kept her home. Jule had been asked to play at the Milford church sociable and she was bound to hear him. She blushed a little, and sensitive Mr. Shrub also blushed, out of sympathy.

"Well," he said, "won't that be fine."

He knew why she was going. There was no secret about it: everyone knew it. But to have been hearty about it would have seemed to him indelicate. And Mr. Shrub, along with the rest of Barly, liked to be delicate about serious things.

Edna too: why did she feel that to be hushed was to be purer? It was like not talking too loud in church. All Barly felt it, all the world felt it. Never be hearty, Edna, or the devil will get you, probably.

There was Anna Barly over to Hillsboro. She did as

she liked once, and had a baby. How ugly all that was; that's what heartiness did to people. Not that Anna had had much joy of it; but there wasn't any doubt if Anna had been less hearty that night on the hay ride, she'd have been happier nine months later. And Edna blushed again, first for Anna, and then for herself, that she should know so much, and think such things.

But when she walked up home again with Julius, she felt only the delicate, shy emotions of her youth, her ignorance, and her love — emotions as untroubled as the sunwarmed air of that drowsy valley shut in from the world by hills not high enough to threaten. She broke a spray of goldenrod and brushed it across Julius' face.

"How was the lesson?" she asked.

"Well," said Julius, hesitating . . .

He had forgotten Lemuel's thumbs. He, too, felt hopeful and peaceful as he walked beside her . . . drowsy, drunk with a sort of beauty, beauty almost without an ache in it . . .

"Mr. Shrub asked me was I going to Milford, to the fair. I said I expected so . . ."

They sat together on a broken stone wall, under a tree. In the north Old Hemlock, blue against the sky's deep blue, lifted itself in the clear bright air. Behind them, in the fields the crickets sang with little voices of earth; and in the south, above Milford, the white clouds of autumn, shining in the sun, trailed slowly over the hills.

Their fingers, clasped between them, rocked together like children in a swing. "What are you thinking, Edna?" he asked.

She had no way of telling him. She pressed his hand. "It's pretty here," he said.

"Yes," she answered. Why couldn't life always be like that, so still and clear and lovely? Her heart was full;

she thought it was peace, but it felt like longing. She drew his hand still tighter; she wanted something of him, something, she would have said, to remember the day by, something to make all that beauty and peace a part of herself, never to be lost, never forgotten. She thought there was something he could say, or she could say . . .

"Talk to me, Jule."

There was such a lot to talk about, and at the same time, nothing. The silence of the fields, of the woods, seemed to be in his blood, and yet there was no peace in it, but longing, longing to tell her — what? That he loved her? No — it wasn't only that he wanted to tell her. He could tell her that over and over, it wouldn't make him ache any less. The words wouldn't come; silence began to get the best of him . . .

"Well," he said desperately, "I love you."

And he looked at her with a sort of dumb anguish which she took for love. She laughed, and looked away.

"I love you, too," she said sweetly. And since that was all he meant to say, she gave up hope of more, and turned to kiss him. Under the tree whose turning leaves covered them with shadow and shine, their lips touched each other with the kindness of children.

At once their longing fell away, leaving them quiet and content. "Isn't it lovely here," she said. "Isn't it peaceful, Jule. I'm quite happy now."

They sat swinging their feet, smiling at one another. But presently Julius sat up, and cocked his head. "Listen," he said; "listen . . . I hear a tune. It sounds like a fiddle."

She bent forward to make sure. "It's above us," she answered, "up the hill. It's Mrs. Sebold's hired man, I expect."

They sat still, to hear. The tune sang to itself, far

37

away; it made Julius frown. "I never heard that piece before," he said. "It's like a dance, isn't it, Edna."

"No," she said, "it isn't a dance. It's too sad."

"What is it, Jule?"

"It's a dance," he said.

It took the peace out of the air, to hear that tune up there on the hill. It made her think of places far away from Barly. She stirred uncomfortably. "Let's go home," she said; "I've got bread to bake."

"Well . . . if you want to, Edna."

As they walked down the road together, they passed Metabel Adams, going up the hill. "How do you do," said Edna with Christian duty, as kind as she could be.

Metabel's face grew red with joy. "Hello," she said bashfully, as she went by. But when she'd gone on a ways, she stopped to look around, her gray eyes wide with adoration. "How do you do," she breathed. "I love you."

She stood looking back at them as long as she could. Then, taking a deep breath, she went on, up the hill, to where she heard a fiddle singing like a bird.

Chapter VIII

"I HAVE a large audience here," said the fiddler, waving his arm to include all the grasshoppers, crickets, and darning-needles. "But they are not very attentive," he added, smiling.

He put his fiddle down. "Come," he said, "sit here with me. This is a fine concert hall. Now we will talk for a while, and listen to some bees. Here . . ." And he held out his hat full of berries.

Metabel settled herself in the grass next to the brown shiny fiddle. How small it looked there on the ground. A little while ago it had been singing in the air; she had heard it from far away. She smoothed out her skirts, and sighed. "It's such a nice day," she said.

"Ah," said the fiddler, "hum." And he took a deep breath, to show her how nice it was.

Then they sat and looked at each other seriously.

"I have a little dog," said the fiddler; "when I play, he dances. You'd like to see that, I'm sure. His name is Musket; and you would both be the best of friends right away."

"Yes," said Metabel. She twisted some grass in her fingers. "I can dance, too," she said shyly. And she added in a grave voice,

"I'm not very godly."

" No ? " said the fiddler.

" No," said Metabel.

" Tst," said the fiddler. And he looked at her with such a merry smile that she had to laugh right out.

" Look," she said, and held out her foot for him. " See that hole? My pa fixed it. That's all the shoes I have."

" These are all the shoes I have, too," said the fiddler, pointing to his own.

She stole a glance at him from under her eyelashes. What a queer, homely body he was; and so shabby, just like herself. " I guess you're not very godly either," she said. " Don't you mind? "

" I expect I don't," said the fiddler.

She leaned back on her hands in the grass. Afternoon light was falling through the trees like sunny water over edges. High on the lanes of air two hawks leaned on their wings with angry-sounding cries. Below them Barly dozed in the valley, in the yellow light, in the early shadows the color of smoke and amber.

" Well," she said, " I do. I want God to love me."

And her gray eyes explored with wonder and longing the hazy sky, the far-off shadowy hills.

The trouble was, she thought, that He'd hardly noticed her, being taken up with more attractive people; she could understand how He wouldn't bother to look beyond Edna Flood. She had nothing, she thought, to attract Him; a shabby little person who caused the preacher to frown. And her heart filled with longing, the child's wish to be noticed.

A bee came droning up the hill, and stopped a moment to look at her. " Go home, bee," she said, " off my leg." As the bee flew away, she added, " Bees have such an elegant look."

The fiddler snapped his long fingers. " There," he ex-

claimed; " now I know who you are. That is, I don't know
your name. But you live under a mushroom."

" No, I don't," she said seriously.

" Then," he insisted, " you live in the bark of a tree."

" No," she said; " I live in a little house outside the
village." And she told him how she took care of her
pa, how she cooked and cleaned and borrowed butter.
" Where do you live, mister? " she asked.

" Just now," he said, " I live in a barn with my little
dog Musket. In the evening when I play my fiddle, the
chickens stop eating and give each other friendly looks."

" I'd like to see that," she said.

" While I am playing," the fiddler continued, " the stars
come out. And the robin goes off in a corner to talk to
a little hen named Matilda. The hills grow dark, night
covers them, it is time to go in to supper. But Musket
still wants to dance, because he thinks he is being admired. The hens watch him until it is too dark to see him
any longer; then they go quietly home to bed, all except
Matilda, who has gone for a walk with the robin."

" Oh, my," said Metabel, " about Matilda."

He looked at her with a smile. " You see," he said,
" I have only a little dog to dance for me. Well, isn't that
a pity? "

She nodded her head. " Dogs don't dance very good,"
she said.

" Come," he said, coaxing her, " if I play a tune now on
my fiddle, will you dance for me here on the hill? "

But she shook her head. " No," she said, " I dassn't.
And anyhow, a tune would make it worse."

The fiddler sighed. " You were right," he said; " you
do not live under a mushroom at all."

And taking up his fiddle, he began to play softly to
himself.

"In this village," he thought, "the young are taught to avoid joy; their elders fill the earth with cabbages rather than flowers. That is because they think there will be flowers enough in heaven. Pain is often very pleasant, in view of the relief afterwards. But what a waste of fertile earth, to improve it with cabbages. And what a waste of childish joy, to improve it with godliness."

Metabel lay on her back in the grass, and stared at the sky. The dry wings of darning-needles rustled through the air above her; and the little yellow butter-flies danced together over the bushes, attracted to each other by longing, and by the clear weather. It was all very well, she thought, to be a little dog and dance as much as you liked, because a little dog couldn't be saved. But a little girl was different; salvation was there, and if she missed it, how dreadful for her. She knew she wasn't godly, but she hoped to be in time; in the end she'd go to church in her yellow dress, and God would notice her.

Was it right, even, to play to hens on a fiddle?

Meanwhile there was a tune in the air above her; she couldn't help hearing it, it sang itself into her thoughts. It wasn't like the tunes in church, making her dreamy; this one was sad, sort of, but it had a dance in it; it was like a dancing bird, or a piece of wind in a field. You could run so well to a tune like that, you could do little hops — a skip there, and then some hops, to get you over to that tree, and then a circle. A girl in a yellow dress would walk along saying how do you do to people, so elegant and kind, but supposing you were out in a meadow with a blue shawl and that little tune, couldn't you hop, though . . .

She sat up, and brushed the hair back from her face. If only she had her blue shawl along . . . well, she'd wave it, like this, and like that . . .

It was easier to wave her arms if she stood up. That wasn't dancing, that was just waving. . . .

The late sunlight, slanting down through the dying trees, softened with its mellow light the angular little body stepping so gravely over the grass, brown pigtails flying out behind, the tattered skirt fluttering. Underfoot the crickets sang; far away, over Hemlock, the hawks cried to each other in the air. Bees went droning home; from the pasture slopes below, the bells of Barly's cows broke into quiet chimes. And over all rose the fiddler's tune, like a dancing bird, like a piece of wind in a field, gayer and gayer, faster and faster . . .

Chapter IX

MR. SHRUB often thought about Mrs. Sebold in an interesting way. He also thought about such things as going to China or Peru; he would stand in front of a map; and after a while he would begin to feel mysterious. Then he would look around him at the dusty postoffice, or at the walls of the little room he lived in at Mrs. Watson's, and then he would think of Mrs. Sebold. Well, one always came home to something after such travels.

Mr. Shrub's room at Mrs. Watson's was like the postoffice, but not so dusty. That was because Mrs. Watson came up to clean it every day. She was proud of the maps on the walls, the pictures of far-away places, the big poster of an express train over the bed. She felt, reflected from these walls on which were hung the names of countless cities, seas, and rivers, the glory of geography. Mrs. Watson had often been as far as Milford, and twice to Attleboro; Peru, she expected, was still farther off.

Everyone knew that Mr. Shrub thought about Mrs. Sebold. It wasn't quite a courting, it was what Mrs. Watson called taking careful thought. Mrs. Watson believed that Mr. Shrub had only to speak, to have the widow fall into his lap like a ripe apple. Mr. Watson, however, thought different. " For a female," he said, " she's right opinionated. You listen to me. She'll turn him down after all."

" I declare," said his wife, " I wish he'd make up his mind, because it's giving me the fidgets."

She hardly knew why she wanted Mr. Shrub to marry Mrs. Sebold. Certainly it was not to get rid of him, for she liked to have him as a lodger; she knew she'd miss him when he went, with his maps and the express train. No, it was more orderliness with her, the way she liked to get things straight; a bachelor and a widow ought to be set together out of tidiness if for nothing else.

She had her own way of doing it. There was nothing Mr. Shrub could say she couldn't lead back to a proper bearing on the subject. Let him talk of what he liked, sooner or later she always managed to exclaim, there's no place like home.

" Well, there isn't," said Mr. Shrub.

But he still thought a great deal about Peru.

He talked of such things sometimes to the Reverend Flood. But the Reverend Flood believed that a foreign country was a place in which there was a great deal of room for improvement. He preferred to talk about Barly, or about heaven, which he expected would prove to be Barly all over again, but on a grander scale. That was not very exciting for Mr. Shrub; he longed for heaven, he got a great deal of comfort thinking about it, but it did not seem as mysterious to him as South Dakota.

Mrs. Sebold did not seem mysterious, either. She was there, down the road; when he thought of her, he thought of all kinds of comfortable things. " She's a good woman," he said to the minister.

" She is," agreed the Reverend Flood. " However," he felt called on to add, " her ideas are a little bold."

Mr. Shrub scratched his head. He was not shocked

by Mrs. Sebold's ideas, because, for one thing, he never really listened to what she was saying. As a matter of fact, he found her boldness something of a comfort; he had an idea he could get behind it and live there peacefully with his travels. As long as she didn't come after him, as long as she didn't bring him home by the ear . . . why, the bolder the better.

He had it in his mind to tell her something like that. "Mrs. Sebold," he said, leaning against the counter of the store, where she was busy, " it's this way: some folks never get any further in their minds than what you can see on a clear day." He looked at the ceiling, and his fingers moved up and down on his Adam's apple. " The world's a big place," he said a little anxiously: " you could get lost in it easy."

" You could, at that," agreed Mrs. Sebold. And as Mr. Shrub seemed to have, at that moment, nothing further to add, she concluded philosophically, " I dare say that's why most of us stay home."

Mr. Shrub nodded his head. " So it is," he said, " so it is. That and other things. Yes, ma'am, home . . . home is a very powerful reason, Mrs. Sebold."

She shook a pound of dried apricots onto the scales. " That's a strange thing to hear from you, Mr. Shrub," she said.

Mr. Shrub looked at her timidly. " I'm a strange man," he said. " There's a load of travel in me. But I don't ever seem to get to it."

" That's like the rest of us," said Mrs. Sebold.

Mr. Shrub was pained. " No, it's not," he declared; " no, it's not. You'd be surprised what's in my mind. But home, as I say, I admire it. Yes, ma'am, I have some very uncommon thoughts."

The widow looked at him shrewdly. " Well," she said,

" I expect there's no cause for alarm. Maybe there's strange things in other folks' minds, too, Mr. Shrub. But we all get along just the same."

He gazed at her fondly. " Maybe there is," he said, " and maybe there isn't. I wouldn't say there was anything strange about you, Mrs. Sebold. I'm a lonely man and that makes me think of things. But I don't aim to be lonely all my life. No."

And he went out of the store feeling that he had made an interesting declaration.

Left to herself, Mrs. Sebold went on measuring out dried apricots. But after a while she began to smile to herself. " There's a courting for you," she thought. And she said to herself in Mr. Shrub's best manner: " There's nothing strange about you, Mrs. Sebold."

" Oh," she said airily to the place where Mr. Shrub had been, " isn't there, just? "

Mr. Shrub walked down past the postoffice toward the lower meadows. When he got to the shallow pond back of the ice house, he saw Tiny Flood and Lemuel Watson on a raft made of boards. The little craft was half under water, the water came up over their bare feet, and tried to reach a small piece of cotton which hung from a stick like a little tired sail. When the two boys saw Mr. Shrub, they cried,

" We're going to China."

Mr. Shrub looked about him with joy. All around him the trees stood up calm and bold with their bright leaves, yellow and red, under the clear autumn sky. Far off Old Hemlock lifted itself like a deep shadow into the air; the autumn hush lay like a mist, like a faint smoke, over everything. In the pond the water splashed over the raft, ran up in little ripples over the bare brown legs, and danced away in the sun. China . . .

" What are you going to do there? "

" We're pirates," said Tiny; " look: there's something coming.

" Boom, boom."

When they had beaten the enemy, they rejoiced at their victory.

Mr. Shrub sat down, and undid his shoes. " I'm going to China too," he said. And he advanced with bare feet into the water.

Then the pirates looked very gloomy, and poled away as fast as they could. " It'll sink," they cried. They would not be pirates any more if the postmaster got on their raft, they would only be boys.

Mr. Shrub rushed after them through the water. " Wait a minute," he cried; " there's room for all of us." But when he tried to get on, the boards tipped over, and the two others had to jump off. Mr. Shrub climbed on the raft alone. " Now, then," he said, " give me a push." And folding his arms, he looked nobly at the opposite bank.

The boys took hold of the raft and pushed it through the water. The water made a little rippling sound against the planks, and washed up over Mr. Shrub's ankles. He began to dream, he began to imagine that he was going somewhere. Were they seagulls or swallows, those slanting wings over the green — oh, surely they were green waters. Where should he land? There — that bay, with the volcano . . . midsummer seas, midsummer seas, and the great clouds piled in the south, over Africa . . .

But all of a sudden he saw the fiddler standing on the bank looking at him. Well, that was the end of it; there he was, on a little raft on the ice pond . . .

He got down with as much dignity as he could, and

waded to the shore. " You know," he said to the fiddler, as he put on his shoes, " that amuses the children."

And he went off down the road again as though he had something important to do. The two boys looked after him with sulky faces. Now everything was spoiled; they did not feel like playing any more; the whole thing looked foolish to them. " Darn it," said Lemuel bitterly, " what does he think he is ? "

Mr. Shrub walked away full of embarrassment. He felt that he had made a ludicrous appearance standing on the raft with his arms folded; he wished that the fiddler had not seen him. As his feet went rapidly along, he began to talk things over with the fiddler in his mind. " Well, of course," he said to him, " you think I'm daft. Maybe I am, a little. There's some strange things in me. My mind's full of foreign lands, that's the whole thing. What are you staring at ? I'm on a raft on the ice pond, but my mind is busy, and that's my own affair. There's no crime in that, so far as I'm aware of."

But he had a feeling that the fiddler did not agree with him. And he imagined him saying, " You are simply making excuses for yourself, because you mean to stay in Barly and marry Mrs. Sebold."

" Supposing I do ? " he argued. " I'm not so young as I was. I'd be a fine one to go off to God knows where, and then where would I be when I came home ? "

" You are a coward," said the ghostly fiddler.

Mr. Shrub's face grew red as he walked; he clenched his fists, and made threatening motions with his elbows. " Maybe I am," he said, " maybe I am. I suppose you're not, but look at you : there you are, a hired hand. Maybe you've done as you've pleased, and what did it get you ? I don't know as you play the fiddle so well, either. You'll

49

end in the poorhouse; yes, sir, that's where you'll end.

"You look happy now, but you'll end in the poor-house."

This consoled him a little; the red left his cheeks, and he began to walk more quietly. He saw himself at home in his old age, rocking up and down in front of a fire; the warm, the friendly light, the comfortable chair, the homely walls on which a man could hang his dreams like maps . . .

The sun sank lower and lower, the blue veils deepened in the trees. From the woods long shadows crept out across the fields, stilling the birds; over the cricket song, through the wet grass, the cows went home with a faint fall of bells. The sky was green, a single star hung like a silver lantern in the west. And there the road went on, over the blue floors of evening, under the quiet sky, over the curving earth . . . The yellow lantern of a farm-house winked at him through the trees. Beyond . . . be-yond . . . He stood there, staring, while his heart, like a river, tumbled to the sea.

In his little room in Mrs. Sebold's barn, the fiddler said to his dog, "Musket, are you happy? You must do what you please, without talking about it too much. Live, my little friend, as if you meant to enjoy yourself, and do not mind what the rooster thinks. He gets his corn every day, but there is another hunger which is worse. There is the hunger of those who have only excuses to make for them-selves. Ah, my friend, that is a hunger of the heart which is very painful."

But Musket was not listening to him. It was time for supper and he was already on his way to the kitchen. And in a few moments the fiddler also went cheerfully in that direction.

Chapter X

THERE was a new cistern to dig at the church that fall, and Pa Adams took work, as he said. It might have been the hole in Metabel's shoe made him do it; that was what Mrs. Watson thought. But Pa was never one to vex himself over a pair of shoes; he worked for something grand, or not at all. He'd beg his own tobacco, if need be, but he'd labor heartily for the trimmings. As a matter of fact, he had something expensive on his mind these days. He wanted to buy Metabel the yellow dress she dreamed of.

He didn't say as much, but then, he never said much if he could help it. He just took his pick and shovel — borrowed from the Lowerees — and went up to the church, and dug. He dug slowly, with a sort of relish, the way he sat; he was a man who did little, but aimed to enjoy it. When he thought of what he was going to buy, he winked to himself over it. He saw the joy coming, and relished it in advance.

Metabel was being friends with Musket and the fiddler. It took up her afternoons; she sat in Mrs. Sebold's yard and watched what was going on. She liked to put her arm around Musket and squeeze him; he was amiable, but he did not enjoy it, really. He preferred to talk to Bartholomew, the rooster, or to explore with his sensitive nose the stalks of grass where he came, from time to time, on tiny friends and admirers. Among them was his acquaintance of the week before, the little bull cricket. When he saw him, he said to him politely, " How is your wife? "

" My wife? " exclaimed the cricket in surprise. " I am not married. What gave you such an impression? "

And he added as an afterthought, " No, where one takes such long leaps through the grass, it is better to remain a bachelor."

" Look," said Metabel to the fiddler. " Musket is talking to a cricket."

The fiddler smiled at her from among the cabbages. " That ought not to surprise you," he said, " seeing that they are both dancers like yourself, and therefore have a lot to talk about."

" Oh," said Metabel with a gasp, " I'm not a dancer." And she looked about fearfully to see if the preacher, or anyone, had heard him. " I'm nothing but a little girl."

The fiddler left the garden, and came and sat down beside her. " Why are you afraid of what gives you joy? " he asked. " Is it a sin to be happy, and to dance? Then we must all of us sin a little bit, my child. I do not believe that you are any more wicked than a rose-bush."

And he added gravely, " It is wicked to be envious, or to make people unhappy. But it is not wicked to dance like a little tree in the wind, or a beetle with a green coat. There are so many who cannot dance or sing in the world, and so they go about scolding those who can. That is what is wicked, as a matter of fact."

As they sat there together, Mrs. Sebold looked out of the kitchen window at them. " There's a pair," she said; and she smiled at her thoughts, which were kind and comfortable. But after a while she sighed. " Heaven knows what mischief he's putting into that dreamy head of hers," she thought, " with nobody to set it right again, poor little soul."

The fiddler was not putting anything into Metabel's head that did not belong there. As a matter of fact, they were talking about the animals in the barnyard. " There is Bartholomew," said the fiddler; " see how proud he looks. That is because he has not noticed that the robin is talking to the little hen Matilda, over there by the garden."

And he pointed to where Matilda stood scratching the ground with an air of abstraction.

Matilda hardly noticed what she was doing, because the robin was talking to her so earnestly. Standing behind a cabbage, where he would not be likely to be seen, he said to her in an eager voice:

" Well, look here, are you really happy? What a life you lead; it must be very dull. And with your husband . . . Oh, there is no beauty in a life like that."

" Well," said Matilda, " it is not thrilling for me, exactly. But that is what life is like after all . . . isn't it ? "

" No, no," cried the robin; " it is not like that at all. Has no one ever sung to you, songs full of love and joy? What do you do when the stars come out, or the moon makes the fields look like milk, and makes such deep shadows among the leaves ? "

" Why do you say these things to me ? " murmured Matilda. " I am foolish to listen to you. However . . . go on."

" You are not foolish," cried the robin; " you are being sensible for the first time. What is there in the world except feeling ? To love, to be sad, to be gay . . . There is so much beauty, if you are in love. Well, you are young now, but do you expect to be young forever ? No, no, my dear, life is going by; take it while you can. As for this husband of yours, what does he know about beauty? Can he sing at all? He cannot even fly. He simply struts around and looks like fighting."

"He is very strong," said Matilda thoughtfully.

"Yes," said the robin, "but is he tender? Does he know what is lovely in the world? There is the song of the thrushes in the morning, it is very sweet to hear when you wake under the dewy leaves next to someone you love. You do not know what it is like to watch the little bats dancing at night, while your heart dances with them. You do not know what it is like to feel anything."

And he added anxiously, in a low voice:

"Don't you feel anything at all?"

She did not reply, but gazed dreamily at the ground. "Do you know," she said at last, "what you say makes me feel very strange. Perhaps I am a little more sensitive than the others. I have often thought that there were other things in life. You are right; it is true, I have never been very happy, and what you say . . . well, I do not know how to answer you.

"You are so young," she added tenderly. "Still," she said, "I am young, too, really."

And she sighed. However, as some other hens were approaching at that moment, she looked around briskly, and exclaimed, "Really . . . I was wondering where everybody had gone."

"Listen," said the robin from behind the cabbage, "listen . . ."

But Matilda had joined the other hens, with her head in the air. "No," she was saying to them, "it is always the same here."

Chapter XI

THAT night there was a wind; the trees creaked, and many apples fell to the ground with little thuds. In the morning Mrs. Sebold went out to see if any birds were down; not that it was likely, she thought, at that time of year, but you couldn't ever tell. The fiddler filled his street-cleaner's barrow with windfalls, and started off for Loweree's Farm, where there was a cider mill. The dew still lay like frost upon the grass; there was a sweet smell in the air, the fields looked warm and gold in the early sunshine. As he pushed along his barrow, filled to the brim with red apples, he began to laugh with joy. "Well, now," he said to Musket, who trotted beside him, "this is the best load I have ever had in here." And he looked fondly at the barrow, on which the initials of the street-cleaning department were still visible.

When he arrived at the cider mill, he took a seat next to the Reverend Flood, who was waiting for some russets to be pressed. "Ah," said the preacher, "what a fine day." And he took a deep breath of the clear morning air, stained with the juice of apples and the woodsmoke of kitchen fires.

Turning to the fiddler, he said to him in genial tones, "You are the man who has a little dancing dog. I have never seen anything like that. But I suppose there is no harm in it."

55

"There is never any harm in dancing, preacher," said the fiddler simply.

"Maybe not," said the Reverend Flood, "maybe not. That depends, I think. There are some things which have the appearance of evil. We must not let our senses get the better of us. Hell is waiting, mister."

The fiddler shrugged his shoulders. "I think of joy," he said, "and you think of evil. What is the good of that, preacher? Are you afraid of the devil? What, on such a bright morning?"

The preacher sighed. "The devil is always busy," he said. "He gets us unawares. Joy, yes . . . but joy of self-denial, joy of good works . . . that is what inclines our hearts toward heaven."

The fiddler looked around him at the fields shining in the sun. "Where is this heaven, preacher?" he asked. "For myself, I think it is very close."

"There is your heaven, mister," said the preacher sternly. And he pointed above him to the sky.

But the fiddler shook his head. "No," he said, "that is not my heaven. Why, it is full of people with gloomy faces. What would I do up there? When I die I hope I shall find myself among people who were happy on this earth, who loved its flowers and fields as I loved them, and kissed each other every day for joy."

"I wonder," said the Reverend Flood, "is Barly just the place for you?"

And although his apples were not yet pressed, he got up and went home.

Left to himself, the fiddler gazed after the retreating figure of Dr. Flood with a smile. "Come," he said to himself, "there is always the host and the guest, wherever you go. Some people do not like to be the guests; they are only happy if they are hosts. They want to be at home, and make the arrangements. Well, well, my dear fellow, come in; here is a harp and a crown. When you were alive, you never gave me any trouble. Now I will do as much for you. There is no wine here, and the women have wings, but no legs. You have nothing to do but be happy, and enjoy yourself in a nice way."

When the cider was ready, he put the jug in his barrow, and went home. There he took his axe, and went to split some kindlings. But after a while it seemed to him that his axe was dull, and he went over to sharpen it on the grindstone. The sparks flew out, the stone sang against the steel. Yes, that was better.

He stooped and picked up a log which looked a little like a man's face. "Here," he said, "is a man of wood. It is the preacher; but his nose is too long." And taking out his pocket knife, he sat down to whittle.

That evening he showed it to Mrs. Sebold. "Here is a picture of the preacher," he said.

"Is that what you've done all day?" asked Mrs. Sebold.

"It is," he said bravely.

She looked at him for a moment; then she burst out laughing. "There's a likeness, at that," she said. But soon she grew grave again. " I could wish you had a little more religion, mister," she said; " folks are liable to take it into their heads you're an atheist."

The fiddler looked at her quietly with his eyes like stones. Then all of a sudden he smiled at her in a wheedling manner. "Mrs. Sebold," he said, in a voice like molasses, " you are a strange woman. That is why I like you, because you are not like everybody else."

"Go along," said Mrs. Sebold, changing the pots on the stove with a clatter.

But that night when the dishes were washed, the cloth

57

folded, and the mending done, she stood at the kitchen door, looking out across the garden. Night was in, the stars shone, and the tree frogs spoke together, kreef kreedn, kreef kreedn, in the darkness, in the mist of night.

In his little room in the barn the fiddler was playing. The tune rose in the quiet air, cold as the dew, clear as a bird's song; it was like a bird, she thought; it flew and sang in the night, it went up, up, it fell in little tumbles, it rose again, sad and sharp, like a bird . . .

She leaned her head against the door and listened. What was it she wanted of that tune? What was it in her heart lifted itself with longing, raised itself with slow, sweet motions, like a flower, like a tree holding out its branches . . . birds nested in trees, they sang their songs among the branches, the leaves covered them, they were at home . . .

"You're a strange woman, Mrs. Sebold. You're not like everybody else."

Well, what do you think of that, Mr. Shrub?

She tossed her head in the darkness.

And Julius and Edna, on the top rail of the fence back of the barn, held each other around the waist, and looked at the stars with dreamy faces. Her head rested on his shoulder, the light fragrance of her body made the night air sweeter . . .

"Are you happy, Jule?"

"Well, I am."

"It's so nice like this. Listen; what's he playing now?"

He shook his head; he didn't know.

"We'll always be happy like this, won't we, Jule?"

He kissed her hair, cloudy and sweet in the darkness. What spoke to him out of the shadows? . . . Her eyes were dark with honey of the heart. He drew her close . . . was that his heart, or hers, beating in his breast?

Oh, wait, wait . . . when they kissed like that, the night changed, the clear sweet air grew heavy . . .

"We mustn't," she whispered; "not like that."

"Oh . . . why?"

"Because . . ."

She put her cool slim finger over his lips.

What was it sang to them in the darkness, filled with longing so like sadness?

"No, Jule . . . please . . . or I'll go home."

He mustn't think of such things, he mustn't think of the soft white body under the flowered muslin, the sweet curving flesh . . . But how it made his heart beat. His whole body was heavy with his heart's wild beating . . .

You mustn't do that, Jule — not ever. It isn't right; there's shame in it. It's hearty, but it isn't right.

In silence they climbed down from the fence, in silence they walked home together under the cold bright stars. The fiddle sang fainter and fainter behind them, and all around them as they went, in the wet grass, in the dark lost branches, the cicadas sang their last songs, droned out their heart's shrill hunger.

"Good night, Edna."

"Good night, Jule. Sleep tight."

The last sweet scent of honeysuckle trembled in the cold.

Chapter XII

THE FIDDLER was teaching Bartholomew to be a fighter. He had made some spurs of wood, and was trying them on in back of the barn. He had also clipped the rooster's feathers a little to make him lighter. "Your weight will be in your favor," he said to him, "provided you are fast on your feet. Let me see. Yup." And he gave him a push into the air.

Bartholomew was pleased with himself. He looked down at his feet: there was no doubt about it, the spurs gave him an air of distinction. It was true he had not done any fighting yet, but he felt already that he looked very martial. He imagined himself with one foot on top of his foe, who was looking up at him with admiration and humility. "Aha," he said to Musket, "now you will see." And he gave the little dog a peck with his beak, in order to practise.

At Musket's howl of pain, the fiddler came hurrying over to rescue him. "Save your pecks, my friend," he said, addressing Bartholomew, "for the fair at Milford. You will have plenty to do there. However, it is like a fighter to want to fight everybody. I am glad to see you have so much spirit."

Musket regarded the rooster with a gloomy air. "I would give you a good bite," he said, "except that I

60

would get my mouth full of feathers, and besides, why should we be enemies? There is enough dislike in the world, as it is."

"You are right," said Bartholomew. "Anyhow, I do not dislike you. If I gave you a peck just now, it was because that was a manly thing to do. I have some spirit in me. Come, let us be friends again."

"Just as you like," said Musket. "And now tell me, what is all this? I leave you one moment grumbling and complaining because you are a married man, and the next moment you have on spurs, and are going around giving people bites. It does not seem to me very reasonable. What have you to say for yourself?"

The rooster looked around him with an expression of satisfaction. "As a matter of fact," he said, "I do not mind telling you. It seems there is a rooster at Milford who is supposed to be practically unbeatable. Well, he has never seen me, that is all there is to it."

"Ah," said Musket thoughtfully. "Oh, so that is it. Well, look out, my friend. There is pride, and there is the fall, and somewhere toward the end there is a good bump."

However, at that moment a couple of young hens went by, looking for something to eat. When they saw the rooster with his spurs, they stopped and exchanged glances of admiration. "Oh, my," said one of them in a loud voice, "what a thrill."

The rooster gave Musket a sly look. "Well," he said, "there you are. Just let me get spurs on, and the women fall over themselves. Still, I can understand that; a woman wants a man to be vigorous. Otherwise, what is the good of it? Look at our robin, he has no manly feelings. If he ever marries, his wife will be disappointed."

"That is none of your business," said the robin, who

had arrived just in time to hear this last remark. "That is my own private life. I will thank you to keep out of it, you bully."

A little while later the robin, pursued by the rooster, passed the Reverend Flood on his way to the store to buy a pound of raisins.

"That man of yours," said the preacher to Mrs. Sebold, as he waited for his purchase, "there's a queer one. A great one for talk. You'd hardly credit what he said to me the other day up to Loweree's cider mill. It's a wonder to me God didn't strike him dead where he stood."

"He's a bold one for speech," said Mrs. Sebold, "but he don't mean half."

"Do you think so?" asked the preacher anxiously. "Do you think so, Mrs. Sebold?"

"Yes, indeed," said the widow. But to herself she said, "Well, you've told a lie now, Amelia."

"I am an anxious shepherd," said the Reverend Flood. Mrs. Sebold replied with a smile, "I guess the flock can stand one goat, preacher."

"No," said the preacher earnestly. "A goat is a goat to the godly. I oughtn't to have to listen to what I had to listen to in front of Loweree's cider mill, Mrs. Sebold."

He received his raisins, and went home. But Mrs. Sebold waited until the fiddler had finished his supper that night. Then she said to him in a dry voice, "The preacher was here to see me to-day."

"So," said the fiddler. And he looked at her happily, with an innocent air. But after a while he found it more comfortable to look at the floor. "Hm," he said. "Well . . ."

The widow put her sewing down in her lap. "Do you know what he came to see me about?" she asked.

"I expect," said Lindeman meekly, "we had some words about heaven."

"Aren't you ashamed of yourself?" she demanded.

"No, ma'am," said Lindeman, "I'm not."

She shook her head impatiently. "Well," she said in tones of finality, "I don't mean to be bothered by folks coming up here to complain about you. I've told you once to mend your tongue, if you had any sense at all. If you want to talk so bad, go into the woodshed, and shut the door after you.

"And then," she added, "if the Lord takes it into His head to go into the woodshed after you, why it wouldn't be the first time things like that had happened in a woodshed, either."

Chapter XIII

IN the morning, before he went to work, Pa Adams said to Metabel, "Maybe I ought to fix up that shoe of yours a little better." But when he bent down to examine it, he exclaimed:

"The gum's gone. You've wore it out again."

And he looked at her reproachfully. It seemed to him that she could walk a little easier on her feet, if she tried.

The truth of the matter was that he was not a very careful worker. He fixed a shoe, or dug a cistern in the same way, without being in the least anxious about it. He took his time, but that was only because he liked to sit down and think about things. His mind was never on the work he had on hand; what he enjoyed thinking about was what it would be like when he got home again. Then he'd sit down to admire the idea. From such dreams he simply got up and went home, leaving the cistern open. He never could bring himself to cover over an empty hole; what was the use, he thought, there was nothing in it.

When the preacher saw the uncovered cistern, he shook his head. "Somebody will fall in that hole," he said, "and break his leg."

"What for?" asked Pa.

"Just the same," said the preacher, "I'd cover it over if I were you."

"Well," said Pa, "I'll try to think of it."

The Reverend Flood had a good deal on his mind. He was, as he often said, an anxious shepherd; but he meant to get all Barly under the bars into heaven if he could. That is, all but the goats. What vexed him was that there should be any goats in Barly at all. The trouble was that one goat could bleat louder than a whole parcel of lambs. And then after a while one heard bleats everywhere.

Take Mrs. Sebold now — what a queer thing she had said to him. " Even the hens," she had said, " need cheer to make them lay. There's no harm in a fiddle, so far as I can see."

Well, maybe not. The hens of pious folk ought to be able to do without a fiddle, but was he responsible, after all, for the hens? If they needed cheer, let them look for it in the earth. When the saints wanted cheer, they looked to heaven; they denied the flesh, and God rewarded them with haloes. The devil had too good a time of it on earth; still, he would suffer for it later. It was a comfort to think that folks couldn't carry their good time with them into eternity. Why should the godly, in a free country, be obliged to watch the ungodly amusing themselves right under their noses? In a free country, mind you . . . What sort of freedom was that?

It made him feel oppressed to think of it.

Meanwhile, one of the ungodly was amusing herself in Mrs. Sebold's store. Metabel Adams was telling herself a story. Seated behind a barrel of apricots, she imagined for herself a world in which all the men were polite, and all the women were elegant. Most polite of all was the king's son, who wore a crown, but looked like Lemuel Watson. As for the women, none could compare in elegance to Metabel in a yellow dress like Edna Flood.

When she got that far in the story, she stopped, in

order to think about Edna Flood. Folks were rude to
Metabel sometimes, but never to Edna. There was something in Edna's face, in her sweet dreamy way of looking, that made people want to be gentle with her. She
made Metabel think of cool things, of things that never
got hurt any.

And the child loved her for that. In her own life,
things got hurt, and things were ugly; she needed so much
to think that further on for her, if she were lucky, life
was all like Edna. Edna was violets in April, and honeysuckle, and holding hands, and songs about love, all as
fond and gentle as a child's kiss.

That was what being godly meant; it meant that ugly
things couldn't happen to you. And all that little dreadful
ache of childhood, that intolerable tiny longing to grow
up and come smack on the lovely things you knew were
there, just out of reach — things lovelier than dewy
mornings, or the first spring flowers, or dancing in the
wind, things as lovely as a yellow dress and having people
say how do you do to you, and being loved —

Being loved, being spoken to so sweetly, holding hands
the way Edna and Julius did . . .

"Edna, darling, I love you very much."

"That's so nice, Julius, dear . . ."

That was all taken care of when she thought of Edna.
Edna was all she could ever think to wish for herself.
Only lovely things could happen to her if she grew up
like that.

And so the story stopped when she got to the preacher's
daughter, and the child sat dreaming, leaning against the
apricots.

She was still dreaming when Mrs. Sebold, coming
around the corner with a broom, nearly fell over her.

"Land's sakes," said Mrs. Sebold, "what a mouse you are. Have you no home, child?"

"Yes, ma'am," said Metabel dreamily.

"Well," said Mrs. Sebold, "I don't mind."

"Thank you," said Metabel. The patched brown skirt wouldn't cover her knees, for all her smoothing it down. "I guess I'll go home now," she said.

Mrs. Sebold looked down at her kindly; her heart, mother of robins and other stray creatures, had plenty of room in it for this shabby little child with the hole in her shoe . . . and her hair, tied in those disreputable strings . . . "Haven't you any hair ribbon," she asked, "at all?"

"No, ma'am," said Metabel.

She stood rocking up and down on her toes, looking with joy at the shelves with their colored goods, at the counter with its red and yellow candies, breathing in the air of this marvelous store where there was so much to admire. But Mrs. Sebold went to the shelf where she kept her ribbons, and cut off a yard of blue, shining as the sky, bright as a cornflower . . .

"Here," she said, "tie this in your hair."

Metabel's thin hands fluttered to her breast, her gray eyes widened and grew dark. "For me?" she cried. "No!"

All at once she threw her arms around the widow, and kissed her.

Then, with flaming cheeks, she ran out of the door and down the road as fast as she was able.

Chapter XIV

LEMUEL WATSON and Tiny Flood lounged in front of Mrs. Sebold's General Store. If they had had a penny between them, they would have gone in to buy a stick of licorice, or an all-day sucker. With five cents they would have bought a bottle of cream soda. They were neither hungry nor thirsty, but cream soda, or even an all-day sucker made people forget their vexations, such as chores, bringing in wood, going to bed early, and practising the piano.

"My ma says," announced Lemuel, "she'll make me learn to play the piano if it breaks every bone in my body."

He put his fingers in his mouth, and danced up and down. "Ow," he cried; "what he makes my fingers do." And he played an imaginary scale in the air, putting the thumb under several times.

However, that did not amuse Tiny so much; for one thing, it gave him nothing to do himself. His attention wandered to the window, to the bicycle with its glittering handlebars. "Look at that old bicycle," he said; "I bet you could go as fast as a horse on that."

"Faster," said Lemuel.

"Twice as fast," said Tiny.

"Yes, sir," said Lemuel; and they both gazed with

admiration into the window across the corduroys and aluminum pots to the bicycle.

"If I had that old bicycle," said Tiny, "I wouldn't do anything else but ride her."

"Neither would I," said Lemuel. And he added, "I'd ride to Attleboro in a day or two."

"I'd ride to Boston," said Tiny, "in about two days and a half."

"I'd ride to China," said Lemuel, "in two days and a week."

Well, that was as far as one could go; now they would have to change the subject. That was easy, after all, for China led them directly upon Mr. Shrub, who had a way of pushing them off rafts . . .

"Darn old fool," said Tiny, with a frown.

But Lemuel knew something about that darn old fool. Drawing his friend out of earshot of the house, and closer to the barn, he addressed him in a mysterious whisper:

"Listen. Last night I was in the kitchen and I heard pa say to ma where's the postmaster to-night, and ma says to pa he's gone up to the Widow Sebold's, and pa says he's gone courting, and ma says she guessed so, and pa laughed, and ma she laughed too, and ma said God will bring together his lonely sheep."

"That's in the Bible," said Tiny.

"Well," said Lemuel, "that's what she said. Anyways, they were going on about that darn old fool, and I guess he was going up to ask Mrs. Sebold would she marry him, because pretty soon he came back and he didn't say a word, he just looked lowering, and he went up to his room, and pretty soon I heard a slam. And my ma didn't say anything, but pa let out a holler and said well I guess he got a mitten, and with that my ma hauled off and smacked me over the ear, and I wasn't doing anything, either."

Breathless, he gazed in triumph at his friend.

Tiny looked back at him with shining eyes. "Oh, my," he said. And he began to dance around. After a while he came up to Lemuel with an air of mirth. "Oh, Mrs. Sebold," he piped, "will you marry me, will you marry me, will you marry me? Oh, Mrs. Sebold, will you marry me . . ."

Their two young voices joined in uncontrollable glee, they fell with joy upon the ground.

The fiddler came out of the barn to see what was going on. "Oho," he said, "I can see that you are celebrating something; I expect that it is someone's discomfort, seeing it affords you so much amusement."

"Yes, sir," said Lemuel meekly.

"Well, that's right," said the fiddler: "the discomfort of someone else is the only thing one can celebrate without envy."

"Yes, sir," said Tiny dutifully. And the two urchins walked soberly home without talking any more. They did not want anybody so old as that to agree with them; it spoiled their celebration.

Lindeman went into the kitchen in a sly way, looking for Mrs. Sebold. When he saw that she was busy in the store, he tiptoed to the cupboard, and took down a jar of currant jelly. Then he hurried back to the barn again, to feed some jelly to Bartholomew, the rooster.

"Here," he said; "perhaps this is not just the sort of jelly fighting cocks are accustomed to, but one cannot always have everything the way one would like it."

Bartholomew looked at the jelly with distaste. But when he saw Musket regarding him with an expression of envy, he made believe that he was enjoying it. He dipped his beak into the bowl, stretched his neck, and looked up at the roof. " Ah," he said, " that is excellent jelly. It makes me feel very manly."

Musket regarded him carefully. "You look thinner to me," he said; " I wonder if you are not a little too thin. You must be careful not to overdo. I hear that this Milford rooster is a terrible bird. He enjoys picking other roosters to pieces."

"Hm," said Bartholomew. "Of course he has had a lot of experience. But my heart is in the right place. I am not like the robin, afraid of everything and excusing myself by saying that I have some ideals. With me, a peck is a peck, and I know where to put it."

" I remember a cock-fight I saw once," said Musket thoughtfully. "It was very bloody. A very handsome rooster was killed right in front of my eyes. One moment he was jumping around, full of what he was going to do, and the next moment he was down under the spurs. Well, for some time after that I lived on farina and vegetables. It was a harrowing thing to see."

Bartholomew cleared his throat; one could see that he was a little taken back; nevertheless he said bravely, " What is the good of being squeamish? I have no patience with that sort of thing. A weak stomach is all very well for a dancer, or a robin, but it is nothing for a fighting cock. As a matter of fact, a fighting cock cannot afford to be weak anywhere. I assure you since the hens have seen me with my spurs on, I hardly get any sleep. It is gratifying, but one has to be a giant. I am thinking of going away for a little while before the bout, to rest myself."

As he walked away, the robin flew down out of a tree, and gazing after him with a look of disdain, said to Musket, "There goes a vulgar fellow. He thinks he is

71

so captivating with his manly talk, but I could tell you a thing or two; I know a few things about him he would not be so pleased to have me know. Well, you see how it is . . . some of his wives also find me a little attractive."

And he ruffled the feathers on his breast. But presently he grew morose. "Unfortunately," he admitted, "they always go back to him again. They seem to be attracted to him at the very moment they are looking at me. Perhaps they even tell him the sort of things about me that they tell me about him. I should not like to think so." And he looked at Musket with a dejected air.

"Women are all alike," said Musket in practical tones. "They do not want things to be always the same. A woman likes to feel a little terrified while she is being soothed, and also the other way around. You have to be a little cruel in order to have success with a woman. She enjoys being sacrificed, my friend; it is her nature. If you will not do it, she will do it for you."

"I suppose you are right," said the robin, with a sigh; "I have often thought that I should be a little fiercer. But can one change one's nature, do you think?"

"You must make up your mind to act a little," said Musket. "For instance, if you feel tender, give your wife a peck, even if you do not feel like it. That will show her how it would be if you were vexed with her. On the other hand, when you feel brutal, that is just the time to be nice to her. She will love you all the more if she feels that you are able to control yourself."

Meanwhile, in the store, Mrs. Sebold was thinking things over. It surprised her how easy it had been to say No to Mr. Shrub. She knew that Barly would take Mrs. Watson's view, that she should have had him, if only out of tidiness. But she wanted something more than tidiness, she knew that now — had always wanted it, she guessed.

Did she want to be loved, perhaps? Glory be . . . she put her hands to her cheeks, red and hot at the idea. Well, then, maybe she did. Not loved, say, like Edna Flood . . . she wasn't so young any more. But least-ways, a little . . . enough to give her heart a flutter. She didn't ask much — just a flutter. Maybe it was wrong at her age, and a widow. Maybe it was; but she'd made up her mind, and if it didn't suit, why then she guessed she'd just stay a widow, and that was all there was to it.

Chapter XV

Sunday before the fair it rained. From the trees the drenched leaves, already dead, drifted in circles to the brown and sodden ground. The air was cold; the rain driven slanting by the wind over the bare fields, fell with a hum upon the church where the Reverend Flood was giving his sermon.

His text was the hundred and twenty-sixth Psalm: They that sow in tears shall reap in joy.

"What does that mean?" he asked, looking around him at the congregation. " Does it mean that God wants you to spend your time on this earth playing and dancing? No, my friends. God is not a loafer. When you think that something is hard to do, too hard, perhaps, for your poor strength, just remember what God had to do. He made the world in six days. He made Adam and Eve overnight. Do you think that was easy, or that He was enjoying Himself? Oh, no. He had to tug, my friends, He had to pull and push."

"Yup," said the fiddler, who was sitting in the rear of the church, and thinking about Bartholomew. The Reverend Flood looked at him angrily, and continued:

" A man came to me the other day and said, What is that I see above me, Dr. Flood; can it be God? He looks at me so sternly. Those were his very words; and they

74

were the words of a lost soul. No wonder God was looking at him sternly, my friends; that man wanted to reap
joy upon this earth. He wasn't thinking of heaven, he
wasn't thinking of being saved. The devil had him by
the hair."

Edna Flood listened to her father's sermon with a
feeling of satisfaction. How nice it was to be right. It
was pleasant to have things to do, and to want to do
them. It was sweet to be pure, to feel what God wanted
you to feel, and nothing else. She felt that she was saved,
and her young eyes filled with happy tears.

Mr. Shrub sat gloomily in the Watson pew and thought
about himself. He had been mortally surprised. Here he
was, after giving up China, in the interests of a tidy life;
and now he'd been given a mitten. It shook his faith in
tidiness. Suppose when he got to heaven, there was another surprise for him? He trembled to think of it.
When he thought of the fiddler, he grew hot. He expected the fiddler was laughing at him. Well, he said
to him in his mind, laugh, and go drat. I'm going to see
the world; I'm going to have a look at something before
I die. Yes, sir, you can rot in this valley, but I'm going
to see Niagara Falls.

"Hell is hot," cried the Reverend Flood; "there are
lakes of fire, and pits of flame. Do you think you will
escape, my friends? Don't imagine it. Those who spend
their time dancing and singing on this earth will sing
another tune when the devil gets hold of them; they will
dance on coals of fire."

"There," said Mrs. Watson to her son Lemuel.
"You'll fry in hell if you don't behave yourself. Put your
tongue in, and listen to the preacher." And she gave him
a slap to remind him.

Pa Adams and his daughter were not in church. Pa

felt a touch of misery in his back, and what with the rain, and six days of digging, chose to stay at home and groan in a quiet way. That kept Metabel at home, too, to rub his back, and look after him; poor Metabel, with a new blue ribbon for God to see and folks to admire.

But the Reverend Flood was pleased: because if Pa stayed away from church long enough, he'd lose his share of the kingdom without the preacher having to trouble himself about it one way or the other. He wished the fiddler would stay at home, too.

The rain fell, the choir sang; in his seat near the door the fiddler looked at his wet boots, and sighed. His eyes wandered about among the faces of the men and women of Barly: eyes, noses, bits of calico . . . They came to rest at last on Mrs. Sebold. Mrs. Sebold had taken the robin to church with her. She was sitting up, looking at the ceiling, while the robin slept in her lap; she seemed to be listening not to the sermon, not to the choir, but to something she was thinking. It made her smile, it made her face fold into gentle lines . . . it made the fiddler's heart grow light again to see . . .

"God bless her," he said to himself.

High up in the choir loft the preacher's little son also regarded Mrs. Sebold. There she was, he thought, praying again, instead of being satisfied. But as a matter of fact, Mrs. Sebold was not praying. She was thinking about her robin; and she was talking to God who used to feed her chickens with her before the fiddler came. She felt that she could ask Him for a wife for her robin. But she didn't pray for it, she just asked Him kindly, as a favor.

"A wife," she thought, "to make a nest with him. Or," she added dreamily, "a husband . . . to sing — what is it robins sing?

76

" A husband to sit in front of the fire . . ."

Edified by the sermon, and blessed by prayer, the citizens of Barly went home to dinners of cabbage soup, corned beef, lettuce with sugar on it, corn fritters, and bread pudding. Such a sermon, mostly about hell-fire, pleased and consoled them; it made their own life seem kinder, to think of what was in store for the ungodly.

Rain fell all through the afternoon, edges of cloud trailed on the hillsides, mists formed and broke over Hemlock. From the ground came the cold sweet smell of the drenching, the air was heavy with the quiet sound of rain. And Metabel, her duties done at last, went shyly up to the church she thought was empty, to sit a while in the dusty light, and show her ribbon to God.

As she passed Sebold's barn, she heard the fiddler playing. It was almost as though he were asking her wouldn't she stop a while, and see Musket and Matilda, and maybe dance a little. But no, she wouldn't; not on Sunday. She went on.

Metabel, Metabel, don't go by — it would be better if you stayed and danced, — yes, even on a Sunday — better than to go where you are going —

When she came to the open cistern, she gave a little shiver. That was where her Pa had got his misery. It was an ugly looking hole in the rain, so dark and deep and wet; a body could fall in there and never get out, likely.

She turned to enter the church. But then she stopped; what she saw kept her from going in. She stood in the doorway and held her breath. " Oh," she said.

Chapter XVI

JULIUS and Edna had gone up to the church to practise the organ. They felt alone there in the rain; the rain shut them in, it put a mist on the roads. When Edna looked out of the window, she couldn't tell what was hill and what was sky. Even the road to Milford was all blurred out, and Milford was lost, far away, in mist, like the top of Old Hemlock. Maybe there wasn't any top to Hemlock any more, nor any Milford . . .

Nor anything in the whole world but the two of them there in the choir loft, and the gray misty air, and the fiddler playing down below in the rain. She'd like that . . . just the two of them.

Julius played fugues and canons with a frown. But after a while he stopped; he didn't want to play, he wanted to talk.

"We're all alone here," he said.

She nodded. " Isn't it nice? No one can see us."

"Listen — down there. That's the fiddler. It sounds queer in the rain, doesn't it — not like a fiddler at all. What is he playing, do you think, Edna — a hymn? "

" I don't know. Father says he makes the hens lay by playing to them. I think that's wicked, Jule."

" It's not a hymn," said Julius, listening, " it's a song. What kind of a song is it, Edna — a love song? "

"Oh . . . Jule."

Under the choir loft, in the doorway, Metabel, un-seen, looked up at them with parted lips. Weren't they beautiful together. But why did Edna act so funny with him? Why did she say, oh, Jule, and push him away? That was a queer thing to do.

Metabel heard the fiddler, too. The music sang to her of love, of a king's son and a queen's daughter. And above her, in the choir loft, was the queen's daugh-ter . . .

"Go on," she whispered, "kiss each other."

Violets in April, the first spring flowers . . .

"Edna," said Julius a little unsteadily, "do you like to be alone — like this — "

She took his hand, folded it between her cool dry palms. "Of course," she said. Her voice was cool too, full of peace, quiet like the rain.

"I don't know. I wish it would clear."

"I like it here," she said; "it's homey."

But Julius was listening to the fiddler. It was queer how it made him feel, that thin, silver song down there in the valley — sad, like, and lonely. It seemed so all alone, in the mist, in the rain — it made him feel all alone too. "Edna," he said huskily. Was she really with him, there in the choir loft?

She tried to draw him away from what was troubling him. "Come and sit next to me," she said, "and let's talk. Then you must practise some more." She raised his brown hand to her cheek. "I want so much for you," she said.

But Julius wouldn't sit down. He stood over her, staring down at the upturned face with its eager curve from chin to cheek, the stretched, white throat, the brown sweet eyes, wide and kind. What makes you so sad,

Jule? Your heart is beating with longing. There, under your hand, the brown and gold, the soft tender body . . . Edna . . . What is it you want of her?

He drew her to her feet. In silence his hands went around her; he saw her dark eyes grow darker still, he felt her body draw back as with all his strength he bent her in his arms. She turned her head to avoid him, she held her breath, she tried to push him away. " No," she cried, " oh, no . . . Jule, no . . ."

Below, in the doorway, the child looked on with anxious eyes, gray as the rain. Edna, Edna, what are you doing? Why do you push him away? That isn't lovely . . . Are you afraid? You, Edna, afraid?

Love is sweet, isn't it? Oh, surely for you . . . honeysuckle and holding hands . . . Why do you cry No, Jule, no . . . Isn't it sweet, Edna? You're making it out so ugly . . . *Oh, is it ugly?*

The child is frightened now. Edna, Edna, please don't make it ugly. Don't let him kiss you like that . . . not if you don't want to . . .

She tried to get away, tried with all her might to get free of him. Her hair fell down her back, her dress tore at the shoulder . . . In the end she let him kiss her. But her mind was cold and dark with the shame of it. He was hurting her and he didn't care. She closed her eyes; the rude kiss hurt her mouth. She gave herself up to being hurt, she didn't even say No anymore, she waited for pain.

Thank God she didn't enjoy it any. An angel couldn't have been purer.

Under the choir loft the child stood weakly clasping and unclasping her hands, her face white as dandelion seed. Edna, the cool, the sweet . . . Oh, what had happened to her? How could she let it be so ugly? Why didn't she make it lovely, the way she was? Why didn't she make it lovely?

And then Edna began to cry. The sound of her crying broke the child's heart; she stumbled out of the church with her arm over her eyes. All that was sweet in the world had let what was ugly get the best of it, all that was gentle had let itself be hurt . . . a girl crying on the floor, a man with a red face, and such pain, such a heart full of pain . . .

She was too sick to cry. Her feet carried her off the path, trembling, hurrying, all but falling. . . . The open hole lay before her, but she didn't see it. Her eyes were shut as tight as she could shut them, never to see that thing again, never to hear again that No, Jule, no . . . never to feel her heart break again at that cry of woe.

She didn't even scream when she fell; there was only a whimper from her drenched little body as the breath was knocked out of her, only a single sob—

"Edna."

Chapter XVII

THE THIN cold rain made cobwebs in Jule's hair; his unhappy feet raised a sound of gravel in the road. His whole body was cold with what he'd done. Well, he'd done it, and no mistake. She'd never feel the same about him again. And would he ever feel the same, he wondered. It was over, love was over. He'd killed it, that was all. Love was over.

At the foot of the hill he met Mr. Shrub walking doggedly through the rain under a great umbrella. "Look here," said Mr. Shrub, "I can't get a rig."

Julius stood staring at the postmaster with dark eyes. He wanted to say to him, "Do you know what I've done?" Instead he said dully, "No, you can't, not on a Sunday."

But when Mr. Shrub turned away, he turned with him. He didn't want to be left alone among those drenched, gray fields.

"I'll go along with you," he said.

And the two of them started down the road under Mr. Shrub's umbrella.

Back in church Edna dried her eyes, and sat up. She was tired, and her dress was rumpled. But on the whole, she wasn't as unhappy about it as she'd expected to be. It was horrid, but, after all, she hadn't kissed him. Her

face grew hot . . . Oh, never, never . . . and the next
time she saw him she'd tell him so. Not until they were
married, and then only in the dark, and she'd close her
eyes. It was her duty then, and so she'd do it. But now it
was so wild, and shameful. It just hurt her, and so she
cried. On Sunday, too.

In the end she went home peacefully. Men were like
that, she guessed, but it didn't amount to anything;
women just had to bear it. And she'd bear it as well as the
next one, but only when she was married, and then in the
dark.

For a while Julius and Mr. Shrub walked gloomily
along without speaking. Julius no longer thought of anything, he was just walking. Presently he'd get somewhere,
and then he'd see. But Mr. Shrub, it turned out, had
something he pined to say. It was something he'd been
thinking about for a long time. "Yes, sir," he declared,
giving the umbrella a bounce on his shoulder, "I've just
about made up my mind. I'm going away. I'm going out
to see something of the world, rig or no rig. I'm going to
walk to Milford, and take a train. It came over me all
of a sudden. Niagara Falls . . . I may get as far as
California."

And he looked around him with an angry air.

"Take that fiddler, now," he continued. "They say
he was a street-cleaner. What good has being tidy ever
got me?"

Julius did not answer.

"Well, that's it," said Mr. Shrub. And they continued
for a while in silence.

"There's Loweree's mill," said Mr. Shrub presently.
"That's the last I'll ever see of Barly."

"Hum," said Julius.

After a while something Mr. Shrub was thinking made

him sigh and clutch his umbrella tighter. "They'll get a new postmaster," he said. "They'll send one up from Milford."

"Yes," said Julius.

"It won't be the same," said Mr. Shrub.

"No," said Julius.

"He won't know so much about the mail," said Mr. Shrub.

And they were silent again.

"There's the trail to Hemlock," said Mr. Shrub. "I'll never see that again."

"No more you won't," said Julius.

"Well," said Mr. Shrub, "I'm doing what's in me. There's a power of travel in me, always has been. Now it's coming out."

But Julius had nothing to say. All he felt, walking like that in the rain, was lonesome. The more he walked, the lonesomer he felt. The farther he got from Barly, the more he wanted to turn around, the more he wanted to get back home again. There was no passion left in him, not much grief even, only a longing to get back into the middle of things, as he'd always had them . . . haying, ploughing, hymns on Sunday, work on Monday . . . back to Edna as she'd been before, sweet, steady, gentle, a comfort to the mind, a not too mortal maid . . . He wanted to go home. He didn't see the dripping trees, the drenched fields; he saw, instead, the little parlor at Flood's where he used to sit, and Flood's godly daughter so cool and quiet and serene, held her again very gently, spoke to her humbly, felt as he walked, the old sweet worship in his heart . . .

He stopped at the top of a rise. Before him the road fell away to the south; he could see, far off, and faint in the rain, the blue hills beyond Milford. He looked at Mr.

Shrub, and Mr. Shrub looked at him. " Well," he said at last, " I guess I'll be going back now."

"Yes," said Mr. Shrub. He stood staring out across the valley to those cold wet hills, to that low gray sky veiled in rain. At last he sighed. " I'll walk back with you a few steps," he said. " I'm in no hurry."

Side by side they started back to Barly under Mr. Shrub's umbrella.

Chapter XVIII

ON the whole, Barly felt that God had visited divine justice on Metabel Adams in a peculiarly heavenly manner. She had been found lying in the water at the bottom of the half finished cistern by the Reverend Flood, on his way home that night from a chance late visit to the church. The open cistern vexed him so much that he went a step out of his way to look in, and saw Metabel lying there with her leg bent under her, and the blue ribbon in her hair. He carried her home, the thin face against his shoulder wet with tears and rain — how gently, and with what pity, no one in Barly at least would ever know or credit. He kept his wrath for Pa, but Pa didn't need it. The little body with its broken leg was enough.

" O my God," said Pa, and went outside and sat down and cried. It was the Reverend Flood who laid Metabel in bed, and held her hand until the doctor came.

" Well," he said to Pa when he left in the dark of the morning, " there's no need of words from me, my friend. If you're satisfied with yourself now, that's your own affair."

And he went home. In the morning Edna went down to see what she could do. But the moment Metabel saw her, she put her head under the covers. So Edna went

home again, thinking that Metabel was an ungrateful little heathen.

So did the rest of Barly. The child had got what she
deserved, for being so forward; and her pa had been
punished for leaving the cistern open. It was enough to
give any one a turn toward religion.

"The Lord giveth," said Mrs. Watson, "and the Lord
taketh away." And seeing her son standing nearby with
his mouth open, she cried, "Just let me see you do that
once — just let me see you."

But Lemuel had no intention of being seen doing anything in the least like it. With his friend Tiny, he sat in
the woods back of the Adams place, and watched the window where Metabel lay. The two young men stared at
each other, looked away, scraped their feet in the ground,
and scratched their heads. "Do you think she'll get
well?" they asked each other in awed tones. They felt
sorry for themselves; they were the same age as Metabel,
and now she'd fallen down a hole. It frightened them to
think of a thing like that happening to anyone as young
as they were.

Old Doctor Bailey paid his visit, from over Milford
way; after a while the Widow Sebold came down the road
with a bowl of soup. She went in, and set it on the stove
to heat. Then she came over to the bed and put her hand
on the child's damp head. "Does it pain you much?" she
asked kindly.

"No, ma'am," said Metabel. Her gray eyes were without light in her white face, her thin bare arms were
stretched out on either side of the coarse brown blanket.
Her braids were tied with shoestrings again; the ribbon,
still damp, and streaked with mud, lay hidden away in the
trunk. "No, ma'am," she said, and smiled; but she might
as well not. She had an air, lying there, of not caring

87

whether she got better or didn't; of not caring what happened to her any more. When Mrs. Sebold asked her how it had all come about, she simply closed her eyes. " I fell into a hole," she said, in a voice so low as to be barely audible. It was all she'd say about it to anyone.

" I expect you'll be up soon," said Mrs. Sebold, as cheerfully as she could. And as there seemed to be nothing more to say, she went outside to talk to Pa. " Look here," she said angrily, " who's going to pay for all this ? "

Pa ran his fingers over his thumb; then he stared at the back of his hand. After a while he looked up at a tree over Mrs. Sebold's head. " Well, ma'am," he said gently, " I figure to pay for it myself; I've a little money put away. I guess I can take care of it, thank you kindly."

He sighed; his eyes went back to his hands again. " I was meaning to buy her a yellow dress," he said at last. " She's always had a sort of hankering for one. But I don't know; maybe she won't want it, now."

And he turned soberly away. " Yes, ma'am," he said, " I guess I can take care of it myself."

Metabel lay on her bed and looked at the ceiling with its dusty cobwebs in which were caught here and there dry wings, or the legs of flies. The fiddler's little dog Musket sat beside her, his cold nose under her fingers; now and then his tail gave the floor a thump, and he moved his nose deeper into the little cup of her hand which trailed from the bed like a pond lily. " Well," he seemed to say, " this is very bad."

Her hand gripped the shaggy neck for comfort. " Musket, dear," she said, " did you come to tell me about a little girl who lived under a mushroom? Well, one day she fell down and hurt herself. And who do you think came to see her but sweet little Musket."

Thump, went Musket.

88

"Tell me about Matilda," she continued, "is she good? Do you remember the day we all sat up on the hill together . . . no, you couldn't, it was only me and the fiddler. And I danced up on the hill, and I guess I shouldn't have.

"Oh, Musket," she cried, "I can't dance any more, my leg's broken. . . ."

Then, as she lay there with the slow tears running sidewise down her face, she heard from under her open window the bird-like fiddle. It wasn't dancing now, it wasn't singing any longer, it was telling her something. "Metabel," it said, "don't cry. You don't need your legs to dance with; dance with your heart, that is better. See how the wind blows in the bush, and the brown leaves fall; hear in the branches the last songs of birds. Is there nothing in the world but a little girl? Out here the shadows of trees bend across the grass; it is lovely still in the meadows above Barly, it is lovely still in your heart, my child. Here are your little friends, the bees in yellow coats; in spring the robins will be back to sing again among the leaves. You will find a new way to dance then. And your heart will blossom again like the apple trees."

Metabel smiled; her eyes closed. The last thing she heard as she fell asleep was the fiddle, and Musket's tail going thump, thump on the floor. The little dog did not dance, although his master was playing; he sat quiet, looking at Metabel out of his true eyes. Then he got up and went home. But the fiddler continued to play until long after the sun was down. The Reverend Flood heard him on his way to bring Metabel a book with pictures of the Christian martyrs being eaten by the lions.

Chapter XIX

BARTHOLOMEW did not like to have his tail clipped because, as he explained to Musket, it made him top-heavy. "It is not vanity with me," he said, "I can assure you. It is simply that without my tail I am apt to fall over on my face, and then my opponent could easily give me a bite when I was not looking."

Musket was watching the rooster at his training. He sat on the ground, in company with the robin and the cricket, while Bartholomew made believe that he was fighting with somebody. Every now and then the rooster stopped dancing around, and came over to discuss things. "I am in fine shape," he said; "I am very confident, and I feel sure that I will soon peck the other bird to pieces. I have one blow which starts from the ground, and is apt to destroy anything. Would you like to see it?" And he started sparring again with an imaginary enemy. Suddenly he rushed at a place in the air, drew back as though to avoid a lunge, and let loose a number of pecks calculated to astonish his adversary. After that he gave the air a beat with his wing, which the fiddler had already clipped. "I measure him like this," he explained, "and then I let him have it." And he brought his beak up in a lunge from below.

"Well, what do you think of it?" he asked, a little out of breath from his exertions.

" It is magnificent," said the cricket. " I would bet on you against anyone." And turning to Musket, he explained in a voice trembling with admiration:

" He is a great fighter."

But the robin was not so easily impressed. " You notice," he said, " that he doesn't use his spurs. Well, actually, he has no science. This other cock is a cunning bird. I flew over there the other day to watch him work. He has a very baffling crouch: that blow will never get started. But he would be easy for a spur. Against a stiff leg he is done for."

Bartholomew replied angrily, " When I want to use my spurs I will do so. But please do not try to tell me how to fight, because that would be too ridiculous."

" After all," said the robin calmly, " I have only your interest at heart. If you don't want to hear what I have to say, why very well, I won't say anything." And he flew away, looking very proud.

When he was gone, the rooster returned to the sparring ground with a thoughtful air, and began to jump up and down. " I must get my legs in order," he said; " the legs are very important, because that is where the spurs are.

" As for this famous crouch, that is just what I like; I will hit him with a spur in back of the head, and then where will he be? "

The robin flew back to the house. On the kitchen porch he came across the hen Matilda; she was looking around to see what there was to eat. " Ah," he said, " I was thinking of you. Well, how have you been? "

But Matilda did not want to pay any attention to him. " I have done a great deal of thinking," she said; " and I don't believe I ought to see you any more. For one thing, you are always talking about the same thing, and in the second place, my duty is to my husband. If I had at one

time, perhaps, a little weakness for you, it is over; you
can never mean anything to me, really, because I love
Bartholomew with all my heart."

And she added, as she hopped down the stairs, "He is
entirely different since he has become a great fighter."

When she got to the ground she looked up and asked,
"Don't you think so?"

"He will be picked to pieces in the first round," said
the robin.

Matilda gave a gasp. "What a wretch you are," she
cried; and as she stalked indignantly away, she added over
her shoulder, "Just keep out of my way after this, you
. . . twitterer."

The robin hopped sadly into the house. Now that
Matilda had no more use for him, he found her more attractive than ever.

That afternoon the fiddler went into the store to get
some rock candy. When Mrs. Sebold asked him what he
wanted it for, he replied that he wanted it for the chickens. Then he went back to the barn and prepared a physic
of cream of tartar and butter, to which he added the rock
candy. "Come," he said to Bartholomew; "this does not
taste very good. But a fighter must be something of a
hero. Close your eyes, and open your mouth . . . because otherwise worse things might happen to you."

"Phoo," said Bartholomew.

When he had swallowed his medicine, he was taken out
for a walk; then he was given a warm mess of bread and
milk, with more rock candy in it. Finally he was shut up
in the barn, away from the hens; and the fiddler went in
to supper.

"Lindeman," said Mrs. Sebold over the supper table,
"I've a little something for you to do for me down to
Milford. I'm not going this year; I haven't the heart for

it, that's one thing; and besides, I've the store to watch. I want you should buy me a yellow dress, for a girl of nine. I'll give you the money for it."

"Mrs. Sebold," said the fiddler, "that is an errand after my own heart. It is the thought of a good woman. I shall bring home something elegant."

"The poor mite," she said. "Well, things like that do cheer you up sometimes."

She was silent for a moment. "I'll tell you, mister," she said: "she don't act right, to my way of thinking. She seems like she's been hurt in her vitals. The child doesn't want to get well, that's the matter with her. She acts like she's had a shock."

And she added gravely, "Children don't fall into holes for nothing."

"I had a little talk with Mrs. Watson," said the fiddler. "Mrs. Watson allows as how the child went up there to the church to dance; and God He up in His wrath and pushed her in. Mrs. Watson is a pious woman, Mrs. Sebold, ma'am."

"Well," said Mrs. Sebold with energy, "I know one thing for sure: if God pushed her into that hole, then He's changed some since I was a girl."

"Good for you, Amelia," cried the fiddler.

And as the red flooded her face, she never thought to be vexed with him for calling her Amelia.

Chapter XX

THE FAMOUS fighting cock of Milford was a Malay cross, a frightful looking bird with a gloomy expression. Musket, sitting on the pitside, shivered to himself; even the robin glanced apprehensively at Bartholomew, who gazed about him with an air of assurance, from which, however, he was not able to banish a certain anxiety. Only the cricket was calm; surrounded by jostling farmers, in danger of being trampled to death at any moment, he looked forward to the combat with composure, and awaited the outcome with pride. " Soon they will see," he declared, " what it means to come from Barly."

The pit was in Silas Bade's barn, cousin to the Ploughmans of Hillsboro. Lanterns hung from the beams, and threw their yellow light onto the faces of the farmers, who crowded each other around the pit, the better to see everything. There was little betting, for it was conceded that Bartholomew had no chance against the Malay cross, who was used to such battles from childhood. Nevertheless, voices were low, and the air charged with excitement, out of fear of the constable, and the expectation of murder.

" For murder," said the robin to Musket, " it will be." And he added inconsequently, " Oh, Matilda."

Outside, in the blue-dark evening, the ladies of the

church were going peacefully down the road to Julius
Penny's piano recital. The old folk went slowly, the better to relish their pleasure; young lovers, hand in hand,
went slower still, and stopped to kiss where a tree hid
them, or whisper in the shadows. In the marshes below
the town the frogs sang with tiny, bell-like voices; woodsmoke drifted in the air, the windows of the cottages, set
back among apple trees, shone with light. Music would
make their love the sweeter, but there was no need to
hurry, it was sweet enough.

Bartholomew closed his eyes. He wished there were
more of his friends there; he would have liked to see
Matilda. The lights were harsh, the murmurs of the men
crowding around the pit were unfriendly and menacing.
The farmers came up to examine him without sympathy;
they went away shaking their heads. His heart sank; he
remembered the sunny mornings in the barnyard, he remembered how the hens had admired him. That was the
way fighting should be, in the sun, with some applause.
Well, he would show these farmers, but it was no longer
a pleasure. His throat felt tight, and he found it difficult
to swallow. Yes, Barly was the place to be happy; how
good it was to go out in the early morning, when the grass
was spidery with dew, and the sun glanced along the fields
warm and slanting, when the shadows were so long, and
the air was so fresh. And how peaceful at night to fall
asleep while the tree toads sang far away.

He opened his eyes again, because, after all, that was
more manly. But the first things he saw were his own
spurs, of shining steel, thin and sharp, curved like a scimitar. There is death, he said to himself, and held them up,
one by one, to look at.

Waiting in a barn like that, the blood grew chilly. Was
it true he might never see Barly again? For a moment

95

he saw himself under the spurs of his adversary, helpless and undignified; and his heart failed him. What, to lose everything? — dignity, vigor, and Matilda?

Panic took hold of him. "No," he said; "better to avoid it altogether." And with a sly motion he started for the door.

The hand of the fiddler seized him before he had gone a step. "Bartholomew," said the fiddler, "it is too late now to run away. But I know what you are feeling. It is always before the battle that one suffers most. Control yourself, my friend. When you are fighting and your blood is boiling, you will forget Matilda, and the possibility of being defeated. That is what makes such things as wars and battles possible. It is only the thoughtful who suffer."

And picking the rooster up in his arms, he went forward with him to the pit. "Barly is ready," he said to the judge, and looked around him with an air of ferocity.

The two birds, placed eye to eye and beak to beak, regarded each other for some time in silence. Aware that the critical moment had come, each looked for some advantage with which to begin the battle. Presently the Malay cross began to lift and lower his head; and Bartholomew did the same, in order to appear knowing, and also to encourage himself. However, his motions did him no good, for all at once he received a terrific blow on the side of the head. The Malay cross had flown at him and pecked him.

Bartholomew sat down, but only for a moment. Filled with rage, but a little dizzy, he arose and rushed at his enemy. The two birds met in midair; their beaks and claws locked, and they fell together to the ground. There they struck at each other, and a few feathers floated away in the breeze.

" Ah," groaned the farmers. " Oh."

" That's it; let him have it."

" There's a pretty bird."

The Malay had risen to his feet, and was leaping on and off Bartholomew, giving him short pecks with his beak. Bartholomew lay on one side; seeing that he needed a wing, the fiddler leaned down to help him. " Be brave," he said; " remember that you come from Barly."

" Ai," groaned the robin, " look at that. Use your spurs, Bartholomew."

The rooster was bewildered. Under the energetic stabs of the foe, he found himself unable to concentrate on what he was doing. He had only one desire, to hurt his enemy, but he no longer remembered how to do it. There was a very clever blow, he thought to himself, which began at the ground, and then went up. But when I try it, that villain is not in the way. And he glanced appealingly at the corner where the robin was hopping up and down with vexation.

The cricket also was excited. " No," he exclaimed " I have never seen such a fight before. I wouldn't believe it possible. What a fighter that other bird is. He fills me with terror."

Down went Bartholomew again, this time on his back. The spurs were in his sides, the beak of the Malay cross pecked at his throat. At that moment as the world spun dizzily about, as even Musket looked away, anxious to spare himself such a sad sight, Bartholomew's spur waving in the air, entered the body of the foe, in such a way that he could not get it out again. At once the fiddler leaped into the ring to unhang him; the farmer also hurried forward, to handle his own bird during the business.

" I expect," said the farmer, eyeing the fiddler sarcastically, " you think your bird's a fighting cock? "

"That is the way we fight," said the fiddler simply.
"Here — take care . . . who is hung, my bird, or
yours?"

"Your bird won't last another round," exclaimed the
farmer, and burst out laughing. At once all his friends
began to laugh along with him. Hahaha . . . did you
see it? Well, he calls that a cock . . . But he won't last
another round.

The fiddler looked around him with a frown. "Who
says so?" he asked.

"I do," said the farmer. He took a few bills from his
pocket and flourished them under the fiddler's nose.
"These say it along with me," he said.

The fiddler put his hand in his pocket; he took out all he
had, the bills Mrs. Sebold had given him to buy a yellow
dress . . . For a moment he looked at them. Then with
a sweep of his arm he threw them onto the floor of the
pit. "I guess that will cover it," he said.

And he stepped forward to pit his bird.

"For heaven's sake," cried the robin, "use your spurs."

This time Bartholomew did not bother to wave his head
up and down. The moment he caught sight of the Malay,
he rushed at him, meaning to drive his beak directly
through his body. The Malay ducked, and Bartholomew
went over his head. Then what he had feared took place:
his clipped tail, making him top-heavy, tumbled him over
on his head. The Malay turned, rose in the air, and
swooped downward, expecting to find Bartholomew on his
stomach. But the rooster from Barly, lay instead, help-
lessly upon his back, his claws extended; and it was into
these claws that the Malay drove. They gripped his own;
and he landed on the ground with a thump which knocked
the wind out of his body.

"Look at that," cried the cricket. "What a fight!"

The crowd roared, and the two handlers jumped forward, ready to claim an advantage. But now both birds lay still, refusing fight. "Are you ready for a count, mister?" cried the judge. And raising his arm, he tolled off the numbers.

". . . Thirty-eight, thirty-nine," he cried, "forty. Handle your birds, misters."

The birds were pitted again, while ten was counted. But neither moved. "Once refused," cried the judge.

"Yup," said the fiddler. And he gave Bartholomew a pinch under the tail.

Twice refused. And again, one, two, three, four . . .

"Bartholomew," said the fiddler, "you are fighting for Barly. You are fighting for Metabel Adams' yellow dress. This other bird is ready to run away. One peck, my friend; that is all I ask."

But Bartholomew was in no condition to peck anything. There was a mist before his eyes; he no longer knew where he was. The murmur of the crowd sounded to him like wind in the trees at home; he felt drowsy, and he wished to lie down. He was very comfortable where he was. Presently Matilda would come walking by with some of her sisters; they would stop to admire him. Then he would crow . . . caroo. Was that croak his own?

Three times refused.

"Ai," groaned the robin, "this is the end." And he put his head down under Musket's belly, and closed his eyes.

Bartholomew was in Barly again, in Mrs. Sebold's yard. "It is you dancers," he was saying to Musket, "who have all the fun. A fighting cock . . . that is the life to lead."

Four times refused.

The Malay was getting his wind again. He looked at Bartholomew with angry eyes; his head went back, he

THE FIDDLER IN BARLY

prepared himself. "There you are," cried the farmer. "Now we'll have it."

The terrible bird gathered himself for the death blow. But at that moment, as the judge droned through the numbers, as the anxious gloomy faces of the farmers grew tense in the smoky light, the door of the barn was kicked open, and a man stuck his head in.

"The constable," he cried.

Out went the lanterns. The fiddler clutched at Bartholomew with one hand, and with the other reached for his money. He received, instead, a stinging blow upon the nose from the farmer, who had taken it, and meant to keep it. And by the time he was able to see again, he was ready for another from the constable who, missing all the rest, was prepared to give the fiddler, at least, a good pounding, before he got him safely to the jail.

Chapter XXI

MRS. SEBOLD was left in no doubt as to what had happened; for one thing, Mr. Shrub made it his earliest business to tell her. "Mrs. Sebold," he said, "you've seen the last of your fiddler." And he went on with the details. "No more you'll see your rooster again," he declared. But he was wrong on that score, at least, for Bartholomew was already at home. He had been delivered that morning by the Reverend Flood, along with a few wholesome sayings from the Bible. The rooster was sound, but he had a thoughtful air, which Matilda found charming. "He has suffered," she told her sister, "but he is all the more attractive for that reason." And catching sight of the robin, she treated him to a chilly bow. "How do you do," she said; "are you still here?"

Mrs. Sebold listened without emotion to the story of her hired man's disgrace. She stood with a dish towel in her hands, and her eyes fixed on the sky above Hemlock, blue as a cornflower. "I want to tell you," said Mr. Shrub: "he was mopped up for fair by the constable. Like this, do you see — " And he went through some motions with his fists. "You're well rid of him, Amelia . . . Mrs. Sebold, ma'am."

After that, Mr. Shrub went home again. He'd missed the cock fight, just as he'd always missed everything else;

but he'd heard tell of it, anyhow. Life was a dark, queer thing, even so near as Milford. Well — no telling, then, when he'd come around a corner slap onto something queerer still, and not have to leave Barly for it, either. Ah, the mystery, all to himself . . .

Mrs. Sebold put down her dishrag and walked slowly over to the barn. There she got together the fiddler's belongings, such as they were, and took them, along with his fiddle, to Mrs. Watson. "I want to borrow your Lem," she said. "I want he should take these things over to my man in Milford. He's in jail there."

"I've a bicycle he can ride over," she added as she turned to go, leaving Mrs. Watson with an open mouth and eyes like saucers. "Oh, my," said Mrs. Watson finally, in a weak voice. Her breath failed her, and she sat down.

Thereafter Mrs. Sebold went about her work as before; she tended store, found time to take some soup or jelly each morning to little Metabel Adams, and did her own simple chores. But her good spirits were gone. Things got along, but she didn't care how. When the Reverend Flood stopped to talk to her, she had nothing to say to him; she listened to the Good Word in silence, and went on feeding her hens.

It was time she was finding a wife for her robin, she thought. The bird seemed mournful; or was it just her own mind she saw in him? He stayed in her room, mostly under the bed; she couldn't get him out, even at feeding time. And not so much as a peep out of him, morning or evening. She stood on the kitchen porch and called, and the hens came running, but no robin. She wasn't interested in the hens the way she used to be. What was that shadow over there, under the tree? Only a bush blowing, that was what. She sighed, and emptied her pannikin. For a moment it looked like a little dog dancing . . .

She passed her hand over her eyes. The wind was rising in the west; there'd be a gale that night, and frost, or nearly, in the morning. She knew the signs, the clear green sky above the hills, the pale, winking stars, that holler of wind high overhead. Winter would be along . . . It was time to think of the wood pile. There it was, as he'd left it. And that old barn — better close it up now. It was so dark over there . . .

She closed the barn, and locked it; then she turned, and went in. Well, she thought, she'd just have to do with what she had. She'd managed a good many years the way she was; she guessed she could manage a few more before it was time to close her eyes on the world's wickedness. He was gone, and her money with him. What was it he said? — when he played, the flowers danced. Ah, she was no flower, and it was time she knew it. Not at her age. Let them dance in some other village — she had work to do. What if her heart felt a little heavy? Nobody liked to be made a fool of.

But for all that, she found it hard to sleep that night. For one thing, there was the wind, making such a racket. And then the shutters banged — he'd have fixed them tight in a week or two, but he hadn't got around to it. She wondered where he was. Not that she cared, she told herself; but it would be cold in the jail, with this snap coming on. Maybe he wasn't in jail any more; maybe he was on the road somewhere, headed south, headed for the city, like as not, and the street-cleaning department. God lead him right, at that.

The truth of the matter was she hadn't looked for a winter alone again. The prospect made her swallow; the

long evenings, with the dark closing so early, the world so
quiet and cold outside, and nobody but the robin to talk
to. Not that she'd be really alone, she thought; she knew
well enough that Mr. Shrub would be after her. Now
that he was home from China and Niagara Falls and
whatever other places he'd never got to, he'd plague the
life out of her to take him in. And the worst of it was she
felt almost fool enough to do it. Not that she wanted to
be second fiddle to a lot of water falling down over a rock;
no, indeed, first fiddle for her . . . listen a minute outside, what a lot of wind, falling down over the edge of the
sky . . .

Maybe a wife would fall along with it for the robin.
A wife . . . to sit in front of the fire . . .

She woke with a start, as though someone had called
her. The sun was up, it was bright and frosty, the cobwebs glistened with dew, or lay soaked and gray in the
shadows. The wind came into her room full and fresh, the
cold, sweet air of an autumn morning, clear as brook
water, sweet as goldenrod. Mrs. Sebold took her basket,
and went out into the garden. But the morning shine and
shadow troubled her eyes. Was that a bird, lying there
under the tree? No, it looked more like a bundle. But
what was that lump there, along with it? She moved
around to see. "Oh," she said, and dropped her basket.

The fiddler looked up at her from the grass. He was
cold and wet; the early sun made a little fog on his clothes.
One of his eyes was darker than the other, and there was
a plaster on his chin. "Mrs. Sebold, ma'am," he said,
"the barn's locked."

She had no words for him; she just felt, suddenly, all
free inside. The very first thing she could think to say
was "where's your fiddle?"

He sat up; from the bundle he carried, he took out a

yellow dress. "Here," he said, "is my fiddle. I am afraid that it will not help the hens to lay any more. But it will help to make a little girl dance again."

And he looked at her with an innocent air. But what he saw must have made him feel uncomfortable, for after a while he looked away. "Mrs. Sebold, ma'am," he said a little uncertainly, "I don't expect you'll want me any more. There's nothing much for a man to do here; and I'm only a trouble to you before the neighbors. As a matter of fact, I came back to say good-bye. Good-bye, Mrs. Sebold, ma'am . . . Amelia. Well . . . I wanted to see you again."

Mrs. Sebold stood still. She wanted to talk, she wanted to scold. But strangely enough, her voice wouldn't come out. There was something heavy, like, in her throat, which kept her from saying, "Look at you, you're a sight," the way she had a mind to. Instead, she took the yellow dress and her basket again. And then, all at once, she turned her head away, and her mouth twisted down at the corners. "You've been a long time coming home," she said. And she fair ran for the house, to keep at least one step ahead of her tears.

To *My Friend* BEN GRUNTAL

The Woodcutter's House

THE ROAD UP HEMLOCK

Chapter I

THAT was the spring poor Ezra Adams died. Trembling and meek, he stepped into Jordan's dark icy water, the cold tide froze him, and he came out again in Zion with a look of peace; he seemed to be saying humbly to the angels, " I don't amount to much, but I feel friendly."

He forgot the home he had left, the small bare shack on public ground at the village edge, the cheerless faces of his neighbors, the preacher's last grave words, uttered without much hope; he forgot his poverty and his pain, and he forgot his daughter Metabel, baptized Mehitabel, to whom he left his bedding, an old hammer, a corncob pipe, some pans for cooking, and a broken chair. She was his only friend; he hated to leave her alone in the world, and died, as he said, regretful. Two days later, in the evening, he was buried.

At that time Metabel was sixteen-going-on-seventeen, small for her age, with rain-colored eyes. Her thrush-colored hair was tied in a knot at the back of her head; and her shoes had holes in them. She did not pity herself, but she felt lonely. Early the next day, she went slowly out of the house and up the hill to the place she loved, a little clearing on the slope above Barly, where she could see Old Hemlock in the distance. The dawn was just breaking; it was too early for birds, too early even for shadows. The trees stood up dark and still in the air cold as water. Metabel drew her shawl around her, and sat down; and Musket, the fiddler's little dog, who had been with her all that night, sat down too, and put his nose in her hand.

Metabel had a lot to think about. In the first place, her pa was dead; he'd forgot her, he'd gone off in the dark, out of sight, out of call . . . gone off over Jordan River. Oh, Jordan River . . . everyday thoughts couldn't get across it. And if you took all your heart and all your loneliness, and went crying out over it, it didn't help you any; as far as you could get, there was only the dark and the empty water. Nobody answered.

Far away, far as the moon, and around curves you couldn't see . . . she didn't pity herself, it was her pa she pitied, all alone in the icy dark with no one to look out for him. Her heart trembled with woe; poor pa . . .

"O Lord," she prayed devoutly, "look after him, he's so meek."

And she added in despair, "Don't leave him all alone by himself."

She sat huddled in her shawl, staring out across the dawn-gray meadows from which the mists of night still rose like the smoke of leaves, uneasy, blown by the wind.

She needed some one to look after, to do for, as she had done all her life for her pa. It was a matter of affection with her, a shy, maternal kindness: she was like a little dreamy mother, with no one to bring up.

And now that he was gone, the loneliness she felt was more for her pa than for herself; she saw him lost and frightened on the road to Heaven, and ached for him.

She knew what they were saying about her in the village; she could almost hear them. There was the preacher: he'd want her to have a good home, and stop dancing in the woods and meadows above Barly. He'd want her to dance like the others in barns decorated with pumpkins or first spring flowers; he'd want her to live with a good woman, and be taken care of. That was the way a girl ought to live, under a proper wing.

They'd all want her under a wing now, she thought, they'd want to look after her, to tell her not to do this, and not to do that. Even the fiddler and his wife — there wasn't much they'd likely disallow her, but on the other hand she'd be of no advantage to them, seeing they looked after each other. And there wasn't any one else in Barly who'd want to take her, except to disallow her; no one wanted her, really, with her shy way of smiling like one who rarely got it back again, and her way of dancing all alone in the woods, which some held queer, and others sinful.

Her hand tighened over Musket's nose. "Who'd ever want me," she said, "unless to change me over?"

And for the first time her eyes filled with tears, not at being left alone, but at being changed over.

The little dog's heart was heavy, but at the same time he did not let his grief for Metabel get the better of him. If Metabel was affectionate, Musket was practical; it was his nature to be tidy and able, to see what there was, and not to tell himself stories. As he sat beside her, with his nose in her hand, he thought to himself, "Probably this is the end of our good times together." But because her fingers hurt him, he moved away, just a little, as though to say, "Excuse me, I am uncomfortable."

Musket had been a dancer in his youth. When he lived with the fiddler, he used to hop about on his hind legs, one, two, one two three; and collect coins in a hat held in his mouth. The fiddler used to say to him, "Musket, you dance in order to live. Nevertheless, I believe that you like to be admired."

111

And he would add with a smile, "Musket, you are a humbug."

But that was long ago, when they were both younger. Now the little dog liked nothing better than to watch Metabel skipping about, her hair flying, and her arms stuck out like the branches of a tree. Too old any longer to dance, he liked to remember that he had also been an artist, in a manner of speaking, and could tell what was good from what was bad.

However, he was of no use to Metabel in this emergency. His tail went thump against the ground, but that was all; he had nothing to suggest. As a matter of fact, Metabel was not paying any attention to him. She sat looking with cloudy eyes across the valleys of her home, to where the night-blue hills already caught the light. The air was fresh, the valleys were dark and still; only in the north, far off, the clear day shone like a fire on the hills. She took a deep breath.

"Musket," she said, "there's the sun.

"It's day on Hemlock."

With hungry eyes she watched the light steal downward on the mountain. There it was day, while she still sat in shadow. Queer, how it made her feel to see; as though life, somehow, were different there on Hemlock, where the rocks and trees shone so brightly in the sun — as though life were freer and kinder in that gleaming air than down in the valley with the preacher and the Watsons and the Lowerees.

"If I were up there now," she thought, "I'd hold out my arms like this. . . ."

Musket moved aside; he thought she was going to dance. Her thin little body lifted itself with longing toward the hills; the day seemed to make things better for pa, it couldn't be cold and dark for him with that clear light shining there on Hemlock. . . .

" That's where my friends are," she said.

She had no friends, except the fiddler and his wife, in the whole world. But she felt as though up there on Hemlock she had friends; as though beyond those fields which nursed the Barly cows, beyond that strip of woods, beyond that rise and valley to the north, in cleaner, sweeter air, in brighter, kinder light, her how-do-you-do would not be left unanswered, her small shy smile be given back again.

It wouldn't be in Barly, that was sure — not by the folks who knew her, and held her no-account. All her life she'd just missed being said how-do-you-do to; she didn't mind, so long as there was pa to look after. But now that he was gone, and there was no one for her to do for, she'd be looked after herself by somebody else; she wouldn't be free any more — free to tell herself stories, free to dance in the woods like a piece of wind, or a little goat — no, not any more; she'd be brought into the fold with the sheep, and driven along the straight high road to Heaven in company with the Watsons and the Lowerees.

And she didn't want to be; she wanted to go after her pa, to do the simple, kindly things for him she'd always done. Her gray eyes ached with it, she wanted it so much.

" Musket dear," she said, " don't look if I cry, will you."

But she didn't cry; the light on Hemlock filled her eyes, instead. It seemed to her as though that were the way he must have gone, up past Hemlock, out beyond the hills . . . not through the dark any more, or around curves you couldn't see, but straight out, through the light. . . .

She stood up, as tall as she was able. "Musket," she said, "I'm going up on Hemlock."

And with her old blue shawl around her, she started out. "We'll be there by noon," she said.

114

"THERE'S NO ROAD OVER HEMLOCK"

Chapter II

MUSKET walked along without enthusiasm; his mind was a prey to forebodings, and he gazed at the ground with a gloomy expression. He did not expect any good to come of this excursion; at the very least, it was a long walk up, and a long walk back. "A hill is never anything when you get to it," he said; "all you see is other hills, which look grander than the one you are on. What I say is, if you wish to look up at a hill, then stay down in the valley where you can see it."

He addressed these remarks to a young May-bug. But the May-bug did not agree with him.

"You are old," she said; "that is the trouble. You sound very wise, but the truth of the matter is you do not feel anything. Any one can be a philosopher, in that case. It is quite another matter with me. An emotion I cannot control fills me with the liveliest joy. Hope lifts my wings. Perhaps by to-morrow I shall be a mother. What an exciting life."

And she flew away, into a spider web. "Even if I am not to be a mother," she murmured, as the spider began to eat her; "I am entirely too young to be a philosopher."

"Musket," said Metabel, looking back, "we'll be there by afternoon."

But Musket did not believe her. With his tail between

his legs and his nose to the ground, he trudged along, through the sweet-smelling, early spring morning. The little white butterflies danced in the sunshine without attracting his attention; the young green grasshoppers leapt full of joy and vigor into the air. And Metabel walked eagerly forward, her gray eyes lifted to the morning sky, the spring's deep blue, blue as the sea.

All about her the tiny voices of earth sang her their little songs of consolation. The first flute of birds in the branches, the early hum of bees, the tree-toad's bell, spoke to her heart, lonely and loving. "Metabel," they said, " are you looking for some one you loved? He is not far away, he has slipped into the shadow of a leaf, he has stolen into the silence after birdsong. Can you tell, my child, where birdsong ends, and silence begins? Perhaps, if your ears are sharp, you will hear him again; perhaps you will see him, if your eyes are clear, over your shoulder like the faint new moon.

" Do not be lonely, little sister, do not think you have no one to love any more. There is still the earth to love, where clover and daisies grow, where the bees fly with golden legs. And he is there, with last year's song of birds, with next year's bloom of rose. They are not very far, they are just out of sight. . . . There, you have missed them.

" Look again, little cousin."

The sun rode higher and higher in the sky, the fresh clear air of the spring morning gave way to the warm fragrance of noon. From the valleys, as the road ascended, there swam up to her through the sunny atmosphere the moist odors of earth and dung, the barnyard smell of cows; from the woods came out to her the hot sweet scent of balsam. A flight of crows rose from a field

116

with noontime cries, a robin sang in a tree, three notes like water falling, and then was still to listen.

"Musket," she said, "it smells so good.

"We'll be there soon." And she gave him a little pat, to reassure him.

But Hemlock was further away than she thought. The sun went down again in the slow spring way, the shadows lengthened little by little to the east; and still the mountain was before her and above her. Slowly the light drew away into the south, the sky over Hemlock grew colder and darker. Was she going the wrong way? She stopped and looked about her. She was far from home, and hungry. What had made her walk so far, she wondered; and where was she?

She was a good many miles north of Barly, she knew that. And as for what had brought her . . . did she hope to find her pa again on that dark lonely hill? Oh no — her pa was dead.

She sat down suddenly by the side of the road. And Musket, anxious and depressed, sat wearily down beside her, and leaned his head against her knee. The shadows lengthened to the east, the sun drew closer to the tree-tops.

It was the lonely hour before dusk, when the sun has no warmth, and the heart grows weary. The sparkle was gone from the air, the little voices of earth were quiet and remote. Soon the light would deepen into blue, soft as a faded cornflower. Then it would be time to go home.

Home?

"We're a long ways from home," said Metabel, and her head drooped. "We're a long ways from supper," she said.

The misty sad spring evening settled down. The frogs began to shrill, a dog barked far away. And Metabel, with a long sigh to keep her chin from trembling, turned her face home.

But this time Musket led the way. The little dog, hungry and dejected, had only one idea, to find his supper as soon as possible. He was tired of walking up and down hills, from which, as he said, it was useless to expect anything. The practical thing was to get home again, or to find, at least, a house with a fire in it, and some one to give them supper. For this reason when, at a turn of the road, he smelled bacon on the right, to the right he went, Barly or no Barly; and Metabel, lost and weary, followed him without thinking.

It was like night under the trees, it was hard to see; the road was narrow, and no more than a path. She went along in a numb way, her feet following Musket, her mind in a cloud; branches whipped at her out of the darkness, roots lay tangled about like snakes under her feet. Presently one tripped her; she caught her foot in a hemlock root, and down she went, thump.

It knocked the dreamy misery out of her, along with the wind. "Musket," she said with a gasp, "wherever are we going?"

But Musket was on ahead. There was nothing to do but follow him, or else sit where she was. She got to her feet, and went forward slowly, feeling for roots with her toes. There seemed an uncommon number of them . . . were they really roots? . . . and not snakes or hairy fingers?

"Musket dear," she said in a shaky voice, "where are you?"

But just as she was ready to feel scary, she caught a glimpse of lantern light at the end of the path. There, between the trees, she spied a low cottage; and in the warm light at the door stood Musket, gazing inside with anxious cheer, while the owners, a young man and an old one, gazed amiably out.

"Come in," they said.

With shy, friendly looks they offered her a chair. It was a rocker, with only one arm, and half the back gone. She sat down in it, and, closing her eyes, held out her feet to the fire. The chair squeaked as she rocked up and down. She was so tired, so hungry and sleepy; it was warm in front of the fire, it was like lying out in a clover field on a sunny day. She rocked up and down, squeak, squeak. . . .

They gave her hot milk to drink, bread and butter, soup, and apple pie. Then when she felt better they asked her questions. They looked at her with awkward smiles, and she looked back at them gravely, out of her rain-gray eyes. The old one made her think of pa; he had no coat, he wore an old red flannel undershirt, and his suspenders were made out of string. The young one wore overalls; they smelled of fresh-cut wood. His eyes were dark — black almost. . . .

"Black as little roots," she thought drowsily, "black as old acorns."

Squeak, squeak. . . .

When she told them she'd come from Barly, they shook their heads, and looked queer. It turned out they'd never heard of it, although she knew it was just down the road a piece. But no, they'd never heard of Barly, neither of them. "And we've lived here, man and boy, all our lives," said the old man.

"There's Lander's Center," he continued, "and the Mill Junction. And Wayne, down the road, and Farmingdale. And there's Green Center, and East Toby. . . . But Barly? No ma'am, there's no Barly, no Barly whatsoever."

"That's where my friends are, Barly," said Metabel dreamily.

The young man scratched his head with a thoughtful air. He, too, had never heard of Barly. Wayne was down the road a piece; up the road was nothing at all. "The road," he said, "goes down, but it don't go up. It stops here. There's no road over Hemlock. There's no road whatever."

"You're lost, ma'am," said the old one; "lost for fair."

"Maybe," said the young one. . . .

"Maybe nothing," said the old one, who knew his own mind. "There's no such place as Barly," he said.

And they both stood looking down at Metabel, who had come from Barly, or from the moon, what was the difference?

She was too tired to argue about it. In the morning she'd find the road again, and go home. Musket lay at her feet, blinking into the fire. There must be Barly somewhere, because there was Musket. . . . Her head drooped, her eyes closed. The last thing she saw was a red flannel undershirt; the young man had eyes like black susanflowers. Clover in a field, the warm sun . . . daisies, black-eyed susans, dancing in the sun. . . .

Squeak.

They brought a mattress in, and laid her on it, covered by a blanket. Then they went to bed. The young one slept on the bare boards, because it was his mattress on which Metabel lay sleeping.

METABEL DECIDES TO STAY

Chapter III

THEY were right; the road before the house was not the road she'd come on; there was no road back to Barly. She found that out for herself the next morning, after she'd walked about in the woods upwards of an hour looking for it, only to find herself back at the house again. The old man in the red flannel undershirt was sitting on the door-step; he smiled when he saw her.

"Excuse me," she said humbly; "I'm lost."

It didn't surprise him any. "You are," he agreed, "you are. I knew it from the first. 'Joseph,' I said to my nephew — he being named Joseph — 'the girl's lost.' And what did he say to me? 'Maybe,' he said. 'Maybe nothing,' I said. Barly — go along."

And spitting heartily into the grass, he gazed at her with satisfaction.

Metabel and Musket stood before him in the sunlight, small and dejected. "What am I to do?" she asked. "Maybe if I went down to Wayne, or East Toby, I could get home that way. But Wayne's way the other side of Hemlock from Barly. So how would I get there?"

"You're in Wayne now," said the old man. "Leastways, you're on Hemlock. Wayne village is down the road a piece. Hemlock peak is about a mile behind you. I don't rightly know how you got here from over the

other side. But being as you're here, I've no objection.
Have a bite of breakfast with us. Joseph's putting on the
coffee now."

" Thank you," she said.

" Well," he added, not unkindly, " a bite won't hurt
us any."

But a sudden thought made him pause. " I expect your
folks will be uneasy," he said.

" I have no folks," she answered. " My pa is dead.
Pa was all the folks I had, beyond Musket here."

" Oh," said he. And he said again, more kindly,
" Come in and have your bite with us."

Seen in the morning light, the nephew Joseph was not
a handsome man. Still he was friendly; he said little, and
contented himself with smiling at Metabel over the top
of his saucer out of which he drank his coffee. Metabel
stared back at him with surprise; she wasn't used to having folks smile at her for no reason; it made her feel
fluttery.

But the old man did most of the talking.

" Right behind you," he said, " is the tallest hill in the
county. I figure that makes us the highest farm in this
section; we're two thousand three hundred and forty feet
up. Still, we don't get much company up here.

" My nephew," he went on, " is a woodcutter. Not a
very good one, neither. Well, I must tell you, that's a
grief to me. I do a little farming myself; I raise the biggest heads of lettuce in the county."

" My Uncle Henry," said Joseph proudly, " is a power
with vegetables."

" Well, that's so," said Uncle Henry. However, very
soon he began to look gloomy and dissatisfied. " This is a
small county," he observed. " I could do with a bigger."

" It's enough for me," said Joseph cheerfully.

"You're too easy satisfied," remarked his uncle.

"That's so," said Joseph, and relapsed into silence.

"We don't have much company up here," said Uncle Henry, "that's a fact." He rubbed his chin, and looked at Metabel with a gleam of hope. "How would you like to see where I've put my lettuce?" he asked.

"I'd like it fine," said Metabel. "Let me clean up first, and I'll go right along with you."

She went over to the sink, and got a foamy suds going. "She uses a power of soap," said Uncle Henry, "it's a right unusual sight."

"It is," said Joseph. And he went off to the barn, where he kept his tools. Soon the sound of his axe could be heard in the woods near by, metallic and clear.

When the dishes were dried, Uncle Henry took Metabel around to look at the lettuces. There was nothing to be seen; it was too early. "Here's where they're going to be," he said; "the biggest heads in Wayne County."

And he stood gazing with pride at the bare brown earth, raked and combed to let the young green lettuce through.

He took her to see the coop he'd made for the hens, the oak handle Joseph had whittled for the pump, the south field near the road where he had planted his corn. They went to the barn to see Isaiah, the meek gray horse, who was near as old as Joseph, he said, but more use. She liked Isaiah, she put her thin hand out to feel his nose; he had Musket's way of looking at a body, so sober and true. The morning was half over before they started back to the house again.

"I ought to be getting on," said Metabel. Wherever Barly was, it was a long way off.

But Uncle Henry was in no hurry to have her go. "Take your bite of dinner with us," he said; "another bite won't hurt us, either."

It didn't take much urging for her to say she would.
But when Joseph made to cook it, she took the pots out
of his hands. She felt at home, and quite happy. " Do
you like Indian pudding? " she asked. " I'll put some on
for your supper.

" Go on out, and set a while. I'll call you when I'm
ready."

She went out to get herself a bowl of dandelions for the
table. The spring sun shone down on her, the moist earth
gave out a sweet mist of smells. Over in the field behind
the house, where the woods ended, Musket was talking
to the old gray horse; they regarded each other earnestly,
exchanging profound looks. A robin hopped out on the
grass among the dandelions; behind her in the woods she
heard a chipmunk scold. " Am I really over Hemlock,"
she wondered. Startled, she looked around at the air, to
see if it looked higher.

When she was ready, she called them in.

" Look here," said Uncle Henry, " there's flowers on
the table." And he added with his mouth full,

" This is the best cooked beans I ever eat.

" Mind how these beans taste, Joseph."

Joseph said nothing; when dinner was over he went
back to his woodchopping, and left Metabel to do the
dishes. Uncle Henry pushed away his empty plate with a
sigh. He drew the back of his hand across his mouth, and
pulled at the strings which held up his trousers. " A fine
day," he declared.

" Isn't it," said Metabel happily.

" It's misty in the valley," said Uncle Henry. " You
wouldn't get a day like this lower down."

" I guess you wouldn't either," she agreed.

" No," he said, " you wouldn't."

He was silent, thinking. " Just the same," he remarked finally, "we don't get much company up here."

And he added, almost timidly, "What for do you want to hurry home?"

In the afternoon silence she went about the house putting things in order. She had nothing else to do, and no way, as far as she could see, of going anywhere. She'd have to start early in the morning to get back to Barly at all. Meanwhile there was plenty to do in the cottage: a corner or two to sweep out, dishes to arrange in the cupboard, a dishcloth to wash; before she knew it, it was time to put the supper on. The stove gave out a ruddy glow, it shone in her eyes and on her pink cheeks; she brushed a wisp of hair back from her forehead, and poured out the Indian pudding.

Supper was eaten in silence. Even Uncle Henry had nothing to say; he sighed happily over the pudding, but beyond that, nothing. He seemed to be tiptoeing about in his mind, as though a thought were up there he was half afraid of: he wanted it there, but feared to scare it off by going at it. As for Metabel, she was used to silence; she'd spoken mostly when she was spoken to all her life, it didn't trouble her any. But when the dishes were put away and the mattress brought out again, Uncle Henry spoke.

"Joseph," he said, "her pa's dead."

"I'm sorry to hear it," said Joseph.

"Yes," said Uncle Henry, "she has no pa. What she's got she says is in Barly."

"That's queer," said Joseph.

Uncle Henry was creeping up on his thought; he was trying to take it unaware. "Barly," he said, "that's a good long ways."

"Where would it be?" asked Joseph.

"Ah," said Uncle Henry, "where?"

Taking up the lamp, he turned to Metabel. "Sleep

tight," he said. And then in a whisper, hoarse and hearty, he added, "Stay as long as you're minded to. . . ."

It was close enough; he shut the door with pride.

"Good night," said Metabel. "Good night. . . .

"Good night, Joseph."

She lay down on her mattress, with Musket beside her; the little dog felt her thin arm around him, tight and loving. "Musket," she whispered, "do you think they want us to stay? I think maybe they do. . . . Anyhow we haven't anywhere else to go. Just suppose there wasn't any Barly . . . what would we do?

"You haven't any friends here, have you? But there's Isaiah. I haven't any friends anywhere.

"Go to sleep, Musket dear. Go to sleep now. . . ."

IN WHICH MUSKET MEETS
A WASP

Chapter IV

So Metabel stayed, and did the cooking and cleaning and mending for Joseph and Uncle Henry. The mountain spring bloomed and blossomed, and Metabel's heart blossomed with it. Even with pa she'd never been so happy, never had so much she liked to do; the little shack outside Barly was bare and ugly compared to the cottage on Hemlock, where the pines stood up dark against the sky, and the dogwood opened like lilies in the wood. The clear warm air brought color to her cheeks; from having lived all her life on an egg borrowed here and a loaf of bread there, she found herself for the first time with more than she could eat. They made a bed for her in the attic; the high narrow room was full of old apples and dried wasps' nests, as sweet a smelling place to sleep, she thought, as ever she'd seen. She still had Joseph's mattress; he allowed he'd sleep on balsam until winter.

But if Metabel was happy, Uncle Henry was happier still. To be sure, it gave him Indian pudding, but what was more important, it gave him some one to talk to. The tiny parade of his own life seemed to him to call for comment: to be, in a manner of speaking, an argument between himself and oblivion. Obstinate, but anxious, he longed to hear that what with one thing and another, between the strength of his opinions and the size of his lettuces, the debate was not altogether lost.

He was the champion lettuce raiser of Wayne County, but he had further ambitions. His own size seemed to him, in a mystical but natural way, to be as big as his lettuces. He longed to excel in cubic content; he wished in his heart to raise the biggest lettuce in the whole state, or in the world. He never spoke of it, but when he thought there might be bigger lettuces somewhere else, he grew very gloomy.

And it was, as he sometimes said to Metabel, a grief to him to think that Joseph was no more than a moderate woodchopper. "What beats me," he said, "is how he can be so no-account, and so content." He admitted that Joseph was neat with an axe; it was the lack of size in his work which bothered him. "He cuts wood," he said, "like it didn't matter. I've seen him squat down in front of a tree a whole morning, before he'd so much as lift an axe to it — studying out how to make it fall neat. Sometimes he won't even take a tree at all; the mountain's full of ash, but he won't take it. Don't care to, he says, though there's a price for ash at the mill. Just tell me what's the sense in that?"

Metabel smiled; it reminded her a little bit of pa — not much, not the neatness part, but the no-account part, the don't-care-to part. "Maybe he's got something on his mind," she said, "besides woodcutting."

"Then what for does he cut wood?" asked Uncle Henry simply. "Taking it just the way it suits him — that's not woodcutting proper. I don't know what it is."

Whatever it was, woodcutting or not woodcutting, it didn't seem to bother Joseph any. He remained quiet and friendly, and without anxiety. She heard his axe like a clear bell in the woods, followed by long silences; some-

times there was a rush and thunder of sound as a tree fell
— neatly, she expected, leaving the forest orderly. At
meals he smiled at her across the rim of his saucer, or over
his plate; he had little to say, mostly to agree with his
uncle, or to express a mild joy and wonder. He was a
happy man, with nothing so far as she could see, to be
happy about — what made him so happy, she wondered?
In her own case it was doing things for people, being
liked or admired, maybe loved, even — but who admired
Joseph? Not his Uncle Henry, at any rate.

Still, there it was: without being admired, he was a
happy man, at least to look at. It had a way of making
her feel happy too. She took to dancing, when she thought
no one was looking, and sang herself little songs. Her
young voice, thin and sweet-and-sour, rose from the
kitchen in lively hymns out of Barly Church, or dancing
tunes she'd heard the fiddler play. Uncle Henry, in the
lettuce-bed, listened without objection. It didn't amount
to much, her singing, but he didn't mind, seeing she enjoyed it.

"Musket," she said, "do you think Joseph is no-
account? He puts me in mind of pa; he takes his time,
and he doesn't care. Pa was no-account for fair, but I
loved him. He never got anything done, mostly. He just
set still and thought about things. And I did for him."

She added with a serious sigh, "I wouldn't have
changed so much as a mouse's tail on him."

Musket did not discuss these things with Metabel. He
preferred to exchange his opinions with the horse Isaiah,
in whose mild dark eyes shone the drowned lights of patience and reflection.

He found Isaiah at the south end of the pasture; with
his head resting on the pasture bars, the old gray horse
was gazing motionless, into space. Dazzled by his friend's

powerful body and enigmatic expression, Musket remained respectfully silent. At last he said,

"It is always the distance which is most attractive.
However, when one gets there, one turns around and
looks back, because in that direction, also, is distance.
What is the use of looking for something which cannot
be found? I believe in being satisfied with what one has,
and not traveling too much. If we had stayed home, we
should still be in Barly, with the fiddler and Mrs. Sebold,
and the rooster Bartholomew."

"Are you homesick?" asked Isaiah kindly.

"Why should I be homesick?" replied Musket;
"wherever I go, my home is under Metabel's bed. No,
I was simply speaking from a philosophical point of view.
. . . Well, just tell me, what is the good of it? These
lettuces for example — suppose they are bigger and bigger? There is no end to that sort of thing."

Isaiah gave his head an indulgent shake. "My poor
friend," he said, "you have led a very dissipated life.
You have been a dancer; I do not object to dancing, but
it is not the same thing as pulling logs to town. You do
not know what it is to work; you do not know what it is to
go to bed so tired that your bones ache. What happiness;
it is the only happiness in the world worth talking about."

Musket gave a shudder. "I have been cold," he said,
"and I have gone hungry to bed many times with legs
worn out with dancing. I suppose you think an artist's
life is all pleasure. You are mistaken: and going to bed
alone is not what I like to think about."

"To go to bed alone," said Isaiah, "is the only way I
would ever wish to go. I stretch myself out, I think of all
the things I have done during the day. . . . That is
better than dancing around in a meadow. To work, and
to respect the work of others . . . that is a natural and

noble life. But I can see that you are a cynic and do not respect anything."

"I am not a cynic," said Musket earnestly; "I simply say there is something else. . . . What is the good of working so hard, when all the rest of the world is playing, when the flowers are blooming, and the little yellow butterflies are dancing together? Why not be happy where we are, and also dance a little because the sky is so blue, or because our hearts are light? To laugh, to cry . . . what does it matter? To feel — that is the thing; and it is better to feel happy than to feel sad, in my opinion."

"I do not feel sad," replied Isaiah; "I work too hard, I have no time to feel sad. What an emotional creature you are. That is because you do nothing all the time. I should go crazy with such a life." And he stamped his foot on the ground, to embarrass some flies who were biting him.

After a while he said in a friendlier tone, "I believe you are living in the attic. That is where the apples are kept." And he added with a thoughtful air, "It is a long time since I have tasted a good apple."

"Allow me to get you one," said Musket, turning politely toward the house.

Isaiah called after him, "One is probably all you can carry. But if it is small, perhaps you would have room for two."

When Musket arrived in the attic, he started to take a large greening in his mouth, to bring to Isaiah. But just then a wasp crawled around from the other side of it, and gave him a gloomy look. "What is all this?" asked the wasp. "What are you doing with my apple?"

"Excuse me," said Musket hastily. "I was simply going to take some fruit to Isaiah. . . . However, if it is your apple, I wouldn't dream . . . there is another one over there which will do just as well."

"That is also my apple," said the wasp. "In fact," he added, "these are all my apples. I am the largest apple-owning wasp in this county. Do you think I have spent my entire life watching these treasures in order to have you give them away to your friends? Do not be so foolish as to imagine it." And he lifted his slender waist with an ominous sound.

Musket went quickly backwards. "Forgive me," he said politely; "I had no idea of it. And Isaiah — I am sure when he realizes how hard you have worked over these apples, he will be the very last one in the world to wish to eat one."

So saying, he returned to the meadow without the apple. But when he told Isaiah what had happened, the old horse's eyes snapped with rage. "What a little fool you are," he said to him angrily; "you might just as well say that this grass belongs to me. You should simply have taken the apple, and come down here with it."

This speech, which he did not expect, caused Musket to grow very thoughtful. He replied stiffly to Isaiah, "You must not expect a dancer to know what belongs to each person, and what does not. Please remember that the wasp was very much in earnest; I have never seen a more serious wasp. . . . Besides, naturally I thought you would wish to respect the work he had done, on which he told me that he had spent his entire life. . . ."

Isaiah said nothing; putting his head down, he began to crop the sweet green grass, through which tiny insects hurried with cries of fright and pain to get out of his way.

132

AND METABEL MEETS THE
LITTLE GREEN MAN

Chapter V

METABEL had taken a pail of milk to Joseph in the woods, in case he was thirsty. They stood together by a giant pine whose straight dark trunk rose beyond tiptoe reach before it broke into branches. "There's a tree," said Metabel dreamily; "look, Joseph, the way it goes up and up, like a noble king. What does it make you think of?"

"Neat cut wood," said Joseph simply.

"Oh," said Metabel. She looked up at it with pursed lips. Yes, she could see it that way, too . . . just neat cut wood. Poor tree.

All at once Joseph had a lot to say. "That tree," he declared, "says to me, 'You can't cut me down as neat as I can stand here.'" And swinging his axe in a bright circle, he drove the blade into the dark trunk, which shivered with the impact.

"But I wouldn't cut an ash," he said, "not for anything.

"I like to see them grow."

Metabel turned away; it made her dizzy to see trees come down; they came down with such a bump from so high up. "Bring me home some knots for the stove," she said, "and some bark for the smell. . . ."

133

She went down through the woods toward the house. The light fell green and yellow through the leaves, birds sang in the branches. A small red squirrel scampered up a birch, flirted himself out through the leaves, and leaped with tiny, outstretched claws into another tree; the slim twig bent as he fled along the branch, noisy as a water-fall, light as a puff of wind. Underfoot the sapling roots pushed up through the dead pine needles; somewhere water sang in the woods, dropped and tinkled. She raised her arms above her head and danced a few steps down the red pine needles and the moss; she remembered the way she used to dance when she was a child . . . this is the way the wind dances, this is the way a rabbit goes, hop, hop. . . .

And with her arms still over her head, hop she went, right into a little man dressed in green, who was sitting under a wild rose bush, quietly talking to some mice.

"Oh," she said, and stood stock-still, as though, all at once, some one had laid a finger on her heart.

The little green man paid no attention to her; he went on addressing the mice, who listened to him with anxious looks. "My poor friends," he said to them, "it is just as important for snakes to have mice to eat, as it is for mice not to have snakes to eat them. Do you expect me to alter the designs of nature? Go away, please; and if you have to be eaten, do not feel that it is a personal reflection on you in any way."

The mice ran away like black drops of water; sighing, their instructor looked up at Metabel, and shook his head. "Ak," he said, "the little anxious mice."

"I'd be anxious too," said Metabel, "if I were mice."

At this his face took on a more serious expression. "If one must be a mouse," he said, "one may as well be cheerful, and accept it as an accident of nature. The

134

gods cannot change these things, least of all a small god, like me."

Metabel looked at him gravely; in the dim forest light he seemed to her no bigger than she was herself. " I knew you were something queer," she said, " the minute I laid eyes on you. But you don't look like God very much — not the one we had in Barly. I used to see Him in the Bible over to the Widow Sebold's, with a long white beard."

The little green man smiled at her — a friendlier smile, she thought, than any she had ever seen, friendlier than Joseph's even, though it reminded her of Joseph's. " I've never been in Barly," he said; " there is no one there for me to visit. I live up here, on Hemlock, because Joseph lives here. I am very fond of Joseph. He is all I have to be fond of, so far as I can see."

And he added sadly, " I am a very small god."

" Yes, you are," said Metabel critically. And she added at once, for fear she had offended him, " Excuse me."

He looked at her doubtfully, with his head to one side, like a robin. " Did I say I cared? " he demanded. " I do not care at all. I have a very good time. During the day I walk up and down in these quiet woods, and watch Joseph chop down trees. How he handles his axe — never too much, just enough. . . .

" Still," he added thoughtfully, " one or two more to be fond of would not do me any harm — if only to have something to fall back on in an emergency.

" Supposing I were to lose him? "

And he gave a shudder to think of it.

Her hands clasped, her head bent, Metabel stood before him in the green spring woods; the sun shone in her thrush-colored hair, shadows of leaves floated up and down on her calico dress. "Why are you fond of Joseph?" she asked. "And why haven't you any one else to be fond of?"

The little man waved his hand in the air. "I am fond of him," he said simply, "for the same reason that you are."

"I'm not," said Metabel with surprise.

"I admire him," he continued, "for his good humor. As a matter of fact, that is what I am god of." And he added sturdily, "I am small, but I am unique.

"As for there being any one else to be fond of, that is not something one can pick up anywhere. . . . You were dancing a moment ago with your hands over your head, looking very awkward, but happy. Shall I be fond of you? You are small, too, but lively."

However, Metabel was not paying any attention to what he was saying: she was thinking about Joseph. "You don't think he's trifling?" she asked doubtfully.

The little man drooped; he seemed to grow smaller still. "What," he exclaimed, "do you want him to be a successful woodchopper? Dear me!

"In that case, I do not think I shall be fond of you at all."

"Nobody asked you to," said Metabel. And she added, with red cheeks, "I don't want him to be anything whatever.

"What do I care what he is?" she whispered.

"Oh," said the little man; "ah. Nevertheless, you think about him a great deal. And you have even sewed up that hole in your stocking, just above the knee, which might never be seen, but suppose you fell down?"

"Well," said Metabel with a gasp.

The little man wagged a finger at her. "Now you are red as a rose," he declared; "but do not lose your temper."

" Why should I lose my temper," said Metabel loftily, " just because you're so rude and silly? "

The little green man drew himself up, not without dignity. " Your remarks cannot shake my divine good humor; " he said, " because for one thing, I am not obliged to listen to them."

So saying, he made her a polite bow, and went off through the woods, humming a song to himself. Metabel stood still, looking after him with stormy eyes.

" Just the same," she said, but too low for him to hear, " I don't think you're very nice."

And she went home without dancing, to pick some spinach for supper.

TWELVE DOZEN JAMS AND JELLIES

Chapter VI

SHE was mending Joseph's socks when Uncle Henry called for her with Isaiah, to take her to town. They went down in the farm wagon; she sat up in front with Uncle Henry, while Musket crouched at her feet and gazed appreciatively at Isaiah's hind-quarters rising and falling as he trotted. " Ah," he thought to himself, " now he is working; this is what he enjoys. I feel a profound respect for him. I would not like to do it myself, but viewed from here, it is heroic." And curling himself up, he lay down against the dashboard, comforted by the thought of Isaiah's sober excellence.

" What's Wayne like, Uncle Henry ? " asked Metabel. Her eager eyes explored the road as it wound down the mountain. She saw the birches on the lower slopes, she saw the stony fields full of berry bushes; they looked sunny and strange to her, seen for the first time from the seat of a wagon owned by a family to which, even ever so little, she belonged.

Uncle Henry gave a swish of his whip at the trees. " I allow it's not a very big place," he said, " that is, looking at it from a sizable point of view. There's a church there, as neat a piece of God's house as any in the county. And we've got the county bank.

"Yes, ma'am," he said, "we've got the county bank."

It seemed to afford him unusual relish; and he went on to talk about it. St. John Deakan owned it, but his daughter Prissy helped him. St. John was a wealthy man, he owned Deakan's Saw Mill as well, but Prissy was the real success. She was not exactly young any more, as young people went, but she handled a great deal of money. A smart woman, was Uncle Henry's opinion of her, with a power of success in her. Likely she could make a success of almost anything she undertook, in the way of business, or — with a wink at Metabel — in the way of a man, either.

"Oh," said Metabel.

And she sat very still and thoughtful.

She knew what it was to make money — Mrs. Sebold used to make money, in Barly. Mrs. Sebold was a success too: she ran the general store, and was kind to Metabel. But she had never made a success of the fiddler, even after she married him. How did you make a success of a man?

She remembered the words of the little green man: You would like him to be a successful woodchopper.

And all at once she felt strange, as though she had a power she'd never known about, a power which had to do with her being a girl and Joseph's not. . . . It was a smart feeling, her cheeks grew pink, and she took a deep breath; but then, just as she tried to get a better hold on it, it was gone, and she was only Metabel and not a smart woman after all.

But the sun was so yellow-hot, and the air so full of sweet smells, and soft on her face, and the light so gentle and glowing on the earth, that by the time the farm wagon, rattling down the road, drew along into Wayne, she had forgotten all about it.

"There's the Deakan home," said Uncle Henry, pointing with his whip to a large, square house, set behind elm trees, and painted a neat white. "That's where they live. I wouldn't mind living there myself, though I wouldn't want to leave the farm. But Joseph, now — the farm's no place for him. That's the house for Joseph."

Metabel opened her eyes wide; she looked at the house, then she looked at Uncle Henry. "Whatever would he do there, Uncle Henry?" she asked.

He put his whip slowly back in the whipsocket. "Well," he replied evasively, "I'm not saying. . . . The trouble with Joseph is, he's lackadaisical. He never did seem to stir up any, like other folks. That wood of his — it don't amount to a row of beans. Two trees a week. . . . It's a grief to me. And no ash whatever."

And as Metabel said nothing, only sat and looked at him with a faint trouble in her eyes, he went on to remark that of all ways of stirring up a man from being lackadaisical, the surest way of all was for a good woman to take hold of him. "You take Joseph's mother," he said, "and my sister: she was a great one for it. My brother-in-law, Joseph's father, never did have much ambition till she got hold of him. He used to carve boats out of wood, to put in glass bottles. Well, a year after she took him, she had him building houses. Yes, ma'am, barns and houses you could live in. One day he fell off a roof, and landed on a hay fork. He never did get over it. She was a great one for stirring people up — one of the greatest.

"Take Prissy Deakan," he said: "there's another one. She'd get the trifling out of a man. A man needs a woman now and then to give him reason to work for. Not me, thank God, I've got my lettuce."

And as he drew up in front of the bank, he added over his shoulder, "She has an eye for him, or I'm a sinner."

He went into the bank with a serious air, hitching up his trousers held by strings, and looking around him in an important but uneasy way. "Where's your pa?" he said to Deakan's daughter; and went off to discuss matters with the banker.

Prissy Deakan had an eye for Joseph, but it was not a young eye. For one thing, she was no longer young herself; she had a sly, secret look, as though she were saying I kept it to myself, you didn't get it. She was a little dry, but able; there was no nonsense about her. "Sit down," she said to Metabel, "and make yourself comfortable." So saying, she turned back to her desk on which lay bills of exchange, bank statements, and other important documents.

Metabel did not wish to admire this older woman who had an eye for Joseph. She would have liked to go past her with her head in the air, and an elegant look on her face. But instead, she felt like a little turnip. And she watched with humble pain and admiration the flourishes Miss Deakan made with a pencil on the bank statements.

"There's roses out on Hemlock," she said at last, shyly; "wild ones, in the woods. It'll be a big berry year."

And as Prissy did not reply, she added with a swallow, "I expect you're too busy to bother."

"Bother?" said Prissy, looking up with a frown; "you mean over berry bushes? I like berries, child; I put up twelve dozen jars last year. That's not counting tomatoes and vegetables, or applesauce. Five dozen raspberries, twenty-four gooseberries, three dozen huckleberries, and a dozen each blueberries and currants. I put them up myself. But large jars, very large jars."

"Oh," said Metabel.

"My . . .

"Well, that's a lot of berries."

Prissy shrugged her shoulders. "What I do," she said simply, "I do so it's done. I cooked myself dark red in the face over those berries. We still have half of them left. This year I'll put up fifteen dozen. Father likes them."

And with a determined look, she returned to her figures.

Metabel sat still, overcome with respect for Prissy Deakan, who knew what she had to do, and did it so it was done. Her own spirit, no more ferocious than a butterfly, felt crushed; she was unhappy; all those jams and jellies weighed upon her heart. She sat humming a little tune to herself under her breath, and staring dismally out of the window, to where Musket stood talking to another dog. She wished she were out there with him, in the sun.

Musket was talking to a young female named Susan who belonged to the banker St. John Deakan. Beneath the legs of Isaiah who towered above them, they were discussing the fact that they had never met before, a fact which exasperated Susan who was accustomed to having her own way. "No," she exclaimed, "this is too absurd. What an amusing time we might have had if only I had known you were here. As it is, I do not find any one to talk to, because no one here is the least bit interesting. I am very fond of stimulating conversation. What fun it will be to go for long walks together, in the fields, or in the woods, where it is quieter . . ."

Musket looked at her with a superior expression. "I am much older than you," he remarked, "and I cannot run about the way I used to. I live up on a hill, and rarely come to town; it is a life which satisfies me, as a matter of fact. When I was young . . . but that is quite another story. I was a dancer. I traveled all over, and I received a great deal of applause. But now, at my age, I must think of the most sensible thing."

"So," she exclaimed with shining eyes, "you are an artist. However, I knew that you were distinguished the moment I saw you. I also do not go about very much; I like older people, because they are interesting. I should like to hear more about your life. A dancer . . . that is most unusual."

"Would you care to see me do a few steps?" asked Musket; and getting up on his hind legs, he began to waltz around very slowly, with an expression of anxiety. Presently he fell down. "Ah," he said; "well . . . at my age, the most sensible thing . . ."

"That was charming," said Susan quickly. "It had a good deal of spirit. What satisfaction you must have from your art. I have often imagined what it would be like to dance; but I fear that I am too clumsy.

"However, perhaps if you were very patient with me . . . after all, I am willing to learn, and I am young."

"Hum," said Musket with a serious look, "that is the trouble. The life of an artist . . . have you any idea of what that means? I should not like to lead you into trouble."

The young female gave a sniff. "Well, really," she exclaimed, "what a surprising thing to say. I confess, I am accustomed to very different speeches. I wonder if I quite understand you. Do you expect me to fall in love with you — is that what you mean? But you are not as attractive as all that, my friend."

Musket moved uncomfortably beneath Isaiah's immobile hoofs. "Do not be vexed," he murmured, "you are really very nice. But I am obliged to be practical. I do not say that you would exactly fall in love with me; why should I think of such a thing? Still you might; it has happened before. What would be the good of it, seeing that I live so far away? At my age . . . well, as I say, I cannot run about the way I used to. No, no, my youth is over. What I want now is peace. Let us forget all this. Do not think about me."

" I see," said Susan slowly, " you are convinced that you would not by any chance fall in love with me. It would be I, not you? . . . That is a novel idea. Set your mind at rest, my friend, I do not find you in the least attractive. I admire your mind, and I would like to talk to you some-times; that is all there is to it. But I am very busy socially: I go out a great deal, I have hardly a moment to myself. However, if you come to town again, perhaps we can have a quiet talk — that is, unless you are afraid, or unwilling. I should not like to interfere with your peace up there on the hill. No, no — go back to your farm and forget me. Forgive me for having spoken to you. . . ."

So saying, she walked away with a sweet and penitent expression, and a gentle swaying of the body. Musket looked after her with chagrin. "Look here," he burst out to Isaiah, " was I right, or was I wrong? You cannot be fair to women, they take advantage of you. One would think it was I, not she, who had made the advances. It makes me very irritated."

" You are a fool," said Isaiah in his deep and melan-choly voice. "You have talked yourself into something with your heroics. Now she will give you no rest. It is the finish of you. She will pursue you, because you have made yourself out unwilling."

" Do you think so? " asked Musket happily. And he gazed after Susan with a speculative air.

However, at that moment Uncle Henry and Metabel came out of the bank, and climbed into the wagon again,

to go home. Isaiah lifted his head, Musket leaped up behind, and off they went, with a creak and a rattle. But this
time Metabel sat silent, with cloudy eyes; and Musket,
instead of looking forward at Isaiah, stared dreamily
back at Wayne as it disappeared behind them. Only
Uncle Henry was talkative, and in the best of spirits.

"Yes, ma'am," he said, "we've got the county bank."

IN WHICH METABEL PLAITS
A DAISY CHAIN

Chapter VII

" Here is the very home
   Of peace, if only you will
   Love me a little. Come
   There is sun over this hill,
   There is quiet under these trees.
   Who sings? Only the birds.
   Who speaks? Only the bees.
   Such tiny words —
   Be still! "

sang Metabel, plaiting a chain of daisies to hang around
her neck. The tall flowers nodded about her; the little
wild-strawberry blossoms lay hidden among them, in the
young sweet-smelling clover where the bees climbed and
sang. The warm air was full of pine scents, the drowsy
fragrance of summer, the somnolent morning-peace of
earth. Her voice, thin as a flute and no more silver, disputed for a moment with the crows who in a distant field
settled upon the grain with tuneless cries.

It was not Joseph to whom Metabel was singing; she
would have said that she was singing to no one at all, or
to anybody. It was a song the fiddler had taught her long
ago in Barly, while he was still a hired man, and before
he had married Mrs. Sebold, for whom he worked.

"There is too much talk in the world," he had said, "and not enough music." He had not played for her to dance that day, because he wished to develop the subject at greater length.

And Metabel agreed with him. "Talk," she had said, "is never as friendly as looks." She thought of it now, sitting in the daisies, weaving a daisy chain. Her young heart beat with joy for the bright sun and the warm earth, for its flowery fields and friendly-looking skies. She put out her arms as though to take it all to her breast: there was no end to it, no end to sun and blossom, to lazy hum of bees, no end to youth, the heart's shy hope, the sweet swift longing, like singing and crying together . . . for nothing at all. . . .

Oh, to do for somebody, to care for somebody. . . .

Joseph came through the daisies, tall and dark against the sun. She waved her hand to him, full of flowers. "Joseph," she cried. But then, suddenly, sitting so low among the daisies, and having to look up so high to him, she turned shy again. "Did you see Musket anywhere?" she asked. And she added in a bright voice, "Do you know what I'm going to cook for your supper? Mushrooms."

"Ah," said Joseph. He sat down beside her, looking quiet and pleased: he seemed to be saying to himself, It is a very fine thing to have mushrooms.

"Uncle Henry likes them," he said as though it couldn't be for any one else she meant them.

But Metabel had already retreated into some happy silence of her own, as though, with him sitting there beside her, there were time and time enough to talk, to-morrow, maybe, or the week after. . . .

"Musket's up to the house," he said, "setting on the door-step, looking down the hill."

147

And he added, curling his long legs under him,
" He's got a trouble on his mind."

She nodded her head soberly. "Yes, he has," she agreed. "He's solemn as a bee.

" What do you think it is, Joseph ? "

" Maybe it's just getting old," he said. "Sometimes it takes you like a trouble. And then again, sometimes it takes you solemn.

" And sometimes," he concluded, " it takes you sort of hand-in-glove with God Almighty."

" Isn't it the truth ? " she said. " You take our preacher down to Barly, the Reverend Flood. He was the hand-in-glove-with-God-Almightiest-man you ever see. I expect he was going on fifty years old. A powerful preaching man. When I fell down a cistern my pa dug, and broke my leg, he gave me a book with pictures of martyrs being eat by lions. It brought on the shivers."

" Ah," said Joseph comfortably.

" He was always figuring to make me over godlier," said Metabel sadly.

" Ah," said Joseph again. And he added kindly, " Well, that's it; somebody always wants you different."

" I expect they do," said Metabel, swinging her daisy chain up and down in front of her. Suddenly she burst out: " Joseph I can't bear being changed over. Folks always want you like they are themselves. Seems like they couldn't be happy otherwise, or else call you queer . . . can't a body be queer by herself without being lonesome? I wouldn't care to change so much as a mouse's tail."

" No," said Joseph.

" Aren't you ever lonesome, Joseph? Because I am . . ."

But that was beyond Joseph's simple thought. " What for would I be ? " he asked.

148

"Not for anybody?" She looked down, her lashes veiled her eyes, dreamy and demure. She was minded to say, not for Prissy Deakan? But the slight flutter of her hands swinging the daisies was the nearest she came to it.

He put out his own big hand, brown and horny, to touch her knee. "I know," he said, "you're thinking of your pa." And he remained reverently silent.

She gave a tiny sigh, wholly in disbelief. "I expect I was," she agreed.

"Would you ever go to live in town, Joseph?"

"What for would I?"

"Oh," she said vaguely, "to get along, or to see somebody."

"I get along all right up here," he answered uneasily.

"I know you do. But to see somebody?"

He stared at her with a frown. "Who would I want to see?" he asked in an anxious voice.

"Oh — somebody." The daisy chain swung up and down harder than ever. "Prissy Deakan."

Prissy Deakan . . . why, yes, he'd go to town to see her, on business at the mill, or with his uncle to the bank. She glanced up at him swiftly, but his sober, puzzled gaze told her nothing. Did he know that Prissy had an eye for him? He never showed it, if he did. Maybe he didn't mind; maybe he felt, despite himself, the power of all those jams and jellies. What if he admired her, too . . . ? Very well, then.

"There was a boy in Barly," she declared, "I used to know. Lemuel Watson. He could play on the piano."

"Yes," said Joseph politely.

She considered a moment, while the daisies swung slower and slower. "There were a lot of boys in Barly," she continued. "My friends," she explained. That was

149

a lie: it almost stuck for good in her throat, and never got out at all.

"It's nice to have friends," said Joseph.

"Yes, it is," said Metabel. She seemed to be picking her way here and there among words: it was almost like a dance, with the little feet of her mind going one two three hop. But the dance wasn't right yet; it wasn't smooth and lovely.

"We went to school together," she said: "Lemuel and me."

Joseph sighed. "I never did go much to school," he remarked. "All that book-learning . . ." And he sighed again, oppressed by the weight of all there was to know and think of in the world.

But Metabel was not to be jogged from what she was after. "You take Tiny Flood," she insisted, "the preacher's son. He was a caution. Do you know what he did? He tried to kiss you at dances."

"No," said Joseph.

"Well, he did," said Metabel. "Didn't get him anything, though."

"I'm glad of that," said Joseph grimly.

The daisy chain was quiet now, on the ground. But deep inside, where nobody could see, she was dancing free and lively. Should she go on, she wondered, about Tiny? What an elegant liar she was, to be sure. For shame, Metabel; who ever tried to kiss you at a dance, or anywhere else, for that matter? But she knew one thing — that Joseph didn't like to think of it.

She could stop dancing now, she guessed, and pluck a daisy's petals.

He loves me, he loves me not . . .

"What does it say, Metabel?"

"Well, . . . guess."

He shook his head. "How would I guess," he asked, "not knowing? This man in Barly, now — this what's-his-name Watson."

She giggled then. "Oh," she said, "him."

And she turned happily back to the daisy petals.

He loves me not, he loves me . . .

The pines took the sun, broke it down through green needles, laid it in flakes of yellow and green on the forest floor. In the meadows among the clover the bees went on climbing and singing, meeting and re-meeting each other with brief, inaudible greetings. The sweet warm scent of daisies hung like a morning mist above the ground; the young summer danced and sang. Joseph was glad Tiny Flood hadn't kissed her.

He loves me . . .

"Come along," she said, "let's look for mushrooms."

IN WHICH METABEL LEARNS
THAT A SMALL GOD'S LIFE
IS NOT AN EASY ONE

Chapter VIII

SHE was walking home through the woods, holding out her skirt full of mushrooms, when she saw the little green man again. He was bending over, peering anxiously into a spider web, in which a young grasshopper, lustily kicking, was being covered with death-shrouds by the spider, preparatory to the first good bite.

"You are just in time," said the little man, pointing to the web. " I am horrified by this tragedy," he exclaimed, " in which I am unable to help either the spider, or the grasshopper. One must not try to defy the laws of nature; it is not for nothing that spiders are not vegetarians. If I were to meddle here, the spider would die of starvation. Nevertheless, the struggles of the grasshopper fill me with a sort of woe. What do you think of it?"

Metabel did not reply; seizing a twig, she freed the captive, and watched the spider flee for her life along the broken rafters of her home.

The little green man shook his head disapprovingly. "Now see what you have done," he said. And he added unhappily, " Ak, the hungry spider."

"I like grasshoppers," said Metabel, "better than spiders."

152

"You are a silly girl," said the little man; "you ought not to interfere in the lives of creatures about whom you know nothing. The spider is much more useful than the grasshopper. She is tidy, serious, and optimistic."

"Still," said Metabel loftily, "I like grasshoppers better."

So saying she started off through the woods in the direction of the cottage.

The little green man trotted along beside her. "How is Joseph?" he inquired. "You have been picking mushrooms; you are going to cook him a fine mushroom stew. Ah, um." And he gave a deep sigh.

"I am only a silly girl," said Metabel, "and I don't know anything about how Joseph is. I suspect he's all right, thank you."

She walked along rapidly, her head in the air; her stride, awkward but dignified, caused several of the mushrooms to tumble from her skirt held out like a basket. The little man picked them up for her.

"Why are you in such a hurry," he asked, "when you have really nowhere to go? If you do not know how Joseph is, it is useless to ask you. . . . I will wait and ask Miss Deakan when she comes."

Metabel stood stock-still; and more mushrooms fell out. "Is she coming here?" she asked; "here, on the hill?"

He replied that the Deakans sometimes came to supper at the farm.

"Oh," said Metabel in a small voice. "Well," she added, in a voice smaller still, "why not?" And she started forward again, faster than ever. But after a while she slowed down to a dawdle.

"I like Prissy Deakan," she said at last, defiantly.

"Hum," said the little man.

"Anyway," Metabel insisted, "I think she's very nice."

The little man looked at her with a wry smile. "Why do you try to fool me?" he asked. "Do you think I do not know the terror which so much vigor and so many jellies inspire in your heart? You are afraid of her, my child, and so am I, because she would like to make a success of Joseph. She loves him for what he will be when she gets through with him. But you and I love him as he is."

"Do I?" asked Metabel.

The little man shrugged his shoulders. "Such questions," he said, "are not important. You will find out for yourself, when the time comes. Then I will tell you what to do. In the meanwhile, you are about to cook him a mushroom stew. Nothing could be nicer."

By this time they had come to a grove of ash trees, whose paler trunks now stood above them straight and tall in the green forest light, while silver leaves showered them with shadow and shine. The little green man stopped and looked about him in a benevolent way. "Here is my home," he said: "this green and quiet grove. Here, among these trees which Joseph loves, there is no one to dispute with me."

Metabel looked up at the trees which seemed to look gravely back at her. "It's lovely here," she said. "It's like what I thought."

The little man continued, musing: "Yes, his heart is like the woods, fertile and friendly. There everything grows, for no other reason than that nature is generous, and does not make distinctions. But Uncle Henry's heart is like a bed of lettuces, grown for a prize. In that dry brown earth there is no room for me. He would like to turn my home into cords of wood."

He smiled at her, and again she thought how friendly

he looked, friendlier than Joseph even. "You are here to help me," he said, "you are here to keep these woods quiet and green. Perhaps I even brought you here, against your will; for the gods must be ingenious if they wish to get along in the world: a god must be a little sly in dealing with other gods, particularly if they are bigger than he is. I am small, but I am sly and stubborn; for that matter, nothing is so obstinate as good humor.

"Well, it is necessary, I can tell you; for the life of a god is not an easy one. For one thing, he is not immortal. Men's faiths, for which they would like to die, or kill one another, do not last very long; in a thousand years, they are forgotten again. Nevertheless, what wars are waged in Heaven in the meanwhile, to the accompaniment of thunder and lightning.

"But here, on this hill" — he rubbed his little hands together — "here in these quiet woods, I can walk up and down day after day, all by myself, without being jostled by Weights and Measures, or battered by the wings of Methodist Angels."

"O my," said Metabel piously; and she glanced up with anxious gray eyes past the tree-tops to where she expected Heaven was, in case it looked dark and indignant. But the sky beyond the leaves shone just as blue as before.

"Well," she said uncertainly, "I don't know. . . ."

Holding her skirt before her like a basket, she walked soberly home through the woods, followed by a mouse who wished to speak to Musket.

There she set herself to wash and cut the mushrooms. She stood at the kitchen sink; her thin hands dipped like tiny swallows into the pot and out again. But her eyes remained dreamy and confused, her thoughts far away. She thought of what the little man had said: "Perhaps I even brought you here against your will." Was she to

155

do battle with the monstrous Prissy Deakan? Her heart beat with excitement. First of all she would have to get over her feelings of terror and respect. And then . . . what? The little man had said he would help her; but what help was he? Not even to a grasshopper in a web. And she saw herself, a tiny David, opposing without weapons the armored Goliath. "I'll just take up my sling shot," she said to herself, "and haul back, and let her have it."

She went through the motions, with a mushroom for a pebble. "Bing," she said to Musket, launching her vegetable into the air.

Musket was enchanted. "She is dancing," he thought; "this is like old times." And he hurried out, to find Isaiah, who had just come back from town.

IN WHICH MUSKET DISCUSSES
MARRIAGE WITH A MOUSE

Chapter IX

He found his friend in the barn, still standing patiently between the shafts of the wagon.

" Well," he said to him after they had exchanged greetings, " what is the news from Wayne? Come, let me hear some gossip: I am sure you have heard something amusing."

Isaiah looked down upon him in surprise. " Why should I hear any gossip? " he asked. " What do you expect? The Stebbins' cow has calved. But surely that is not what you wished to hear? "

" Yes, yes," said Musket, trying to be hearty, " that is very interesting. But it is not exactly what I had in mind. I thought perhaps . . . some social bit . . . well, tell me, were you at the bank? "

" Aha," exclaimed Isaiah, " so that is where the wind blows. Yes, I was at the bank. I saw your little friend Susan, also; she appeared to be enjoying herself, and in the best of health." His voice dropped to a graver note. " She was not alone, my friend."

" Why should she be alone? " asked Musket easily; " I hardly expected she would be. She has many friends. So she was enjoying herself; that is a good thing. I should not like her to be unhappy on my account." He gave a

157

deep sigh. "After all," he said, "I am not young any
more. The best thing for me is a quiet place like this,
where there is nothing to do."

"She was not even thinking of you," said Isaiah.

Musket replied irrelevantly: "The thing I like about
her is that she is intelligent. Do you remember how interested she was in my travels? Also the fact that I was an
artist appealed to her."

"Well," said Isaiah kindly, "it appeals to her no
longer. You told her to forget you, and she has done so.
What are you anxious about?"

"It is not always easy to forget people," said Musket
in a gloomy voice.

"Nonsense," said Isaiah; "a lot of exercise, or good
hard work, and the thing is done. There is nothing like
getting up a sweat, to take the mind off its troubles. But
do not worry about Susan, because I doubt if she was as
much attracted to you as you imagine. From what I saw
yesterday at the bank, I should say that she was something
of a flirt." And he gave a chuckle like a low whinny.

"Ah," said Musket thoughtfully, "women: there's a
strange thing for you. One never knows what to expect.
They are like you, Isaiah, always looking in the distance.
All a woman wants is to want something.

"Did she say nothing about me at all?

"Very well," he concluded; "one makes up one's mind,
and then what happens? Some one else, who has also
made up his mind, comes out ahead. But what of it? One
must be a little philosophic about such things."

And he moved away with an enigmatic expression. Suddenly a mouse ran out of a hole and gave him a sharp bite
on the leg, at the same time exclaiming, "Excuse me; I
took this means of attracting your attention."

With a polite look, the mouse added, "I am engaged

to be married. However, my thoughts are all at sea. Marriage is not what it used to be; I do not know my way about any more. What do you think? You have had so much experience."

"Not," said Musket thoughtfully, "with marriage. But it is true that I have thought a great deal about such matters. What is it you would like to know, my friend? However, first tell me: is this a marriage of convenience, or the result of passion?"

"Alas," said the mouse, "I do not know." His voice sank. "My fiancée," he murmured, "is not a virgin. She has already been unfaithful to a number of my friends. Nevertheless, to be near her fills me with rapture. But I am obliged to admit, it will be more convenient for her than for me."

"Women," said Musket in a noble manner, "are unfaithful by instinct, inclination, and the force of circumstances. So do not let that trouble you. I remember once when I was dancing in a little town . . ."

"Yes, yes," said the mouse hastily; "but what about me?"

Musket looked down at him with a superior expression. "Well, tell me," he said, "why do you wish to marry her?"

"Because," said the mouse, "she wishes to settle down in a respectable way. She says that she knows what she knows, and that life is not all what-you-may-call-it. As for me — God help me; I love her.

"However, should I marry her? That is where I would like to hear your opinion. I do not understand these modern ways."

Musket replied musingly, "She has had experience; and she believes that life is not all what-you-may-call-it. She would make you an excellent wife, my friend. As for what she knows, that would only make her more intelligent. For one thing, she has learned that vigor without wit is of no use to her. I congratulate you."

"You mean," said the mouse dizzily, "that it is I who am the fortunate one? You think, then, that I should go on with this?"

"At once," said Musket, "before the lady, who believes that life is not all what-you-may-call-it, changes her mind. Marry her, my friend, but do not believe her. Enjoy yourself as much as though you were not married at all."

"Thank you," said the mouse. "This is very helpful." And he ran off through the grass in a dazzled way. Musket heard him calling, "Elizabeth, I have something to say to you."

Isaiah, who had been listening to this conversation, exclaimed sternly:

"Musket, you are a scoundrel."

"Isaiah," replied Musket firmly, "you are going at it from the wrong end. I am not a scoundrel; I am simply on the side of the wife. Well, look here: she expects love to be lofty. She is married; and her virtuous husband attacks her with appetite and embarrassment. By the time he is ready to go to sleep, she is sunk in despair. Phoo, what a ridiculous thing. That is because there is some attempt to be pure. If it were a sin, they would enjoy themselves.

"Women should sin a little before they are married, for the joy and the experience."

"No," said Isaiah; "you are a scoundrel, that is all there is to it."

Musket shrugged his shoulders. "After all," he said, "you have spent your life on a hill. And much of it has been, as you say, devoted to perspiration. I have not been a dancer for nothing; I know what I know. It is the woman who is not ashamed to love. Left to herself, she would make heaven out of such things. Unfortunately, she has been kept in the background."

"That is the place for her," declared Isaiah.

He added uneasily, "I do not like this sort of talk, it makes me very uncomfortable." And he looked around, to see if there were any females within hearing.

Musket looked up at his friend, who towered gloomy and surprised above him. "You are an old fogey," he said. And he trotted off in the direction of the kitchen, as Uncle Henry came into the barn to rub the gray horse down.

MUSKET MAKES A SENTIMENTAL JOURNEY

Chapter X

THAT evening Musket sat a long time on the door-step before the house. The blue dusk deepened about him, the stars came out in the sky like frosty lights. Behind him, in the warm kitchen, in the yellow lamp-glow, Metabel stood dishing out mushroom stew to Joseph and Uncle Henry. "The best mushroom stew," said Uncle Henry, "I ever eat." But Musket did not care. Around him in the darkening air trembled the voices of his friends; the crickets sang, and the cicada, the tree-frogs creaked *kreef kreedn kreedn* . . . voices of earth in the warm sweet night, voices of love, lonely and longing. . . .

The last light faded from the sky, the lamp in the cottage was extinguished. New stars arose, the crickets hushed their song. The night poured like a slow wind over the earth, and vanished in the west; the dew of morning, silvery and cold, fell upon the little dog who lay with his nose on his paws before the kitchen door. He shivered in his sleep, and woke and yawned.

Shaking himself, he walked across the yard, lifting his paws above the dew puddles, stretching himself in the gray morning light. He was hungry and cold; he wished he were snug in bed with Metabel. He stood a while, dejected and uncertain, before the barn, where he could hear

Isaiah moving in his stall. " I am a fine one," he thought, "at my age, to stay out all night. In the morning my bones ache." But when the red sun rose, and all the earth grew warm again, he felt more gay. No one was up: the gray horse was still in the barn. If he were to go for a little walk, no one would ask him where he was going. . . .

The birds were waking, their voices skipped and sang among the leaves. The whole earth seemed to stir with joy, to give forth sweet odors, to quiver with happy sounds. Musket's heart beat with pleasure. "What a morning," he said aloud, " to be going for a walk. Supposing one were to meet some one one were fond of . . . a lover's meeting on a summer morning. Ah well, such things have happened to me before."

A beetle who was going by replied pensively, " Why do you wish to meet any one? For every meeting, you can look forward to a parting. The same two who are so irresistibly drawn to each other to-day, will be just as irresistibly drawn apart to-morrow. Life hurries them by on other business, often tearing off a leg or a claw which has become too inextricably entangled. No, no, my friend; go alone, I say."

" I was not speaking to you," said Musket; "however, I thank you for your friendly interest. As you see, I am alone; nor am I apt, I imagine, at my age, to find a companion. I simply thought I would take a walk — a stroll in this delightful air. Down-hill is the way to go. But I do not expect to go as far as Wayne."

"Enjoy yourself," said the beetle, waving a claw at him. A moment later, with one claw still in the air, he stumbled over a twig, and fell upon his back, where he lay, looking at the sky. " When one is alone," he reflected, "one does not have to consider the safety of a second party. Life and death are often no more than a twig apart. What an undignified difference." And feeling already in his body the talons of some hungry ants, he closed his eyes to the inevitable.

Musket continued on his way, heedless of the groans of the unhappy beetle. When he came to the first turn in the road, he thought he would go a little further, in case there were anything to be seen down there. . . . There was another turn, which he took for the same reason. He felt happy without knowing exactly why; he was excited, but he did not wish to ask himself for what reason. However, when he had come within a mile or so of Wayne without meeting any one on the road, his spirits began to sink, and he moved more slowly. "It is too early," he thought, "for any one to be up.

"What did I come all this way for?"

But just as he was about to turn back, he caught sight of a small brown figure trotting along the road in his direction. His heart gave a thump; and he remained as though paralyzed. Then, with an awkward motion, he went forward to meet her. It was Susan.

"Just imagine," he murmured, "finding you here."

"Yes," she said, "how strange. I was out for a little walk. . . ." And they stood regarding each other with shy looks.

Presently Musket turned his head away, in order to let Susan examine him more closely. When she had finished she also stood erect, in a favorable position, and delicately looked aside while he regarded her. Then without a word, they started up the road together in the direction of the farm.

Susan was the first to speak. "I am glad to see you," she said simply. "I have thought a great deal about you."

"Indeed?" said Musket. He spoke in a low voice, so

164

as to conceal the fact that he was pleased and confused.
He felt wary; nevertheless his heart seemed to grow
larger. He bent upon Susan a friendly eye. "You have
been happy?" he asked.

"Happy?" she replied slowly: "yes and no. I do not
lead a very interesting life. For the most part, I am
alone."

"You were not alone yesterday," said Musket mildly.

She gave him a glance of surprise. "No," she admitted; and looked away. She seemed to be changing her
mind about something. "No," she continued brightly, "I
was not alone. Indeed, far from it." She gave a light
laugh. "Do you know with whom I spent the afternoon?
He is supposed to be irresistible."

"Ah," said Musket; "so he is that sort. Well — did
you find him irresistible?"

And he awaited her answer with anxiety.

She did not reply at once, but went to the side of the
road to examine a fungus. Then she came back again with
a languid expression. "To tell you the truth," she said,
"I do not like to have proposals made to me so soon, or
with such assurance."

Musket was conscious of a disagreeable sensation in
his stomach. "He must be a very impudent fellow," he
exclaimed.

"He is not unattractive," said Susan, "although for
my taste, personally . . . the truth is that he has had too
much attention. He does not care for any one but me,
he said. Of course, I do not take all that very seriously.
For instance, I do not believe that he lost his heart to me
really . . . he simply found me sympathetic, because I
let him talk about himself."

"Yes, yes," said Musket. And he added, under his
breath, "Do you expect me to believe you?" But it did

not help him to think that Susan was a flirt; he seemed to himself to grow more unhappy than ever.

Come, he thought; pull yourself together.

"Sympathy," he said, "is a very dangerous thing: like pity, it looks to be more than it is. Then you find that certain things begin to be taken for granted. It can be very embarrassing. Once when I was dancing in a little town . . ."

"Exactly," said Susan; "but one cannot change one's nature; if one is naturally sympathetic and friendly, there is no use trying to be anything else. Besides, it makes life more agreeable. Of course, one is apt to be misunderstood; but so far, I have never had any trouble. As for my friend last night — I admit, he was a little forward. I do not like to have things taken for granted."

"I hope that you were very short with him," said Musket.

"No," said Susan, "why should I be? He knew that he would not be allowed to presume. . . . After all, there is no harm in talking. I like to be gay in my talk, and a little intimate. For one thing I feel that it is expected of me. But I can assure you, I said nothing which might have made him think he had a right . . ."

Musket replied dryly, "One does not make proposals unless one has first been allowed to hope. If he insulted you, it was because you let him think that it would please you, and that your answer might be yes."

Susan gave a gasp. "That is absurd," she said. "Besides, I did not say that he insulted me."

"It is not absurd," answered Musket gloomily. "He made you proposals; they surprised you. That is what is absurd, as a matter of fact; because you know very well what to expect."

She stood stock-still, and looked at him with indigna-

166

tion. "It is you who insult me," she said. "I wonder why? What right have you to say those things to me? First you tell me not to think of you — as though that were all I had to do. . . . Well, that was insulting enough, or would have been, if it weren't so ridiculous. And now you say that I know what to expect. No, really, I would rather walk alone, if you please; I came out to enjoy myself."

"So did I," replied Musket. "I came out for a pleasant walk. Instead, the entire time, I am obliged to listen to some proposals a stranger made to you. Of course, it is nothing to me. But I cannot help seeing it in its true light. First you lead him on; then you complain. Probably you are very cruel."

"At least," said Susan stormily, "I am not cruel to you, because you can leave me at any minute, and go back where you came from. You are perfectly free; so why do you vex yourself by staying in my company? I am quite able to get home alone, thank you."

Musket gave a shrug. "Or you in mine?" he asked. "Besides," he added, "if you will notice, I am actually on my way home."

"You are insufferable," said Susan; "it is really too bad, because I thought, when I met you, that I liked you. I thought that you were intelligent, and kind. But you are like all the rest, stupid and conceited."

"I am not," said Musket angrily. Then, growing more dignified, he added, "I too, thought that you were different. But you are like the others, vain and untruthful. I am glad I am not your lover."

"I would not have you for my lover," said Susan, "for anything in the world."

"It makes me happy to think," said Musket, "that you are nothing to me."

"Or you to me," said Susan.

"Fortunately," said Musket, "I live so far away that we are not even apt to meet each other very often."

"Fortunately indeed," said Susan.

With these words she turned around, and started back to Wayne. When she had gone about a hundred yards, she looked back over her shoulder and remarked, "I am not cruel at all."

Musket did not hear her because at that moment he was exclaiming in a loud voice:

"I am not conceited."

Chapter XI

" WHAT do you think about good humor, Uncle Henry? "
asked Metabel.

" Haven't I got it? " said Uncle Henry.

Rain had settled over Hemlock; gray cloud tatters
trailed on the mountain, the air was searching, cold and
sweet. Icy drops fell from the trees on to the bushes; in
the drenched garden Uncle Henry was taking this last opportunity to thin out his lettuces.

Metabel stood beside him in a rubber cape, the hood up
over her head. The cape was too long for her, it came to
below her feet, and lay in the puddles. The thrum of the
rain was in her ears as it moved, driven by the wind, across
the fields and through the woods; it made her want to
dance, but when she put up her arms, cold trickles of water
fell down her neck. So she stood still and peered anxiously
across the garden to the black sopping woods, where the
little green man lived.

" I wonder is he comfortable? " she thought.

Uncle Henry, with an oilskin over his red flannel shirt,
knelt on the ground. " Haven't I got good humor? " he
asked. " I always figured I had. Look at the way I go
after these lettuces, rain or shine; and what thanks do I
get? But I don't complain. Look at the way I am with

169

Joseph: there's good humor for you. Here's a head for the table. It's got a spot on it."

And he held out to her a lettuce soaked with rain. She put it under her cape.

"I don't think that's what he meant," she said thoughtfully.

"What who meant?" asked Uncle Henry.

"Nothing," she said; "I was just thinking."

"You do a powerful lot of thinking," complained Uncle Henry, "and what with the dancing you do, you're liable to waste most of your life.

"Like Joseph," he added gloomily. "He has the whole side of a mountain to lumber, and what does he bring out of it?"

"Neat cut wood," said Metabel. It popped out of her mouth, to her own surprise.

"I wouldn't give you two cents for it," said Uncle Henry. He pointed to the lettuce. "There's my prize head," he said. "When they see that, they'll know who's living on Hemlock. There's not much bigger grown."

Metabel gave the lettuce a polite look. "I like the little ones best," she confessed. "They taste sweeter."

"For eating," agreed Uncle Henry, "for eating. But I'm not raising lettuce for eating. I don't care for them myself. It's a work with me. I don't like it, but I do it. Do you know who gets the good of it?"

"No," said Metabel honestly.

"The county," said Uncle Henry, "the county gets the good of it. Wayne County, where they grow lettuces as big as a barn. Folks hear of that. And I'm the one up on Hemlock, in Wayne County, that grows it. It's a way I have with vegetables. But the county gets the good of it. And why do I do it? Because I've got an opinion of

170

my fellow men. I've got an opinion of myself. I'm a help to this county.

"Take Joseph, now." And he prepared to continue this subject which vexed and perplexed him.

"He has no opinion," he said sadly. "It's a grief to me.

"But wait till a good woman takes ahold." And he rubbed his wet hands together, thinking of what was going to happen to Joseph.

"I know what you mean," said Metabel.

"That's it," he said cheerfully; "that's the one for him. She'll take hold of him good. No more setting and thinking for Joseph. No more neat cut wood for him.

"I can see it in her eye. Last time I was at the bank she said to me, 'How is Joseph?' 'Come to dinner,' I told her, 'and see for yourself.' 'I will,' says she. There's a woman for you: 'I will,' she said, just like that."

Metabel looked out across the rain-soaked fields with startled eyes. It gave her a turn, his saying that; it made her feel as though there weren't so much time ahead as she thought. Time had always seemed something infinite to her, stretching out ahead of her, full of lovely things — all she had to do was to find them, and then live happily ever after. Ever after, for always and always. But this was different: something was trying to happen which would change everything. Time wasn't infinite, it was moving very fast, it was coming to an end. . . .

Her breath caught in a sudden panic. If it happened, the thing which was trying to happen, then there'd be no loveliness ahead any more. She didn't stop to think — she simply knew. One couldn't just take one's time about things — one had to do them quickly — sharp and sudden — I will, or I won't, just like that. That was the

giant one had to face with no more than a sling shot —
not Prissy Deakan. Well, she'd face him, in whatever
panic, and let him have it.

Remembering what she had seen in Barly, in the Book,
she exclaimed, "He fell upon his face to the earth."

"Who?" asked Uncle Henry. "Not Joseph?"

"No," said Metabel, "not Joseph."

And she tramped off through the wet grass to the barn,
already fragrant with clover-hay, her long rubber cape
making a trailing whisper as she went.

In the barn she found Joseph, sewing an old harness
for Isaiah. He smiled when he saw her. "Hello, Metabel," he said, "I was thinking about you."

She stood still, taking the cape down from her shoulders. "Were you?" she asked, hardly believing it.
"What were you thinking?"

He replied seriously, "I was thinking were you happy
here?"

"Oh," she said. She looked at him with eyes gray as
the rain outside. "Don't you know, Joseph?" she asked
quietly.

No, he didn't rightly know. "I always think folks are
happy," he said musingly, "till I stop to think. Then I
think maybe not. It's a queer thing, happiness. I expect
it's not the same for everybody. I declare to God, you
might just as well let them be.

"Don't you ever wish yourself home again? Tell me
true."

Metabel wanted to say No, right out. But then she
stopped; the little sly part of her got up inside and looked
around. The rain fell with the wind against the barn in
a long sweet whisper. Barly . . . Barly . . . why did
Joseph care?

"Who's in Barly," she asked, "would want me back?"

172

"The preacher's son?"

She smiled to herself. He hadn't forgotten that much, at any rate. "Well, he might," she said, lying. "But I don't mind staying."

Joseph looked earnestly at the harness in his hands. "I'm right glad to hear it," he said. "It wouldn't be the same hereabouts, if you went. Uncle Henry's got that used to you."

Uncle Henry? Was that all? "Not you too, Joseph?"

"Yes . . . too. But I mightn't always be here."

Her heart went down with a swoop. "You're figuring on going away?" she asked, looking at her feet, and trying to keep her voice from trembling.

He wouldn't look up, either. His voice sounded trifling — too trifling, almost. "I don't know," he said; "I don't exactly aim to. But Uncle Henry keeps pestering me; he wants for me to go down to work at the mill. Winters."

He gave a sigh. "I guess maybe I'm just no-account," he said anxiously.

Again she bit her tongue to keep back the No which started to come out so fast. What was it kept her from saying the thing she wanted to say? It was almost as though she were set to give herself a hurt if she could. "You'd be right near to Prissy Deakan," she said, "if you went to town."

"I would, too," he admitted.

She stood looking at him for a long while. Then, slowly, and with a shiver, she put her wet cape on again. "Why don't you go?" she said. And turning on her heel, she marched out of the barn into the rain.

It cooled her face, it made her pulse go slow again. The cold, wet air steadied her, started her thoughts to going orderly. Whatever was she up to, marching out like that? He hadn't said he'd go — he hadn't even said he wanted

173

to go. There she was; she'd met Goliath, or at least had a look at him; and what had she done? Run away the first crack out of the box. Hadn't even stayed long enough to sling one stone. "Glory," she thought, "we've got each other all mixed up."

And suddenly she seemed to see the little green man at her side again. "Where's your good humor?" he was saying to her. "Nothing is so obstinate as good humor."

She took a deep breath of the sweet, searching air: it stung her nose. "All right," she said aloud. And back she went to the barn again.

"Joseph," she said, "do you want to go to Wayne?"

He shook his head. "No," he said. "I declare, I don't."

"Then don't go," she said. And with a firm, peaceful expression, she sat herself down next to him, and took over her share of the sewing.

THE DEAKANS COME TO DINNER

Chapter XII

BUT that didn't keep the Deakans from coming to dinner. All three of them, St. John the banker, Prissy, and Susan, came up in the Deakan automobile one hot summer day, drawing the dust behind them. Uncle Henry and Joseph met them at the road, all in their Sunday best: over the faded red flannel, Uncle Henry had buttoned a blue and white checked cotton shirt, which Metabel had carefully washed and ironed; while Joseph, with his hair wetted down until it shone, had got himself into a corduroy jacket, hot but elegant.

Metabel herself was nearly distracted, what with the cooking she was expected to do, and the looks she wanted to give herself — not that she had more than a ribbon or two to add between her worst and her best, but even the ribbon, she felt, ought to take fixing. She was all for the cooking and letting the looks go, until she saw Joseph's shiny face and wet-down hair; then she was all for the ribbon. It gave her a hot feeling in her heart to see him getting himself up so grand for any one else.

She stopped before her little mirror, and gave herself a long, disdainful look. " You're an ugly piece," she said, " and what good's a ribbon going to do? You might as well tie it on to Musket; all you've got is an old dress, anyhow, with holes in it." So saying, and with a dreamy air, she arranged the ribbon at her shoulder, and pinned it on with a black safety pin. Then she turned around, and gave a skip on her toes. "How do I look, Musket?" she cried.

Musket did not reply. He seemed excited, and at the same time his thoughts were elsewhere. He trotted to the door, and looked out; then he came in again, and sat down in a corner. But in a moment or two he was back at the door again, peering down the road with an uncertain expression which he hoped would be taken for indifference.

Metabel turned back to the mirror, and gazed at herself with falling spirits. Then she gave a sigh. "Oh well," she said, "I don't care." And she went back to her pots on the stove, from which the steam presently wilted the ribbon until it drooped like a shoestring.

It made no difference, for the moment Prissy came in, she felt like a little humble toad again. Prissy in her store clothes, looking large and cool and able — looking as though she knew more about cooking than Metabel, more about lettuces than Uncle Henry . . . but not, Metabel thought with a quiver, more about cutting down trees, quiet and neat, than Joseph did, thank heaven. . . .

"We had to bring Susan," said Prissy; "she came running after us, and wouldn't be left. I'm glad to be here; it's cooler than the valley." And she looked around the room in an ample way. "There's been changes," she said.

Her eyes fastened on Metabel, bending anxiously over the stove. "That's right," she said; "I forgot you had a hired cook."

Uncle Henry brought a chair forward for the banker. "Sit down, St. John," he said, "and ease yourself."

St. John eased his large spare body into the chair, and

176

mopped his face. "It's hot, Henry," he complained. "There's like to be thunder by night. It'll sour the milk." He exhaled a long breath; it was his habit to talk about things like milk while his mind was going over figures. He believed in being strong inside, and amiable out; it took a little longer to make an impression, but it made it deeper. After he had been amiable for a while he'd bring out his figures, and strike other people, who had no figures, dumb. Uncle Henry was used to it; as soon as the banker started talking about milk, Uncle Henry began to think in terms of acres and lumber. He'd be ready when the time came.

"Yes, sir," he said proudly; "thunder up here is the loudest in the state."

Musket and Susan stood together in the doorway, looking out across the yard. "Isn't it funny, my being here," said Susan; "will you believe it, they insisted on my coming. As a rule, the woods do not attract me. However, there was no help for it to-day."

These words did not fool Musket, who wished to say, "You were obliged to come, but not for the reasons you have given me." Nevertheless, he held his tongue, content for the moment with his advantage. "I am glad you came," he said gallantly, "even against your will."

Susan looked at him out of one eye. "Perhaps it was not wholly against my will," she murmured. And as Musket said nothing, she added in a faint voice, "It is so hot in here; shall we go out?"

"Why do you dislike the woods?" asked Musket as they trotted down the steps. "They are cool and quiet and green; the little moths fly about in the half-light; there are caves under the rocks, and houses under fallen trees. It is just the place to be on such a hot day. Besides, you are not likely to be disturbed. It is very peaceful."

"What an alluring picture," said Susan. "As a matter of fact, I do not dislike the woods. Some unforgettable things have happened to me there. . . . I suppose that you have some little place of your own to which you usually go; a soft carpet of moss, a hidden hollow with the sound of water falling, green branches overhead making a sweet half-light . . . you see, I am not unfamiliar with the woods. Of course, you would naturally know of such a place."

"Yes, indeed," replied Musket; "I am most anxious for you to see it. Let us go a little faster; then there will be more time afterwards."

"What a romantic creature you are," said Susan. And as they disappeared among the trees, she was saying, "I like things to be made a little attractive. The brutality so in vogue to-day does not appeal to me."

At dinner Metabel did the serving, sitting down to eat with the family, and hopping up again to fetch things from the stove. Her hair was wet and stringy, her thin face red with work; the wilted ribbon on her shoulder hung without dignity from the black safety pin. And Joseph sat there, saying little, with the same friendly smile for Prissy Deakan that he had for everybody.

"If only," thought Metabel, "even once, he'd look as if he didn't like her."

But not Joseph; he continued to look as though he liked everything and everybody. On the other hand, when Prissy looked at Joseph, her eyes grew secret and hard, just as though she were looking at what belonged to her, and having a sly thought about it.

And the worst of it was, there didn't seem to be anything for Metabel to do, except to go on hopping after the dishes. After all, she wasn't David; she couldn't just sail up to her foe and let her have it in the forehead.

178

Prissy looked so sure and able; maybe he did belong to her.

She grew hotter and hotter, her face turned redder and redder; and Uncle Henry and St. John Deakan discussed politics.

"We could send this road right over the hill," said the banker, "if we had more dairy interests. This is a dairy state, Henry. You'd ought to raise cows."

"It may be a dairy state," said Uncle Henry firmly, "but it's a vegetable county. This road has always gone down. What for would it go up?"

"Up and over," said the banker. "A road right over Hemlock. New roads, new farms; bring the wood down. There's a lot of lumber on Hemlock."

"We could use a little more mountain ash down to the mill," said Prissy.

Joseph seemed not to hear. "They want some ash down to the mill, Joseph," said Uncle Henry in a wheedling voice. "There's a lot of it up above us."

"There is," said Joseph. "But you can't reach it."

"They'd give a price for it at the mill," said Uncle Henry.

"Ah," said Joseph.

"We could put a road right up the hill," said St. John, "and bring the wood out. Instead of being obliged to go around by East Toby, like we are now. Ash is what we want. You'd have a tidy property, Henry. A road's a good thing, too, for coming and going."

"There's nowhere I want to go," said Joseph.

"You've no opinion," said Uncle Henry angrily. "Never did have. For all the time you set and think, where's your opinion?"

"That's right," said Joseph amiably.

"*Joseph,*" cried Metabel, inside her heart.

"I don't like to take out mountain ash," said Joseph quietly. He didn't seem to be arguing about it; he just said it.

Metabel took a deep breath. "He has his own opinion," she said out loud, "and that's enough for anybody."

At once it seemed to her that she heard a sound of handclapping, very small and faint, just outside the window. Inside the kitchen, every one stopped talking and stared at her. Only Joseph himself seemed unmoved by the declaration. "I expect you're right, Metabel," he said. It made her want to shake him, out of vexation.

"Everybody has an opinion, miss," said Prissy coolly. "Some folks do well with theirs, and others don't. Some folks live in rags" — her hard secret look swept over Metabel's small figure — "and others don't."

"That's it," said Uncle Henry; "that's saying something. Do you hear, Joseph? Rags for some, and riches for others. Take your choice."

"What riches," said the banker in his slow voice, "will you ever get out of lettuce, Henry? Cows are the thing. And a proper road for lumber."

Uncle Henry's face grew solemn. "It's my lettuce draws the farmers, St. John," he said. "The county gets the riches from what I do. I get my own riches.

"But that don't let Joseph out," he added gloomily. "You take your axe, Joseph, and go up and have a look at that ash above us. Prissy'll go along with you. I declare, I'm sick of your fancies. St. John, you come with me; if there's to be a road over Hemlock, I want to see."

He went out, to figure cords of wood, to show the banker his lettuces, to follow the road in his mind up the hill and over. Joseph and Prissy went off to the barn, to get an axe. And Metabel took her dishes to the sink, and got the suds ready. As a rule she enjoyed washing up, the warm water, the bright, shiny china in stacks on the table; but now she had no patience at all. Her thin fingers flew and stumbled; she felt all of a hurry, as though she had no time for what she had to do. She pressed her wet hair away from her face with the back of her hand. A road up Hemlock, and the trees down? Her heart gave a flutter of fear. And why did Prissy look at him like that? Was there something between them? She had an eye for him . . . she certainly had an eye for him.

"There never were so many dishes," she cried, "in the whole world. Oh, go on — get clean, for goodness' sake. . . ."

A STORM IS GATHERING

Chapter XIII

HEAVY heat lay on the hillside that afternoon, heat almost as heavy as a mist. The birds were still, even the crows forgot to caw; only a locust stung the silence with the drill of his sound. At the wood's edge Metabel came upon Musket; the little dog's head was hanging, and he dragged his feet wearily. Susan walked beside him; she took mincing steps, and gazed at him in a hopeful way. But Musket did not return her glances. When he passed Metabel, he hung his head lower than ever. Finally his legs collapsed, and he sat down. " Ak," he said. " Yoo. My legs are not what they used to be."

Susan wished to console him. " Never mind," she said; " I am not sad about this, really. Supposing that in the future we simply confine ourselves to conversation? Come, cheer up; life is not all what-you-may-call-it."

Musket gave her a startled glance. Then he closed his eyes with a groan. He did not feel consoled at all.

Metabel went across the dry grass into the woods. There it was more silent still: the green leaves, dusty with heat, closed behind her, and drowsy shadows peered at her from out the tree trunks. Dark, gloomy, the trees gazed down at her; and again she felt the need to hurry, as though something were pushing her. Was it the trees, pushing her? They were so very still. There was something queer about them; the very silence itself, up there among the branches, seemed to be thinking a strange thought. Or was it a fear? Yes — it was more like a fear. The forest was afraid. It made her feel scary.

"Little green man," she whispered; "little green man . . ."

But no one answered; and the silence grew deeper. A dry twig broke under her feet with a pop; she began to run. "Wait a minute," she said to something; "wait . . . I'm coming . . ."

The faster she ran, the more frightened she felt. It seemed to her as though the forest were running with her, as though shadows skipped along behind her and about her, from tree to tree. *Pat pat pat* went her feet, but all she could hear was the sound of silence, like a great hum. She closed her eyes. "Wait," she cried; "oh, please . . ." Her foot went under a root, and down she came with all the world's pain in her ankle.

When she opened her eyes, she found herself buried in a sumac bush, at the edge of a little clearing into which Joseph and Prissy were at that moment slowly walking. In the center of this clearing stood a great ash tree, toward which Prissy was directing her steps.

"Ah," said the banker's daughter, "that's a tree. Look how straight it is, Joseph. Like the mast of a ship. A tree like that would bring money at the mill."

"Would it?" said Joseph, without enthusiasm.

Prissy laid a hand on his arm. "Joseph," she said seriously, "I want to talk to you. I'm right fond of you. You know that."

"I like you too, Prissy," replied Joseph.

Her face grew pink, the eyes softer, then harder. "I'd like to see you get along," she said.

"I do get along," said Joseph; "I get along fine, Prissy."

She spoke a little impatiently. "Yes," she said; "but that's not what I mean. I'd like them to say about you down to the town, 'He's a good man.'"

"Don't they?" asked Joseph with surprise.

She turned and looked at him honestly. "No," she said, "they don't. And you know why, Joseph? They say you're no good with a tree, and that's the truth of it."

Joseph looked unhappily at his axe. "It pleases me, the way I cut," he said. "I cut slow, but the tree goes where I want it. I've taken out a chestnut between two birch, and never cracked a limb on either of them. That's the way I like to cut, Prissy. What's the matter with that?"

"It don't get you anything," said Prissy. "It don't get you cordage. That's what we count at the mill. Not what you leave, but what you bring out."

Her fingers twined on his arm. "Joseph," she said in a low voice, "bring me a load of ash to-morrow."

"I don't want to, Prissy."

She looked at him, all softness and wheedle for a big woman. "Start on this one, Joseph," she said. "Bring it down for me.

"Bring it down fast and neat. I've never seen you cut."

In her sumac bush, Metabel, with one hand on her ankle, and her mouth screwed tight with pain, was looking for a stone. "God give me a stone," she said to herself.

"Who's that called my name?" asked Joseph.

Prissy glanced around in surprise. "Nobody," she said; "there's no one about. I didn't hear anything."

Joseph looked at the tree and sighed. "I'll bring you down an oak, Prissy," he said coaxingly; "that's a lot better than an ash. I can cut fast if I've a mind to. It's only that I've never had a mind to. A fine stiff oak. You'll see."

184

"The mill's full of oak," said Prissy wearily. "What we need is ash. This would be just for me, Joseph. You said you liked me."

"I do like you, Prissy. But you're asking me to go against what I've a mind for."

"Then you're plain no good with a tree. That's what they say in town. Well, they're right."

"They're not either," said Joseph. And he advanced slowly but angrily to the tree.

"Look here," he said, turning around, "somebody threw a stone at me."

"You're crazy," said Prissy, with a gasp; "go on — begin. Let's see you cut. Let's see you . . . if you can."

Up went the axe, and down it came on the tree, which gave a groan. In her sumac bush, Metabel closed her eyes; her heart was going like a little trip-hammer. Goliath had his big knee on her. "Help," she croaked, inside herself.

"I don't want it to fall on that sumac over yonder," said Joseph chopping away.

"Faster," cried Prissy, "faster . . ."

"I can't get direction so good when I'm going fast," puffed Joseph.

"It doesn't matter," cried Prissy. "Faster, Joseph . . . oh . . ."

The tree creaked and cracked; the upper branches shivered, the leaves gave one last desperate dance, and down it came with a swoop and a roar — square on the sumac bush.

"There you are," said Joseph. "I didn't get my direction very good. Do you want me to chop it up here and now?"

But Prissy was satisfied; her face was pale, she looked languid, almost drowsy; when she spoke, her voice was thick and sweet, like molasses. "No," she said, "come home." And she took his arm. As they moved off, her legs seemed to wobble under her.

The fall of the great ash had flattened Metabel out like a little pancake. It came down on her like a wave, all rushing and roaring; she didn't feel anything, the thunder and the fear seemed to blot out all feeling. She gave one faint cry, "Oh, pa . . ." and closed her eyes. For all she knew, she was dead; broken to pieces. It was the end of her.

In the quiet after echoes, she looked around again with eyes all ready to brim over with pain. But it was queer, the pain held off; nothing hurt her, except her ankle. Was she numb? Was she so smashed she couldn't even feel pain? She looked anxiously for blood, or broken bones, but nothing was broken or bloody. "Oh," she said with a groan, "ow." And she waited wide-eyed to see if anything ached.

But nothing did. Instead, a voice at her ear exclaimed, "What are you groaning for?"

There at her side was the little green man.

"Now look," she cried; "just see what's happened."

And she explained earnestly, "A tree fell on me."

"I know it," he said.

Then she saw that he was holding up one of the branches in such a way as to make a sort of shelter over her. He did not seem in the least vexed or uneasy; as a matter of fact, he was smiling.

"I could have died," she said; "I could have been smashed to kindling."

"Yes," he replied; and then, "nonsense."

She looked at him for a long time, while her rain-gray eyes grew darker and darker. Finally she pointed a trembly finger at him. "You did it," she said. "You made it fall on me."

He nodded his head. "I did," he admitted.

"Well," she gasped, "I never. What on earth for?"

He did not reply. Instead, he looked thoughtfully up at the sky. "The hot spell is broken," he said. "Soon there will be a storm. Thunder on Hemlock is the loudest in the world."

And as he spoke she heard above her in the tree-tops, a heavy sough of wind.

"I'm going home," she declared.

At this the little green man looked anxious and gloomy. "No," he exclaimed hurriedly, "that is impossible. A tree has fallen on you."

"But it didn't hurt me any," cried Metabel.

"That makes no difference," he said. He added earnestly, "What do you think I did all this for! It is not a pleasure for me, exactly, holding up this tree. . . . But what an opportunity. Go home indeed — no, no, my child, that would spoil everything. Supposing it is a little uncomfortable for you; never mind, it is a time for courage. One does not win battles by going home at a critical moment. Do you know what is going to happen? In the morning Joseph will come to look for you; led by Musket, he will find you under this tree, which he cut down against his will, for Prissy's sake. What a night he will spend, looking for you. And what a morning, when he has found you. O my. That is the end of the road up Hemlock."

"But," objected Metabel, "that isn't fair for Joseph. I'm not hurt; I could crawl home easy."

"Think how much nicer it will be," said the little green man cunningly, "to have him carry you home, all anxious for what he has done to you. And once you are in his arms . . . well, hmn. Now do not argue any more, but make yourself comfortable. While we wait, I will tell you some stories. What would you like to hear? I remember everything."

"You're so obstinate," said Metabel beginning to sniffle; "I hate you. I don't want to hear stories, I want to go home."

The little green man gave a chuckle.

"Nothing is so obstinate as good humor," he said. And settling back with a contented sigh, he began: "Once upon a time . . ."

THUNDER AND LIGHTNING

Chapter XIV

THE LIGHT faded ominously with the day, leaving the woods in darkness hidden from the stars. The wind increased; sighing, it passed overhead, among the leaves, which rustled in the air. Thunder rumbled up from the west; at last, between flashes of lightning, the rain came rushing over the tree-tops with a marching sound. The upper branches bent beneath that rush of water. But at the foot of the trees, the drops fell with a loud, hesitant patter, their solid fall broken and scattered by the leaves.

The little man drew down the branches of the tumbled ash to make a cover for Metabel; it did not keep her wholly dry, but it kept off some of the rain. When the lightning broke too brightly through the clinging dark, she closed her eyes and moaned. The little man held her hand and comforted her. " Come," he said coaxingly; " there is nothing to be afraid of. I do not think he really means to hit us. Besides, his aim is poor; he is always hitting the wrong person, and then taking the credit. However, to be sure, I have put a small piece of steel in the branches of a tree a few yards away. Originally it was a mouse-trap. You are safe with me; but do not let go of my hand."

"Do you mean some one's trying to hit us?" cried Metabel. "Ow."

The little green man replied seriously, "The gods are

189

always fighting. I alone have no such desire; and that is what makes me unique. I do not even urge my rabbits to attack Uncle Henry's lettuces. What is the good of quarreling? But the gods do not feel amiably inclined toward those who will not fight with them. Accustomed to arguments and battles to prove that the other gods do not exist, they cannot bear a mind in which there is neither envy nor disapproval. Like you, I have almost no friends in Heaven, because I do not wish to fight about anything. That is what attracts me to you."

" I wanted to fight about Prissy," said Metabel soberly, " but a tree fell on me."

"That is different," said the little man. However he did not explain how it was different. He continued: " While their mortal admirers slaughter each other upon earth, Heaven resounds with divine slaps and blows. The god of the Jews has had his nose pulled many times. But he is tough; almost as tough as I am. I respect him for his obstinacy. I would like to be friends with him, but he will not have it. ' There is no good humor,' he assures me proudly, ' among the Jews.' And he covers up his beard with his hands, to keep an enraged archbishop from pulling it out."

"I didn't know it was like that in Heaven," said Metabel.

At that moment a blinding flash of lightning, attracted by the mouse-trap, lit up the forest like day.

Metabel sat up with a start, shivering from fright, and from the cold water which fell on her from the trees. " I want to go home," she said.

Letting go of the little man's hand, she exclaimed with energy:

" Why did I ever leave Barly?"

The little man seemed to dwindle at her side. " If you

go on like that," he said, "I shall soon be too small to hold up this tree any longer. Then you will be squashed for fair. Or Satan will get in here, and throw me out. He is very ugly; if he knows you are frightened, he will come at once. Already I hear his wings in the dark; my nose detects an unmistakable odor of sulphur and molasses. Give me your hand; hold on to me tightly."

And he exclaimed in a loud voice, "Go away, Satan; nobody wants you. We are all brave as lions here."

"All right," said Metabel in a tiny voice, "I won't be scared. Don't leave me." And she held his hand as tightly as she could.

They were silent; the trees dripped down on them, the storm rode sullenly off into the east, banging and blazing. The girl closed her eyes and dozed; when she woke, the little green man was stirring uncomfortably.

"It is nearly day," he said, "and I have a crick in my arm. In a few minutes the sky will begin to turn gray, and cocks will crow in the villages. Soon Joseph will be coming through the woods crying 'Metabel, Metabel.' It is time for me to leave you, my child. I have arranged a stick to hold up the tree until he gets here.

"But before I go let me give you some advice. You are in a very favorable position. Do not bungle this opportunity. When Joseph arrives, act a little hurt; weep a little, make some touching moans; if possible, faint. Remember that a tree fell on you; it was his fault, and you have every reason to be upset.

"And think that what you are doing is not entirely for yourself. As a matter of fact, that part of it does not interest me. It is for the woods, it is for me, it is for Joseph himself that you must act wounded this morning. The eyes of many little mice and rabbits are upon you. Farewell."

191

With that, he was gone. At the same time, the light in the woods turned gray; cocks began to crow; and Metabel heard through the trees the anxious voice of Musket, and Joseph calling, " Metabel, Metabel."

Musket was the first to reach her; he poked his cold nose into her face and jumped about.

When Joseph saw her under the tree, he turned pale. " O me," he said. And he began pulling at the tree like a demon.

Metabel gave a melancholy groan. " Joseph," she said faintly, " is that you? A tree fell on me."

Seeing that his back was turned, she gave Musket a sharp slap. " Stop licking my face," she whispered, " for goodness' sake. . . ."

The little dog sat down and stared at her in dismay. " Ai! " he exclaimed.

" I've been here all night," said Metabel in her faintest voice.

" Are you hurt? " cried Joseph. " Are you mangled? "

" I'm mangled," said Metabel. And she closed her eyes, intending to faint. But then she opened them again, thinking she'd put it off for a better time.

" My ankle's swole," she announced.

Dropping to his knees beside her, Joseph exclaimed with anguish, " It was Prissy's doings. I'll never forgive myself, nor her, neither. O Metabel, look what I've done to you."

Now, thought Metabel, was a better time to faint than the other. But before she let herself go limp, she sat up and exclaimed with energy, " You'd never let her do it again, would you, Joseph? "

" Never, so help me," said Joseph fervently. He gathered her up, white and wet in his arms. " Ah," she murmured, " oh." And she acted like fainting as well as she could.

Home they went through the gray wet woods; from the dripping branches little squirrels looked down at them with happy faces; mice gazed up at them from under logs green with moss.

" Hurrah for Metabel," they cried.

" She is a noble creature."

Joseph paid no attention to these sounds, which seemed to him like so many squeaks. He held her close and light as a feather; her face rested against his shoulder; it made her heart beat, to feel the rough cloth of his shirt, and the strong arms around her. But after a while his feet began to lag, for he kept looking at her. " No," he said, " I'll never get over this. She's fainted. Metabel. Don't faint. We're nearly home."

So saying, he put his face down next to hers, to make her feel better, probably.

She stretched one thin arm up around his neck. " Joseph dear," she murmured, able to talk, " you won't let them make you over, will you? "

" No," he said. And he gave her cheek a brave kiss.

" Ho," he added thoughtfully; " well . . ."

Her arm tightened about his neck. " Hold me closer, Joseph," she said, " because I'm wet. I'm mangled, and my ankle's swole. Did you give my cheek a kiss? "

" Yes," he said.

" Oh," said she. She closed her eyes contentedly. " It felt like it," she said.

He brought her home, and set her down in the chair. Uncle Henry gave one look at her, and went for hot water. " I knew you for a fool," he said, " the minute I laid eyes on you; but I didn't figure you for the biggest fool there was. Couldn't you get out from under a tree before it fell on you?" However, when he saw her ankle, blue and swollen, he grew merrier. There was no question about it, it was an important swelling.

While the ankle was being bound, Musket went off to find Isaiah. The little dog's tail drooped, and he looked forlorn. "What a night," he said to the gray horse; "looking here, looking there . . . I was not prepared for it.

"Tell me, why do they try to fool each other? If they feel anything, they should say so, and be done with it. What is all this, hiding under trees, and giving me a slap? . . .

"There is something queer here."

ONE STAR OVER THE PASTURE BARS

Chapter XV

UNCLE HENRY went to look at his lettuces for the last time. One more day and it would be too late, they'd go into seed. Already the smaller ones were high in the middle; one or two, even, had a great stalk darting up through the leaves.

Uncle Henry looked at them for a long time. While he gazed and gazed, the sun sank slowly in the west, and a chill stole out of the woods, in the shadows. There, before him, lay his size and his glory, but he felt weary. He was a worshiper, from whom the ecstasy had departed. He had grown those lettuces, teased and coaxed them to be bigger; that was what he loved, raising them. Now that they were grown, something stopped in his mind; he was just so big, they were just so big, and there was nothing more to be done about it. If only the spring held over, and things went on growing. But no; all the great effort of June, and were you any bigger by September? Christmas time you were as small as ever.

Not quite, perhaps — there was the prize up over the fireplace, and farmers from as far as East Toby spoke of those famous vegetables.

Yes, they spoke of him. His bosom swelled, but not very much. He wasn't young and hopeful any more, he'd learned how big the heads would grow — so big, and no bigger. What he wanted was a lettuce to go on growing through July and August, through October and November. . . . He sat and thought of other things, things like roads; yes, there wasn't any end to them, you could go on building them bigger and bigger, further and further. . . . Perhaps he should have been a road builder. Perhaps he should.

He drew in a breath; his nose detected the fragrance of Indian pudding from the kitchen. Weary, but consoled, he returned to the house. There, at least, was something couldn't be better.

In the cool evening light Metabel and Joseph stood together by the fence above the pasture where Isaiah, with a faint *clop, clop,* was moving slowly through the grass already wet with dew. Below them, near the woods, the fireflies were darting like little golden sparks into the air cold with the mist of night; while above them, over the dark, still trees, trembled the evening star, white and alone.

His arm was around her, her thrush-colored hair lay against his shoulder. Serious and happy they stared without winking at the green clear sky above the tree-tops. Then they wished together on the evening star.

"Very first star I see to-night,
Wish I may, wish I might . . ."

Ah, Metabel thought, why not? Here was the world all full of a light which made it look so lovely . . . the green twilight from the sky, perhaps . . . why shouldn't she wish for what she wanted to come true? There she leaned in Joseph's arm, with her head against his shoulder, loving him; and and did he love her back? He had his arm around her, anyhow. Her heart almost spilled over with happiness. To be loved, even a little. . . . What a strange, shy burning it put into her eyes when she looked at him, across the table, or suddenly coming in through the door. . . . And the way her heart beat, now and then, all of a sudden, making her want to dance, only that she didn't know, ever, how to dance as gay and free as her heart felt. She loved him, he had his arm around her, and oh, how sweet the evening smelled. . . .

She blew a kiss into the air. "That's for a little green man who lives in the woods," she explained.

"What a fancy you've got," said Joseph.

"Never mind," she cried gaily. But her mood passed, leaving her solemn and anxious.

"Joseph," she said, "are you glad I came here from Barly?"

His arm tightened about her, but he said nothing; he stood quiet and smiling. He was never much for talk, was Joseph.

She went on, in a low voice, with her head against his shoulder: "I told a lie, I haven't any friends there. There was just the fiddler who ever cared for me. But that was different, too. He didn't put his arm around me. He was an old man."

She looked up at him sweetly. "I guess I always knew I'd be happier some day," she said.

"You and pa would have got along fine."

"Wouldn't we?" agreed Joseph.

"He was no-account," said Metabel humbly, "but he could be smart when he wanted. He used to plug the holes up in my shoes with gum." She took a long quavery breath. "Do you like me, Joseph?" she asked in a tiny voice.

He bent his head. "Yes," he said.

"Better than . . . anybody?"

197

"Oh . . . better."

"Better than Prissy Deakan?"

"Yes."

"Well," she said as bravely as she could, "I'd marry you if you wanted."

"That's what I aim for," said Joseph simply.

She did not know that her heart had stopped, until it began to beat again. An awful joy took her by the throat. "O my," she said; and she closed her eyes faintly.

After a while she opened them again, on the green sea of the evening sky and the dark shore of the woods. "You're my sweetheart now," she said with solemn wonder.

"Yes," said Joseph, giving her a happy hug.

"I love you," she whispered, but only to herself. She was shy; it was such a thing to say: she tried it over. "I like you," she said.

"I never liked any one before."

The calm and happy night touched her heart with loving fingers; a late last thrush sang in the dusk a few sweet evening notes. How happy, how happy she was . . . and strange to say, how sad; a little wandering grief trembled in her joy like a leaf in the wind. It was nothing, it was too much happiness, it was the night being so beautiful, it was that star shining so bright, it was because she wanted to cry. . . .

"You're crying," exclaimed Joseph, astonished.

She shook her head; two tears rolled down her cheeks. "I'm not," she said.

"It's your pa," said Joseph kindly. "There." And he laid a timid kiss in her hair, like a small bird in a nest.

She turned with a cry, and took him in her arms; thin, eager, they twined around his waist. She buried her head against him, just below his breast, where it came. "I don't need a pa," she cried, " if I have you.

" I don't need anything."

And she looked up at him, her face pale, her eyes wide and dark as water.

Then Joseph surprised himself; he bent down and kissed her. Her face was cool, her mouth was softer than roses, softer than flowers . . . he stared at her, and she stared back at him.

" I never kissed any one before," she said slowly.

" Me neither," declared Joseph. He brushed his mouth with the back of his hand; he took his arm away from her; he put it back again; and they gazed solemnly at the sky together.

" Ah," they sighed; " hum."

The thrush was still; far off in the valley sounded a tonk of bells as the cows went home to their barns. The cold night air seemed to gather sweetness, a murmur of wind sounded in the trees. Sighing, it touched their cheeks, and passed on to the field where Isaiah stood lost in dreams.

" Is your foot easier? " asked Joseph at last.

" It's still swole a little," she replied.

Arm and arm they returned to the house where Uncle Henry sat sad and thoughtful, gazing at the stove.

But in the forest there was silence; and the ash trees trembled.

IN WHICH THE ASH TREES TREMBLE

Chapter XVI

WHAT a big change it made in the world, being in love — or was it being loved did it? It was like having a merry-go-round in her heart, with people going around and around, laughing and gay, and the music playing . . . in the morning she'd jump out of bed with a gasp; and then jump back in again, to be quiet a moment, to feel how happy she was.

She hugged her happiness to her thin breast. Her happiness — innocent, and without end, it trembled around her and before her, sweet as singing, light as dreaming. Life would never change now; she would never be lonely again.

And the woods, her woods, her fields, her little paths, all gave it back to her again and again, spoke to her in new and friendly accents. They seemed to say to her, " Now you are part of us, now you belong to us. It is only the lover who sees, it is only the beloved who hears. Little sister to the birds, little cousin to the bees, now that you have given your heart, there are no more secrets left. Under your feet and in the air about you throng your sisters and brothers, their tiny bodies making a music of love, of meeting and parting. Under the wings which

flutter overhead, beat hearts filled with longing, poignant
and mystical. It is the longing which fills your own heart;
it is the pain which makes your eyes so bright, it is the
joy which makes your steps so slow."

When she passed a beetle crawling through the grass,
she stopped and said to him, "Can I help you? Where
would you like to go?" And she admired his shiny coat
and ferocious expression. Her heart was full of kindness
because she was in love.

"Go on," she said to the birds, "sing louder."

She went to dance in the woods by the fallen ash tree,
wild roses in her hair. She hummed to herself, she floated
over the moss . . . one, two, and turn, one, two, and skip
. . . but in the middle of it she stopped to ponder, to hug
her happiness again: is it me, is it Metabel? Joseph's axe
clinked in the deep woods; the sun, falling through the
leaves, lighted her face, dreamy and pale. Her slender
body stood quiet as a tree among the sister birches, rooted
to the earth from which the summer fragrance rose upward to her heart.

In the cool shade of the barn she sewed herself a wedding dress; it was of cotton, yellow and faded. Musket
sat at her side, his black, weary head in her lap. "Musket," she said, between stitches, "do you remember how
I used to wake up in Barly, in my little room, and look
out of the window, and say, 'It's day on Hemlock'? Oh
. . . Barly . . . What would the fiddler think if he
could see me now? I'll write him a letter, and tell him;
the postman must likely know where Barly is; it can't be
far.

"I'll say, 'Dear Fiddler, I'm living up on Hemlock
Mountain, and I'm going to be married. I'm making myself a yellow wedding dress. We're not going to have a
wedding trip, because my husband is not a success.

There's a rich girl here called Prissy Deakan, but I slung her with a stone and she fell to earth. Very Sincerely Yours, Metabel Adams.'"

Stitch, went the needle proudly, *stitch.*

"Musket dear," she said after a while, "do you remember my pa? He never was a handsome man like Joseph. He was right smart at gumming up the holes in my shoe, but he wasn't strong, rightly — he was thin and trifling to look at, like me."

Stitch.

She dropped her sewing, and sat gazing quietly at the green fields glowing in the sun. In the cool barn tiny motes of dust swam in a fall of light down through the cobwebbed windows. All was still; she saw a bird go by, and heard, outside, the little hum of summer in the grass.

"Musket," she said soberly, "do you think I'm very trifling looking?"

"Poor Joseph, he's not getting much."

She saw Uncle Henry go by, with his brows drawn in a frown. He stopped a moment, put his head in the barn door, to wave at her. "I'm looking for Joseph," he announced. "I want to show him where a road would go, right up past the north field, if we were minded to build it. Those dairy people, they have all the roads. We'd ought to have one, anyhow . . . a good one."

And he went off again, shaking his head. Already he saw the road he wanted . . . the longest road in the county, it went on and on, nowhere in particular.

Presently Joseph came in from the woods with his axe over his shoulder. Seeing that no one was looking, not even a swallow, they kissed each other shyly; then they sat down together on the feed bin, swung their heels, and gazed at the floor with embarrassment. "What are you sewing?" asked Joseph.

"It's a dress," answered Metabel. "A yellow dress, for being married."

He took it up to look at; his strong brown fingers felt it and gripped it. He sighed; his feet stopped swinging against the side of the bin. "You'd ought to have a store dress," he said bravely. "I'd ought to buy you a silk."

"Go along," said Metabel; "buy me . . ."

"Well, it's the truth," said Joseph.

Metabel sat silent, while a great wonder spread slowly through her heart. That Joseph should . . . like her . . . was a strange thing; still there it was, thank God for it, it was like a dream, not very real, but how lovely. But this thing about a dress — that was different. That was everyday real. She was going to belong to Joseph, they were going to be one; and he wanted to buy her a dress, the way you would for your own folks. . . . What an amazing moment. Possibly marriage itself would be more astonishing, but it wasn't likely.

"I could as lief make you a shirt out of this," she said timidly, "instead of a dress for me."

She longed to give him something, too; something of her own. . . . As long as they were one, what did it matter who had the wedding dress?

But Joseph shook his head. His face was clouded; he had it on his mind to buy her something. Not doing it was going to make a difference.

It had only just occurred to him.

He was a poor man.

At their feet Musket was talking to the mouse whom he had advised to get married. "Look here," said the mouse enthusiastically, "how are you? You do not look well. I am very happy, myself. My wife's experience is a constant source of gratification to me. All I have to do is forget where she got it."

Musket replied irritably, " Do not ask me how I am; I am old, and my bones creak. Nothing is what it used to be, except my folly and my appetite."

" You should find some one with experience," said the mouse happily. " She would make you forget your bones."

" Go away," said Musket, " and do not bother me."

And he went gloomily out of the barn to find Isaiah. When he saw him, he said to him dejectedly, " Are you sure that it was she? It could not have been somebody else? We were to meet in the woods, half-way; she said that she wished to spend the day in quiet conversation. When she did not come . . . you do not think that she was indisposed? "

However, he did not wait for Isaiah's answer, which he already knew by heart. Hanging his head, he went back to the house, and lay down under a chair.

Chapter XVII

METABEL went on sewing her wedding dress, and Joseph went on chopping wood. But his axe seemed to ring faster, off in the woods; the old, lazy, comfortable chime was gone. He went out earlier, he came home later; and his face, thought Metabel, looked different. It looked sharper, but puzzled. Was he getting opinions, she wondered. He had something on his mind.

One day he said to Uncle Henry, "I'm going up the hill, and have a look at that ash. Maybe I'll send a load of it down to the mill. I could use some money." And he looked at Metabel as though to say, "We could use it, I mean."

Metabel glanced up in dismay. "The ash?" she exclaimed. "Why, Joseph . . ."

"Well," he said, a little sharply, she thought, "I guess I'm as good a man on ash as the next one."

Uncle Henry looked around with gentle joy. "Ah, Joseph," he said; "ah. Now, then." And he began to think of what he'd say to St. John Deakan about that road. They were going in for lumbering.

But Metabel felt her heart turn over. She followed Joseph out to the barn where he'd gone to sharpen his axe, and took him by the sleeve. "Joseph," she said to him anxiously, "you're never going to cut that ash?"

He looked unhappy, she thought, but stubborn. "I expect I'll have to," he said. "I've got new things to think of now, Metabel."

"You mean about me?"

"Yes," he said. And he added firmly. "I mean to give you what you've a right to."

"Oh," she cried, "but Joseph — if I don't want it?"

"That don't signify," he said. And he said again, "I aim to give you what you've a simple right to."

She stared at him with wide, doleful eyes. Whatever had come over him?

"Joseph," she cried again, as he started off, "where are you going?"

"Don't fret," he said.

But all she could do was fret. In the house again, she went about her tasks with a heavy heart, while Joseph's axe sang on the hill faster and faster, sharper and sharper. Oh, where was the little green man? If the ash trees went . . .

She stopped in the middle of her dishwashing, to wring her hands faintly. If the ash trees went . . .

Would he ever forgive her?

Late in the afternoon a little mouse approached her, and sat up on its bottom. Metabel and the mouse exchanged a long look.

"What do you want, mouse?" asked Metabel.

The mouse did not reply. Instead, he got down on his paws, and started out of the door, with soft backward glances.

Metabel went after him; for she knew who had sent him. Anxiously she followed the mouse through the woods until she came to a clearing where four ash trees lay broken on the ground. On the trunk of the largest sat the little green man, looking very dismal and smaller than ever.

"So," he said. "There you are. Do you see what has happened?"

"Yes," said Metabel unhappily.

"I suppose that you are proud of yourself," said the little green man.

"No," said Metabel, "I'm not." She looked around her at the desolation, the four trees down, their branches tossed along the ground. "He's cut the ash," she said with honest horror.

"He has," cried the little man, "he has. And why? To buy you a wedding dress, that is why. And what do you want a wedding dress for? Ah, you greedy creature."

Metabel stood and looked at him. "So that was it," she said. She shook her head proudly. "I didn't tell him to," she declared. "I was making it myself, out of goods. I didn't want him to cut the ash. I'm not a greedy creature."

The little green man looked at her for a long time in silence. When he spoke at last, his voice was gentle, but sad. "I believe you," he said. "Perhaps you did not ask him to buy you a wedding dress. Still," he added uncertainly, "that is what he wishes to do." And he gazed at her keenly.

To save her life, Metabel could not help thinking, "It's sweet of him to want to." Her heart grew warm; she forgot to be sorry for the trees. But she did not want to admit it. "O dear," she said, like a hypocrite.

The little green man mimicked her. "O dear," he echoed. "But that will not put the trees up again, or keep Joseph from cutting down what is left of them. He is like a crazy man, his axe is like a buzz-saw . . . rip, rip, everything must come down."

"Well," said Metabel firmly, "never mind; I won't let him."

"Ah," said the little green man doubtfully.

"I'll stop him," said Metabel. "I'll tell him I don't want a wedding dress, or anything else. There — are you satisfied?" And she gave him a sweet smile.

But the little green man was not satisfied; for all at once he got to his feet on the tree-trunk, and leveling a tiny finger at her, exclaimed indignantly, "You — Prissy Deakan."

Metabel stared at him in dismay; then she looked down at herself, to see if she was changed. But she was just the same as always. "Why," she cried, "I'm not."

"Yes you are," he insisted.

"But I'm not," she cried again, "and you know it."

"Well," he said, "you might as well be.

"You've done her work."

"Oh," said Metabel, while an anxious feeling began to take hold of her. Was it more than a wedding dress? What did he mean? The sun was low in the sky, the trees stood about, gloomy and shadowy. Night had entered the woods far away, it was stealing nearer.

"I haven't done anything," she said again, in a whisper. And all at once she began to cry.

"Oh, please . . ."

But her tears had no effect on the little god; his small, divine spirit remained as untouched by her grief as it had been unmoved in the past by her indignation. "Yes," he said quietly, as though he himself were sure of it for the first time, "you have done her work, although you did not intend to. Last night the gods went through these woods, the Powers and the Dominations, the Weights and the Measures. Their heavy feet trod down the ferns under which mice had taken refuge. They were laying out roads, they were adding up lumber, they were dividing these woods among themselves. When I heard them coming from the valley, I ran away and hid in a hole under a tree. That was a fortunate thing. Finally I put my head out and said to one of them, 'What are you doing here? Go away.' He did not even stop to answer me. But another one replied, 'It is no longer a question of good humor up here. Joseph is going into the lumber business.' I threw a stone at him, and he gave me a kick. Look."

And he showed her a large lump on his forehead.

"O my goodness," wailed Metabel weeping. "O dear."

The little man went on gently, "Here, in this forest, is my only home. There is no road here, to Milford or Peru; here there are only friendly paths, which return again to where they started, or lose themselves in ferns and shadowy branches. What does it matter that you wish me well, how does it help me that you love it too? Joseph has found a strange duty in his heart, now that he loves you, now that he wishes to marry you. His peace is gone; he longs to be spry and active, for your sake. He aims to give you what he has not got; he will destroy this home to build another, to lay roads, to create a lumber business. You cannot stop him, my child, since it is for you he does it. Talk him out of cutting trees? First you must talk him out of loving you."

"Never," said Metabel tearfully.

"I did not think you would say that," remarked the little green man sadly, "although I confess I feared it. What is it that you want? A wedding dress? That is what the neighbors have. Look for it where Uncle Henry sells his lettuces."

"I didn't ask him to buy it," Metabel repeated pitiably. "I didn't want him to."

"No matter," said the little god inexorably, "since he wants to. He wants to take care of you, to do for you as

well as any one could. Is that what you want, to be
taken care of? To knock down a forest for a wedding
dress. . . . O Metabel . . . to steal away his peace of
heart to feather your own heart with? Some day he will
hate you for it. But first of all you will dislike yourself,
my child."

"No," whispered Metabel.

She stood before him, a forlorn, bewildered little figure,
clasping and unclasping her hands, the tears wet on her
cheeks. Evening was in the woods, the day was gone, only
a green dusk lay like moldy light upon the trees. Night
was on its way, already it had stolen past the east, it was
coming. The woods were silent; it grew darker.

"I will not let you make Joseph over," said the little
green man quietly. "I will not let you change him into
the likeness of every one else. I have fought for him too
long. . . . If I must turn against you, too, why then I
must. Joseph the successful woodchopper . . . squeezing the woods, squeezing his heart, to have what the neighbors have. . . . No, no, my child, I will never allow it.

"Go back to Barly, Metabel, and leave him to me."

"I won't," said Metabel.

He shook his head impatiently. "Will you try to stay
in spite of me?" he asked. "Sooner or later I will throw
you out, as I threw out the other one."

"I thought you were the god of good humor," said
Metabel bitterly.

"I am," said the little green man, "but I am obliged
to fight for my home. Already I have a lump like a toad-
stool on my head. The ash trees are down; and trees are
down in Joseph's heart. He does not think of me now, he
thinks only of you. But he will remember me, some day,
when it is too late to find me any more. He will look for
me in the lumber business; and when he does not find me

there, he will blame you. What will you do then, my child?

"You had better go home now, before it is too late."

Metabel looked at him quietly through her tears. "Must I?" she said. "I haven't anything at home. Here is all I have."

"I will come and visit you sometimes," he said.

He got to his feet; and together they started back through the woods. She could not see very well, it was too dark; but the little green man glowed before her like a firefly, and she followed, dumb and doleful. The trees made a path for them; not even a root rose out of the ground to trip her. The night came stealing up behind her, full of small sounds, dark and whispering. "Oh," she cried, "hurry."

All at once the little green man stood still; and she saw that they had come out of the woods, and were upon a road. "Here," he said gently, "is the road to Barly. It is all downhill. Good-by my child; I will come and see you some day."

She clutched at him wildly, but already he was gone. "Wait," she cried; "no." Behind her the trees rose like a wall, severe, unyielding. She flung herself back at them, they caught her in their branches.

"Joseph," she cried, "Joseph."

Far off, in the deep woods, a drowsy bird, cheated of his sleep, woke with a cry.

"Joseph . . ."

THERE'S NO ROAD THROUGH

Chapter XVIII

ALL summer long the valleys around Barly are green as
the sea. But in autumn they are like yellow pools; over
them the clouds swim slowly in the sun, trailing their
cold blue shadows across the hills. Goldenrod climbs the
slopes, the maples are just turning. How far away the
hills look now, touched by the gentle haze of fall, faint,
acrid, sweet, like the smoke of a leaf.

It is the time of quiet, the time of crickets and drowsy
bees; their voices, faint and sleepy, mingle with the rustle
of leaves dying on the branches. Even the blue seems to
deepen in the sky, to shine again, as in spring, with other
light.

The tassels on the corn are black; the yellow squash, the
green cucumbers ripen on the ground. In the window of
Mrs. Sebold's general store, the muslin dresses and straw
hats are taken down, and corduroys and woolens put out
instead. But the bicycle, hard candy, and pocket knives
remain as they were.

Once again Metabel sat on the slopes above her little
cottage, and watched the red sun rise. Musket was with
her; her hand, thin and brown, lay on his head. Her heart
was quiet; and her eyes, long dried of tears, searched with
dreamy looks for the first beam of day. Her summer was
over; she had come home to work for Mrs. Sebold, to

dance some day again for the fiddler — not now, but in the spring — to dance, maybe, for more than just the fiddler, in other towns than Barly. . . .

Far in the north Old Hemlock caught the sun; light shone like a fire on its crest. Metabel caught her breath. " Musket," she said, " there's the sun.

" It's day on Hemlock."

Below her in the valley the smoke of Mrs. Sebold's fire rose through the early air, thin and blue, curled at the end like an Indian pipe. And in her heart nodded and whispered the green untroubled woods of Joseph's home, where the sun shone when Barly was in shadow. The forest stood on Hemlock; there was no road through.

Serenely she rose, and returned to her cottage. There, at the door, smiling, stood the little green man.

" Good morning, Metabel," he said.

The Bishop's

Wife

Chapter I

ALL about, in the cities and in the villages, the country was being built. No longer parched by deserts, devoured by wolves, and scalped by Indians, the descendants of the pioneers were erecting buildings of marble and steel, hundreds of feet into the air, and covering acres of ground. Everywhere were mines, mills, bridges, cities, farms, and power-plants. Nevertheless, the pioneers still persisted, since everybody was a pioneer. But there were certain differences.

These differences were of a practical nature. That is to say people were not obliged to suffer discomfort any longer. As a matter of fact, the entire country groaned with comfort, although it had not yet reached its full development. This gave rise to an extraordinary state of mind. At the moment that whole cities were being torn down in order to make room for something larger, it was generally conceded that everything was perfect. So it was possible to admire the country's perfection, and at the same time to assist in its improvement.

In the schools, children were taught that four is twice as large as two; and to despise foreigners. As a result, there emerged from the schoolrooms of the nation a race of men and women filled with pride, and anxious to increase two into four. Nothing was allowed to stand in the way of this ambition.

It was the duty of the Church to illuminate with the light of piety the vigorous battles of the industrial world. This was not considered difficult or astonishing, in view of modern exegesis.

The bishop's house stood on a hill above the city. From one window he could see the river; and from another, the gray cathedral, which stood on the same hill, pointing with sharp, stone fingers at the sky. The city made a steady noise all about; and the cathedral also made a sound, with its bells. They rose in peal upon peal from the gray walls stained by the pigeons, and disputed with horns, shouts, squeals, rumbles, and human cries.

The bishop's study was on the ground floor of his house. Along the walls stood his bookcases, containing the works of the Fathers of the Church, and biographies of eminent business men. In the one he had studied theology: from the other, he had learned administration. For the bishop had many problems. He controlled, as regent of God, not one, but two cathedrals, twenty churches, twelve parish houses, two deans, three archdeacons, more than one hundred curates, deacons and sextons, seven female auxiliaries, and a great deal of money. To assist him in the discharge of his duties, he employed a secretary and several clerks. Now he sat alone in his study, considering some problems of administration.

They did not cause him much concern. For the most part, and in matters of routine, his assistants did very well; they took care of things. However, they could not help him procure a new archdeacon for the cathedral; or, for that matter, a larger cathedral. Such problems as these he was obliged to settle for himself, as head of his church.

He was kind, upright, and vigorous. It could be said of him that he had enthusiasm, for he was still, in a manner of speaking, a young man. And he dreamed of a magnificent cathedral able to do honor to the city, and to his diocese. He imagined it rising into the clouds, and including upon the grounds an office building with elevators and improvements. It soared upward, in the direction of Heaven, immaculate, marble, and set back in pyramids according to the building code.

However, there was no hurry about it. In the meanwhile, there was the matter of the archdeacon to be attended to.

The bishop gave a deep sigh.

There were many candidates for this office, but none, thought the bishop, of the stuff of which an archdeacon is made. And he went over in his mind the qualities he wished to find in his assistant. In the first place, the archdeacon of St. Timothy's must be a man of firm and fundamental views. He must believe in Heaven and Hell, and in the miracles. He must believe that God was watching . . . that was no reason, the bishop thought, for him to be tactless. God, he reflected, and the bankers, love a tactful man. For himself, he had, he felt sure, piety enough for both; but he needed help with his accounts. A good hand at figures, a tongue of fire in the pulpit, a healing way with the doubtful, a keen eye for the newspapers . . .

Where, thought the bishop, is there to be found a man compounded of equal parts of piety, tact, energy, and ability?

"What I need," he exclaimed, "is an angel from Heaven."

And he raised his eyes to the ceiling, although he did not expect an angel to appear.

Nor did an angel at that moment make his appearance. Instead, the bishop arose, and went to look for his wife, whom he found seated before the mirror in her room. She was brushing out her long golden hair, before she pinned it with a neat and womanly twist at the back of her head. It rippled under the brush, it flowed across her wrist, as she turned to smile at him.

"Dear," she said, "is there anything you want? I'm on my way to the park; and I must hurry, for I'm late already."

And she gave him a hurrying look, over her arm.

The bishop did not want anything at all. As he gazed at his wife he experienced a feeling of satisfaction. He saw eyes, nose, hips, hair, arms, all in order: he saw her all complete. How well she attended to everything: she dressed herself, she fixed her hair . . . yes, she did everything very well for herself. And for this reason it was a comfort to watch her. She was attractive, but she was capable; she did not ask him to help her with anything. He believed that he satisfied her as a bishop; and felt that nothing further was expected of him.

Nevertheless, he was uncomfortable because she was going out; it saddened him, for it left him alone with the archdeacon. He would have liked to remain looking at her — watching her adroit hands and amiable expression, taking comfort from her tidiness. She seemed so certain of herself . . . seemed so to him, at least . . . was there such a thing as doubt in that pretty golden head of hers? Never, he felt sure; and in her deft and quiet presence, treated himself to feelings of peace.

"You're like a child," she said, "standing there. . . . Is anything the matter? I must go, for I've promised to meet Juliet in the Mall, and take her from the nurse. Can I do anything for you? But not too much, dear, or I'll never get off."

She drew on her hat, twisting her hair beneath the brim, patting the crown into shape. And she stood there smiling gently into the mirror, in which she saw only vaguely, her thoughts being dreamy, her own slender figure.

"Julia," said the bishop, "to-night I should really like to stay at home. I have a great deal on my mind."

Her look flew over him as lightly as a moth. "You're sure you're all right, dear?" she asked.

"I dare say," replied the bishop, "that I am." He paused; he would have liked to look a little dismal, for sympathy. But there was really nothing to complain of. He felt lonely, and his problems troubled his mind, empty, for the moment, of divine grace.

"Well," said Julia brightly, "that's all right, then; we're at home to-night, and the nurse is out. So . . . now what else is there? Have you an errand for me? Then good-by; come and talk to me this evening, after Juliet's bath."

"I have put a few socks," said the bishop, "on my bed. There are some holes in them."

"I'll see about that," said Julia, "when I come home."

But the bishop did not want his wife to leave. "I would like to talk to you," he said. "About the ladies of St. Mary's."

"That also," said his wife, "will keep."

And she added, smiling indulgently, "Was that all you wished to say?"

The bishop went on hurriedly:

"What are you going to do this afternoon, you and

Juliet? The carousel is closed in this cold weather. But I suppose the Mall is full of children. I wish I had nothing to do, and could go with you. Perhaps a walk would do me good. If it were not that I am very busy . . ."

"Good-by," said Julia, giving his cheek a kiss; and she went out to meet her daughter in the park.

The bishop stood alone among his wife's chairs and tables. The cold light of early winter, striking through the curtains, tried in vain to chill the room which remained warm, disorderly, and delicately fragrant. As he stood, gazing thoughtfully at the walls, his mind began to feel relieved of its troubles, and his thoughts to take on a certain importance. The perfection of his home consoled him in the midst of the most perplexing problems. He was like a collector who loves his treasures because they are complete, and because they belong to him. It is the love of a child for his toys; such a passion, without desire and without despair, sustains the human race which leaves to its heirs collections of stamps, porcelains, books, and furniture.

The bishop did not compare his wife to books or porcelains. Nevertheless, he closed her door as one closes the door of a museum, and went down-stairs to his study with renewed spirit. In his house all was comfortable and complete. Very well: in the midst of this peace, in which nothing was lacking, he would equip himself with courage to continue his work in a world where everything was still being built. His cathedral took shape again before his eyes. And he wrote down on a sheet of paper:

Mrs. Guerdon . . . . $ 5000

Mr. Lanyarde 2nd 10000

Mrs. Hope 500

Then, after a pause, he wrote:

Mr. Cohen . . . . $ 5000

But presently he crossed this out, and wrote instead:

Mr. Cohen . . . . $ 1000

And he continued his list with a sigh.

Chapter II

WHEN the bishop was ten years old, a picture of Sir Galahad hung from the wall above his wardrobe where he kept his linen, some books by Horatio Alger, and a sort of shrine, composed of two candles and a picture of Jesus embraced by a crown of thorns. Here, before the candles whose significance was lost to him, he would stand, trembling with adoration, lifting up his heart toward God, whom he supposed to be older than his father, and a little bigger. Overwhelmed by the noblest feelings and impulses, he wished to be pure: to lead a life, like Bayard, without fear and without reproach.

At the age of sixteen, in answer to his misgivings, his father, a wealthy manufacturer, addressed him thus: "My son, the time has come for me to inform you about certain matters. Your mother believes that you are old enough to know how it was that you came into the world; although, for my part, we could wait a little. . . . In the first place, let me remind you that to the pure, all things are pure. There are certain simple rules of hygiene. . . . Then there are the birds and the flowers . . . well, how marvelous that is. In this way, life is caused to continue from generation to generation. Remember," he added sternly, "that marriage of a man and a woman is above

224

all a pure and holy thing. As for the rest . . . there is a certain matter of hygiene . . . Do not trouble your head about it."

His mother on the other hand, drawing his head down to her bosom, exclaimed with a sigh, " My poor son." And she remained silent, lost in mysterious thoughts which troubled and perplexed him.

Presently she added, " I can assure you that what you imagine to be so important, is not important at all."

And because she was of a devout turn of mind, she concluded mysteriously, " Faith alone will help you to bear the disappointments of life. The Church is a great refuge. Never forget to say your prayers."

The future bishop had no occasion to doubt anything his mother had said to him.

When he was ordained, she did not attempt to conceal her satisfaction. But when he told her that he wished to be married, she grew very gloomy. And her dejection was only increased by the sight of Julia, glowing with youth, ignorance, and bliss.

For Julia looked forward to her marriage with the most radiant hopes. She expected to discover, in her husband's arms, that felicity about which she had thought a great deal. At the same time, she had a horror of ugliness: her ardent nature longed to express itself only in terms of beauty and sentiment. She was generous and loving, but she knew that she was ignorant and that life could be painful: and for this reason she respected the young minister whose ideas, like his religion, comforted and reassured her. She felt that life with him would be beautiful, like a church service.

Nevertheless, she insisted that she wished to share everything with him, not only joy, but sorrow; and trembling with apprehension, she exclaimed:

" We will always be happy together, because you are my ideal."

And he would reply, " No, it is you who are my ideal."

" But perhaps you will grow tired of me. I am stupid; really, I know nothing."

Then he would declare, " I am glad you know nothing. You are so innocent; and I love you."

And he would clasp her in his arms, but not so hard as to crush her.

The marriage took place in the cathedral, and was attended by many people of society. Surrounded by flowers, the bride and groom gazed at each other through happy tears. She thought that her slender body, which trembled with love as virginal and tender as a child's, was soon to partake of a terrifying but beautiful communion. Then her ignorance would be gone, drowned in happiness. She was upon the threshold of felicity.

She gave herself joyously to the sacrifice, sustained by a thousand hopes.

That night, in the darkness, the young divine entered the room where his wife bravely awaited him, the covers drawn about her throat in which she felt a choking sensation.

Tenderly, and not without embarrassment, he explained to her the unimportant nature of what he was obliged to do. As he described it, it seemed to her no more than a simple act of hygiene. In the face of that necessity, severe, and without beauty, she held herself taut but meek. It was soon over. She was a married woman.

And while her husband lay sleeping beside her, she lay with wet eyes, reconstructing her hopes. So that was the great secret, for which she was made woman, and he man. This, then, was marriage — this strange and painful moment, followed by an ashamed silence. Felicity . . .

" No," she murmured wearily to the dawn, " it is not important. It is not important at all."

And with a gesture of infinite resignation, she bent over to give her sleeping husband a kiss, cool as a lily petal, motherly, and reserved.

Seven years later, Juliet was born. It was this child, now four years old, whom Julia was on her way to meet in the park.

Chapter III

JULIET BROUGHAM, at four and a half, took after her
mother, which is not surprising, seeing that it was only to
her mother's intense longing for a child that she owed
her life at all. For the period following her wedding was
not a very happy time for Julia. The young bishop-to-be
had much to engross his mind; his duties, as he saw them,
no less than his convictions, kept his thoughts severe. At
night, on those rare occasions when he came to her, she lay
unhappy and reserved, made ashamed by the feeling that
God was watching to see that her thoughts were pure;
and knowing only too well that business was waiting behind the door to claim her husband afterward, in case
slumber missed him. The dreams of her youth, baffled by
his devout and practical manner, repelled by his caresses
without beauty and without joy — her deep and ardent
affections, which her husband seemed only too anxious to
avoid, turned in upon herself; in which state of mind, and
after five unhappy years, she conceived and in due course
of time gave birth to a daughter.

She was named Juliet — after his wife, the bishop
thought. But that was not what Julia meant at all: she was
far too modest to think of calling her child after herself.
Juliet, for her, was the name of that young girl of Verona

whose tragic love has everywhere helped to make youth and sorrow better friends.

However, she would never have admitted it.

She did not believe that love was all and only what her husband told her. Deep in her heart she believed that passion and tenderness might go hand in hand, that ardor and shame need not follow each other. But she said no more about it. She was a good wife: she made her hubsand comfortable. Only in her dreams, and dim and far away like a lost light, she still held to her hope: she could not see it, but she knew that it was there. And to her daughter — who had sprung, so it seemed to her, from her own longings alone, whom, on a night of passion turned in upon itself, she had drawn up into life and air from some deep, unused region of her being — she gave the full and aching love her husband would have found embarrassing.

"You belong to me," she would say, gazing dreamily at the tiny being in whose conception and birth her husband seemed to have played no more than a technical part.

"You are my child."

Juliet saw everything in the sweet and misty light of her mother's love for her. She saw everything as real, and everything as loving. She expected the wooden horses on the carousel to run away with her; and the angels her father recommended to her prayers lived for her as joyous children older than herself, with long white wings.

Nothing surprised and nothing saddened her, unless it was some sadness of her mother's. Then her little face grew crestfallen, and her lips trembled with sympathy. But mostly she ran happily about, up and down, amusing herself with her own motions, which were those of an awkward little animal.

If she had any longings at all, they were to be admired,

and to be grown up. She approached her mother in the Mall with a serious look. " Well," she said, " what do you think? Am I rumpled? "

" No, my dear," said Julia, " you're not. But don't be so neat. Go and rumple."

" I don't need to," said Juliet. " I'm playing a not-very-rumpling game."

She gave a hop. " Mother," she said.

" Yes, my darling? "

" Do you think I'm very grown up? "

" I'm sure of it."

" Well," she said, " I like it when you take care of me." And she gazed with a lofty expression at her little cousin, Potter Guerdon, whose mother never took him from his nurse in the Mall, for fear he might be naughty.

Potter was bashful, for Juliet dazzled him. He regarded her with an admiration which he refused to admit either to her, or to himself. In her presence the rages with which he impressed himself upon his nurse or his mother, turned into petulance or tears. Now he stood at a distance, and stared at Juliet with his mouth open. He seemed to be saying: Is it really? . . . What a wonder, what a wonder.

But Juliet paid no attention to this look with which she was familiar. " I'm more grown up than him," she said. " He's only a little child."

Julia smiled across at Potter's nurse. But her thoughts were small and sharp, like needles stitching in her heart. Yes, she thought, you are very grown up, my darling. You are not a baby any more. You can do things for yourself, think out things for yourself. The little hands which fumbled for life, already point in not-to-be-disobeyed commands. And Potter obeys them, with his mouth open. Soon you will not need me at all, not even to take care of you in the Mall. You will turn to some one else. Will he leave you heartsick, too, for the beauty you hoped to find, for the love you meant to give?

And what will I do then? What will happen to me when you do not need me any longer? Shall I sit down in a corner like an old woman? But what have I to remember? Only . . . only the great love I wanted to give some one who was too busy — and too ashamed . . .

"Bother," said Juliet; "I've broke my chalk."

And she looked hopefully at Potter.

"No," said Potter.

"Give me your chalk, Potter," said Juliet, holding out her hand, "and then we can both play."

"I won't," said Potter.

Juliet looked at her mother, as one woman to another. "He won't," she said simply. And she added, as though that explained everything,

"He's only a little child."

It made no difference to Potter. Squatting on his heels, he began to draw uncertain circles on the pavement. As soon as he had drawn one, he jumped about in it; then he drew another. One would think that he had forgotten Juliet, who stood watching him with an expression of patience. But when, a moment later, she ran off, waving her arms in an important way, and uttering happy cries, he dropped his chalk and ran after her. At the corner of a distant bench they stopped, and regarded each other with surprise. Then Juliet came back, and picked up the chalk.

"This is my hop-scotch," she told Potter. "You can't play in it."

And she applied herself earnestly to the circles and squares.

The afternoon sun, low in the south, filled the Mall with a yellow, watery light, in which the children played in front of bronze busts of famous men and under trees bare of leaves. The pigeons with cooing cries walked between them, or flew in low arcs among the benches. Over all rose the tiny shouts, the plaintive voices of children disputing, laughing, complaining, going solemnly about their games in which already they displayed qualities of nobility, sobriety, impatience, and dislike for everybody else.

But the quality which distinguished Juliet was love. Not love in her father's sense; nor yet, perhaps, entirely in her mother's. For she not only wanted affection, but, unlike her mother, she quite meant to have it; there was nothing meek about her. She supposed that God loved her, but in a personal way; she took it for granted that He admired her. And had she met one of those angels about whom her father so often spoke — as she was, indeed, later destined to do — she would have said to him — as she did, in fact, say — " Do you love me? " and if he had said No, she would have stared at him uncomprehending, with eyes full of tears.

Now, as the evening fell blue in the streets outside, she sat in the warm water of her bath, chasing a rubber fish from one end of the tub to the other, happy and absorbed. Her mother, with a wide towel across her knees, sat on a stool beside her, scrubbing her back as well as she could, soaping the wash-rag and wringing it out again. This was a happy hour of the day for Julia, this hour which was hers alone to make warm and gay; she could have cried with happy sorrow over the tiny shoulders, so round and fat, which depended upon her for soaping. " Ah," she cried, " I could eat you! "

Juliet looked up at her with a smile. " Mother," she said, " I'm not going to play games with Potter to-morrow. I'm going to hug him. I'm going to hug him like this."

And she gave the fish a watery kiss on its rubber snout.

"He won't like that," said Julia wisely.

Juliet brought the fish down with a smack in the water. "I'm going to, anyhow," she said.

She was drawn up, dripping and protesting, on to her mother's knees, muffled in towels, dried pink and rosy. Then she was put to bed, with her doll Maryannlouise and her book about the four bears, Howly, Prowly, Scowly, and Growly. She sat up, and looked at her mother moving busily about the room.

"Mother," she said, "do you love me?"

"I do, my darling."

"I mean do you really truly?"

"Really truly . . . truly."

"Well, come and do it then."

But when she had been loved enough, she pushed her mother's face away. "Now let's read," she said.

And she listened with rapture to the story of Howly and Scowly, which she knew by heart. When the reading was over, she lay back and said her prayers. She asked blessings for every one. But for herself she asked God's unending admiration, although she said nothing about it.

Julia put the light out, and stepped into the hall, still feeling around her neck the pressure of her daughter's small round arms. She was smiling, her heart was humming : life was full and even. On the landing she met her husband, the bishop.

"I cannot make up my mind," he said, "about the archdeacon. Nothing but an angel from Heaven will solve my difficulties."

She looked at him mist'ly ; she hardly saw him. "Well," she said vaguely, "ask God to send you one." And with her heart still humming, smiling to herself, she left him standing staring on the steps.

Chapter IV

THE BISHOP sat at his desk, writing a letter to the newspapers. It was an answer to the report of a committee in favor of restricting the grounds for divorce to adultery alone, and eliminating all other reasons. The bishop agreed with these findings, about which the newspapers had asked him for an opinion.

"Our conclusion is," he wrote, "that the New Testament recognizes but one ground for divorce, namely adultery. When we go beyond that ground, and sanction divorce and remarriage upon other grounds, we have parted company with God's express commands. If a strict adherence to the delivery of Our Lord on marriage and divorce seems a severe course to follow when dealing with particular cases, let it be remembered that loyalty to His command can work but good to mankind in general. The divine laws are not given us in order that we may indulge ourselves, and the very book which contains the revelation of the law of God exhorts us to deny ourselves and subordinate the pleasures of time to the principles of life everlasting.

"Divorce is now competing with death as a dissolver of marriages in this country. One out of every six marriages ends in the divorce courts. It is easy to demonstrate from history that the increase in divorce, the thawing of family

234

morality, and the breakdown of the sanctity of the home have ever been the heralds of national decline."

As he wrote, filled with a pure indignation, he saw in imagination the entire country given over to pleasure, to ruin, and decay. His mind, informed with apostolic vision, foresaw strikes, riots, the blowing up of buildings, and the decline of religion. And he signed his name with a firm hand to this document designed to avert such disasters: " Henry Brougham D. D."

It was not to be expected that the Right Reverend Henry Brougham would take any other attitude toward divorce. Adultery was a great sin: for one thing, it sounded like a sin. The word still caused him a flutter of anxiety, as it had when he was a boy. It was like a sound out of Hell, suggestive and obscene.

For Hell and the Devil were real enough to Bishop Brougham, although he could not exactly describe them. Over and against the forces of evil were ranged the hosts of joy: the Trinity, God the Father, the Son, and the Holy Ghost, the Virgin, the Powers, Thrones, Dominations, Angels and Saints, Bishops, Deans, Canons, Deacons, Cathedrals, Churches, Chapels, and Homes. The bishop knew that nothing here could be overlooked: that if the bottom collapsed, the whole would come tumbling down. And for this reason he applied himself with energy to the homes. He could not banish evil from men's hearts, he could not bring about the millennium on earth. But he could — and would — keep man and wife together, for the glory of God, and the good of the country.

These thoughts caused him to bring the palm of his hand down on the table. " Divorce," he exclaimed, " is an instrument of the Devil." And he made a note of this remark for future reference.

Like the pioneers before him, and for the same reasons,

the bishop's creed was simple and stern. To serve God, and thereby mankind; to love the meek who were to inherit the earth, and also the strong, to whom it already belonged; to waste nothing; to give no more to pleasure than duty allowed; to believe in the Holy Bible word for word, in the English translation; and to deny such cravings of the flesh as seemed to have no moral purpose, served him at once as code, creed, and practical philosophy.

For this reason, in addition, he considered himself an excellent husband.

He prided himself that his wife also considered him an excellent husband; and he was right. Men were like that, she expected; they had business instead of beauty. It hurt her, but she did not doubt it; for she respected his opinions. She never spoke of the lonely ache in her heart; he thought he did very well. When he denied his passions, he believed that she benefited by it.

And in a sense, she did, seeing that the note of haste and purity he managed to inject into his transports left her singularly dejected. She was happier without them.

She could not bear to think that her beauty stirred him so little, wounded him so little. Like other women before her, she took it out in works: she kept herself busy, and created from his likes and dislikes, and her willing efforts, an almost perfect home.

It was this home the bishop thought of as he sat in his study.

About him all was quiet; he had just dined on his favorite food, smiling across the table at his wife. A good dinner, a good wife, and a good bishop; a good house. What was it the prophet said? A silent and loving woman is a gift from the Lord. . . . But that was absurd, that was not what he meant at all. Where were his thoughts?

He had meant to think of something hearty from the Old Testament. Those Jews knew what they were about. An invading nation in an angry country, beset by the Devil in the form of Philistines, Hivites, Amalekites, Moloch, Bel, the Golden Calf, Anakims, Jebusites, Amorites, Sidonians, Canaanites, Hittites, and sensual pleasures, they attended to duty, and built up the home.

The result was Solomon and the glory of Israel, St. Paul, Justinian, monogamy, Luther, and the reformed nations of the earth. Through their history ran the strong golden thread of the Bible and the miracles. . . . Ah, the miracles; that was it, that was what he was coming to. Why were there no more miracles, he wondered. Was it because they were no longer necessary? No; for the world was as badly off as ever. Men needed light, as always. And he rehearsed in his mind the miracles in order, from the parting of the waters of the Red Sea, to the healing properties of the bones of certain saints in the fifteenth and sixteenth centuries. These bones did not interest him; what interested him was the visit of angels to the earth. They used to come, he thought, long ago, to assist and to strive with mankind. There were the two angels who visited Lot; and there was the angel who wrestled with Jacob. Heaven was full of those sons of light; they came and went between Heaven and earth. Their divine presences made fragrant the homes of the Jews.

He was silent, reflecting. Around him the house lay hushed; dimly, through the curtained windows, sounded the wintry sirens of the city. The light from the lamp on his desk streamed across his face, bathed him in a soft and yellow radiance. Outside, in the streets, men and women hurried with lisping feet in search of pleasure; sin sounded in their footfalls. Up and down they went, up and down, searching, anguished, picking at the old to make way for the new. The house rocked gently; and the bishop brooded.

"Are we to have no further help?" he thought. "Must we stumble about by ourselves with clouded eyes and groping hands? My strength is nothing, Lord; my wisdom is inadequate. Help me to save the homes of this nation which bears witness to Your glory."

And he sat bowed in painful thoughts.

At that moment the door opened, and a stranger entered the room. The bishop looked up quickly, with a beating heart.

"Who are you?" he asked in alarm.

The stranger reassured him with a smile of ineffable sweetness. "My name is Michael," he said. And he added simply,

"I am your new archdeacon."

Thinking that some one had played a joke upon him, the bishop exclaimed with vexation, "What I need is an angel from Heaven."

But the stranger held up his hand with a gesture of great dignity.

"I am that angel," he declared.

Chapter V

MICHAEL thought of everything. When the bishop, excited and overjoyed, wished to announce to his congregation the heavenly nature of its archdeacon, he replied: "Do not do anything of the kind. It is true that your cathedral would be crowded with people who wished to see me; but in the end you would only lose money. Startled by the imminence of divinity, the members of your own congregation would cease working in order to devote themselves to prayer and contemplation; and your church would perish for lack of funds."

And he continued to speak in a practical and inspired manner. But he refused to speak from the pulpit. "Do not ask me to give a sermon," he said, "which might conflict with the teachings of your bishops. Remember that to the sons of light the universe presents a different aspect from that in which it is viewed by mortal man. I have not lived through Genesis, Exodus, Deuteronomy, and the thirty-nine books of the Old Testament for nothing; not to mention the twenty-seven books of the New Testament from Matthew to Revelation, the Apocrypha, the Talmud, the Code of Justinian, the Augsburg Confession, and modern Exegesis. . . . It has been a stirring experience. But you cannot expect me, after being present at the Garden of Gethsemane, to trouble myself with problems of transubstantiation. . . . Or can you?"

239

The bishop agreed that it was unthinkable.

The angel continued:

"What but the church is capable of comforting mankind for the practice of those austerities without which no nation can hope to live? A church must have rules and codes and bishops to administer them; otherwise there is no organization. But in Heaven we do not occupy ourselves with such matters. Where everything is perfect, naturally there is no need for regulations."

"That is understandable," said the bishop. "However," he added, "this is not Heaven."

"That is why I am here," replied Michael. And he went on to explain how he happened to be there. "I must confess to you," he said, blushing slightly, "that I have spent more time with the poets in the past than with the clerics. In this I have only followed the customary angelic practice. However, the poets who used to extol the familiar virtues have been succeeded by a new race of philosophers. A moment ago I had just come from a gathering of artists, poets, critics, and musicians, in which not a word was spoken concerning art, poetry, music, or literature. Instead, the hostess threw herself upon the bosom of a visiting novelist, while her husband took a young lady into the pantry to tell her something. What the other guests spent the evening discussing, I cannot tell you, out of deference to your cloth. Such things do not help to establish the home. It was while I was sorrowfully pondering this fact, and recalling to myself those divine discussions under the porches of Ephesus, among the tables at the Mermaid Tavern, and in the drawing-room of the Villa Saïd, that I passed your door and heard your prayer. At that moment I saw my duty. 'I will assist,' I exclaimed, 'this good divine in his struggle to uphold those domestic virtues without which the arts decay, religions decline, and nations disappear.' "

His face took on a divine radiance. " I do not look forward to being an archdeacon," he said, " but even an angel has certain duties to perform; and having seen my duty, I do not see how I can decline to do it."

And he held out his hand, which the bishop grasped. At once a strange and heavenly warmth ran through the Right Reverend Henry Brougham's veins. Rising to his feet he exclaimed,

" So be it, for it is the will of God."

" Well, tell me," said Michael, " why do you wish to erect a cathedral into the skies, like those tall towers of Akad and Erech built at the desert's edge by the Sumerians to remind them of their hills of home? You are not a mountain people. If I remember correctly, your own religion flourished first among graves and catacombs, deep in the bowels of earth. Now it soars into the air, along with the banks and the office buildings."

" The whole country," replied the bishop, " soars into the air. It aspires. Man has learned to fly, and has already made an altitude record of thirty-eight thousand feet."

" That is very high," agreed Michael gravely, " even if Heaven has not yet caught sight of him. However, I would like to ask you a question. Is it really toward Heaven that these buildings aspire? I am not sure, my friend. There are two ways of going up: one is to reach for what is above, the other is to spurn what is below. That is a difference in the point of view."

" It is only," remarked the bishop, " by spurning what is below that one can reach what is above." And bringing out the plans for the new cathedral, he showed them to his companion. " Here is the nave," he said, " and here is the transept. Here is the basilica, here the dome . . .

and here, to one side, is an office building which will also be very lofty."

The angel replied practically, " Will not the cost of this building be very great?"

The bishop sadly admitted that it would. "I have a list," he said, " of men and women whom I believe I can count on to help us." So saying he showed the list to Michael, with a sigh. "It is inadequate," he admitted.

The angel took it with a thoughtful air. When he saw how little was expected of each contributor, he was astonished. "The ancient tax of a tithe," he declared, " was a wise measure. In taking a tenth of each man's wealth, the Church expressed the conviction that wealth cannot be enjoyed without moral support. Just tell me, who would be wealthy in a country where nothing was sacred? No, no, wealth owes much to the Church, and should pay for its privileges."

So saying he seized a pen, and began to double the list of contributions. When he came to Mr. Cohen, he paused. Finally he wrote down opposite Mr. Cohen's name twenty-five thousand dollars.

" But Mr. Cohen," expostulated the bishop, " is a Jew. And you have just increased by twenty-five times the contribution I thought — but only thought — to ask from him."

The angel replied: " I know Mr. Cohen better than you do. It is true that Mrs. Lanyarde would not contribute to a Jewish synagogue. But she would gain nothing by such a contribution. Mr. Cohen, on the other hand, knows that when you have nothing, that is the time to give something to your wealthy neighbor. Cast your bread upon the waters, Bishop. That is a Jewish saying."

The bishop looked perplexed. "I recognize the text," he said, " but not your use of it. However, if the cathedral goes up, I do not care who builds it. I dare say that Mr. Cohen's wealth is made for him by Christians. So in the end, it simply returns to the Christians again. That is the best way to look at it."

The angel smiled. "In those accents," he declared, "I recognize the voice of the administrator."

And he continued to revise the list upward, in a radical manner.

While they were engaged in this pursuit, the door opened, and the bishop's wife entered the room. A beam of light from the hall followed her across the threshold, breaking upon her golden hair in a spray of light still more golden. When she saw the stranger, she stopped. "Excuse me," she said.

The bishop rose from his chair. "Ah," he said, "my dear." And he added in a voice trembling with joy, "Julia, I have found an archdeacon. He is a . . ."

But a warning look from Michael silenced him. The angel, standing in the shadows, seemed to glow with a faint radiance, as though the light which fell about the wife found an echo there. No one spoke: but it seemed to the bishop as though the room were full of shadowy beings moving slowly and with divine sweetness between them and around them. He felt the presence of the hosts of joy, their heavenly pinions brushed his soul.

"His name," he said, "is Michael."

Julia moved slowly forward, her grave blue eyes fixed upon the stranger. She held out her hand. "How do you do, Michael," she said.

A stronger radiance filled the room. The angel no longer stood among the shadows, which seemed, instead, to have gathered in the corner where the bishop stood lost in dreamy bliss.

"How do you do, Julia," he said.

Chapter VI

"WHAT a strange young man," said Julia later to her husband, the bishop.

The Right Reverend Henry Brougham was silent: he meditated. Were he to inform his wife of the true nature of his assistant, were he to make known to her the divine essence of which Michael was formed, could she, as a pious woman brought up in the Church, do any less than worship him? It was a serious problem for the bishop: it occurred to him for the first time that the advent of an angel might have its disadvantages.

He did not want his wife to adore a stranger.

And on his own part, too, there were certain difficulties. He was not overproud; he did not doubt that he needed light as much as any one else. Faith, science, love . . . he did not, like his wife, approach them with hesitation and longing, but came upon them with the tread of conviction, and strong in hygiene. Still, there were moments when he felt the buffet of unfriendly powers: and stood, like Joshua, halted before the walls of Jericho. On such occasions he called upon the trumpets of faith, which never failed him. Then the walls of the evil city fell before the horns of the pioneer, positive and not to be denied.

But it was one thing to blow the walls down himself;

and quite another to have an angel direct from the God-head do it for him. He was not the one to follow some one else; faith, for Bishop Brougham, was an act; it was works; it was the muscle of his spirit. And now it seemed to him that his spirit felt uncomfortable; for some reason the way before him appeared clouded. The moment when the battle ends is not always a happy one; to fret and strain against evil is an act itself dear to a hearty spirit with convictions.

There was no question but that the bishop cherished his convictions. They had won him a wife, and they had made him a bishop. He did not like to think that the Real Presence in the Eucharist was of less importance in Heaven than it was on earth. He did not, at his age, relish the idea of learning his dogma all over again.

And so, being mortal, he came finally to a mortal decision; troubled and human he resolved his trouble in a human way. He decided both to believe, and not to believe. For himself, he did not doubt that Michael was an angel; he simply decided not to admit it. And he forgave himself for this deception when he remembered the angel's advice to him. "Do not tell any one," the angel said, "because, for one thing, no one would believe it."

Then the angel had added even more practically: "It would be presumptuous for an angel to take precedence over a bishop in earthly matters."

He determined to enjoy without further thought the services of his assistant. There was no doubt about it, Michael was a rare deacon; like his wife Julia, he was quite perfect for his part. What if he hid — as his wife did too, perhaps, she being a woman, and given to frailty — some mystery still, beyond what the bishop thought it best to see? The wisest thing, one might say, was not to see it.

Therefore he replied to his wife in tones of enthusiasm, "The new archdeacon is a very amiable young man. And very well up on church affairs. Quite astonishing with figures."

"I'm so glad," said Julia honestly. She was pleased for Henry's sake; but she was not really thinking about it.

"Do you know what I think, Henry," she said; "I think he is a very reserved young man."

"Ah," said the bishop doubtfully; for he remembered their meeting.

Julia also remembered it; she felt inclined to blush a little at the memory of it. She was not used to having people call her Julia — that is, at first . . .

"It was strange," she mused; "I almost thought for a moment that we knew each other. Did you say anything about me, Henry? Before I came in, I mean."

"What?" exclaimed the bishop; "certainly not."

And he added a little sharply,

"He had never heard of you."

"Well," said Julia, "it was very queer, anyhow."

"Nonsense," said the bishop.

"He is," he remarked, "a stranger here."

And he added as an afterthought,

"His ideas are a little liberal."

But Julia was not to be put off. She knew that something out-of-the-way had happened to her; and she wanted to know what it was. "It was very strange," she said, "and I don't understand it."

The bishop looked away; his eyelids veiled his gaze. He felt, in his heart, an anxiety he could not entirely account for.

"Must you, my love," he asked, and his voice was even and heavy, "understand everything?"

Julia sighed. "No," she replied. She knew the question and answer by heart. "No," she answered meekly, "I mustn't."

But to herself she counted out, like a little girl on her fingers, the things she could never hope to understand. God first, in three parts, and Heaven and Hell and the Garden and Adam and Eve. Nobody could hope to understand it; fortunately it was considered enough merely to believe it. And then, on the other hand, science. . . . And why did passion, like a frightened child, go creeping out of the marriage bed? And now the new archdeacon . . .

"There are some things," said the bishop, "beyond the power of understanding."

He rose to go. "I have some business to attend to," he said. "Can we dine at seven? Then I must work."

Julia nodded her head. "Of course," she said. "Shall you be alone?"

"Doctor Michael will be with me," said the bishop.

He could not see that her heart quickened its beat by the least shade. "Could you come home a little early?" she asked. "Then you could say good night to Juliet. It means so much to her to have you come in for a moment."

"I shall try," said the bishop briefly: and left.

Julia sat still after he had gone, with her hands folded in her lap. The new deacon had called her Julia, and she had called him Michael. But now it appeared that his name was Doctor Michael. How silly of her.

Still, it had all seemed very natural.

Perhaps Henry was right; perhaps it wasn't important to know everything, to understand everything. Perhaps the important thing was just to feel happy and hopeful — about nothing, maybe. At any rate, whether it was right or whether it was wrong, it was a sweet feeling.

Juliet had it, about almost everything. Still, when Julia

was that age, she had had it, too. It was like a lamp shining, making things clear — even things you didn't know the name of. . . .

Michael had it, too, she felt sure. Doctor Michael, she meant to say.

Smiling, she rose, and went to look for Juliet.

Chapter VII

It was Michael, however, whom she found. He was standing at the nursery window, staring vaguely before him. His slender body, dark against the light, seemed to her, for a moment, almost like a bird, on tiptoe, and ready to fly. She stopped on the threshold in dismay.

"Why," she exclaimed, "whatever are you doing here? This is the nursery.

"I thought you were at the cathedral with Mr. Brougham."

To which Michael replied moodily, "His Grace was so good as to invite me to go with him. But after we had talked for a while, I grew tired; I thought I would come home and play with Juliet."

And he smiled at her sweetly, like a child making an apology.

She was at a loss for an answer. "But," she said, "I thought . . . of course, if you were tired . . . still . . . to play with Juliet?"

Then, since she could not keep from smiling, she turned her face away. "How funny," she said. And thinking of the bishop left alone with his figures, she began to laugh. "No, really," she exclaimed, "it is too absurd."

She soon grew sober again, and gazed at him curiously.

"But what did my husband say?" she asked.

The angel looked distressed. " He was a little vexed," he admitted. " He said that he had expected better things of me. He seemed to feel that I ought to be more serious."

" Well," said Julia severely, " oughtn't you ? "

" I do not think so," said Michael simply.

He continued : " In the past, to sing and to play were always a part of my duties. In Jerusalem the children used to play with dolls made of clay, and with knuckle-bones of ivory and horn. I should not like to think that these enjoyments are closed to me now that I am an arch-deacon."

He is mad, thought Julia, but he is attractive.

" What strange ideas you have," she said, " for a churchman. Knuckle-bones . . ."

" You were not in Florence in the fifteenth century," he replied, " or even in France during the reign of the great cardinal. So your knowledge of churchmen is limited. However, you are right; I have no business being an archdeacon. I was considering this fact when you came in. How could I have made such a mistake ? "

Julia flushed at his tone, which was gloomy and critical. Nevertheless, she answered in an even voice, " Perhaps it is not too late for you to change your mind. Shall I speak to my husband about it ? "

He considered this for a moment in silence. Finally he approached her, and, gazing into her face with an absorbed and thoughtful expression, remarked in a low voice, " No, do not say anything about it."

At once she experienced a feeling of relief whose intensity surprised her. In order to hide her confusion, she replied hastily :

" We should be sorry to lose you. That is, the church . . . and my husband, the bishop . . ."

"Your husband," he said gravely, interrupting her, "is engaged in an important work. He wishes to build a cathedral, loftier than any which have preceded it. I do not doubt that this building will give the Church a greater impetus in this country. He is an able man, for he also realizes that the strength of the Church lies in the home."

He stopped and looked about him at the nursery, from whose corners dolls and rabbits made of cotton and linen peered at him with mild expressions. "Had I such a home," he declared, "I should not desire to leave it, either."

"While you are with us," said Julia earnestly, "you must consider this home as your own."

"Thank you," said Michael.

"Where is your home?" she asked after a pause. "Where do you come from?"

He replied without thinking, "My home is in Heaven." Then he corrected himself. "That is just a manner of speaking," he explained.

"Of course," she agreed.

"I come from a sort of school," he said. His eyes brooded for a moment; he saw before him the flash of angelic wings, he heard in his ears the sounds of heavenly joy. "Ah," he said with a sigh.

"You are an orphan, then?"

"God is my father and my mother."

What he means, said Julia to herself, is that he comes from an orphan asylum.

Poor soul.

"God is everybody's father and mother," she said in her best manner.

She expected him to be grateful. But he looked at her in surprise; he smiled and his gloomy thoughts seemed to vanish. "Probably He is yours," he said; "but you do not take after Him. Confess that you do not feel like God at all."

She did not know whether to be angry or amused. "Well, then," she said with an uncertain smile, "what am I like?"

"Being mortal," said Michael, "you will live a little longer than a grasshopper, but not as long as a turtle. Knowing that you must die, you are full of longing: you wish to experience something, and have it last for ever."

"Isn't that natural?" asked Julia.

"For what do you hope, my child?" answered the angel. "For joy? It is all around you. Hold out your arms to receive it, but do not believe that it comes to you from Heaven."

And, glowing and beautiful, he took a step in her direction.

Julia backed away hastily.

"I think I hear Juliet coming," she said.

But Juliet did not come home just then. And Julia could think of no reason for leaving the nursery. "I don't know if what I want is joy," she remarked nervously. "I think perhaps that duty . . ."

"Duty and joy are one," said Michael. "That is," he corrected himself, "they ought to be. But man has taken upon himself duties which never were intended for him. Man was made to love, and to rejoice: I refer you to the second chapter of Genesis. He was not expected to distinguish between good and evil. That is in the third chapter, which relates the fall of man."

He was silent for a moment, gazing somberly before him. "In the morning of the world," he said, "when the dew still lay upon the Garden, man was created so that there might be some one to enjoy it. In order that he might relish beauty, he was given a soul; and having a soul, he was given speech, since without speech, it is impossible to understand such abstractions as the soul. That was a mistake, but I do not see how it could have been avoided. In those days the wings of angels moved with slow and graceful motions through the air which upheld also the flight of birds exquisite as flowers. Everywhere was beauty, everywhere was peace; and man was the witness of this peace and beauty. He was like a child, innocent and whole; his duties were to live and to give praise; and to give praise and to live were equally a joy, and equally natural. He was, indeed, little lower than the angels whose choirs sounded above him; made of earth, rather than of air, he could not fly, but he was repaid for the loss of wings by receiving earthly sensations unknown to the sons of light."

He paused and was still, remembering the peace of the Garden, the bliss which lay upon Eden. At length he sighed and continued:

"Such a light lay then upon the earth as you will see some mornings in the spring, when all the flowers are blooming, and the grass is young and green. The birds sang, and trod one another: they did what they were meant to do. Man lay with woman, and rejoiced. He understood the Infinite and the Eternal; since all was One, he saw no end to it, and had nothing to fear.

"Then came the fall of which you have read. Man ate of the fruit of the knowledge of good and evil.

"Alas for Eden when man learned that there was evil in the world. Where is the Garden now? You are far from Paradise, my child, although I do not doubt that you are closer to Heaven. How little you think of joy. Only in your dreams, when you remember the Garden. . . . There is no help for it. Even I, to do God's will, must aid you with your duties; must help your husband make his church secure, help him to build his cathedral, help to protect his homes. But my heart is heavy, for I remember the morning of the world, and the light which lay on Eden.

"I would rather bring you joy, I would rather help you find the Garden again."

Julia stood as in a trance, with her eyes closed. She hardly heard what he said; her ears were ravished with sounds of heavenly sweetness, her mind roamed among the most fragrant meadows. Her soul, roused by an angelic voice, strained upward in her breast; she hardly breathed.

Suddenly she felt upon her mouth a kiss of extraordinary sweetness and vigor.

"Oh!" she exclaimed, and, starting backward, opened her eyes with dismay.

She was in time to see Michael disappearing through the door. She sat down slowly on the edge of Juliet's bed, and put her hand to her face, which burned with a strange fire. Slowly her thoughts assembled themselves; slowly she passed from wonder to consternation. The fire cooled on her face, leaving a mortal blush. She touched her lips lightly with the tips of her fingers.

"What on earth," she began.

But she was unable to feel angry, although she wished to. At length she smiled and arose with a matronly air. "He is like a child," she told herself.

"But in the future he must be kept out of the nursery —at least . . ."

Chapter VIII

JULIET came home from the park with red cheeks. She had a new friend, and she was full of her adventures. He was smaller than Juliet, and round as a little apple; his chubby legs carried him at breakneck speed up and down the Mall, and back to his nurse, where he buried his face in her lap. This small, round, and happy child answered to the name of Johnson: what other names he had, Julia never discovered. He remained to her for ever Johnson.

" I lent him my skates," said Juliet; " and he fell down, and cried. He came down bump, and he hit himself bump. So then I fell, but I didn't cry. I came down more bump than he did.

" Only little tiny children cry.

" Mother, can I help you brush your hair? "

Seizing the brush in her hand, she drew it slowly, and with infinite care, across her mother's golden hair. " What would you do without me? " she asked.

" I can't imagine," said Julia. And she hid, behind a gentle smile, the sudden anguish of the thought.

" I know what you'd do," said Juliet wisely. And thinking of the stories her nurse read to her at night, she exclaimed, " You'd weep and moan."

" That's just what I'd do," said Julia. And she tried it out as well as she could, to see what it sounded like. " Ow," she moaned. " Oh. Oo."

Juliet dropped the brush and flung herself at her mother. "Oh, don't do that," she wailed. "Oh, don't do that. I won't go away, I won't go away."

"Well . . . do you promise?"

"I promise."

And she gazed at her mother, whose heart she feared she had broken.

Julia gathered her to her breast. "All right," she said, "I won't do it any more." And she added, laughing, "What a little love child it is."

But underneath the gay storm, she felt a sudden terror. Suppose something were to happen to her; suppose something were to happen to Juliet. Love was frightening, it put out such greedy hands. Ah, there was nothing eternal about love. Death took it, and left real weeping and moaning. Ought one not wish, rather, for strength to be without it? Ought she not teach her child . . . Was it not her duty . . .

Her duty . . .

She remembered Michael's words; and she drew the little golden head closer. "It is my duty," she said almost defiantly, "to love you."

"Yes," said Juliet with great satisfaction.

"Now tell me what you did all day."

"No," said Julia. "You tell me what you did. All you said was that you fell down."

"Well," said Juliet reflectively, "I fell down." Her eyes widened. "Potter was there," she declared. "When I cried, he came and patted me. So I gave him a hug, and he ran away."

Julia nodded her head. "That happens, too," she said. "But I thought you didn't cry when you fell."

"Well," said Juliet, "it was only a very little cry. And

256

so," she concluded quickly, " I played with Johnson, and he played with me."

" And what did Potter do, my darling?"

" He played, too. But he wouldn't love me. He played things like soldier, and walking on cracks, and running away.

"Mother, do you think maybe Potter doesn't love me?" The young lips trembled.

" Perhaps it's just his way," said Julia. But she felt a pang as she said it. " Little boys are like that," she said gravely. " They like to play their own way."

" Johnson isn't," said Juliet. " He hugs me."

" Still," said Julia wisely, " hugging isn't everything."

" Well," replied Juliet, " it's something."

And she gazed at her mother with a serious air.

" Mother," she said, " can I help you dress for to-night?"

They chose together from the closet a cloth of gold with a buckle made of a rose-leaf: it fell over Julia's narrow shoulders like a shower of light. Juliet looked at her mother critically. " Will I have a dress like that when I'm old?" she asked.

" Yes, dear . . . I hope so."

" Are you going out in it?"

" No; we have company for dinner."

" Who?"

" Only Doctor Michael."

Juliet clapped her hands. " Mother," she cried, " will I see him? Will he say good night to me? Will he come and kiss me in my bed?

" I'd like him to come up and kiss me in my bed."

She liked any one to kiss her good night. Once there had been a scene because she insisted that the plumber, who was working in the house, should say good night to her. Her father objected; deprived of the plumber's love, she had cried herself to sleep.

On such occasions Julia felt a very lively anxiety for her little daughter. What will become of her, she thought, when she grows up? And she imagined for Juliet a life full of sorrow and despair. Then she would talk to her seriously about such things as service-to-others, and for-getfulness-of-self; and Juliet would listen with an abashed and tender air. The next day she would come home and tell her mother that she had given away her doll to a little girl in the park.

" She was poor and dirty, and I gave her a kiss."

Then Julia would be more anxious than ever. To Juliet living was loving, and loving was kissing and hugging; and that was all there was about it. What had put such ideas into her head? They frightened her mother; she won-dered sometimes if deep in her own heart . . . But surely not in so generous a manner . . . plumbers . . . poor little girls in the park . . .

Of course it was all quite innocent. But just the same, this dream of a world of people all loving and kissing one another must be stopped; she must put an end to it.

It would have made the bishop very gloomy if he had thought about it. But the bishop did not think about such things. A child belonged to the Kingdom of Heaven throughout its childhood; the important thing was to learn the catechism. The little bundle of curiosity and longing belonged to God as long as she remained tech-nically innocent; she might inherit from her parents a nose or an eye, but inside all was bound to be simple and serene and taken care of. As pure, the bishop liked to say, as a lily, or a little child. He might have added, " As pure as my wife's thoughts "; it would have meant the same thing.

He came home from St. Timothy's frowning and concerned with something else. "This deacon of mine," he said; "well, really . . . All at once, in the very middle of what I was saying to him, he disappeared. I looked up, and he was gone. Have you seen him, my dear? I am not used to that sort of thing."

"No," said Julia. She had not meant to say No; it shocked her to hear it come out. Nevertheless, at the moment, it seemed the right thing to say. She blushed for herself, and remained silent.

"Well," he said with a sigh, "I had already asked him to dine with us, so he may turn up after all. I suppose there is no use in losing one's temper. He is a very reserved young man — as I believe you pointed out."

"Reserved?" said Julia stupidly. And she burst out laughing.

The bishop looked at her in surprise. "Didn't you say so?" he demanded.

"Did I?" she asked. "Perhaps I did." She struggled to take firm hold on herself. "I suppose I was thinking of something else."

But the bishop was irritable; he disliked having people disappear under his nose. "I wish you would pay a little more attention to what I say," he complained. "I was telling you that in the middle of my remarks . . .

"Oh . . . well, well . . . hum . . ."

And he remained glaring in astonishment at Michael whom he observed at that moment unconcernedly descending the stairs.

"Where have you been?" asked Michael. "I lost sight of you at the cathedral."

And he added happily, "I have just been up-stairs to kiss Juliet good night."

Chapter IX

ST. TIMOTHY'S rose above its hill, gray and stony, into
the wintry sky from which the winds had driven the deeper
tones southward over the sea. High on the paths of air
the light clouds traveled over the city from the west;
they shone white in the sun above the flocks of pigeons
which wheeled and gleamed like little silver pieces above
the city. But the houses below were in shadow; and
shadows lay like dark splinters across the streets where
the breeze turned into long rivers of wind, brawling and
uncertain.

The city was being torn up to make room for the new
city, which raised itself to incredible heights in the shape
of obelisks, pyramids, mountainous crags, monasteries,
temples, lozenges, pavilions, and medieval fortresses set
upon rocks. In the midst of this confusion, St. Timothy's
preserved its composure, and remained an excellent imi-
tation of the cathedral at St. Didier, built in the thirteenth
century in honor of that saint whose bones were believed
to cure rickets.

On Sunday the bells of St. Timothy's were rung, the
carillon was played, and the air in the neighborhood was
disturbed for a distance of several blocks. Seated in their
pews, men and women gave themselves up to feelings of

260

solemnity not untouched with sadness. The deep organ tones pulsing through the air which rose arched and motionless above them, led them to pious reflections, to thoughts of eternity, and to proposals of powers beyond their comprehension. The light streamed downward, dim, quiet, affecting their hearts with peace, untroubled and unchanging, a light not of this age and not of this earth. Beneath it, in seats supplied with cushions, Bibles, psalmodies and hymnals, the congregation remained hushed, while fathers and mothers turned over more comfortably in their minds the problems which awaited them at home.

The bishop delivered the sermon. Reverend but practical, he led the members of his flock in pastures which attracted them: he assured them that it paid to be devout. They did not doubt it; but it pleased them to hear it; and while the organ played and the choir sang, their hearts, uplifted, took part as celebrants in a divine communion.

" Our day," said the bishop, " has its martyrs. The fact that we are no longer martyrs to faith, speaks for the triumph of that faith. Where can a man die to-day for his beliefs? Nowhere — thank God. To-day we have other battles to wage; and other martyrs to admire. To-day Satan would like to tempt us away from our work. The devil comes to us garlanded with flowers, and bids us put away our sober habits, our industrial tools, and embrace the joys of the flesh, idleness, and sin.

" Now, in this season of the year, a great spirit rises in our hearts to oppose him. It is the Christmas spirit: the Christmas spirit, which will save home and Church from the immoral teachings of present-day paganism. The star of Bethlehem, the Christmas star, shines with a pure light in the sky, and strengthens our hearts with holiness.

" Take, then, to be your own at this season that orderly,

261

devout and forward-looking spirit whose motto is, Peace on earth, good will to men."

In the midst of this sermon, Professor Wutheridge, whose scholarly books on Rites, Purifications, and Festivals nobody had read, got up and went home. The following day he lectured to his class at the university:

"When Gilgamish, King of Erech, conquered the city of Akad, the festivals of the Akadian gods continued to be celebrated — with this difference: they were celebrated in praise of the tutelary deity of Erech. Beaten in battle, the ancient cities lost their gods, who were adopted by the conqueror and joined to his parthenon, along with their festivals and celebrations."

His departure did not disturb the wealthy congregation of St. Timothy's whose members, in the holy light, saw one another in the form of oil companies, mining concessions, mills, factories, and gilt-edge securities.

But Julia sat quiet, with her own thoughts. She closed her eyes; and as her husband spoke, she answered in her mind, half in reply to him, half to herself:

"My dear," she said seriously, "what did they do before there was a Christmas? Weren't people happy, anywhere? Was it all sin? I suppose so. Not sin, really; but not salvation. Not the sort of happiness that counts — that we have now, for instance. It must have been a very sinful world . . . garlanded in flowers, as you say. Did people kiss each other . . . suddenly, I mean, and without being asked? The way — the way he kissed me? Yes, he did; but I didn't ask him to. He simply quickly and all at once . . . It was like fire and ice, it did something to my heart."

The choir sang:

> "On earth a child is born,
> And in the manger lies."

The congregation knelt; and the bishop prayed. "Lift up our hearts, Oh Lord," he urged, "and draw our thoughts nigh unto Thee at this season, in order that we may exalt Thy Name among the nations. Let us not think too much of the joys of the flesh, but rather of the spirit which denies the flesh, the spirit which has built this great country as a lasting monument to Thy glory for ever and ever, amen."

And Julia, on her knees, went on: "The Christmas spirit will put an end to paganism. We'll have a tree for Juliet, with red and blue lights; and Juliet will give out the presents. One for the cook, one for me, one for Michael . . . My dear, you've never been kissed suddenly, against your will — so how do you know? But if you had been, and if you knew, then you'd know what a man thinks . . . afterward. He never spoke of it. I wish I knew. One ought to know so much, and, after all, what does one know?

"Ought I be ashamed, or angry? But he almost seems to have forgotten it, the times I've seen him since. Maybe it never really happened. What if I think it never happened?

"Perhaps that would be wisest.

"Very well, then: he never kissed me, never, not at all.

"Will he kiss me again? Will he ever dare? Well, I should think not.

"For we have done what we should not have done, and what we should do, we have not done; there is no good in us."

She knelt; but her gaze wandered in search of Michael. The bright young golden head with its strange radiance was not to be seen; the archdeacon was invisible.

He stood, leaning moodily against a pillar in the rear

of the altar, listening to the service. He had heard many services, but they never failed to impress him. There was an organist, he remembered, at Weimar long ago; how he played; it was like being in Heaven merely to hear him. "This bishop," he thought, "does not use much eloquence, but he is sound. What energy there is in the world to-day, what force. We must direct it in the proper channels, otherwise there will be further changes in Heaven."

And he reflected soberly on the changes in the past: how at first the angels used to come and go between Heaven and earth, passing up and down Jacob's ladder with folded wings and peaceful expressions; he thought of the slavery in Egypt, the flight through the desert, the endless wars, the short-lived triumph of Judah. He remembered the destruction of the Temple by the Roman legions, and the lean years which followed, among the martyrs and the hermits of the Thebaid: there was nowhere then for an angel to feel at home except in the arena among the lions, or in the desert with the jackals. He remembered how Heaven began to fill with saints, some of them without heads, or hands, or feet, some pierced by arrows, some burned to a crisp; he remembered the triumphal entry into Rome with Constantine, the martial years of the crusades, the exciting time spent in hunting witches; he remembered how Heaven rocked the day that Darwin was born, and how they sang hosannahs on Canon Wilberforce's birthday. Now a new era had dawned upon the world, which quivered with the impact of tremendous forces, of discoveries and inventions. Man rode upon the air, sent his voice across the seas, divided the indivisible, and penetrated the impenetrable. Audacious, optimistic, and indefatigable, he might even forget God altogether, and raise his limitless towers like altars to none other than himself.

"No," said Michael, "that must not happen." And he added firmly,

"It is time for every angel to do his duty."

Nevertheless, an unaccountable weight seemed to lean upon his heart, saddening him. "I will save the homes of this diocese," he said; but he felt oppressed. He thought of his own lodgings, which consisted of a single room containing a bed, a bureau, a table, and a chair. "I shall not be there long," he said to console himself. He thought of Juliet; and he sighed. "Perhaps God will send me one of the little cherubim to keep me company," he said.

But he realized that such an act would cause embarrassment to the bishop.

The Right Reverend Henry Brougham came down in his episcopal robes from the pulpit. "Well," he asked, "what did you think of it?"

"Splendid," said Michael; "splendid."

"I thought it went over very well," said the bishop.

But he seemed, to Michael, a little absent in his mind, as though the real test of opinion were not to be found in the cathedral at all, but somewhere else; and soon afterward, avoiding the members of the congregation who wished to congratulate him, he hurried home to his wife, to ask her in his most casual tones,

"Well, my love, what did you think of it?"

She did not answer; instead, she put out her hand, and motioned him to sit down with her. "Henry," she said, "come and talk to me a little. Tell me about yourself. Are you very busy these days?"

But the bishop stood still, his hands full of papers, an expression of disappointment on his face. "As usual, my love," he answered politely, "as usual. Business, arrangements, calls . . . Is there anything wrong? You seem a little preoccupied."

She wanted to say to him, Yes . . . I'm lonely. She wanted to cry out to him, I'm frightened, Henry — and I don't know what I'm frightened at . . . at least, I'm not sure.

Would you hold me tightly, please, for a little while?

But that was impossible; as she looked at him, she realized how impossible it was. There was nothing in him waiting to talk to her loneliness, or comfort her fear. He loved her; he stood there, straight and tall, looking down at her with kindness, and affection. But he never saw in her the things he didn't want to see. And if she told him that she was lonely, he'd not see that, either. He'd look at her the way one looked at a child. . . . There, there, my dear, don't cry; see, there's nothing to be afraid of. Grown up people don't cry over nothing. . . .

How sure he was, how certain of himself — was there such a thing as doubt in that severe, finely chiseled head of his? Never, she felt sure. Not even for her. How could she say to him, I'm lonely and frightened? What would he say back to her? Nonsense, my love. And then, probably, I am very busy. . . .

"I suppose," she said, having to say something, "it's because I have Juliet a little on my mind these days."

"Ah," said the bishop comfortably. "Well, my dear, what is wrong with Juliet? Has she a cold?"

"No," said Julia, smiling faintly, "she's quite well. But she's growing up, Henry. Sometimes I think of all she'll have to learn — all we'll have to teach her. I wonder if I know enough."

"There are teachers," said the bishop, "whose duty it is to know enough. She is growing up, like any other child. What can happen to her? Nothing."

Julia sighed. "Are you quite sure?" she asked. And

she added, half under her breath, "Such strange things happen."

"Quite," said the bishop. And he went on into his own room, bearing his papers before him. "Don't worry," he said: "we'll attend to Juliet's education at the proper time."

But at the door he stopped, and turned back again. "You didn't tell me," he said a little sadly, "what you thought of my sermon."

She roused herself with a start. "Oh," she said; "yes . . . so I didn't. It was very interesting, dear. I thought it very interesting. All that part about Christmas . . ."

Chapter X

GEORGE HERMAN WUTHERIDGE, Lanyarde Professor of
Semitic Languages at the University, lay asleep in a bed
without a pillow. His hands were folded across his breast,
below his short, white beard; and his face was already
lighted by the early sunshine. As he slept, he smiled; then
he looked like one of those good saints such as the happy
Florentines used to love to draw. But presently the sound
of a cart rumbling over the cobbles below, awoke him;
and he opened his eyes. " Here is the day again," he
said to himself. And he shut his eyes tight, hoping thereby
to hold, for a moment longer, those fading dreams which
had amused him.

" No," he said at last, " they are gone. Up with you."
With the stiffness of old age he arose, and began to pre-
pare for breakfast.

As he drank his coffee, he glanced, as was his custom,
at the morning paper. As usual his face grew thoughtful
and sad. " It is always the same," he said to himself.
" I, too, could write the morning's news. One man takes
away another's bread; that is the news. Why do I vex
myself with it ? "

Then, as his gaze traveled down the paper, he continued :

" In Athens a woman known as Tamara has been found

268

guilty of murdering eight men whom she had first converted to Christianity. She confesses to these murders with candid joy; to make sure that they would not recant, and to insure their eternal salvation, she admits that she killed her converts immediately after baptism."

He read: "When the police reached Tamara's room, the girl was in prayer. Reverently waiting until she had finished, the officers heard her expound her own worthiness for salvation because of the souls whose eternal bliss she had assured by sending them to the next world at the moment when they were in Heaven's grace."

Putting down his cup, Professor Wutheridge exclaimed, "It is quite possible that this woman is a saint, and deserves canonization. One must acknowledge the sublimity of her intentions, the practise of which has drawn down upon her the disapproval of the police.

"Still, when one comes to think of it, how many saints would be allowed to practise their martyrdom to-day? The confessions of another Augustine would be censored by the Church; but they would make their author's fortune. And that pious girl who gave her maidenhead to a ferryman, having nothing else with which to pay him, lest pride should keep her from her pilgrimage, would receive no attention.

"In this particular instance, however, we are dealing with a form of sacrifice not unknown to the priests of Bel, of Moloch, and of Ammon. It is true that in the case of Moloch, to whom only virgins were sacrificed, there is no mention made of a divine hereafter for the victims. Nevertheless, it is by death alone that man lives; in which he partakes of the nature of all life."

Pleased with these reflections, the professor of Semitic languages left to attend his classes at the University.

In the afternoon he went for a walk. Snow was in the

air, in the close gray sky, under which the wind sang a slow, northern tune. The water in the river looked wrinkled and cold, dark, and heavy; on the windy street corners, before boxes for the poor, red-hooded Santa Clauses rang their little tinkling bells. Holly wreaths were to be seen in the windows; in front of florist shops and grocery stores the damp air was perfumed with evergreens.

Professor Wutheridge left the streets in which men and women, anxious to get their shopping done before the holidays, hurried with stern and serious faces; and entered the park. There he could look at the city across a foreground of winter-withered trees, and admire the lofty rooftops from a distance. As usual he laid his course through the Mall, for he enjoyed watching the children whose games reminded him of the festivals of the past, joyous, or tragic, and intense.

He had in mind one child in particular, whose small dark face radiated enthusiasm and love. When he saw her, he could not restrain himself from turning to the young man in whose care she seemed to be, and remarking,

"What an unusual child. She reminds me of those children of Cyrene whose happy forms and innocent thoughts have come down to us in the writings of the poets."

And he quoted:

> " ' Crethis their first in tale or play,
> Sorely the Samian maidens weep;
> Their pretty taskmate, prattler gay,
> Sleeps, as must they, her fated sleep.' "

To which the young man replied, "I am not familiar with the Greek Anthology. However, I have studied the works of other poets, one of whom writes,

"'Bow down his neck in his youth,
    And smite his loins when he is a little one.'"

"The verse you refer to," said Professor Wutheridge, "is the work of the son of Sirach; and was composed in the second century." He gazed at the young man with curiosity. "I see that you have golden hair," he said; "and your features resemble those of the great archangel of Donatello, now to be seen in the Bargello at Florence. Nevertheless, I feel that there is something Oriental about you."

"It is true," said Michael; "I come from what was originally a Semitic family." And he added simply, "I am an angel; and this young girl, whose nurse I am at the moment, is the daughter of the Right Reverend Henry Brougham, Bishop of Saint Timothy's."

"I am glad to hear it," said the professor; "I am glad to hear it. Tell me something: when the tribe of Habiri crossed the Jordan, did they, as I suspect, mingle with the Philistines; and were the Philistines, as Mr. Golding insists, a Minoan race, from Crete? Come; what is the truth of all that?"

And he gazed eagerly at the angel, who, however, shook his head.

"I know nothing about the Philistines," he said, "except that our people overcame them. Their tenacity in the face of divine disapproval was something of a surprise to me. However, the entire period is a little vague in my mind. It was not a very happy time for me, socially speaking: I believe that we did nothing but fight for the ownership of a few hills and a desert."

"Just the same," insisted the professor, "I cannot help wishing I had been there. What an opportunity for research. I console myself by visiting the park, and watch-

ing the children at their games. When one of them is
made a victim by the others, I read in his pained and ·
lonely expression the entire history of the race.

"This charming child whose father you tell me is the
Bishop of St. Timothy's does not resemble her parent. I
have often listened to his sermons; which have always
struck me as betraying more common sense than scholarship. But then what use would scholarship be to a bishop
who wishes to erect a new cathedral? He has already approached me, through the University; and I have sub-
scribed ten dollars. I suppose that you are interested;
which is why I tell you this."

"I am interested, naturally," replied Michael, "having, in addition to my heavenly duties, taken over the
office of archdeacon to the cathedral. You see me at the
moment playing nurse to the bishop's child, while waiting
for her mother to join us. This is my happiest office; in
which I am assisted by a tiny spirit not unlike a cherub,
who goes by the name of Johnson."

And he pointed to where Juliet, rushing through the
Mall, was pursuing her friend with sparkling eyes and
cheeks red from the cold.

"But tell me," he continued; "did I understand you to
say that you had already contributed ten dollars to the
new cathedral? That would explain why you are not
down upon the list, which contains the names of many
eminent professors."

"Are you sure," exclaimed the professor in surprise,
"that my name is not upon the list? Wutheridge, George
Herman. . . . Well, tst . . . there's a strange thing."

The angel made a courteous gesture. "The list," he
explained, "contains only the names of those whose contributions are in excess of fifteen dollars."

"Ah," said Professor Wutheridge.

272

" I noticed the names of the Heads of the Departments of Economics," said Michael, " of History, of Romance Languages, of Physics, of Hygiene, and of the Business School. There are also many Associate Professors of Mathematics, of Fine Arts, and of Astronomy . . . on the whole, a very distinguished list of names. We intend to publish it soon in the Sunday papers, under the shield of the University, and surrounded with a design of laurel leaves."

" Ah," said Professor Wutheridge again. And he added in a gloomy voice, " There has been a very serious mistake here. My contribution was to have been exactly fifteen dollars . . . However, in making out the check . . . Well, well. My friend, do me this little favor; set this matter right for me. See that I am down for fifteen dollars . . . if it is not too late. . . ."

And raising his hat to Mrs. Brougham, who came hurrying up at that moment in search of Juliet, the professor took his leave to continue his walk through the park, under the wintry sky.

Chapter XI

"WHAT were you talking about?" asked Julia. Her face was flushed, and she was gay; she told herself that she was happy because she was meeting Juliet in the park. "You looked so serious, Michael."

He replied, thoughtfully, "I was thinking that soon I shall have to visit Mrs. Guerdon, and Mr. Cohen, and get them to build us a new altar, in the name of commerce."

Julia's face puckered into a child's frown. "Oh," she cried, "you think of nothing but business. You and Henry. . . . Do you ever talk of anything else? Aren't you glad to be in the park with Juliet and me?"

"Yes," said Michael, more serious than ever.

She laughed. "Then tell us about it," she cried. And she held out her arms to greet Juliet, who flung herself at her mother with cries of joy.

"Johnson, look, there's mother."

"Come and love her."

Julia let herself be dragged to a bench, the children's arms around her knees. "Sit down here with me, Michael," she said, "until we get cold. And tell me about yourself. I never get a chance to ask you. . . . Have you a nice room on the hill? Henry says it gets the morning sun . . . I wonder, if I sent you over an old rug or two from our house . . .

274

"I must come some day to see it. . . ."

She bit her lip; she corrected herself. "I'll ask Henry to bring me," she said.

"But tell me, are you really settled now? You must come and see us more often. Your being a stranger . . . and then, my being your bishop's wife . . . of course . . ."

She broke off. Was he listening? She wondered what he was thinking about. The new altar . . . Mr. Cohen . . . It was too absurd. He hadn't been thinking about Mr. Cohen that evening in the nursery. . . .

There — she hadn't meant to think of that again, not ever. Why couldn't she simply forget it — the way he did, apparently.

"I'll look through my things at home," she said. "We have so much put away that we never use." And turning with a motherly air to Juliet, she remarked,

"See, there's Potter. Perhaps he'll let you ride on his wagon."

But Juliet barely glanced at her friend. "I don't want to," she said. "He's not very distractive."

And turning her back on Potter, who continued to trudge solemnly up and down with his wagon, she skipped off in advance of Johnson, who followed her like a bee or a bullet.

Julia let herself sink back with a sigh. It was so peaceful in the park, even though it was cold. She supposed her nose would be red, presently; but it was healthy for Juliet. So it was only right for her to . . . she smiled to herself. What had he said that evening in the nursery? You think so much of right and wrong. . . . Well, but one had to. And so, for that matter, did he; he thought of nothing but duty. He was a very able archdeacon; and she was glad of it, for Henry's sake.

" Michael," she said, " will you help us trim our tree this year? We fix a little tree for Juliet, on Christmas Eve. Of course, if you have anything more exciting to do . . . But perhaps it would amuse you? "

" Thank you," said Michael. " I had nothing to do. To tell you the truth, it is so hard these days to find anything to do that is both joyous and devout. To trim a tree for Juliet would be both, I think. May I bring her a present, Julia? A trifle for her stocking? "

" She gets so much; why should you, too, bring her something? "

He replied: " In Heaven, on Christmas Day, we give the cherubim gifts of fruit and a sweetmeat; and then they sing for us. Perhaps Juliet will sing for us too, an old carol or a madrigal."

Julia's eyes grew tender. " He speaks of his home," she thought, " as though it were Heaven. An apple, and a stick of candy for each orphan. Oh, the poor soul."

And she replied gently,

" You shall bring Juliet a doll made of peppermint. And I'll teach her a carol to sing."

" I should love that," he said simply. And he remained silent, gazing across the park at the city.

She looked up at him from under her golden eyelashes. What a strange person he was! She knew that wherever he went people followed him with their eyes. But she knew, too, that it was not so much his beauty as his expression which attracted them: it was proud, insolent, and full of longing. It puzzled Julia. " He doesn't really love people," she thought; " not the way Henry does. And yet he's sweet with Juliet — sweeter than Henry, even."

She leaned back and looked at him thoughtfully. He was the only man — except her husband — who had ever kissed her; and he seemed to have forgotten it. That was

276

a queer thing for her to have to face. She rather thought it would hurt, in time. Perhaps it did already. And yet there was nothing careless, or satisfied, about him; even now, sitting there in silence, he seemed to be moved by some obscure but quite unbearable longing. The strange thing about it was that it moved her, too — whatever it was. It took her peace away, and left her restless. She wished she knew why.

"I suppose," she said apologetically, "you've many friends who'll want you on Christmas Day."

But he shook his head. "No," he said; "I have no friends at all, to speak of. How would I have? I am a servant, Julia."

She smiled; but it was to hide a sigh of disappointment. She was so used to that sort of answer; how tiresome it was. "Yes," she said; "I know. Henry is a servant, too — we all are. Still, one can serve, and have friends. One can serve, and . . . love . . ."

She checked herself sharply, and looked away.

And Michael, too, was silent for a moment before he answered. "Julia," he said at last, "since I have been an archdeacon, I have heard the word love spoken all around me. What is this word, whose meaning in the sense I hear it used, escapes me? I am used to love; but not in religious matters. I have often heard it discussed among the poets."

At Julia's expression of surprise, he continued earnestly; "I know that such thoughts are not expected of me. In the past I have often been obliged to hide my true nature, in order to fit in with the theology of the period. It was simpler in the old days; for the emotion which animated the Jews was not so difficult to understand. They rose out of Canaan like a sky-scraper; and they did not wish any one to share their blessings with them.

"Now everything is changed; men speak of love, they have new definitions. But they act as they used to in the old days, when those who were chosen despised those who were not. It is natural; but I would not call it love."

"You say such strange things," said Julia, "for a deacon. You talk of the Jews, and of us, as though it were all the same thing. The Jews taught us an eye for eye — don't you remember? And then God taught us to love our enemies and turn the other cheek. That's the difference, Michael."

But Michael shook his head. "God does not love His enemies, Julia," he replied soberly. "He wishes His enemies to love Him. That is entirely different."

"You spoke once," said Julia, "of joy; you told me it was all around me."

"I said it would not come to you from Heaven," said Michael.

"But you were speaking of love," murmured Julia.

"Was I?" asked Michael wearily. "I do not remember."

She bowed her head, and looked at her hands folded in their leather gloves. Had he really forgotten, then; did it mean so little to him, after all? Of course; for what was a kiss to a man? How very horrid, she thought. And to happen to her, of all people. It was not as if she were used to that sort of thing. No one had ever dared before. And now he had simply forgotten all about it.

He looked at her in a friendly way. "Your cheeks are red," he said: "are you cold?"

"Perhaps I am," she answered. "Shall we walk?"

They rose, and passed slowly among the children down the Mall, between the benches. Pigeons wheeled from under their feet, rising into the air with creaking wings, like dry leaves scattered by the wind. Little boys ran past them, with loud cries; little girls gathered in groups, earnest, and secretive. All about them sounded the childish voices, shrill, eager, and without pity.

Can I play?

What's your name?

Don't let her play with us.

Look — I'll be the mother.

No, no — it's my doll.

Fraulein, they won't let me play with them.

Can I help it? Don't bother me.

There; now you've fallen.

"When you speak of joy," said Julia as they turned slowly back again, "I sometimes wonder if I know what you mean. What joy is there, beyond doing what we have to do, and doing it well?"

But Michael's eyes were dull; the radiance was gone from his face. As he looked down the long lane of children; he seemed to see, at its cloudy end, a vast and shadowy church, up through whose spires, piled stone upon stone, tiny voices seemed drawn like a thin smoke, like a mist of sacrifice.

Let us pray here.

What is your name?

Oh, no, you cannot pray with us.

Here is the truth.

But it is I who discovered it.

Can I help it? Don't bother me.

"Michael," exclaimed Julia with vexation, "you're not paying the least attention. I said, is there any joy beyond doing what we have to do, and doing it well?"

He roused himself as from a dream; he seemed to lift himself from some deep place beyond her power of reach. He looked at her for a moment with eyes gray as stone.

"I do not know," he said.

Chapter XII

POTTER, with his wagon, trudged up and down the Mall; he imagined that he was being busy, that he was drawing behind him an important load. For this reason there exhaled from his diminutive figure an air of dignity mixed with melancholy; he gazed at the other children who were only amusing themselves, without envy. Nevertheless, he wished them to admire him; and when his nurse asked him to sit quietly beside her, he refused. Upon her insisting, he galloped away, drawing his cart after him; and when she overtook him, he kicked her shins.

Juliet observed him later, plumped upon a seat, and crying bitterly. " He's only a little child," she explained to Johnson, who nodded seriously.

But she found it difficult, under the circumstances, to draw her design of hop-scotch anywhere but in front of the bench where Potter sat. " One — two — three . . . you have to jump over this," she told Johnson, " with your legs out."

She leapt; and landed, as she said, with her legs out. Then she glanced at Potter, who remained, however, lost in grief. She thought that next time she would leap a little differently: to land with the legs out was not very becoming.

It was a strange thing about Potter: he was not much fun to play with. For one thing, he never played what she wanted to play, the way Johnson did. And then, he kicked people's shins. Still, when he wept, she felt it: she was touched. And she respected his grief, which kept him from admiring her.

She hopped on one leg. Probably the most charming thing to do was simply to stand still.

The grief of little children, piercing and abandoned, touches other children in a strange way: it seems to warn them of sorrow in the world, to advise them of pain; yet they do not wish to be left out of anything. Juliet could not bear indifference to herself, even in tears. She did not want Potter to cry; but if he must, she wished to play a greater part in his grief than hopping up and down on one foot, unnoticed.

However, Potter was in no mood to admire anything. Deprived of his importance, he sat in the shadow of his nurse, and wept.

"Look," said the nurse, "there is Juliet. She is wondering at you. Aren't you ashamed, such a big boy? And my leg, which you have kicked."

She addressed the heavens. *"Um Gottes Willen!"* she exclaimed, not unreasonably.

"Come, Miss Juliet, and look at this wicked boy, who weeps."

Juliet drew near, and gazed at Potter with deep concern. Then coming closer still, she slipped her hand shyly into his, and stood beside him, looking into his face with sweet earnestness.

"Don't cry, Potter," she said: and she endeavored to embrace his foot, out of sympathy, and the desire to be active.

"I wouldn't cry," she said to Potter's nurse; "would I?"

"There," said the nurse, "do you hear that? Juliet

wouldn't cry. No nice child would cry, and kick his nurse's leg."

"I'd smile and laugh," said Juliet. "Wouldn't I?"

She wanted some one to admire her. But she spoke too soon. For all at once Potter, with a howl, drew back his leg, and shot it forward again. And down went Juliet on her back in the dust.

For a moment she said nothing; sprawled on her back, she presented a picture of silent consternation. But when once she had risen to her feet, the realization of what had been done to her overwhelmed her. Her tiny face broke into creases, her mouth went down; and she burst into tears.

"My dress is dirty," she sobbed. "I don't like my dirty dress.

"He kicked me. He kicked me."

And rushing from the clasp of Potter's outraged nurse, she fled to the convent of her mother's arms.

Julia received her calmly, brushed her dress, rearranged her bonnet, wiped her eyes, and helped her to blow her nose. Then she took her firmly by the hand. "Come," she said, "walk here with Michael and me. Little boys are often very rude; you mustn't mind such things. He didn't mean to hurt you, darling. Look, there's a little girl feeding the pigeons. See how many there are, and how they gobble. The sparrows gobble, too; they steal pop-corn from right under the pigeons' noses. Goodness, what greedy little birds."

Juliet's face lost its woebegone expression; with one hand held high in Michael's clasp, the other in her mother's, she gazed with gradual interest at the pigeons. Now and then she gave a sniffle, but not because she meant to. "What greedy little birds," she echoed.

"I wouldn't be like that, would I?" And she gave an uncertain laugh.

The shadows of afternoon were lengthening in the Mall. The air was colder, the sun no longer warmed the wind. The first blue veils of evening, faint and misty, lay upon the benches and drifted, like deeper light, among the trees. It was the hour of the sadness of children, before the lamps are lighted. They are cold, and tired, the day is over with its games; soon they will be back in their warm and quiet nurseries. But not yet; first they must part, and follow their nurses home, lonely and dreaming. The chime of voices fades, good-bys are said, half sung, half whispered; the Mall grows empty. The wind sweeps sadly across the walks on which the ghostly chalk-marks still linger.

Potter went home in disgrace. But he was not unhappy; he pulled his wagon along, and looked around him in a pleased way. His nurse hurried ahead of him, without speaking; but he was used to that. He did not think of Juliet; he forgot that he had kicked a little girl. His mood was a rich one; he remembered only the attention he had received. For to Potter, at that age, attention and admiration were all the same; he did not draw any distinction between them.

But Juliet did not forget. That night, before she fell asleep, she discussed with her mother the manners of little boys who kicked their own cousins, and dirtied their coats. She lay in her tiny bed, the light blue covers thrown back from her arms, the short hair loose on the pillow. Only her eyes' dark light held sleep at bay.

"He gave me a kick," she said, "and I didn't kick him back. Did I, mother?"

"I should hope not," said Julia.

283

"I wouldn't do such a thing, would I?" continued Juliet.

"It's not a sweet thing to do," said Julia; "kicking people."

"No," agreed Juliet, "it's not." She mused for a moment; and sleep drew nearer. "I like sweet things to do," she said. "I was doing one when he kicked me. I was giving him a kiss."

It was not strictly true; but it seemed so to Juliet, as she remembered it. She sat up in bed, moved all at once by a serious thought. "Mother," she said, "he never wants to play nicely with me, like other children do. He wants to play all alone, and I have to watch him."

But Julia was thinking her own thoughts. "Ah," she said.

"It's not much fun for me," said Juliet.

She sank back again, and gazed with dreamy eyes around the room. "Mother," she said, "could an animal like there are in the zoo come into my room and hide in a corner?"

"Why," exclaimed Julia, "what an idea."

"When it's dark, I mean," said Juliet. "Could he, mother?"

"No, darling, not possibly."

"Couldn't a lion or a tiger?"

"No, no."

She sighed. "That's good," she said. And more drowsily still,

"Will Michael come up and kiss me good night?"

"Later, my darling. Go to sleep now."

She put out the light; but she did not leave at once. She stood for a moment on the threshold, half in light, half in shadow; she felt her own heart beating, she heard the blood singing in her body.

284

She closed her eyes. Here, in this room, where her child lay half asleep, he had kissed her. He had forgotten it; but would she ever forget? What had he said? Nothing . . . only the sound of his voice, beautiful as it had been then, and that taste on her lips, like fire and honey. Her heart beat more strongly. Would it never happen again?

She clenched her fists; all her body yearned in the darkness, her breasts, her lips . . . surely he was there, the fire burned, the voice sang. . . .

She gave a long shudder, and opened her eyes. There was the empty darkness, the little bed. . . .

"No lions or tigers," said the little voice, heavy with slumber.

She closed the door behind her. "Henry," she called down the stairs to her husband, "Juliet wants you to say good night to her. Come quickly, dear."

Chapter XIII

THE DAY before Christmas Michael went to call on Mrs. Lanyarde. He discovered the wealthy lady in a small house near the river, furnished in the style of the last century, which is to say that everything was uncomfortable. She received the archdeacon in her library, in which there still remained a few books. The essays of Mr. Emerson and Mr. Holmes, and the novels of Mrs. Glyn rested side by side upon shelves which were also devoted to pieces of bric-à-brac, and bits of jade of no value.

The angel wished Mrs. Lanyarde to increase her contribution to the cathedral; with this in mind, he set himself to describe the long and triumphant history of the Church. But he soon saw that she was not interested in the events which he portrayed with fire and relish. She did not care for the triumphs and conversions; she preferred to hear about those whom the Church had excluded.

" I have often thought," she said, " that it is a mistake to wish to convert so many people to the faith. If every one believed as we believe, we should find ourselves worshiping in the company of Jews, Negroes, and other nonsectarians. The Church would lose its dignity, my dear Doctor, which depends upon the social prominence of its members."

Michael replied, " The new cathedral will attract by

286

its glories twice as many worshipers as the old. Since the seating arrangements are equally restricted, we shall be able to exclude twice as many people as before."

A few minutes later he left the house with Mrs. Lanyarde's contribution, in the form of a promise, in his pocket. He went at once to see Mr. Cohen, the banker.

"What is the use," said Mr. Cohen, "of my contributing to a church where I cannot even get a seat to sit down?"

Michael gazed about him at the scrolled and paneled walls of the banker's study, on which were hung paintings by Goya, Memling, Reynolds, and Van Gogh. He leaned back in his chair, which seemed as soft to his bottom as a cloud, and blew a ring of smoke from one of Mr. Cohen's cigars in the direction of the ceiling, beamed with oak from an English manor house.

"Mr. Cohen," he said to him at last, "let us talk frankly together. Let us speak as one Jew to another."

"What?" exclaimed the banker. "How can that be?"

"I am also," replied Michael, "of Jewish extraction. And my youth was spent entirely in the company of Jews."

Mr. Cohen was astonished. "No," he exclaimed. A moment later he added, "I have a nephew who is blond, like you. Still, I would never have believed it, to look at you.

"Have another cigar," he said. "Put it in your pocket."

And he gazed at his visitor in a friendly way.

But presently he gave a sigh. "It is not easy," he said, "to be a Jew. Even God has grown tired of it. I don't blame Him; what pleasure did He ever have with us? What a marriage that was, between God and Israel."

"I remember it," said Michael.

"Yes," said Mr. Cohen. "Nothing but quarrels."

"You are a philosopher," said Michael.

"Every Jew is a philosopher," replied the banker, "if he stops to think. What else is there for him to be except a Christian? My grandparents had a little shop in Tratsk, in the Ukraine. They did no harm; but they were killed in a pogrom. Now their grandson should build a cathedral. Well, why not? We Jews are always building homes for other people to live in. Do the prophets sleep in the pyramids?"

"I, also," said Michael, "have no home."

"Nebich," said Mr. Cohen.

"Because I am rich," he continued, "I shake hands each day with the bishop and Mrs. Lanyarde. But it is my wealth which shakes hands with them, my Goyas and my Memlings — not my heart. My heart? Do they want my heart? On the end of a stick."

"Has it never occurred to you," asked Michael sensibly, "to turn Christian with the rest of us? For I believe that the Jewish religious practises do not interest you, although you help support the Temple."

Mr. Cohen leaned forward in his chair, and put his hand earnestly on Michael's knee. "You are right," he said; "religious exercises do not interest me. Getting up and sitting down, praying, fasting — what does that amount to? But do you think it is any better with a bishop than with a rabbi? What do you quarrel over, in your church? The reservation of the sacrament? All right — in the Temple, we have quarrels, too.

"No, my friend; if I do not turn Christian like so many others, it is not because of the religious practises. It is because I do not want my grandchildren to hate the Jews. There is too much hate in the world as it is; in this country it flourishes like the weed. Here even the poets hate one another. Very well, I stay a Jew, I do not go over on the side of the haters. I do not buy my way up, so that I too, can spit down on my people. Do you think I love the Jews so much? How can I tell, when I am one? But I am sick of those who hate them, because I am sick of hate. What we need is more politeness in the world. Let people shake hands and say, Come in.

" Do you think it is a pleasure to be kept out of everything?

"My grandparents were killed in a pogrom in the Ukraine, but they were poor people, gentle and sweet to everybody. Shall I shake hands with those who hated them, simply because it is an easy thing to do? Very well I will shake hands with them; here I am, let them come and shake hands with a Jew. Let them be polite to a Jew, and see how much better the world gets on for it."

He ceased; and, taking out a large handkerchief, mopped his brow, wet with the sweat of indignation.

" I respect your sentiments," replied Michael, " which are those of an obstinate man. In your words I recognize the spirit which, combined with guile and aided by the irresistible power of the Lord, made Israel invincible in the past. Nevertheless it is not as a Jew that I approach you, but as a business man."

Mr. Cohen sat back in his chair; his body relaxed, his face assumed an anxious expression. " Why didn't you say so," he asked, " in the first place? "

" I grieve for your grandparents," continued Michael. " But after all, that was in another land, and in a different time. I need not point out to you the advantages of the Church to this country in which you operate. It is the Church which saves the home, by confronting with a determined mien the practises of immorality. The home, following the Church, conforms to design, and consists of the father, the mother, and the child. That home, Mr.

Cohen, furnishes the basis for your credit in the markets of the world. The father produces, the mother buys, the child consumes. I ask you: can you do without it? Do you wish to see this country sunk in wickedness, the father drunk, the mother divorced, the child debauched? Would you like to see the mills idle, the mines closed, the farms overgrown with weeds?"

"God forbid," said Mr. Cohen.

"Against the dragons of sin," went on Michael in a voice which sounded strange to his own ears, "stands the Right Reverend Henry Brougham, lance in hand; and behind him rise the towers of the new St. Timothy's to be called St. Agatha's, drawing men's thoughts from ways of the flesh, encouraging their hearts to labor in the Vineyard."

The banker sighed. "Who should know better than I," he said, "where my credit comes from, and what a market is worth? My business and yours are the same, Doctor Michael. They go together. What do you want me to do; just tell me. Shall I endow a bay? Shall I give you a new altar?"

"An altar will do very well," said Michael wearily. He rose to go, and held out his hand. "I cannot promise you a pew at St. Agatha's," he said, "but you will find a number of free seats in the rear."

So saying he left. But as he walked slowly down the marble steps of Mr. Cohen's great house, he shook his head with an air of bewilderment. "What has come over me?" he said, half aloud. "What is the matter with me?

"Doctor Michael, archdeacon of St. Timothy's, were you once an angel?"

Chapter XIV

IN the meanwhile the bishop faced, in the privacy of his room, a thought he could not very well avoid. It was that Julia, his wife, had suffered a change of spirit toward him. It was hard to put his finger on the change itself; but there it was, he felt it. Not that she was cold to him; for one thing, she had no reason to refuse him anything, since he asked for nothing. Between his room and hers, the door remained closed except during the day; and things had been so since before Juliet was born.

Yet he was aware of a subtle difference in the spiritual atmosphere of his home. Some element of peace was gone; and at the same time he believed that his wife was enjoying an inner happiness from which he felt himself excluded. But perhaps happiness was not exactly the word for it; gaiety would be better. An inner gaiety, then — strangely without joy, he thought. And most decidedly without peace.

He was accustomed to being excluded from her dreams; he knew that there was a part of her life that he had never quite satisfied. But it was a part he had never meant to satisfy, in any gross sense; a part of life it were wiser and healthier to deny altogether, or at least as far as possible. Nevertheless, he had always believed that her dreams had their center around him; and that she found, in her life as a wife, if not all the terrifying passion of youth, at least the sweet, long-breathed duty of womanhood.

Now where were her dreams? He felt that they were gone astray. At the same time he found it impossible to believe it.

Nothing was altered; her small, fair face greeted him in the morning with its customary smile. Did he imagine that sometimes, when he watched her, she looked away with a troubled expression? Her voice, when she addressed him, was warm and serene; the housekeeping went on without disturbance. When he was in his study, all was made quiet for him; the house was in order, the toys stood upon the nursery shelves, the maids went calmly about their work. The wifely presence abated no fraction of its graciousness.

And yet, there was something withdrawn about her. She seemed to be gazing at him from a distance: not that distance from woman to man, which lay in her eyes after their wedding-night; a greater distance still, a distance of the heart. It was as though that part of her to which he had addressed himself with tight-shut eyes and beating pulses, no longer asked of him even the grace of a denial.

Well, then, what was it? What had happened? The bishop arose and walked absently to and fro, his hands behind his back; he held a colloquy with himself. I have been a good husband, he said; I have been faithful in thought and deed; I have succeeded in my profession, I am a bishop, and generally admired. My wife also admires me; but there is a snake in Eden.

Nothing has happened — of that I am sure. That is, nothing there are words for. But are there words for everything? I have always thought so, but what of that? Let us say that she is weak and feminine, which is, after all, no more than might be expected. Very well, I ought not to be surprised in that event. She has her moods, what of it?

Come; let me put my trust in the Lord, who has already sent me an angel to help me with my cathedral.

He stood still, and stared at the wall, while his face assumed an incredulous expression. Had he forgotten the unearthly beauty of his assistant? He had never told his wife that they were entertaining an angel. He thought: she sees him simply as a young man possessed of indescribable charm.

The bishop gave a groan, which he stifled at once. He began to think back, he began to put two and two together. She is fond of him, he thought; there is no doubt about that. She is decidedly fond of him. He remembered she had invited Michael to help trim the tree. He counted the number of times the archdeacon had been asked to dinner; then he reckoned up the number of weeks since his first appearance.

And he walked more slowly up and down, while his face grew longer and longer.

Now that he thought of it, he was obliged to admit that a change had taken place in Michael as well. When he looked at his assistant, through the microscope of anxiety, the bishop saw something disturbing: it was evident that Michael had taken on a certain earthly quality. To-day he was an archdeacon first, and an angel second. An earthly lassitude, a mortal dulness, had overclouded the pure radiance of that first appearance. He seemed to have something on his mind; he had an anxious look, more the property of archdeacons than of angels. Was Julia the reason?

The bishop stopped in his pacing, and frowned. Perhaps he had been a little too much inclined to forget the divine nature of his assistant. In that case, he was being properly punished. Michael was a great help to him, there was no doubt about it; he had taken over the most pressing burdens from the ecclesiastical load. The bishop had gained an invaluable assistant. But what had he lost?

The problem was too much for him, it overwhelmed him. Was Julia too fond of Michael? Was Michael, in turn, more fond of Julia than it was right for an archdeacon to be? The bishop knew what was right for an archdeacon; but was Michael an archdeacon or an angel?

There, he thought, he kept forgetting: of course Michael was an angel. Didn't that make it all much simpler? Being divine, Michael loved Julia with a pure and heavenly love. The bishop determined to give his assistant a holiday directly after the New Year. He said to him already, in imagination, Come, Doctor, you are losing your freshness; these mortal cares are too much for you. Go away for a while, and refresh your spirit with less material considerations.

That would solve everything — supposing, as he supposed, that there was anything to solve. He must make a firm angel of Michael again, that was all there was to it; if necessary, he would even tell Julia. Do not think too much of our friend, he would say in a light manner, for he is divine, and not meant for mortal love.

But a sudden thought made him pause. Was the divine spirit really unfitted for mortal love? He thought of the men of Sodom, and the visitors at Lot's house; he remembered Io, Danäe, Leda: he thought of other women visited by the Godhead in one form or another; and a faint perspiration moistened his brow.

No, he exclaimed, this is monstrous. And he summoned to his aid the resources of comparative theology. What had the heathen gods to do with the heavenly hosts?

Theseus, Perseus, Herakles . . . were these sun myths to be taken seriously? Sons of a god and a mortal woman, they represented their countries on the field of battle. Only the Son of Man ever interested himself in religious disputes.

Nevertheless, the picture of Leda caressed by a swan, caused the bishop to tremble. He believed that his weakness was caused by indignation, and in the trouble of his mind retired to the oldest fastnesses of faith. Feeling that the tempter was near by, he addressed him by means of the formula,

"Get thee behind me, Satan."

At once he felt more peaceful; but at the same time he also felt a little ridiculous. "Forgive me," he said humbly in the direction of Heaven, "for doubting Your intentions. What — am I to imagine that You would send an angel into my house for the purpose of seducing my wife?"

So saying, full of suspicion, his heart ready to burst with jealousy, the bishop descended the stairs to the study, where he could hear the happy voices of Michael and his wife laughing above the Christmas tree.

Chapter XV

THE LITTLE tree bloomed and blossomed under their busy fingers; there ripened upon the evergreen boughs a miraculous harvest of colored balls, cornucopias, peppermint canes, and strings of pop-corn. On the very tip was set a silver star, a double star in honor, as Michael gravely explained, of a shepherd boy who later became a king. "Juliet," he said, "believes that all fairy tales are histories. By the light of modern exegesis, it is the other way around; but the truth lies in between."

"Don't be tiresome," said Julia. "This is Christmas Eve."

Michael smiled at her; he held in his hand an angel, or a fairy, made of wax, with silken wings. "Do you know what this is?" he asked. "It is a sylph. They were often seen in the fifteenth century. They are little creatures of the air, whose home is in that element. This portrait is in wax; but there is no reason to believe that the sylphs no longer exist simply because we do not hear of them."

"Nonsense," said Julia wisely, "that's an angel. Look at its face; it has a heavenly expression. It looks like you, Michael. Don't put it too near the candle, it will melt. There — that's a good place for it."

She moved busily about the tree, her hands, like deft birds, darting in and out of the branches.

Michael was happy; he felt that he was engaged upon a delightful occupation. From this tree nothing would develop of interest to the cathedral, or the community; it had no moral purpose. It was not a part of his duty as assistant to the bishop to arrange wreaths of pop-corn, or hang up little Christmas apples for a child.

"This tree," he remarked, "reminds me of a time when every one was happy. Of course, where I came from, we had no such trees. But we had festivals; and we had lamps not unlike these candles. Perhaps I am mistaken when I think that every one was happy. No one was comfortable; and there were many quarrels. But I was happy once, I think."

"And now?" asked Julia gently.

"I am homesick," replied Michael simply.

Julia wished to say, "For what are you homesick?" but a feeling of delicacy restrained her. Instead she murmured politely,

"Yes . . ."

Michael did not reply at once. He swung an apple on his finger by a loop of colored twine, and followed it with his eyes. "You wonder," he said at last, "what I, who never had an earthly home, can find to be homesick for. What do I know of children and households, of mortal cares and earthly responsibilities? But you are wrong, Julia; a warm hearth often brings to the homeless wanderer an unexpected sadness. He thinks: I could be happy with this; and he remembers the past, when he was happy, in another land, or in another time. For every one has been happy once, no matter how long ago."

"I know," said Julia, "I was happy too, when I was a child. I dreamed and dreamed; and I was always the heroine of everything. I thought something wonderful would happen to me." And she gave a rueful smile.

"At first," said Michael, "almost before I can remember, I lived with my people. It was a rude life, but a free one; we had no past, and as far as we knew, no future. We lived like the Arabs at the edge of the desert; in the evening we could see the sun go down like a poppy in the west, and the blue flower of night unfold among the eastern hills. Then, in the purple darkness, fires were lighted, and everywhere there was singing. In the spring the desert flowers perfumed the air; and the grass seemed to dance under our feet.

"That is what I remember, Julia; and the beauty and innocence of our youth, before men drew us to their battles."

"In a minute," thought Julia, "he will kiss me again." And she shut her eyes and held her breath, half in delight and half in terror.

But hearing her husband upon the stairs, she opened her eyes again in a hurry. "How you must miss it," she said, with a frightened laugh; "poor Michael . . ."

Michael continued without noticing the interruption: "The life of freedom was soon over. We had our duties . . . we made laws, or helped to make them, and we upheld the edicts we had helped to make. We learned strange forms of suffering; I found myself often in the company of men with emaciated faces who scourged their pitiable bodies and died in an ecstasy of pain. My duties led me into the darkest cellars as well as the most beautiful cathedrals; often I found the cellar illuminated with a holy light, and the cathedral dark. I taught the law, and visited the sick; I moved in a world of sorrow, where men denied themselves joy in order to be innocent. Demons with dreadful faces and voluptuous forms rose from those struggles of flesh and spirit.

"Where am I now? In a land where those who do not enjoy anything make laws to deprive others of their pleasures; where God and prosperity are worshiped as one, and men are taught to hate before they are taught to love. Since God is prosperous I must serve prosperity; since His people hate, I must hate; and when they build cathedrals, I must arrange for contributions. Do you wonder that I am homesick, Julia — although whether it is the past for which I long, or this quiet hearth where man, with woman at his side, forgets the battle and the pain, I cannot tell you."

The bishop, who had entered the room during this speech, replied,

"God made man in His image, Doctor. The battles that we wage on earth are fought in His name; and Heaven rewards the victor with eternal peace."

"It is you," said Michael shortly, "who are the theologian, not I." And turning to the tree, he hung the apple on the branch next to the wax figure with silk wings.

The bishop remembered that Michael was an angel. "No, no," he said hurriedly, "you probably know much more about it than I do." And he looked gloomily at his wife, who was, however, paying no attention to him.

"Michael," she cried, "catch this;" and threw across to him a package wrapped in tissue-paper, and tied with red ribbon. "That's for you," she said, "but you mustn't open it yet. Put it at the foot of the tree, and wait for to-morrow."

The bishop moved uncomfortably; he felt that he was being left out of things. "Yes," he said uncertainly, "in matters of dogma you are naturally wiser than I am, Doctor."

"Henry," said Julia sweetly, "must you talk business? It's Christmas Eve."

"Business?" exclaimed the bishop, bewildered; "no, really, my love . . . business?"

"We've the tree to do," said Julia.

"Here's a present for the cook. Put it there, Michael, next to nurse's. Isn't it fun? I love to watch their faces, they're so sweet and grateful. And Juliet's so serious about it; she's afraid they mightn't like their presents."

"Business," said the bishop reproachfully; "Julia."

"Were we talking business, Michael?"

But Michael turned away from him.

"What do I know of dogma?" he cried petulantly. "Am I a bishop? I come when I am called."

"I should think," began the bishop with dignity, "that being an angel . . ."

"Michael," cried Julia, "look what you're doing. You'll upset the tree."

". . . an angel," went on the bishop bravely; but no one heard him.

"There," said Julia, "now look; all the pop-corn is broken. We'll have to throw it on the tree and make believe it's snow. Oh, dear, everything goes wrong. Really, Henry — was that necessary?"

"Was what necessary, my love? As I was saying . . ."

"Here," said Julia busily to Michael, "you hold the string, and I'll tie it up again."

Her bright face bent, pouting, over Michael's hand; but before she had tied the knot, her own were trembling. She moved away quickly. "What white hands you have, Michael," she said evenly.

The bishop felt his throat contract. "Perhaps I am in the way," he said stiffly. "Shall I go?"

300

She gave him a bright smile, but absent-minded. "Go along, dear, if you have business," she said; "we won't need you. Michael and I will do the tree together. It's almost done, anyway."

"You don't need me?" croaked the bishop incredulously.

"Of course not. Do go along now, and leave us alone."

"I am not needed," said the bishop. And he went heavily out of the room and out of the house. They heard the front door close.

His heart was beating heavily; a dull misery burned behind his eyes. What was happening in there, in that softly lighted room behind him? He saw his wife smile absent-mindedly, he heard her say again, "Go along, dear, we don't need you. . . ." How cruel it sounded, out there in the dark. To be in the way — to be sent off — such a thing had never happened to him before. Well, it had happened now. . . . His heart sank low in his breast.

He stood in the street in bitter loneliness; and his thoughts trod his heart down with heavy feet. How beautiful they looked together, the divine stranger and the smiling wife. He saw her turn to Michael, bend over the angelic hands . . . He saw her lift her face, he saw her eyes grow tender. . . .

It was hard to tell where all the pain came from. If they kissed . . . The blood rushed to his head, he felt sick and dizzy. But whether they did or not — they had sent him out, alone, in the dark. They didn't care where he went or what happened to him, Julia didn't care. She had robbed him of dignity, of all that made him a man, and a bishop. She no longer looked up to him. All she saw was Michael. . . .

His dignity? What was his dignity against the heavenly hosts? what helplessness . . . what helplessness.

He tried to steady his thoughts, to be humble and calm. But all he felt was pain; and a dull rage, like a child's. It passed, and left him weak and cold, with dragging limbs. He turned, half blindly, to the cathedral. . . . It was not God he wanted, but his business — his cool, mothering business. The street lamps were ringed with fog; a fog seemed to envelop him, to blow him along between the houses whose tops he could not see, himself a fog-like figure, stiff with misery, starched with woe.

As he entered the cathedral, the first snow fell softly over the city. Below, in the distance, by the river, a freight went by, clanging its lonely bell.

Chapter XVI

THE SNOW touched with a whispering sound the windows
of the bishop's house, where Michael and Julia stood gazing at the tree whose candles were already lit. Their hands
were clasped, like children in a swing between them, trembling and happy. The swing went up a little, and back
again, and the fingers clasped one another tighter.

"*Stille Nacht,*" sang Julia to herself, "*heilige Nacht.*"
She looked peacefully around the room. "I suppose
you must go soon, Michael," she said.

"Not yet," said Michael. He remained silent, musing.
"I am happy," he said at last. "Why should I go?"

"I'm glad," said Julia. Then she said doubtfully,
"Won't there be services to-night, and Christmas music at
the cathedral?"

"There is more music here," said Michael.

Something in his tone made her heart beat out a warning. She tried to draw her hand away, but he held it
firmly. "I hear no music," she said hurriedly; "only a
freight train's bell . . ."

"Listen," he said; "be still. All around us there is
singing."

"Ought we to listen?" she asked faintly.

"We cannot help it," he answered.

"No," she whispered; "how can we?"

"You hear it, too," he said.

303

"The carillon," she murmured, "from the cathedral."

But he shook his head. "This is no Christmas carol, Julia," he said.

She turned and looked at him; she held her eyes level with his. And in that moment her heart ceased its uncertain stir, and waited, free and cool.

"What is it, then?" she said. "Tell me, my dear."

And she threw back her head with a proud and tender gesture.

The perfume of the tree, warmed by the candles, sweetened the air. There was a fire in his eyes; blue, blazing, they held her still as a charmed bird, her throat alone trembling. As he drew her close, she had time to notice everything, — the windows blue with night, the glittering tree, one corner of a curtain caught in a fold. . . . This was what she had been waiting for all those long weeks. She did not know what it would be like; but she knew it would not be like her wedding-night. She thought that she would not be frightened; but she was mistaken.

And Michael, too, felt in his veins a long-lost, heavenly fire melting the mortal coils in which he had wound himself. It seemed to him that he heard about his ears the thunders of the host, the music and hallelujahs of his brothers, long silent; their shadowy wings passed and repassed about his head, filling the room with a radiance he remembered. Gone were the bands of the cleric in which he had dressed himself; nothing was left to him but the emotion of which he was created, the love and the glory, the beauty and the longing.

Was it a mortal woman he held in his arms? He could not tell. It seemed to him like once, long ago, in a garden, before a tree; it was his youth he held there, close to his breast. His brothers crowded about him, their voices sang in his heart the lonely and lovely music, their wing-tips brushed his shoulders. He bent his head to hers; with closed eyes, they dreamed of Heaven and youth, of Eden, and of joy.

I remember, I remember . . .

Yes, it was true . . . before evil, before the tree, in the world's morning, there was this longing, there was this joy . . . this heavenly pain. . . .

Julia was the first to rouse herself. "Michael," she breathed; "we mustn't."

He did not answer, only pressed her closer to his heart. She rested her head against his shoulder, her hair making a little golden cloud below his cheek. "It's so strange," she whispered. "What has happened? Is it I? You seem to have great shadowy wings . . . I'm so silly . . . my heart is beating so . . ."

"Be still," he answered, "it is I. Dream yet a little."

She moved uneasily in his arms; her hands fluttered against him. "I can't," she said. "I daren't any more . . . it frightens me. This isn't right, Michael. We must stop."

And she made to disengage herself. But he held her tight; he was all angel, his spirit, burning, passed over her mortal strength like a flame. . . . "Stop?" he cried; "we cannot stop, my Julia. See, this room is filled with divine and happy beings. Heaven bends to earth to leave this kiss upon your mouth, and the choirs break into shouts of hallelujah. Shall I shed this mortal coat, and fold you in my wings? You would die, my darling, of longing. Close your eyes; do not look too carefully. Let me seal them with this kiss, and this.

"Once, when I was young, I heard such music, long ago . . ."

She strained backward, away from his breast. "This is a sin," she moaned. "What are we doing?"

305

He paused; the divine voice faltered. "Hush," he said, laying his finger across her lips. "Hush, my darling. Do not speak of sin. Speak of joy."

"I cannot, I cannot. . . . It is wrong."

He seemed to shudder; touched by a mortal chill, his arms loosed their hold upon her. "You will drive me away," he whispered, "if you say such things."

"Yes," she answered desperately, "I must. It is true."

"Let me love you," he pleaded; "only let me love you."

"No, no, I am frightened. This is too much. . . ."

"Do not drive me away as you did once, long ago. . . ."

She answered in a voice infinitely remote, infinitely sad, "I do not forget. I do what I must."

And still he fought for his life against what man had made him. "Wait," he cried to the shadowy figures which thronged around him, watching his struggle with sad and pitying faces, "do not go yet. Help me; speak to her of joy, cover her with your wings, sing to her of Heaven and earth, whisper to her of paradise."

The ethereal forms gathered about her, enveloped her in their wings, sang to her with the voices of her childhood:

Julia, remember . . .

The fresh, pure joy, the young, sweet rapture, the wonder . . .

Her eyes closed: half in a dream she lifted her face to receive again that kiss, which she felt less upon her lips than upon her heart.

My darling, my darling . . .

What happiness.

But again, and for the last time, she tore herself away. "Michael," she cried, her hands in front of her face, "what are we thinking of? We are mad."

She stood staring at him with wild, shocked eyes. "You," she said, "of all people . . . and I. An archdeacon — my husband's helper . . ."

Tears gathered in her eyes and ran unheeded down her face. "It was my fault," she said bravely. "I have only myself to blame. I should never have tried . . . I should have known . . . my child . . . my duty . . ."

She broke off, speechless. And Michael, too, said nothing; he stood still, while the fire died slowly in his heart. Duty . . . he was an archdeacon.

What else could he expect? Had he forgotten all that had happened in the world?

He was cold; he felt the bands of the clerical collar about his neck, his ears hummed with silence.

"Forgive me," he said quietly; "I will go now. I should not have spoken of joy — no, not in this world."

She came up to him, her hands outstretched, pleading. She no longer feared him; an overwhelming pity for him filled her heart, pity for herself, for the sad two of them. "Michael," she said, "it is I who must ask forgiveness. I wanted you to love me. I didn't know it would be like that.

"Perhaps I love you, too. I don't know. It was too much. It frightened me."

She took his hands, and pressed them against her cheeks. "I don't know what I'll do," she said; "I've got to think.

"Go now, my dear."

He took her once more, gently, in his arms; he kissed her cheek, dabbled with tears. "Good night," he said. "Do not be frightened. Eden is far away."

So saying, Doctor Michael, Archdeacon of St. Timothy's, turned and left the house.

She put the candles out on the tree, one by one. When the tree was dark, she went soberly up the stairs. At

Juliet's door she stopped to listen, but all was still. On tiptoe, then, she crossed the hall to her own room, and shut the door. Her mind was empty; she was exhausted, she thought of nothing.

But Juliet was not asleep; excitement had roused her long before the dawn. She sat up in bed, and looked at the place where her stocking was hung. Was it full yet? She couldn't tell, it was so dark. She wanted to get up, and go over to see; but prudence restrained her. Suppose her mother had been wrong about the lions and tigers? Under the bedcovers they couldn't very well reach her; but on the bare floor, in her nighty . . . what an easy morsel she would be. A lonely freight went by outside with a faint hoot at the river's edge; she shivered a little, it made such a lonesome sound. With a sigh she reached for her doll, Maryannlouise, who slept, tidy and untroubled, beside her. " Never mind," she said to the doll; " go to sleep now."

Outside in the night, she heard the soft, spitting snow; and a peal of bells from the cathedral. Her own eyes closed again; the little hand fell back from the doll's smooth face. " Don't be afraid," she murmured. " Nothing can hurt you. God won't let it.

" Merry Christmas to-morrow morning, Maryannlouise."

Chapter XVII

In the early morning, Michael presented himself at the house of Doctor Wutheridge, Lanyarde professor of Semitic languages at the University. He was pale and weary; his eyes burned deep in his white face, like low blue flames. Although the sun was barely above the roof-tops, he discovered the professor seated at table, enjoying, in the snowy light, a breakfast of fruit, cereal, eggs, bacon, waffles, toast, and coffee; and reading the paper, over which he uttered occasional groans.

"Well," he said, "what do you think: Mr. Litvinoff has demanded that all the nations of the world lay down their arms. But Monsieur Boncourt and Lord Cushenden have courageously pointed out that such a scheme would leave their countries open to the danger of an invasion. These men are patriots; but they also deserve to be called philosophers."

Putting down the paper, he regarded Michael with a gloomy countenance. "There will always be wars," he declared, "until every man, woman, and child is enrolled as a common soldier, and obliged to join the army in the field. When that occurs, there will no longer be any one to exclude from that glorious military company; and an experience common to all will no longer attract any one.

"Will you join me in some Christmas toast and coffee?"

"I am in mortal trouble," said Michael.

The professor buttered a slice of bread. "It does not surprise me," he said. "However, continue."

"I am in love," said Michael, "with a married woman."

"You are right," said the professor: "that is a mortal trouble. It is the curse of human beings to desire always what does not belong to them. It was Epictetus who said: True education lies in learning to distinguish what is ours from what does not belong to us."

And he added, with his mouth full,

"Did you put me down on the list?"

"She is a good woman," said Michael, "but she loves me. As archdeacon of St. Timothy's I can find no excuse for such a passion."

"Certainly not," agreed the professor.

"But as an angel," continued Michael, "it fills me with felicity. It reminds me of the time when all was love, before there was evil in the world, and when man's only duty was joy, which he shared with the angels.

"Alas," he added, sighing, "she cannot rid herself of evil. Like Eve she banishes me again from paradise, by talking to me of right and wrong. Imagine: there I stand, while the divine fire dies in my veins — overwhelmed and embarrassed by the consciousness of original sin. The angel disappears, to make room for the archdeacon who is naturally horrified at such behavior."

"Naturally," said the professor. He added, sensibly, "Will her husband divorce her?"

"Her husband," said Michael, "does not favor divorce, except under one extreme condition, which her purity forbids."

"Tst," said the professor; "well, there you are."

And he shook his head disconsolately.

"Perhaps it would be possible," he said hopefully, "to

have the marriage annulled. Such things have happened: I notice that the marriage of an English duke to an American duchess has recently been declared invalid after twenty years of wedded bliss. The two children of their union are not affected by the decree which makes sinners of their parents. According to the opinion of an eminent and scholarly divine who was questioned in the matter, the parents may have lived together, but they were not married. Nevertheless, it is his contention that the children remain legitimate and of noble blood. As they belong to another church, this decision, moreover, makes no difference whatever."

"The practises of one church," replied Michael, "do not conform to those of another. Nor do the customs of the past lend themselves to the present. David, King of Judah, sent Uriah the Hittite to his death, in order to possess himself of Uriah's wife, the lovely Bath-Sheba. It was a scandal in Jewry; he was first roundly scolded by Nathan, the bitter apple of God; and later punished; but he acquired Bath-Sheba. Still, I am not in David's position."

He held out his hands pleadingly to the professor. "Tell me," he cried, "how can I possess this woman whose face is the face of Eve dreaming in the garden, whose heart is full of joy, like my youth?"

"My dear Doctor Michael," answered the professor, "if your bishop will give you no other cause for divorce than adultery, then you must commit adultery."

"Ah," said Michael. "Hum."

"Unfortunately," the professor went on, "that is impossible."

At the archdeacon's startled expression, Professor Wutheridge allowed himself a dry smile. "You forget," he said, "that you are an angel. And nowhere in my researches have I come upon an angel of Semitic extraction capable of performing such a feat.

" You are immortal; a spirit, a child of light, a pure and perfect being. How can you feel a mortal hunger? How can you, not being made of earth, experience an earthly desire? What you feel is a divine discontent, an eternal longing. Do not mistake this emotion for love. The love of man and woman is a different thing entirely. It is full of pain, and human hunger; in the unending desert of eternity, it is an illusion of comfort, it is a mirage of consolation. It is also, in addition, an irresistible impulse of a purely animal nature. I know nothing about it myself, but I have studied the poets.

" No, no, my friend, the love you offer your lady would first frighten, and then disappoint her. It is not meant for earth. Remember that your discontent is divine, and your longing endless; and that you can neither experience nor give earthly satisfaction. That is, perhaps, a little sad for you; but such an explanation would not satisfy your mistress, who would expect at least a satyr, after so much longing."

" You are right," said Michael : " how could I possess her? I might have thought that out for myself, with more time."

He seized the professor's hand in both of his. " Thank you," he exclaimed, " for saving me from such an impossible attempt. I can see that the longing on which we immortals feed, and of which we are created, is no food for mortal men and women. We can only speak to them of a beauty not of this earth; we can only visit them in dreams, and stir their hearts with a vague longing, troublingly sweet, and soon forgotten."

So saying, and with a face from which every trace of anxiety had vanished, he turned to go. " Good-by," he said with a radiant smile; "God will reward you."

"Good-by," said the professor. "Don't forget to put me on the list."

With these words he turned back to his paper, in which he found the following piece of news:

Philadelphia, March 14 — The first female statue of early date to be found in Mesopotamia, together with bronze and silver objects of great intrinsic and historical value, has been uncovered at Ur of the Chaldees in the ruins of the remarkable Temple of the Moon, excavated by the joint expedition of the British Museum and the University of Pennsylvania Museum.

Vessels in which the last meal of Sumerian priests was cooked more than 4,000 years ago have been dug from their mausoleum of sand. Coffins of hammered copper were unexpected finds.

Among the fragments which combined to make up vases and other things of alabaster or diorite dedicated by kings and pious worshipers in the shrine of the moon goddess, was found a diorite statue of the goddess Bau, patroness of the poultry yard. The statue represents a squat and solid figure in an elaborately flounced dress seated on a throne supported by angels. It is the first statue which has been found complete, for only the nose is missing, and it is the first female statue of early date ever found in Mesopotamia.

The professor closed his eyes luxuriously. "Doctor Michael would have enjoyed that," he thought; "I should have shown it to him."

Chapter XVIII

THE CITY lay shining under the white fall of snow; the sun burst into a thousand sparkles, the houses stood out boldly in the clear, blue air. "Come," they seemed to say, "this is something elegant." Already little children with shiny new sleds coasted on the hills in the park, calling to one another with happy voices. Every one was gay because it was Christmas, and because the weather was fine.

At the bishop's house all was in readiness for Juliet's Christmas party. She had seen the tree, she had received her presents — overcome with surprise, as always, that there was more than one, and presently with weariness because there were so many; she had given gifts to the nurse, the cook, the maids, peering up into their faces from a position level with their knees, to make sure that all was well; and she had given a box of cigars to Mr. Sams, the policeman on the block. There was nothing more to do, then, but wait for Potter, her only guest. For Julia wisely thought that on such an exciting occasion, and at four-going-on-five, one guest was enough.

She herself had not slept all night, although she had decided nothing. She was weary, but she was busy, and for that reason relaxed from anxiety; though she knew that before the day was over she would have to come to a decision. What it was she was obliged to decide she really did not know. That she should leave her husband had never entered her head. Nor did she mean to sin, exactly. Possibly the decision would arrive of itself, without too clear thought — just as the situation itself had arrived apparently without her having had much to do with it.

Without . . . ? Well, at least, she hadn't meant it to happen just that way. That is to say, of course . . .

She bit her lip, and bent to straighten the ribbon around Juliet's waist. " Be nice to Potter, dear," she said to her. " Give him his present very sweetly."

" I'll very sweetly give him a little kiss," said Juliet. " That is," she added doubtfully, " if he lets me."

But when Potter finally arrived, his feet in their boots and leggings powdered with snow, his cheeks red from the clear frosty air, she simply looked at him and turned away. He was not surprised; nevertheless, while his nurse undid his jacket, he watched Juliet out of the corner of his eye. And as soon as he was free, he trotted over to where she sat squatting on her heels, playing with a toy from the tree.

" Look at my suit," he said, placing himself in front of her.

And he stuck out his stomach, over which his mother had placed a velvet coat and a shirt with lace.

" Look, please," he said.

" Yes," she replied. " I see it." But she did not look up.

" Don't you love me in my party suit?" he asked in surprise.

" It's very nice," said Juliet calmly. She arose, and went over to her mother. " Mother," she cried with her utmost gaiety, " do you remember how I gave Mr. Sams a present? What did he say, mother? Did he say I was a sweet little girl?"

"Yes," said Julia without enthusiasm. "But just the same, darling . . ."

"And do you remember," went on Juliet, "how I gave the presents to everybody? And how I came down in the morning, and saw the tree, and I said, oh . . ."

Julia took her daughter firmly by the hand. "Come," she said; "let's give Potter his present now — shall we?"

They went over to the tree, and found a box marked with Potter's name. Juliet held it out to him without a word; he took it silently and started to unwrap it. When he saw that it contained a clown made of wood, and able to move its arms and legs, his face fell. "What else have you got for me?" he asked, looking hopefully at the tree.

Julia smiled and sighed; she had known what to expect. She unhooked a small drum from a branch, and held it out to him. At the sight of the drum he grew gloomier than ever.

"I don't like that," he said. "I don't like my presents very much."

And he sat down with a sigh, to play with his clown.

Juliet's face quivered. She approached her mother with her head bent, and put her arms about her knees. "I haven't any clown," she said in a trembling voice. "I love a clown. You gave my clown to Potter. It's my tree. It's my party. You gave him my lovely clown."

She began to weep. "I haven't any party suit," she sobbed. "I haven't any nice new party suit."

Potter paid no attention to her. "Here I go jumping," he remarked, throwing the doll into the air, "and here I fall down, bang."

"Darling," said Julia, hugging her daughter, whose heart was broken, and wiping her nose from which the tears also were running, "it was you who gave the clown to Potter — don't you remember? It's because it was

316

your party that you gave the clown away. Nobody else could possibly give the clown away, at your very own party . . . you gave it away because you loved it. That was a very sweet thing to do. That's the nicest thing of all, to give away the things you like yourself. That's a grown-up thing to do."

Juliet's sobs ceased. "Did I give the clown away all myself?" she asked.

"You did, my lamb."

"Was I sweet, mother, to give him my clown?"

"Yes, darling, you were sweet . . ."

Smiling and gracious, though a little inclined to hiccup, Juliet marched over and sat down beside Potter.

"That's the funniest clown," she said. "Look how he jumps."

"I can jump, if I want to," said Potter.

And then, surprisingly he added,

"You have a nice dress, too."

That was enough: leaning forward, she enclosed his head in her arms, and gave him a kiss like a little bird, on the cheek. Then going to the tree, she reached up on tiptoe and took down the angel. "Here," she said, "you can have this. I don't want it any more."

"Say thank you," said the governess, hopefully.

"I don't want to," said Potter.

And he added, not unreasonably,

"I don't like it, anyhow."

Julia, watching the two of them, found her thoughts taking shape again, almost without her knowing it. What was it she had said to Juliet? "That's a grown-up thing to do." To give away the thing you wanted most of all. . . . But what was it she wanted so much? Was there anything she wanted more than Juliet?

Poor soul, she thought, she's all alone, really, except

for me. There was Henry, of course, but he was so busy; and she and Juliet were women together, she could almost say friends together. Not friends, perhaps, as one could be with a little brother or sister of one's own; but still, they understood each other. Why was there no little sister for Juliet to play with, and whisper to?

There might be, of course. Strange, how it made her heart beat to think of it. But she was changed; she wasn't the same any more. Something had happened to her.

She had to face it; something was aroused in her now, something she had never had to face before. She didn't know what it was exactly; but it felt like longing. Not like the old dreams: this was new and heavy, this was in her throat, in her breasts, in her whole body. She clenched her hands: what was she to do with it?

There was beauty in it, too — even in the pain. But how could she ever reach it, how could she ever come to it? If she went to Henry . . . Beauty? She gave a dry sob.

No, Henry would give her no beauty. But if he gave her life to carry, wasn't that beauty, too? Wasn't it beauty enough? Must she have everything?

Henry could give her life to carry . . . another child, like Juliet all her own, made of her dreams, her desires, her blood and bone. . . .

Yes, there was peace in that; it spoke to her heart with peace. Quiet again, serene, she turned to face herself. Was this, then, what she wanted — another child, for Juliet's sake, (or for her own, what was the difference)? Those long, slow, dreaming days, the new life heavy in her, under her heart . . . the months at the breast, the tiny, sweet, helpless hands . . . why had she been so long without it?

Soon Juliet would be grown indeed; and who would

318

need her then? She stood very still; with eyes which saw nothing she stood staring at the children. Already the longing had turned inward: the fertile fields of her nature, warmed for a moment by an unseasonable sun, dreamed of the harvest.

She thought no more of Michael — not then, not yet. There would be time for that later, in the long days to come. He had taught her heart; what more did she want of him?

He had not said it was a sin to love.

It was no sin to love — no, not even that way, not with all the hunger of her body. Henry was wrong; she would tell him, she would make him see.

She shook her head slowly. She could never make him see. She would never feel, in his frightened arms, the rapture, the pain, of that unforgettable moment before the tree. She would close her eyes and bear it — as he would, too. And behind her closed eyes — whose face would she see? Her whole body trembled; she took a long, sighing breath. There was no help for it, she had no courage for anything else. Or was hers the stricter courage? "That's a grown-up thing to do. . . ."

Something told her, at that moment, that she would never, in all her life, be able to answer that question. She bowed her head.

Chapter XIX

THE WINTER passed; and in the spring, with the new life stirring within her, she walked in the Mall among the children, between the flowering trees. The carousel was open, she could hear the music, gay and out of tune, as the children rode around and around on the wooden horses, lions and giraffes. The first yellow tulips were out, in beds below the rocks; like them she drank in the sun, untroubled and grateful.

She sat on a bench, near the sweet green grass, and gazed out across the drive at the city misty in the soft spring light. The pigeons strutted at her feet; a robin sang, near by, three watery notes, his head tilted to one side.

She smiled, and sighed; and the man sitting at the other end of the bench turned and looked at her. "How do you do, Mrs. Brougham," he said.

At her slight start of surprise he arose, and bowed. "You must pardon me," he said. "I am a contributor to your husband's cathedral."

She smiled wearily. "How nice," she remarked. And she added, with a polite wave of her hand, "What a lovely day."

"As a matter of fact," he continued, "I was present on one occasion when you came to join your daughter in the

Mall. I was talking to Doctor Michael at the time; and you came up to us with your cheeks red from the cold. Naturally you would not remember me; but I have more reason not to forget you."

"Yes," said Julia, "I remember. It was before Christmas." And she gave him an amiable smile.

"Have you had a pleasant winter?" she asked. "I'm so glad it's spring again."

The professor shrugged his shoulders. "My winters are all the same," he said; "one is like another. But tell me — what has happened to my friend, the archdeacon? I do not see him any more in the Mall with your charming daughter, or at the cathedral on Sundays."

It was a moment or two before she answered. "He has gone home," she said at last, evenly. "He left us soon after Christmas. I think he found the city a little distressing."

The professor nodded his head wisely. "I am not surprised," he declared. "So he has gone home again. Hm."

And he added somewhat plaintively, "I was hoping to ask him some more questions.

"Ah, well — perhaps he could not have answered them.

"And your husband, Mrs. Brougham, the bishop? Is he very busy? I suppose that his plans for the new cathedral absorb most of his time."

She bent her head. "Yes," she said in a low voice; "he is very busy. It has taken all his time this winter . . . naturally."

"I believe," remarked the professor, "that it will cost many millions of dollars; and that it will take rank among the greatest cathedrals in the world."

"That is true," she admitted; "but that is not what my husband cares about, really. What he has in mind is not the Church, but the home. He always says that we are a nation of homes, not of churches."

" A very sensible remark," declared Professor Wutheridge.

" My husband," said Julia, "has always been a very sensible man."

And with the faintest sigh in the world, she turned to her daughter, who was approaching her with a serious expression, followed at a decent distance by Potter, who did not look at all hopeful.

" Mother," said Juliet, " we want to go on the carousel. Please will you take us on the carousel, mother? We'd like to ride around, and around . . . and around. . . ."

For Joan's Great-Grandmother
FRANCES GRUNTAL
the gayest, truest, quickest, and most lovable
of all my friends

The Orchid

PROFESSOR PEMBAUER

Chapter I

SPRING, on her way up from the south's sweet gardens, from the mocking-bird still singing in the Judas-tree, has quartered herself for a fortnight in the city, before leaving with bud and blossom for the country. All at once the lawns and meadows in the Park turn green, the elm trees put out their leaves, and already the first robin, under a bench in the Mall, has sung his lonely, liquid song. The Park Commissioner has planted his tulips along the drives; and beneath the stone wall near the zoo, the slender cherry trees shake out a snow of blossoms. The great buildings rising on all sides like mountains or terrible rocks, shine in the sun, watered with air from the sea; and ladies and gentlemen go rowing in little flat-bottomed boats on the lake where a few ducks gaze at one another with an eye for marriage, or some folly.

Nearby, in tiny cages hardly large enough to allow them to turn around, the wild animals of all the continents of the earth stare out at the spring without enthusiasm, but with a certain natural restlessness.

This restlessness of the season, which in the case of these miserable captives is made evident in grunts, roars, bleats, and sighs, expresses itself in the case of the other inhabitants of the city in arguments and the desire to travel. Everywhere it is possible to hear a debate upon some important subject; while in the theaters devoted to the moving pictures one can enjoy scenes from almost every country in the world, consisting of rivers, towns, trees, and cattle, going slowly by to the accompaniment of music.

Soon troops of children, dressed in lace and tinsel crowns, will put up their May-poles in the Park; then the air will be full of small voices shrill as magpies. But it would be a mistake to imagine that these children are happier, or more friendly than their elders. It is only because, like the birds, their shouts are so piercing, that one does not hear the groans, the sobs, and the outbursts of despair to which their own brutality causes them to give way from time to time. Fortunately, their anguish does not last; soon they are making plans again as though there were no such thing as sorrow in the world.

It is this hope which illuminates for a moment the faces of those who pass each other in the streets. Come, they seem to say, where are you going this summer? I am going for a little trip during the hot weather; it will be an adventure for me. Perhaps I shall be very happy for a while; or I may meet someone . . . Who can tell? Is it possible that you might be that one?

It is very unlikely; but they do not lose hope on that account. The shops are full of summer dresses, valises, traveling bags, tennis rackets; it is impossible to look at them without feeling hopeful. And this curious malady, for which there is no reason which is not in the blood, is felt most keenly by those who have the least right to it. It is a fact that the city, during these first spring days, draws such tonic from the air that even those whose lives have led them to expect nothing of fortune, glow a little in the sun, like those great towers from whose rooftops it is possible to see the ocean and the Jersey hills.

How strange, how unreasonable is this illusion of happiness in the spring. There, we say, there in the distance is the heart's true home. It is far away, it is uncommon, it is different from the ground under our feet. What a lovable land; and full of our friends and admirers. How happy we should be if we were there. Alas, it is only an illusion, a mirage to confuse us. It is ourselves we long for; it is ourselves for which our hearts cry out.

That is why, thought Anton Pembauer, the truly wise man stays at home, or, if he travels, it is not in search of happiness, for that is one of the things he takes with him.

Professor Pembauer had no intention of going anywhere; for one thing, it would have been quite impossible. The small amount of money he received for giving piano lessons allowed him to live, but not much more. It was fortunate that his wants were simple, and that he was a practical man. In this way he managed to remain cheerful, and even happy; and in the serene melodies of the past, consoled himself for the discords of the present.

Once he had had great hopes of a career; he was young, and his friends at home expected him to be another Rubinstein. There were not many of them; like himself, they were teachers, or students, at the conservatory. When at last he gave his concert, they showered him with compliments. What *Empfindung,* they exclaimed, what repose. But the critics did not say anything; as a matter of fact, they did not even bother to attend.

So Anton Pembauer, pupil of Taussig, associate instructor in piano at the conservatory at Rothenburg, and one-time soloist with the Muenchner Philharmonik, came to America to give his concerts. Alas, in America he did not even have friends to tell him that with a little more practice he would be another Rubinstein. So in the end there was nothing to do but give piano lessons.

All that was long ago: the disappointment was over, scarcely remembered, even. And finished, too, were those first terrifying years when there were all too few pupils, or even none at all. Professor Pembauer was not so busy that he was obliged to employ an assistant; but at least he could now afford a room big enough to hold his grand piano, and he could treat himself to a new suit now and then, and a seat in the balcony at the symphony once a week.

It was not the life of a virtuoso, but it suited him; and at all events, it was the life of an artist. He rose early in the morning, in order to work for a while on the concerto or the sonata he was writing. He never expected these compositions to be performed; but he could not resist working at them. While he was busy in this fashion, and for weeks thereafter, his own melodies and harmonies would fill him with secret excitement, with a sort of dizzy exaltation. Then he forgot them; and if anyone asked him what he had written, he answered " Nothing," without even thinking.

He cooked his own meals on a little gas stove behind a screen. In the morning, and again in the afternoon, his pupils came to see him, or he went out to see them, depending on their age, or their importance. The good ones, who were poor, and paid very little, came up the stairs mopping their faces, or blowing on their fingers, according to the season. Then they would take a Bach Suite, or a Brahms Ballade, out of their music-rolls, and seat themselves at the piano. From a corner near the window Pembauer would listen, without saying anything. Then he would show them how it ought to be done.

First of all he would remark, sitting down to the piano: " You must learn to control yourself, you must have a little repose. If you have emotions, you should do something else with them, not play the piano."

Then he would play simply, and with a manly tone, the piece of music under his nose.

To his pupils he always said: "The piano is a masculine instrument: its father was Beethoven. So do not be too poetical; and try to keep the wrists quiet."

Nevertheless, he enjoyed teaching the children, whose young minds were filled with mystery, with curiosity, and with impatience; who had no ambition and did not desire to become virtuosi. It is true, he thought, that they do not understand why Brahms was greater than Chopin; but on the other hand, if they are sad, or in love, they play some other game, they do not play the piano.

Now, after a lunch consisting of bread, cheese, tea, and a baked apple from the delicatessen, Professor Pembauer was seated at the piano, playing for himself. His strong, stubby fingers, no longer young, beat down the keys like little hammers, gently, or with force, but without hesitation or sympathy. And from the strings four voices, clear, strong, touching and sweet, rose, met, tumbled and twined, and filled the little room with music.

Pembauer was improvising. With closed eyes, he let his fingers sing for him whatever came into his head. He sat quiet, barely moving; and listened with appreciation to the music which he himself was composing, and which he would forget again as soon as it was finished. He did not ask much of it musically: only that it should not be too sweet, and that it should be sensible. By this he meant that he wished his music to be thoughtful, and clear, and not too full of pity for himself or for others. One must have faith, he liked to say, if one is to be an artist. But he did not know how to explain what he meant by faith.

With a sigh, he stopped playing and, turning, sat for a moment looking out of the window. The sunny light of spring shone on the streets washed still with the blue shadows of winter, and on men and women as they stepped along rejoicing in the sun and the mild air. Well, he thought; there it is: now they believe something about life, or about themselves. But could they tell anybody else what it is they believe? Some would say that they believe in God; and others would say it is a fine day. That is how the artist must be, even when he is sad. Either he must have God, or a fine day in his heart, all the time.

Then, seeing that it would soon be the hour for young Master Grogarty's lesson, he closed the piano, and rose to go. Taking his hat and his coat, in case the weather turned cool, he went slowly out of his room, locking the door behind him, and down the stairs to the street. There he took a deep breath of the warm air, in which were mingled together all the odors of the city, the fumes of gasoline, the smell of asphalt, the odor of vegetables from the grocer and of drugs from the druggist, and also a faint but unmistakable smell of grass and trees from the Park two blocks away, because the wind was in that direction.

Yes, he said to himself, it is easy to believe something, on a day like this. It is impossible to avoid a feeling of enthusiasm for the fact that we are alive at all, or for even less than that.

And with that he started off cheerfully in the direction of the apartment where the actress, Rose Grogarty, lived with her young son William.

MISS GROGARTY HAS HER HAIR BRUSHED

Chapter II

ROSE GROGARTY sat before her dressing-table, inclining her head with its treasure of copper-colored hair into the hands of Mrs. Connor who stood behind her, and wielded the hair brush. Miss Grogarty's strong but slender neck was curved back in the most delicious arch; and she gazed at herself in the glass with thoughtful criticism. Mrs. Connor, on the other hand, kept her eyes on the hair, which she was brushing out with long and rhythmical strokes. There was nothing new in all this for Mrs. Connor; but it never failed to charm her. That was because she could see things as they looked to other people. And as she brushed Miss Grogarty's hair, she realized that each night hundreds of eyes were focussed with enthusiasm on its owner. So much admiration moved her; and as she brushed, she trembled with an inward joy.

She made no mistake about herself; she knew that she was not an artist; she was a professional woman. And for that reason the artist seemed to her an amazing object. To be beautiful, or to be famous, and to be admired; what joy, what happiness! That was art, that was for the artist.

This hair, rippling so softly over her hands, sparkling under her brush, gave her strange ideas, lovely and terri-

fying dreams. She saw herself on the stage, with everyone looking at her; she saw herself acting a part. Her
breath came faster; she advanced one foot before the
other, and smiled mistily into a corner.

But Mrs. Connor was a sensible, quiet body, and she
kept these thoughts to herself. She did not have to be
told that for a professional woman, or a woman in business, common sense comes first, before enthusiasm. So
she brushed on, with a long, easy sweep, and tried to be
quiet and soothing, having in mind the natural delicacy
of the artist.

As a matter of fact, there was nothing in the least
delicate about Miss Grogarty. It is true that she had
made a success, but not without hard work, discourage-
ment, and good luck. She had arrived, but only because
she knew the way, and had no illusions about where she
was going.

To the reporters who came to interview her, she always explained: I owe my success to the public, who have
had the kindness to love me. In this way she threw a kiss to
the thousands who delighted in her appearance, and her
art. But to herself she admitted that she did not understand the public at all. It frightened her; it kept her
anxious, and alert. And she remarked to her hair-dresser,
" Connor, what is the public? Perhaps you can tell me;
because I suppose in a sense you are part of it."

" I suppose I am," said Mrs. Connor gloomily, " in a
way."

" What a beast you are, then," said Miss Grogarty
promptly. " You terrify me, Connor. Suppose all at once
you didn't like me any more?"

" Go along," said Mrs. Connor.

" It's all luck, Connor," said Miss Grogarty dreamily.
" Luck, and being careful. Still, I love it. But you're

never quite sure . . . Well — if it comes to the worst I can always set up as a hair-dresser."

" I'm sure of it," said Connor soothingly.

Miss Grogarty touched her curved, taut throat with long, capable fingers. " I suppose you think," she said, " I wouldn't be a success as a hair-dresser." And she gave Mrs. Connor a defiant look in the glass.

" Why," cried Mrs. Connor, " I never thought anything of the kind."

" Yes," insisted Miss Grogarty, " you did. You think I wouldn't be a good business woman — don't you, Connor?"

" Well, of course," the hair-dresser admitted, " it's not exactly in your line . . ."

" You see," exclaimed Miss Grogarty; and she made an impatient gesture with her head. " Ouch!" she said.

" Sorry," murmured Mrs. Connor.

" As a matter of fact," said Miss Grogarty, settling back again, " I'm a very good business woman. For one thing, I'm practical, and good at detail. I could run an office, and a house — and bring up a family. As a matter of fact, I do."

And she listened a moment to the sounds from the next room, where William was going over his scales with Professor Pembauer.

" Some day," she said, " I'll have to dye my hair." And she gave a shiver.

" Never," said Mrs. Connor firmly. " Not for a long time, anyhow."

" Is there any gray in it at all?" asked Miss Grogarty.

Mrs. Connor peered critically at the roots. " Not much," she said.

" Oh," said Miss Grogarty.

Presently she burst out:

333

"No one can be beautiful forever."

Mrs. Connor agreed that such a thing was impossible.

"Connor," exclaimed Miss Grogarty; "I'm going to leave the stage. I'm going to open a shop."

Mrs. Connor, who had often heard Miss Grogarty express this determination, said nothing, but continued to wield the hair brush, and to make certain, soft, clucking sounds such as she had once, in her youth, heard a stableman address to a horse.

"And all day long," continued Miss Grogarty with gloomy relish, "I'll sit in an office completely hidden from sight."

"And how you'll dislike that," said Mrs. Connor.

"I'll loathe it," agreed Miss Grogarty.

"Cluck," said Mrs. Connor.

"It's beauty," the hair-dresser remarked after a moment, "gets on in the world, for a woman. Brains are all very well, but where do they get you? You can have mine."

Miss Grogarty waved her hand vaguely at this offer.

"You," continued Mrs. Connor reproachfully, "an artist — to talk of a shop. You're above such things, Miss Rose. That's all very well for someone like me. But you were built for glory."

"Thank you, Connor," said Miss Grogarty with pleasure.

"Not at all," said the hair-dresser. "That's the simple truth."

"Nothing is simple, Connor," said Miss Grogarty; "not even glory."

"Of course," agreed the hair-dresser, "being an actress might easily have its troubles; that is, if you count them troubles. But nothing like the troubles of a business woman. And looking like you do, besides . . ."

" I know," said Miss Grogarty; " you needn't say it. Am I so appealing, Connor? "

" Very appealing, Ma'am," said Connor.

Miss Grogarty opened her eyes wide, and stared at herself in the glass. " I suppose I am," she said sadly.

" That's what men love," said Connor, giving the hair a vigorous twist. " It brings out the fatherly in them."

" Ouch," exclaimed Miss Grogarty. She tossed her head, to bring one loose red-golden strand across her shoulder. " Look," she said: " the ends are split."

Mrs. Connor gazed without anxiety: she knew that Miss Grogarty had something else on her mind.

" Connor," said Miss Grogarty earnestly, tossing her hair back again into the hair-dresser's hands, " God save me from a fatherly man."

" Just show me one," said Mrs. Connor with a grim smile, and hope in her heart.

" I suppose," said Miss Grogarty, " you'd rest on his bosom, and let the hair fall out of my head."

" I would," said Mrs. Connor; " right on his bosom."

" You're no use to me," exclaimed Miss Grogarty; " you bring out the worst in my nature. Go on, then — leave me; put in the combs, and go home."

She sat a moment, her sweet bright face drawn up into a thoughtful frown. " Connor," she said; " as you go out, step into the library a moment, and ask the professor to come to see me when his lesson is done. I must find out how William is getting along. It's time he was learning something besides scales."

MRS. HEAVENSTREET RECEIVES
SOME DISQUIETING NEWS

Chapter III

SEATED at her desk in the library of her home, overlooking a small rear garden in which a dejected but entire ailanthus tree was already breaking into leaf, Alma Heavenstreet gazed with flushed cheeks at the report of the State Secretary to the Daughters of the American Revolution, a copy of which she held in her hands which trembled with indignation. Her mild brown eyes, distended with surprise, alarm, and the determination to oppose with her last breath the enemies of her country, encountered the following paragraphs:

" It is almost beyond belief that these sinister forces are reaching out through our churches, our clubs, our schools to bring about ends that well-meaning people who belong to these organizations would be the first to condemn. But we have proof that this is so. Some of the most astute minds in the world are employed to deceive us. They have no end of money at their disposal to perpetrate deception so no one need be surprised or humiliated at the discovery that she has been deceived."

" Great heavens," murmured Mrs. Heavenstreet. She read further:

" We have the very grave menace of socialist legislations, the far-reaching and pernicious youth movement, but of all the destructive propaganda, probably none is more dangerous nor more widely embraced by good people than the pacifist movement. It is a well-known fact that the countries that are doing the most in the way of military preparation are backing the pacifist program of American churches, women's organizations, and youth societies."

Mrs. Heavenstreet also read of how the President General of the Society had been presented to King George of England. " During her trip," said the report, " the President General expects to arouse interest in the activities of the D. A. R. abroad, and thereby bring about a better international understanding."

There followed a list of twenty-eight societies whose activities were judged to be harmful to the country. These included the Foreign Policy Association, The National Association for Child-Development, and The World Alliance of International Friendship through the Churches.

" Nevertheless," continued the State Secretary, " it is ridiculous to say that we do not support the President of the United States of America."

When she had finished this report, Mrs. Heavenstreet sat for a moment in stunned silence. Then, trembling with indignation, and with the desire to express this sentiment, she seized her pen, and began a letter to the *Times*. First she wrote down the title, which was to be simply Patriotism. Mrs. Heavenstreet felt ready to exclaim with her cousin, the Senator: Let us not leave ourselves an easy prey to enemy countries by giving up the fifteen cruisers to which our wealth and our impregnability entitle us. Were we to join a world of nations all of whom have laid down their arms, how then should we defend ourselves from attack?

Alma Heavenstreet, known to the directors of Heavenstreet Structural Steel as Julian's wife, was not by nature made for wars. Brown, plump, and with a charming timidity which daily expressed itself in a thousand diffident gestures, she was far more at home in the drawing-room than on the battle-field, whether political or military. However, her first experiences of marriage, like those of most good women, had left her with the desire to defend herself against strangers. Naturally, if they were foreigners besides, that was all the more reason . . .

To tell the truth, Mrs. Heavenstreet did not really like battle-ships; and she detested the sea, for it made her ill. When she was obliged to look at moving pictures of those enormous vessels, solemnly rising and falling in one another's wake, she felt seasick. When they belched black smoke from their guns, she simply shut her eyes. However, when it was over, she experienced a feeling of patriotism, mingled with pride.

These were her defenders; behind their bristling guns she felt safe. That they might, in turn, give offense to anyone, never entered her mind. She was a mild, submissive little woman, whose secret hope was to be friends with everybody. And by this alone, she had been undone. Unable to avoid taking sides with those around her, she already found herself elected to membership in three committees, two boards, and the Society of the Daughters of the American Revolution.

Poor soul; how she would have enjoyed being Julian's wife, and nothing more. Fate had reserved another position for her: she was destined to become a leader in civic affairs. Those whose opinions she took as her own, and repeated with the excitement of the discoverer, were delighted to agree with her, and praise her enthusiasm. But alas — who is fooled? Always the wrong people. That her husband, of all people, should have been mistaken in her, perplexed and disconcerted her.

For Julian, whose mind for twelve hours of the day

concerned itself with the problems of Structural Steel, saw his wife, when he saw her at all, not as she was, but as her public life had shaped her; which is to say that he saw her in the form of committees, boards, and councils; and not at all for the shy small person that she was. And as his powerful mind and energetic body prevailed in a manly manner over what sometimes seemed to him less a woman than a quorum, he felt pleased, but a little sad to think that after all there was no one for him to take care of in a personal way.

Now Mrs. Heavenstreet sat chewing her pencil, and trying to think about battle-ships. But her thoughts came back again and again to her own problems. What could she do, she wondered, to make Julian see her as she was, a feeble female, in need of assurance, and protection? In his presence she felt inadequate almost to the point of awe, or of tears; yet, apparently, he considered her a woman of importance. But was she of importance to him? Was she, oh, was she still of importance to him? She bit her lip; and wondered.

Presently she picked up the telephone, and called his office.

" Hello, dear," she said briskly; " what's new? "

Julian, at his desk on the thirty-fifth floor of the Structural Steel Building, far downtown, replied that there was nothing new.

" No," said Mrs. Heavenstreet a little vaguely; " nothing has happened here, either. I'm writing a letter to the papers about the naval limitations."

" Ah," said Julian.

" I'm saying," went on Mrs. Heavenstreet, " that . . ." She looked at her letter, to see what she was saying, only to discover that so far, at least, she had said nothing. " Well," she remarked, " I think it's pretty bad."

"Yes," said Julian.

"And Julian — I was wondering if on your way home from the office . . ."

Julian replied that he was sorry, that he was not coming home from the office.

"Oh," said Mrs. Heavenstreet.

"I shall be home in time for dinner," said her husband; "but if I am late, sit down without me, as I do not expect to be hungry, anyhow."

"Yes," said Mrs. Heavenstreet feebly.

"Goodbye," said Julian.

Mrs. Heavenstreet returned to her desk, where the letter to the *Times* lay waiting. She picked up her pencil again. "Shall we," she wrote, holding her breath, "surrender our defenses in the name of peace which everybody knows is but a dream . . ."

At that moment a tear, unexpected even to Mrs. Heavenstreet, fell without reason upon the fifteen battleships, where it made a small blot.

THE CAROUSEL

Chapter IV

"Sit down, Professor," said Miss Grogarty. Her hair still fell about her face and down her back, like a fiery shower. "Make yourself comfortable," she said.

Professor Pembauer sat down, and gazed at Miss Grogarty with pleasure. "It is right," he said, "to hold beauty within orderly bounds; then, when it is loosened, the result is surprising, it makes the heart beat quicker. Such an effect is obtained in the piano concerto in B flat major, of Brahms. I am thinking in particular of the first movement. It is all very fine, but toward the end of the movement there is something special. Suddenly the piano descends; and the horns give out an august phrase. Then the piano ascends again, and climbs so sweetly, while the horns sing below . . . well, there is nothing astonishing about it; all the great masters wrote such things."

"Ah, yes," sighed Miss Grogarty, who was unable to distinguish one tune from another; "that must be very lovely . . ."

"The sight of your hair," continued the professor gallantly, "is like the first sound of those horns."

And waving his arm in time to the music, he sang in a husky voice, "La, la la."

"Thank you," said Miss Grogarty. "That's very sweet. . . . And now tell me — how is William doing?"

"William?" said the professor blankly; "oh — William. He is doing very well."

"Don't you think," said Miss Grogarty, "that he could begin to learn a little piece now? Something like" — she searched her childhood memories — "*The Happy Farmer?*"

"That would sound even worse," said Professor Pembauer simply, "than the scales. However, if you wish it, I will let him learn *The Happy Farmer.*"

"Thank you," said Miss Grogarty again. "That is very kind of you."

"However," continued the professor, "if I speak to you as one artist to another, then I must speak with common sense. . . . Why do you bother with these lessons at all? William is a good boy; but a musician? Never."

"Perhaps you're right," sighed Miss Grogarty.

"I suppose," went on the professor, "that you want your son to have all the advantages. But to play a little music badly is not an advantage. From a practical point of view, there is nothing in it."

"Ah," murmured Miss Grogarty. Drumming with her fingers on the dressing-table in front of her, she regarded the professor with thoughtful interest.

"Professor," she said at last, "you are a great musician. I believe that you understand me; and so I feel that I can talk to you honestly."

"I am not a great musician," said Professor Pembauer.

"No matter," insisted Miss Grogarty; "you are an artist. Tell me, do you think I am the sort of woman who needs to be taken care of?"

"Taken care of?" murmured the professor; "what does that mean, 'taken care of'?"

"I mean," said Miss Grogarty, looking at him steadily,

342

but growing a little pink, " if a man . . . supposing . . .
that is to say . . ."

And she remained silent and confused.

Professor Pembauer put his fingers together, and
peered over them at the young woman with the beautiful
hair. " Are you poor ? " he asked gently; " do you need
money ? No, no; I do not believe that is what you mean.
What is it, then ? A man, you say . . . if a man . . . I
can imagine that someone wishes to take care of you.
There is nothing strange about that; what could be more
natural ? A man who has nobody to look after, soon begins to pine; he wonders if he is manly after all. But what
has the artist to say to such an offer ? An artist has already learned to take care of himself. Who else knows
so well how to make use of joy, of love, and of sorrow,
for the advantage of his art ? It is the artist whose head
is hard, who is nothing if not practical.

" And then, consider : with what does he come forward,
to wring a living from the world ? He is no soldier, with
cannon and a uniform, or a rich man with iron and steel.
His weapon is a little cat-gut, or a bit of lead no longer
than his finger. To get along with a tool like that, one
must have something else, Miss Grogarty, one must have
courage, and above all, common sense."

" That," exclaimed Miss Grogarty, " is what I wanted
to hear." And sitting up very straight, she gazed earnestly
at herself in the glass.

" That is what I believe, too," she said at last. " And
yet, since I am only a woman, you can understand that it
is easy for me to think myself mistaken." She leaned forward, and rested her hand for a moment on the professor's
knee. " Life is hard," she said, almost as if she were appealing to him to agree with her; " I do not know if it is

harder for a man, or for a woman. But they tell me no, it is harder for a woman. Men have so much: they build houses, and bridges between them; they have something, with all that. A man has so many factories, so many companies. But I — I have only my looks, and a little art; and not forever, either."

Her hand dropped. "Perhaps they are right after all," she said in a low voice; "perhaps I am just a woman who is not young any more."

Professor Pembauer replied in dry tones, "I also have no factories, Miss Grogarty. And I am neither young, nor handsome. Still, I am content to get along by myself; I should not like anyone else to look after me. There is nothing so exacting, or so difficult, as being looked after. That is why we like to think that God is all-wise, all-knowing, but above everything else, all-forgiving. If it were simply a matter of taking care of ourselves, there would be no need for all that forgiveness. As it is, we are always afraid that in some way or other, we shall vex those who take care of us."

Miss Grogarty sighed; and then she smiled. "That is a very sensible remark," she observed; "and I will remember it when I am tired, and feel that it would be pleasant to be looked after a little."

Realizing that there was nothing more to say without admitting more than she felt ready to admit, she rose to her feet, and held out her hand. "You've been very helpful," she said. "Thank you. We must have another talk very soon."

As the professor went out of the door, she added, "Don't forget *The Happy Farmer*."

On his way home through the Park, Professor Pembauer stopped off to greet his friend Mr. Gambrino, the proprietor of the carousel. This amiable man, who considered himself a musician first, and a business man second, claimed to have studied singing under Ragini in Milan. It was undeniable that he had a passion for opera, and often sang along with the steam calliope which accompanied the horses. Alas, here too, as in Italy, Mr. Gambrino found himself singing in the chorus, due to the fact that the calliope did not play any tenor arias.

Nevertheless, he enjoyed his business, which seemed to him tuneful, attractive, and useful; in addition, it did not take up too much of his time. "Everywhere children," he explained to Professor Pembauer, "must be amused: but in this way they learn music, and also to love the animals." So saying, he pointed to a lion made of wood upon whose back a young lady of four or five was rapidly circling around with looks of rapture.

"As for the music," he added with a shrug, "for myself I would rather have *Salve Dimora,* or *Celeste Aïda;* but I am obliged to take what I can get; besides, for riding around in a circle, probably the anvil chorus is better, anyway."

And rushing forward, he assisted a dizzy child to alight from a camel on which he had already crossed the deserts of Arabia and the sands of the Sahara.

"There is too much emotion here," he said, returning to the professor. "You would think that each ride was a performance at La Scala. With so much enthusiasm, I assure you, and also with a little health, I would have been a *primo tenore.* However, as you know, when the opportunity came, my stomach went sour."

"Yes, yes," said the professor, who did not wish to hear his friend's history all over again.

"A *primo tenore,*" said Mr. Gambrino dreamily, "and a great success."

"Console yourself, my friend," said the professor,

" with the reflection that in addition to being happier as you are, you are also more unique. One should sing for joy, as you do; not for a living. It is true that this calliope is not a symphony orchestra; but looked at from one point of view, that is an advantage, because if your stomach turns sour, you simply do not take the high B flat, and no one is the wiser. I assure you, a man is well rid of his ambitions. I have just come from the house of a famous actress who, in addition to the anxieties of her profession, has more troubles than you could imagine, although she did not exactly tell me what they were."

Mr. Gambrino looked with distaste at the carousel, filled with children and nursemaids. " You are a lucky fellow, Pembauer," he said.

" No," said Professor Pembauer earnestly, " I am not lucky. That is what I am trying to say to you: no one is lucky, unless he is very humble. Then no one bothers to disturb him. The poor man has only peace as a guest — unless he is so poor that he is starving."

The singer gave a shiver: he remembered his student days in Milan. " Or if he is in love," he said. " Or, with bad luck, maybe both."

" Love," said Professor Pembauer with a snort of contempt; " is there nothing else in your mind? That is what comes of listening to too many operas. You should study Bach, my friend; he did not write any operas."

So saying, the professor took leave of the proprietor of the carousel, and continued on through the park in the mild, sweet-smelling air. A robin sang in the grass, the faint shouts of children sounded from the Mall. Far off, across the lawns, above the trees, the great gray towers of the city shone dreamily in the sun; and the professor hummed a tune as he walked. He was content: he was satisfied with the conversation in which he had just taken part, and in which he felt that he had expressed himself clearly, and with intelligence. He was not aware that he was being followed. Mrs. Connor, who was also going home through the Park at that hour, had seen him pass, and was now walking a little behind him, in a modest manner, but with a thoughtful air.

A MAN ACCUSTOMED TO HAVING HIS OWN WAY

Chapter V

ENJOYING an early dinner at the Crillon, Mr. Julian Heavenstreet remarked to his companion, "You look a little tired, my dear; your play has run too long; it is time to go away for the spring months, during which so many people have influenza."

So saying, he offered Miss Grogarty the dish of celery, at the same time glancing around to see if any one recognized her.

Miss Grogarty smiled, and replied drily, "My dear Julian, I am not doing a monolog in vaudeville. If I were to stop working, a large and prosperous business, employing a number of people, would be obliged to close down. Or would you like me to hand over my part to an understudy who is charming, certainly, but in my opinion too young for this play, which demands a woman of thirty, God help me."

Mr. Heavenstreet shrugged his shoulders, for it seemed to him that Miss Grogarty was unreasonable. Nevertheless he adored her for what he considered the most feminine quality of all. "What you need," he said, "is some one to look after you." It was not the first time he had

348

voiced this opinion, which always caused Miss Grogarty to sigh noisily.

"You can balance my check books if you like," she answered.

That was not exactly what Mr. Heavenstreet meant; but it was something. He leaned back in his chair, and regarded her through narrowed eyes. What an extraordinary woman she was, with that bright face of hers overlaid with sweetness you could almost touch . . . and that amazing hair. She looked such a child — and she had check books to balance. In addition, people turned around to look at her.

Mr. Heavenstreet believed in looks, but he did not always understand them. That is to say, he believed in what looks made him feel; and when he looked at Miss Grogarty, he felt that he wished to take care of her. That is easy to understand, and besides, he was not the first; but he was relentless and audacious. It was to such qualities as these that the Heavenstreet Structural Steel Company owed its success. In short, Mr. Heavenstreet believed his eyes, which told him always one thing, to hope and to have courage.

And since, to be the owner of what so many admired seemed to him no more than what he was entitled to, it was easy for him to believe that this young woman needed the protection held out to her.

Miss Grogarty was not insensible; but she was cool. It must be remembered that love was not a novelty to her. Night after night she wooed her audience; and felt, so to speak, its thousand hands in her hair. And this emotion, which filled her heart to overflowing, drove itself like an arrow or a waterfall into the bosom of her leading man, for whom she felt nothing, or very little, and

who, in turn, five times out of ten, found it hard to forgive her for being a woman.

In this way she had learned that things are not always
what they seem.

So now she replied to Mr. Heavenstreet, with the same
bright, grateful smile, and the same secret thoughts which
ran as follows: Do you really love me? Or do you simply
wish to own me? I don't in the least wish to be owned.

" My wife," said Julian, not without a certain gloomy
pride, " is writing a letter to the papers. She does a great
deal of that sort of thing." And he sighed, as though to
say, I am a lonely man because my wife spends her time
in public works.

Miss Grogarty's face lost none of its brightness, but
she was aware of a feeling of depression. She did not
like to be reminded of another woman at such a time.
Even a questionable situation, she felt, should be kept as
fragrant as possible. And besides, Mr. Heavenstreet's
offer to look after her had touched her; for no matter
what she thought of it, she was unable to avoid feeling
pleased by a compliment.

And there was no denying the fact that Mr. Heavenstreet was paying her the compliment of a passion of some
sort. In fact, it seemed to interfere for a moment with his
breathing. Crushing a piece of bread in his fingers, he exclaimed in a low voice, and with difficulty, " I was meant
to be a family man, and to come home each evening to a
little cottage in the country."

" What a charming idea," said Miss Grogarty, " so
peaceful and pastoral." She was vexed because in her
heart she also longed for the same thing. " Do you see
me, Julian," she asked, " waiting at the garden gate,
swinging a sun-bonnet up and down? And one day, when

350

you came home, there wouldn't be me any more; there'd just be a cow, with a tail, and some horns." And she gave a sad sounding Moo.

Mr. Heavenstreet smiled painfully. "Yes," he said. "Well . . ."

"Wasn't it Io," continued Miss Grogarty, "whom Juno turned into a cow, so the flies would bite her? Poor Io, Julian." That was not very fragrant she thought, but after all, it wasn't her fault there was a Mrs. Heavenstreet.

"Rose," said Julian . . .

Miss Grogarty's face was flushed; and she hurried on: "Was it Io's fault that Jupiter was married? She was just tired, and she lay down to rest . . . and look what happened . . ."

"All this talk about cows," said Julian, "is beside the point. Nobody wants to make a cow out of you, Rose. I want to take you away, that's all. To a little cottage in the country . . ."

"Yes," said Rose, still struggling; "and you, Julian? . . . what about you? Can you just go here and there, as you please? Out in the morning, and home in the evening. . . . Is there nothing to stop you?"

Drawing himself up with dignity, Mr. Heavenstreet replied in the accents of Zeus, or the President of the Heavenstreet Structural Steel Company,

"I am a man accustomed to having his own way."

Miss Grogarty smiled. Well, she thought to herself, that's unlikely in the future, at least. And unconsciously echoing an earlier remark of Mr. Gambrino's, she added to herself, There's too much emotion here altogether.

Therefore, in order to change the subject, she asked,

"Are you going abroad this year, do you think?"

To this unfortunate question, Mr. Heavenstreet replied by throwing down his bread with an angry gesture. "Without you?" he cried.

Receiving no reply, he continued:

"Why should I go abroad? Europe is nothing to me, if you're not along. I've seen it all, a thousand times." Bending a little forward, he gave her a beseeching look. "Rose, why don't you come with me? Paris . . . and the Bois in the afternoon, with the light coming down through the trees the way it does . . . and the shops, Rose — millions and millions of shops . . . and cocktails at the Ritz . . . and lying out all morning in the hot sun at the Cap, diving off the rocks into water so clear you can see the bottom . . . and the moon coming up over Annecy, and shining on the mountains, on the snow . . ."

"You're very sweet," said Miss Grogarty. "Thank you." She gave a quick glance at her wrist-watch. "Good heavens," she cried, "I'm late. I've got to go."

(*How young and eager he was, when he spoke like that; almost poetical . . .*)

"The moon," cried Mr. Heavenstreet, leaning desperately across the table, "on those snows high up . . ."

Miss Grogarty rose to her feet. "I mustn't keep the curtain waiting," she said.

(*The full round moon in Venice, heavy and golden . . .*)

"The curtain," said Mr. Heavenstreet, "can wait. Listen to me."

(*Listen? Listen? the one thing in the world she mustn't do, was to listen. . . .*)

"We'll take a motor," cried Mr. Heavenstreet, "and drive . . . to Vienna, to Buda Pesth . . . there's an island in the Adriatic where everybody goes . . ."

"Goodbye," said Miss Grogarty; and fled, with a mist in front of her eyes, but with a sedate motion.

Mr. Heavenstreet paid his bill, and went home. There he found his wife, who had finished her letter to the *Times;* and a large dinner. " I am sorry, my dear," he said. " I have no appetite."

" Couldn't you," asked Mrs. Heavenstreet timidly, " try? "

" I told you," replied her husband, " that I would probably be late, and that I would have no appetite." So saying, he retired to his study, to smoke, and to look over business reports, financial bulletins, and maps of Europe.

In her dressing-room at the Embassy Theater, Miss Grogarty painted blue shadows under her eyes, and gazed at herself in the glass. " Come, Rose," she said; " there's work to do. Gather yourself together, my girl. Understudies are waiting."

London in the spring . . . the long, warm nights on the river, the slow happy dawn . . .

And Fiesole . . . the pines and the flowers, the dark sweet cedars . . .

" Oh dear," said Miss Grogarty.

MRS. CONNOR IS NOT EASILY FRIGHTENED

Chapter VI

THE NEXT time Mrs. Connor encountered Professor Pembauer in the hallway of Miss Grogarty's apartment, she remarked with a smile, "I hear that you are a great artist." At the same moment her glance seemed to say, But you do not look like one.

Professor Pembauer did not take the trouble to reply to these words; instead, he remarked drily, " It is through the eyes that we are most often deceived. On the other hand, the ear is able to distinguish between the smallest fraction of a tone. Possibly it is the desire to be fooled a little which causes us to prize our eyesight more than our hearing."

Abashed by the tone in which he uttered this reflection which she did not understand, Mrs. Connor answered vaguely.

"Will you believe such a thing? I can't even so much as carry a tune."

"You are not obliged to," said the professor.

With these words, he moved toward the door, because he was on his way home. Mrs. Connor, who had also finished her work, accompanied him.

"Still," she declared, "I do enjoy my bit of music now and then."

At this the professor burst out laughing. "Mrs. Connor," he exclaimed, "you are irresistible."

Mrs. Connor blushed. "There," she cried; "go along. You artists — you are all alike."

"Not at all," said Professor Pembauer genially; "not at all. I am on my way this very minute to visit another artist whose business is located in the park near a lemonade stand. All day long he makes music, in a humble way, to be sure, but with real enthusiasm. In his company you can enjoy your music, as you say, and also a glass of lemonade now and then, while going on the most delicious journeys whose only fault is that they leave you just where you started."

And humming a phrase from *A Hero's Life,* he strode briskly down the street, followed by Mrs. Connor.

"However," he added suddenly, "looked at from another point of view, perhaps that is a virtue."

Although the professor's remarks seemed to be directed at her, Mrs. Connor felt left out of the conversation.

"What do you think," she said, hurrying after him; "Miss Grogarty may be going abroad after all. Do you know what she said to me to-day? 'Connor,' she said, 'put a band in my hair, like the Greeks; I want to look like Io.' Io indeed — whatever that may be. 'Io?' said I. 'The flies bit her,' she said, but she's always like that, making fun. . . . So finally she said, looking at herself from the side, 'It's just in case I travel.'"

The professor slackened his pace, and directed a thoughtful glance at his companion. "So," he murmured.

"Well, at that," said Mrs. Connor, pleased to be doing the talking, "it's high time she was getting away, after the long run she's had; another month or two, and she'll go stale. Even now you'd ought to hear her about the gray in her hair; irritable isn't the word for it."

"Nevertheless," said Professor Pembauer, "we must keep her here, Mrs. Connor." And raising his forefinger in admonition, he solemnly declared: "I am convinced that it will take our very best efforts to do so."

Mrs. Connor gave a gasp, and at the same time a skip to keep up with him. "What for?" she asked. However, as they were rapidly approaching the carousel at that moment, the professor did not reply. Instead, he pointed to his friend, Mr. Gambrino, and exclaimed,

"There is the man of whom I spoke. I assure you, he has had all the advantages. He is a tenor, and has sung in opera."

Mrs. Connor gazed at the proprietor of the carousel, who was just then collecting tickets for the next ride. "A tenor," she murmured, "at the opera; yes, I can believe that." And although she understood that Mr. Gambrino was in reduced circumstances, she easily imagined him with a wig and a cloak, performing the part of Cavaradossi, or Rodolfo.

Professor Pembauer made the introduction. "Gambrino," he said, "this is my friend, Mrs. Connor, who has had a great success in the hair-dressing business. Mrs. Connor attends personally to Miss Grogarty, the actress, in whose house we first had the pleasure of meeting each other."

Faced with so much success, Mr. Gambrino sighed. "I am enchanted," he declared, "to meet any friend of my friend's, and in particular, such a woman as Mrs. Connor." And he gazed hungrily at her, as though to say, Do you really touch the hair of the beautiful Miss Grogarty?

Mrs. Connor smiled vaguely: she was unable to make up her mind how to act. This indecision lent to her face an expression at once irresistible and humble. However, this expression, so unlike that of the sopranos with whom he had sung in the past, was lost on Mr. Gambrino.

"I am also a business man," he said. "I manage my own show." So saying, he waved his hand at the carousel, which was slowly coming to a stop. Then, struck by what seemed to him a happy inspiration, he added, "Perhaps you would like a ride."

Mrs. Connor blinked; it was years since she had been on a wooden lion, or a horse. "For nothing," Mr. Gambrino added as an afterthought.

Well . . . why not?

So it was that Mrs. Connor and Professor Pembauer found themselves riding around side by side, faster and faster, to the strains of the wedding march from *Lohengrin*. Seated on a giraffe, Mrs. Connor embraced the neck, and gazed at the scenery with a sensation of dizziness. Then she looked down at Mr. Gambrino, who stood beside her with a negligent air. "Reach for the rings," he encouraged her; "put out your arm." When she did, and nearly fell off, he propped her up again.

"Bravo," he said. "What a handful."

Behind them and before them the animals circled on their platform, to music, and to the happy shouts of children who, clutching the reins, or the neck, and drunk with dreams, sailed off on mysterious journeys of their own. The professor, astride a horse, gripped the wooden saddle with his thighs, and remained sunk in revery. "Thus," he mused, "seated on the steed of our illusions, we circle forever among strangers whose goal is as obscure to us as ours is to them. And in the end we descend where we started. Oh, happy ride; oh, never-ending curve!"

At that moment the calliope, playing flat, caused him to shiver with anguish.

357

" Do you ever go to the opera ? " asked Mr. Gambrino, gazing fondly upwards.

Mrs. Connor admitted that she was familiar with *Trovatore, Tosca, Bohème,* and *Aïda;* but not with the music, since she was unable to carry a tune. What she wished to say was that she recognized the costumes, and enjoyed the occasion.

" You must have me sing for you," said Mr. Gambrino graciously. " When I did the *Celeste Aïda* in Malfi, in Italy, I held on to the B flat for a minute and three-quarters by actual count. The orchestra was obliged to wait for me, and I had a great success."

" Still," he added, " I am better off here, on the whole.

" Although," he put in as an afterthought, " I am think-of giving a little performance again, some day."

" That would be lovely," said Mrs. Connor. " Then you could sing for me."

" For you," replied Mr. Gambrino gloomily, " and many others. No — for you I have in mind something a little more intimate." And he looked with meaning at Mrs. Connor, who saw herself already, like Mimi, seduced and dying, but victorious in a moral sense. " Go along," she murmured, and reached for the rings.

The carousel, with the power shut off, coasted more and more slowly through space ; and finally came to a stop. Children fell off their horses into the arms of their nurses ; fresh riders crowded forward, shouting and jostling one another, to find the animal which suited each one's fancy. Mr. Gambrino helped Mrs. Connor to alight ; she rested for the fraction of a second in his arms, which trembled beneath the burden ; then he escorted her to the pavement. Neither of them took any notice of the professor, who, lost in thought, remained on his horse and went around again.

" Allow me," said Mr. Gambrino, " to treat you to a glass of lemonade." Grasping her firmly by the elbow, he directed her to the lemonade stand, where, while she sipped her acid drink, he gazed at her with an expression of generosity.

" I would do even more for you," he said, " if you would let me."

" Perhaps I couldn't stop you," replied Mrs. Connor feebly.

At these words, Mr. Gambrino allowed himself to pinch her arm.

" We will see," he said. " Something very intimate."

They returned to the carousel in time to assist the professor to alight. " Thank you, Gambrino," he exclaimed; " I have had a very pleasant ride. There is nothing like being on a horse to help one's thoughts. However, it is late, and I must be getting home. Shall I leave Mrs. Connor here with you; or is she going further in my direction? "

Mrs. Connor held out her hand to the proprietor of the carousel. " Goodbye," she said; " I have to go. Don't forget . . ."

" Never," said Mr. Gambrino; and he put his hand on his heart.

As Professor Pembauer continued on his way home through the Park, he said to Mrs. Connor: " An artist should not mix himself up too much in the affairs of other people, because when he sees a problem, he is obliged to solve it; it is his conviction that he understands everything. So, for his own sake, let him stick to his last, like a cobbler."

And, when Mrs. Connor made no reply, he added: " What do you think; will Miss Grogarty go abroad this summer? "

359

"When?" asked the hair-dresser, who was not paying any attention to him; "Miss Grogarty? Yes; perhaps . . . what was it you asked?"

"No matter," replied the professor. "I do not think that you know the answer. However, I believe it would be a serious accident to art, and an even more serious accident to Miss Grogarty."

"Accident?" murmured Mrs. Connor dreamily; "there's been no accident; at least, not to my knowledge."

The professor replied inexorably: "I am speaking of a spiritual accident, Mrs. Connor. That young woman must not be allowed to destroy herself."

"This friend of yours," said Mrs. Connor, "this Mr. Gambrino . . . I suppose he's married?" She spoke airily, and not without hope, but ready to be told the worst.

"He is not," said the professor.

"No doubt," continued Mrs. Connor, "he has had many opportunities. A tenor in the opera . . ."

And she heaved a sigh.

"So far as I know," replied the professor acidly, "no one would have him. However, I am not interested in all that. As I was saying . . ."

"I don't believe," said Mrs. Connor, "that nobody would have him. I know about tenors; they lead a wild life."

She walked along on her toes for a minute. "I suppose you think that would frighten me," she said.

The professor shrugged his shoulders. "There is a song of Schubert's," he remarked, "in which the poet admits that only in his art does he find peace. However, the peace for which you are looking is of another variety. If glory attracts you, then farewell to peace; or, at least, to art."

These words made no impression on Mrs. Connor, who continued to walk beside the professor in a manner at once lofty and exasperated — startled, but at the same time resigned to the surprises of life. The arrow had touched her; the invisible archer, aided by the season, and by her position on the giraffe, had loosed his dreadful shaft. As yet the damage was slight; but there it was, the wound. . . . How unexpected. And how unsuitable.

Perhaps, if she could put it a little differently, it might not appear quite so unsuitable. . . .

"What I like about Mr. Gambrino," she said, "is the way he reminds me of my father."

A LITERARY TEA

Chapter VII

THE FIRM of Laocoon Ltd., publishers, was giving a tea for the Australian novelist, Matilda Arbuthnot. The company, whose imprint was thought by some to represent publishers struggling with a group of authors in the form of serpents, wished to introduce their distinguished guest to the journalists and writers of the city. For this purpose they had hired a reception room, and a bar at which it was possible to procure whisky, gin, or champagne made of cider, vichy, and alcohol. There was also a ballroom, for those who wished to dance.

Miss Arbuthnot stood in the reception room, and shook hands with every one who came up to her. She had spent twenty years of her life writing books; she had even made a modest living for herself out of it; but she realized that no one had ever heard of her. Perhaps, she thought, my new novel will sell enough copies to enable me to go back to Australia first class, instead of second. However, neither Miss Arbuthnot, nor her novel, were of the slightest interest to the critics, journalists, editors, poets, and other novelists, who crowded into the bar with cheerful cries, or took each other by the arm to dance in the ballroom. They believed in life, not in literature. Poor Miss Arbuthnot.

She was a very distinguished writer. Once she had almost been given the Newbold Medal, for a tragedy entitled *Mary of the Lane*. She liked to think of it now and then. Perhaps the new book would be taken by a book club; it dealt with some people in very sad circumstances in Australia. A book club would be even better than a medal. And Mr. Rasselas, of Laocoon Ltd., had thought it quite likely. The fact that the book was English, he said, would count very heavily in its favor — people who were miserable abroad being so much more liked than those who were miserable in America. Well — England, or Australia; what was the difference? She smiled grimly; and went on shaking hands.

Mr. Rasselas also believed in life. He had quietly left Miss Arbuthnot's side earlier in the afternoon, and was now in a corner, explaining to a young lady from the *Follies* exactly what it was he believed in. The young lady listened with a dreamy expression; she believed in what she could get; and she felt that she was about to get something.

Miss Arbuthnot thought that being polite to everyone would help things along. She could not have been more mistaken. " Who's the old lady shaking hands left and right? " asked Mr. Peters of the *News*. " She acts like she owned the party."

The young woman to whom he spoke, eyed her drink composed of gin, lemonade, ginger ale, and a little champagne for the experience. " Who cares? " she replied. " Maybe she's the lady novelist from England. But it's nothing to me. I never heard of her, anyhow."

" Neither did I," said Mr. Peters. With these words, he seized his companion by the waist, and steered her toward the ballroom. " Shall we dance? " he asked doubtfully.

" Let's," she said. Nestling her head against his cheek,

she began to kiss him in the ear, in a friendly way. A tendency to hiccup, however, caused her to withdraw. "Heigho," she sighed; "what a life."

And she stared dreamily at Stang, the great Irish critic, whose eyes, cloudy with dreams of the queens of Ireland, and a little off true from drink, stared hungrily back at her.

"Ho," said Mr. Stang, looking after her. "What a shape. . . . The trouble with Anatole France," he continued to the poet Stoffel, " is simply this: he has no content. He is all form. He is finished. He is dead. What are you drinking, my dear fellow?"

"Gin," replied Mr. Stoffel. He snapped his fingers to express his contempt for the creator of *Thais* and *Penguin Island*. "Form," he exclaimed: "I spit on it. It is finished. Phoo!"

"Oh my," exclaimed Mr. Stang, looking back into the ballroom; "what a shape."

"Quite, quite dead," muttered Mr. Stoffel absently.

Mr. Stang gave a sigh. "He was a good writer," he admitted, "but he was not an Irishman. What are you drinking?"

"Gin," said Mr. Stoffel, as before.

They turned back to the bar together, where a dozen men and women stood waiting with outstretched glasses. "I believe in life," said Mr. Stoffel. So saying, his free arm, used to gesture with, encircled like a tendril the stout waist of Miss Morrison of the *Telegraph,* whom he found standing beside him. Without saying any more about it, their lips met, for a moment, and in an absent manner. "Yes," said Mr. Stoffel gloomily; "life."

Meanwhile, a few feet away, on the floor of the ballroom, Miss Grogarty was exclaiming to her companion, "Whatever brings you here, my dear? I'm so glad to see you; but just fancy, meeting you here, of all places."

Mr. Heavenstreet regarded the young woman in his arms, while his feet kept time to the music. "I told you," he said, "that I always got what I wanted. Our advertising man once worked for Mr. Rasselas. Are you really glad to see me?"

Miss Grogarty shrugged her shoulders. "Why not?" she asked. "Don't be so peculiar, Julian."

"Well," said Mr. Heavenstreet, "you've been avoiding me."

"Have I?" asked Miss Grogarty innocently. But to herself, she added, Yes — and it was bad luck finding you here at all, my darling. Bad luck for me — and for Alma — "How is Mrs. Heavenstreet?" she asked sweetly.

And she looked up at him with a smile. What a good-looking man he was, so solid and able, in the midst of all this confusion. And such a nice face, really, when you came to look at it among all these other faces. A clean, able face.

"How well you dance, Julian," she said.

Mr. Heavenstreet smiled back at her.

"I've been having lessons," he admitted. "Look."

And he did a few steps in a corner.

Miss Grogarty was full of wonder. She put her head down on his shoulder, and gave a shudder. "Let's do them," she said.

He felt her body come close to his, and relax in his arms. At once the music, like a spider, ran over them, and bound them together with filaments lighter than silk and stronger than iron. Assisted by saxophones and violins, and by a cornet under a hat, their bodies celebrated a mysterious marriage: for a moment there existed between them only one pulse, one heart beating strong and slow in the music, one breath, one song; then they swung apart, to look at each other with vague smiles, half bewildered, half consoling.

"Rose," said Mr. Heavenstreet hoarsely; "we must dance together more often."

Miss Grogarty said nothing; but with the palm of her hand on his back drew him closer. Mrs. Heavenstreet — Alma — didn't dance, then; or, at least, not very well. Poor busy Mrs. Heavenstreet. There was so much she didn't do — swim at the Cap, for instance, or stay up to watch the moonlight on the snows — where was it? No matter; Alma didn't do it. That left it for Miss Grogarty to do, if she wanted. Even as the second Mrs. Heavenstreet, perhaps, if she made a point of it. What an awful idea.

"Don't let's talk," she said. "Let's just dance."

Mr. Heavenstreet looked about him. At his side Mr. Peters of the *News*, his eyes closed, his face pressed against that of an unknown young lady, moved his legs in what he trusted were the steps of a dance, while with his free left hand he caressed his partner's bosom, without, however, causing her to lose her air of indifference. Staring hungrily out of the bar were Mr. Stang and Mr. Stoffel, with glasses in their hands and argument on their faces.

"Only in Ireland," said Mr. Stang, "is the great realism being written."

"Ireland," said Mr. Stoffel; "phoo. If you never were a Jew on the east side of New York, you don't know realism at all."

"There's Rose Grogarty," said Mr. Stang. "What a girl it is."

"Let's have a drink," said Mr. Stoffel.

Mr. Rasselas had retired to a position directly behind

Miss Arbuthnot, taking the young lady from the *Follies* with him. Part of her was on his lap, in exchange for certain promises; but the whole was more or less hidden by the guest of honor, who, with her face firmly forward, continued to shake hands with everyone, in a despairing way, and for the second time.

Mr. Heavenstreet felt more determined than ever to take Miss Grogarty away from a life of this sort. He wished to tell her about it.

" Rose," he said.

" Yes ? " she murmured, looking up at him. Her lips, half parted, were close to his; an intolerable sweetness, beaming in her eyes, pierced his heart.

" Oh," said Mr. Heavenstreet.

And with a groan, he bent to kiss her.

" Look where you're going," exclaimed Mr. Peters, bumping into them. " Who do you think you are ? "

Mr. Heavenstreet did not hear him. He was not even ashamed of himself. But he was unable to make any more steps, because his knees felt weak.

Miss Grogarty also did not wish to dance any more that day.

MISS GROGARTY HOLDS A
COUNCIL OF WAR

Chapter VIII

In her dressing-room at the Embassy Theater, Miss Grogarty held a sort of court, which is to say that she received Professor Pembauer, and his friend, Mr. Gambrino, while Mrs. Connor attended to her hair. Mr. Gambrino, who had been in opera, and had once shared a dressing-room with four other artists, wished to show that he felt at home, and easy in his mind; but the size of Miss Grogarty's room, the silver ornaments on her dressing-table, the beauty of her hair, and the charm of her presence, all combined to depress him, and caused him to make movements with his feet, to feel in his pockets, and to yawn from time to time.

"It was good of you to come," said Miss Grogarty. "I have heard so much about you from Mrs. Connor."

"Yes," muttered Mr. Gambrino. "Well — I have heard about you, too . . . naturally. However, it is some time now since I was on the stage."

"Mr. Gambrino used to be a tenor," said Mrs. Connor, giving him a starry look. "In the opera."

"Ah, yes," said Mr. Gambrino.

"But now I am a business man."

"I'm sure," remarked Miss Grogarty, "that you are still a tenor. Some day you must sing for me. Mrs. Connor tells me that you have a very powerful voice."

"When you sing with a steam calliope," admitted Mr. Gambrino, "you develop . . ."

"Art without muscle," said Professor Pembauer, "is nothing. It does not even exist." And he looked thoughtfully at his own strong stubby fingers, each one capable of crushing a beetle or a nut in a single motion.

"Isn't it true," agreed Miss Grogarty. "Professor Pembauer always says the right thing. Even an actress must have strength; if she is sensitive or delicate, where does she get? Nowhere."

"I am sure," remarked Mr. Gambrino gallantly, "that Miss Grogarty is as delicate as anybody. When you look at her, you can see how delicate she is."

Miss Grogarty shrugged her shoulders. "Thank you," she said. "That's very sweet. I know," she added, "that I am very appealing looking. But underneath . . ."

And she lifted her arms, as though to say, Look how strong I am.

"Mr. Gambrino is an artist," said Mrs. Connor. "He's always saying gentlemanly things."

And she gave him another glance, proud and admiring, but a little withdrawn, as though to say, I am here too; what about me?

"Not quite so hard, Connor," said Miss Grogarty. "You're pulling my hair."

"Pardon me," said Mrs. Connor.

Miss Grogarty sighed, and settled herself again. "An athlete's life," she murmured. "Does one never rest?"

"For a little while, perhaps," said Professor Pembauer. "And to regain one's strength. But not long enough to grow soft." And he gazed meaningly at Mrs. Connor, who returned his glance with indifference, while giving a vigorous swoop with the hair brush through the air.

"Yes," continued the professor thoughtfully; "the artist must always be in training. If he is a singer, his vocal cords, larynx, pharynx, sinus, palate, and entire digestive tract must be in the very best condition. If he is a violinist, or a pianist, his arms, hands, fingers must be like iron and elastic. A painter's eye must be fresh; a writer's mind must be clear as a mirror, and active as a kaleidoscope. You cannot be an artist by rote, or by habit; and there is no filing system to help you. You have only the muscles of your art with which to attack people suffering from hunger, envy, boredom, grief, indifference, and a thousand illnesses."

"That's it," said Mr. Gambrino vigorously. "So, for myself, I add some wooden horses on a platform, and entertain the children. Nobody calls it art; but in this way I ease myself. Pembauer here — he teaches. Nobody calls that art, either. *Do re mi fa sol* — and something with the thumb. Bah.

"But my high B flat, or even a B natural . . . That is, when I'm feeling good, as he says . . ."

Mrs. Connor dropped her brush with a clatter. "Not here, Gambrino," she begged. And blushing furiously, she recalled to herself the first — and last — B flat she had heard, when stunned by the volume of sound, and coaxed by the occasion, she had fallen dizzily into the tenor's arms, only to be treated to a discussion of his art, with further examples.

Nevertheless, she felt that the high B flat belonged, in a way, to her alone.

The actress also begged Mr. Gambrino not to sing, but for different reasons.

"You have said nothing," she observed to Professor Pembauer, "about the actress. Or perhaps you don't consider her an artist, strictly speaking."

"Ho," exclaimed Mrs. Connor; "indeed."

"It's not my larynx or my fingers that ache," said Miss Grogarty. "It's the whole me that aches. Do you know what it is that gets so tired inside you? Perhaps it's the soul; at least, it has a heavy feeling, like a soul."

"That is, indeed," said Professor Pembauer, "a melancholy way to speak of the soul. I should think it is more likely your nerves. For my part, the soul is a lively sort of thing, it is like a scherzo, or an allegro. The last movement of the last of the quartets of Beethoven — that is the soul. Must it be? he asks; and he replies, It must be. His manner is proud, and energetic; it is written allegro, but it is to be played con gusto."

"Still," said Miss Grogarty, "I ache. And so I think how nice it would be to rest." She sighed. "To go swimming in the sea," she murmured; "to dive off rocks into water as blue as the sky . . ."

"There you are," said Mrs. Connor in a loud whisper; "we're going to travel."

"Tell me, Pembauer," said Miss Grogarty; "was a woman meant to struggle like this? Wasn't she made, rather, for care, and having things done for her? I'm tired, Pembauer; I want to go to Venice, and be waited on."

Her voice trailed away; she bent her bright head lower. "I want to be loved," she whispered.

Mr. Gambrino sat up with a start. However, Mrs. Connor's eye, lifted and enquiring, caused him to sink back again. Nevertheless, he presently burst out:

"Miss Grogarty, that is the speech of the heart; and I respect your feelings which are like my own. I also would like to go to Venice, and be waited on. To be wafted gently along the Grand Canal, bowing to the friends, waving to the acquaintances . . ."

371

" You can do that," said Mrs. Connor, " here."

" But not," replied Mr. Gambrino, " with the same ease."

" All you think of," said Mrs. Connor, " is ease. I could think of ease, too, if I tried. Here I stand on my feet all day, waving a hair brush. Well — I could sit, and wave something else, without feeling bad about it."

Professor Pembauer broke in at this point. " I can see, Mrs. Connor," he remarked, " that your ankles must grow weary. But the weariness of which Miss Grogarty speaks, is a different thing altogether. It is a weariness of the heart, Mrs. Connor; it is a fatigue of the muscles of the spirit. These are the muscles which lift you to the heights of emotion once, or perhaps twice, during a lifetime. In Miss Grogarty's case, they must be used daily, or perhaps twice a day. It is not as far to go; but it is tiring work."

Miss Grogarty nodded her head. " Yes," she said; " and what is the reward? A little applause, an empty theater, and then the whole thing to do over again, the next night."

" What nonsense," broke in Professor Pembauer : " the reward is not that at all. It is in the art itself, or it is nowhere. To act — that is your reward. So why do you talk about applause, and empty theaters ? "

These words, delivered in tones of the greatest indignation, caused the young actress to smile. " What a tyrant you are, Pembauer," she said; " am I to have no weaknesses at all ? "

Professor Pembauer was about to reply, when he was interrupted by a knock on the door, and a florist's boy entered with a square white box tied in green ribbon. She took it on her lap to open, and Mrs. Connor peered over her shoulder.

"Oh, my," said Mrs. Connor; "orchids."

Miss Grogarty looked even rosier than usual. "One of the rewards of art, Connor," she said gaily. And pinning the orchids on her shoulder, she rose in time to greet Mr. Heavenstreet, who entered the room on the heels of his flowers.

"Julian," she exclaimed, holding out her left hand in what Mr. Gambrino recognized with a stir at his heart as an intimate gesture; "how sweet of you to come for me . . . and these flowers, Julian . . . really . . . they're too lovely altogether . . .

"These are my friends, Professor Pembauer, Mrs. Connor, and Mr. Gambrino, who owns some horses. We were discussing art, Mr. Gambrino is a great singer; he has many friends in Venice."

And she gave the owner of the carousel a dazzling smile.

"I am charmed to meet a friend of Miss Grogarty's," said Mr. Gambrino gloomily.

The actress put on her hat; she stood in front of the mirror, and pulled and pushed, with her head first on one side, and then on the other. When the hat was on, she turned, and took Mr. Heavenstreet's arm. "You will excuse me," she said to the others, "if I leave you now. Thank you for coming; you have all been very helpful. You, Connor, and you, Professor — I shall see you again soon, I know. And you, Mr. Gambrino, perhaps — who knows? — we may wave to each other across the Grand Canal, before so very long. . . . But perhaps I may come to see your horses first, some day."

So saying, she departed with Mr. Heavenstreet, leaving the others to gather their hats, and follow when they pleased. Mrs. Connor and Mr. Gambrino looked at each other with wary eyes. Mrs. Connor seemed to be saying,

Do I still appeal to you, after so much glory? . . . and Mr. Gambrino appeared to reply, What I think, or do not think, is too intimate to concern anyone but myself. As for Professor Pembauer, he remained sunk in thought in his chair.

" My friends," he said at last, " I begin to believe that art is losing the battle. Orchids, gondoliers, and the impulses of the season, are too strong for us. It is time to act; it is time to get in a decisive blow. This giant of business, this sentimental ogre who wishes to run away with our friend in order to take care of her, must be discouraged once and for all; and those practical elements in Miss Grogarty which have been the cause of her success even more than her looks, or her art, must be roused to save her. Just how we are to do this I do not at the moment know; but I have an idea. It concerns you, Gambrino, and your carousel. Let us now all go to supper; and I will tell you what I think."

INTERNATIONAL CONFIDENCES

Chapter IX

Miss MATILDA ARBUTHNOT, of Smithtown, Australia, sat at tea in the home of Mrs. Julian Heavenstreet of New York, and listened with an expression of quiet stubbornness to what her hostess had to say. This was not very much, although Mrs. Heavenstreet had a great deal on her mind. She had decided to ask her guest, whom she had met at the Friday Women's Literary Luncheon Club, what she thought of marriage in general, and Mrs. Heavenstreet's in particular; she wished to learn about love. Her heart, bruised by misunderstanding, longed to throw itself upon the bosom of a sister, Miss Arbuthnot, the author of *Mary of the Lane,* which had a pastoral sound.

"I mean to read it," she assured her guest, "at the very first opportunity."

"Ah," said Miss Arbuthnot. It occurred to her at that moment that Mrs. Heavenstreet had not read her book.

"It must be very wonderful," said Mrs. Heavenstreet, holding out a tray of muffins, "to write such wonderful books. About such wonderful things . . . about people, I mean, and . . ." She meant to say "love," but she was unable.

And glancing shyly at the novelist, she thought, To look at her you would hardly think that she had led such an interesting life.

375

Wonderful? thought Miss Arbuthnot to herself; well
. . . I dare say. And she went rapidly over in her mind
the titles of her books, which concerned themselves only
with the most unhappy people. " I assure you," she murmured, " there is nothing wonderful about it at all."

" You are modest," declared Mrs. Heavenstreet. " But
that only makes it easier for me to talk to you. I cannot
bear immodest people, or people who are always talking
about themselves. Being English, of course you will understand that."

" British," said Miss Arbuthnot; " not English."

" Yes," agreed Mrs. Heavenstreet; " British. As I
was saying, life is so full of . . . what you can't possibly
expect — don't you think? I mean, life is not always . . .
or, that is to say . . . marriage . . . well? A muffin,
perhaps? "

" Thank you," said Miss Arbuthnot, and reached gratefully for a muffin.

" My husband," said Mrs. Heavenstreet, " would be
so glad to meet you. He has some friends in the theater.
I believe that he has met Miss Grogarty . . . once or
twice. Perhaps you've seen her in *The Orchid* . . . the
play by that Hungarian — or perhaps it's an Austrian —
at the Embassy Theater? I never remember the names of
foreigners. Except, of course, the English; but they're
so like our own. A very handsome woman."

" I haven't seen her," said Miss Arbuthnot.

Mrs. Heavenstreet clasped her hands in her lap, and
gazed thoughtfully downward. " I suppose," she said,
" that marriage is the same all over. I mean, in England
too. . . . That a man must have his friends . . . his interests . . . and a wife must have hers."

Her voice dwindled off, and she made a few inarticulate
murmurs. It was altogether too difficult, really; because,

for one thing, her visitor made no effort to help her. What she wanted to say was simply: What am I to do about Julian? How am I to make him notice me — see me as I am, not as he thinks I am? How am I to tell him that all these things I do, all these clubs I belong to, amount to less than his little finger . . . that if he were to leave me . . .

What am I to do, Miss Arbuthnot? You are so wise, because you have written books. Books like *Mary of the Lane,* which sounds so peaceful. Do you think that some-one will take Julian away from me? Do you think that already, perhaps, she is thinking about it? Take Miss Grogarty, for instance; a very handsome woman. No — actually pretty. Oh, dear . . .

But it was impossible to get into it without her visitor's help, without Miss Arbuthnot saying something, at least, to invite her . . . such as, You have something on your mind, Mrs. Heavenstreet, can I be of any help to you? . . . But there she sat, instead, munching on a muffin and with such a look of quiet stubbornness — yes, stubborn-ness was the only word for it — on her face . . . or was it indifference, perhaps, the true British phlegm? But that was like the English, she thought, they were so im-personal, they would never talk about anything but the weather, or the shooting. Well, at least, we'd not give up our navy . . .

Boom, went all the fifteen battle-ships, at once.

Nevertheless, "And so," she was saying, "I'm on all these committees; and that pleases Julian so much. Though, for myself . . ."

Miss Arbuthnot's refined face remained passive and composed. She was not interested in what Mrs. Heaven-street was saying, because she wished to do the talking herself. It was true that she was British, and indifferent, but that is only to say that she was indifferent to the recitals of others. Such recitals seemed to her in the worst possible taste.

What an impulsive thing to do, she thought, to tell me that she is on committees.

" My dear Mrs. Heavenstreet," she exclaimed, " if we must indeed discuss marriage, let me warn you that I am, thank God, still a virgin."

At these words Mrs. Heavenstreet gave a jump.

" What is more," continued Miss Arbuthnot inexorably, " I consider the entire institution of marriage the most foul disaster that can overtake a woman. The very thought of being fondled, in an intimate way, by a man, repels me. I could not bear the humiliation, Mrs. Heavenstreet; nor the discomfort."

" Hum," said Mrs. Heavenstreet, growing pale.

But Miss Arbuthnot was beginning to enjoy herself. " The body," she declared, " has never attracted me, in a sexual sense. That is to say, the male body . . . I confess, the female contours often draw me irresistibly. But so far nothing has come of it — nothing serious, that is."

And she gave Mrs. Heavenstreet a thoughtful look.

" Do have a muffin," said Mrs. Heavenstreet.

Miss Arbuthnot went on, with her mouth full of muffin: " As a child, my father fondled me rather a bit. A great, moist, hairy man, my father; I took quite an aversion to it. As a matter of fact, I'd a deal rather he'd fondled mother; and I think she thought so too. He died when I was still a girl — too much drink, and one thing and another. And then another time I had rather a beastly experience: walked smack into my nurse and a man . . . even today, if I close my eyes, I can see the whole thing all over again. There was a good bit of thicket around the house —

378

bushes, you know, and shrubs . . . and there they lay, the two of them . . ."

"Do forgive me a moment," broke in Mrs. Heavenstreet, "I remember I must say something very important to my cook. . . ."

Safe in her own room upstairs, Mrs. Heavenstreet dabbed cologne on her forehead, and took a deep breath of her smelling salts. Then she went bravely down again.

"He was her husband," said Miss Arbuthnot simply, as her hostess entered the room.

"Ah, yes," said Mrs. Heavenstreet; "well . . . dear me."

And she gave a hollow laugh.

At the same time she noticed that there were no more muffins left on the tray.

Miss Arbuthnot rose to her feet. "I must get on," she said.

"Must you?" said Mrs. Heavenstreet. She also rose, and held out her hand. "If you must, of course," she murmured.

"I'm afraid perhaps I ought," said Miss Arbuthnot uncertainly, gazing at the tea table, where there still remained some cream, and the sugar.

Mrs. Heavenstreet lost no time in ringing for her maid. "It was so good of you to come," she said.

"Not at all," said Miss Arbuthnot. "I hope I haven't bored you?"

"Oh, no," replied Mrs. Heavenstreet. "Oh, no, indeed. The English point of view . . ."

"British," said Miss Arbuthnot. "Australian."

"Goodbye," said Mrs. Heavenstreet. "Do come again."

She went slowly back to her desk, and drew out a list of the things she had to do.

Committee Colonial Dames, Mrs. Gwinnet 8.30.

Answer letter *Herald Tribune.*

Four yards blue ribbon.

Ask Julian shall Edith buy steel common or sell.

Ask Julian opera tickets.

Tea Arbuthnot 5.15 (Read *Mary of the Lane.*)

She crossed off *Mary of the Lane.*

PROFESSOR PEMBAUER READS
THE EVENING PAPER

Chapter X

A SLIGHT sizzling sound and the smell of frying, with some smoke, filled Professor Pembauer's apartment, where that worthy and practical man was engaged in cooking for himself a small chop which, with some soup in a can, bread, tea, and radishes, was to constitute his supper for that day. Professor Pembauer liked to cook; when he thought of what he was doing he was happy. But he made no pretenses to himself. " I am not the best cook in the world," he admitted, " but for that matter, who is ? It is true that the cooks of France can do a great deal with a mushroom, or a little *estragon,* but take it away, and what is left ? Simply a soufflé, and some pastry. In Persia only stews are eaten; in Germany everything is fried; and in England it is all boiled. And in America there are no cooks at all, except in the canning factories. So on the whole I consider that I do very well for myself."

Consoled by these reflections, and with his mouth watering, Professor Pembauer sat down with his chop, and opened the evening paper. In this way he read the news of the day, and made his chop last longer. At once his eye was attracted to the following paragraph:

50 Sit in Trees in Hope of Fame.

" Chicago, — Tree-sitting today was the most popular pastime in the Mississippi valley.

" Boys of all ages, and girls too, perched among the treetops, each determined to win everlasting fame by remaining there longer than any of the others.

" They sat in oak trees and elm trees, hickories and catalpas, in Iowa, and Missouri, Wisconsin, Michigan, Oklahoma, and Illinois. However, none so far has disputed the claims of 14-year-old John Wittaker of Kansas City that he is the champion. Today he had been up nearly one hundred hours, which was some sixty hours more than the original record set by Freckles Lloyd of Racine, Wis.

" ' I'll stay up here until school is over,' said John.

" In another Kansas City tree sat Mary Beer, 12; she was left alone last night when Charlotte Heldstrom, 11, who had been sitting with her for thirty-nine hours, decided that she didn't want to play any more.

" One Chicago boy, Lionel Bettles Jr., was forced down after sixty-five hours because of internal trouble. Too many sandwiches and bottles of soda pop gave him an old-fashioned stomachache."

When he had finished reading this bit of news, Professor Pembauer gave the table a thump. "There you are," he exclaimed; "that is what happens when everybody wishes to be famous. Such a thing could only take place in a democracy, where even a twelve-year-old girl has the right to sit all night in a tree. I tell you, this desire to be renowned will end by making monkeys out of us. Already it has brought into our music tug whistles, motor horns, alarm clocks, and a thousand unmusical sounds. So there is no reason to study harmony any more. Besides, there is no longer any privacy, in which to study. Unfortunately, a longing for public life is only seen to be ridiculous when infants begin to sit in trees. Like the delirious crusades of the children in the twelfth century, it can have only the worst possible ending; and here I see that already Mr. L. Bettles Jr. of Chicago has indigestion."

So saying, and being much moved by the eloquence of his own reflections, Professor Pembauer seated himself at his piano, and struck with energy the opening chords of the Chorale, Prelude, and Fugue of César Franck.

Chapter XI

IT was while he was engaged in this manner that a timid knock sounded on the door, and a moment later Mrs. Connor entered the room. With an uncertain smile, she made several steps in his direction; then, bursting into tears, she precipitated herself upon his bosom.

Professor Pembauer was terrified; but he was not surprised. "Come, come," he said, patting Mrs. Connor on the shoulder, "control yourself, my friend. I assure you that nothing is worth such an outburst of grief, which racks the system."

At these words, Mrs. Connor wept louder than ever. Immediately Professor Pembauer felt that his fears were justified; and he grew pale.

"The scoundrel," he exclaimed. "But do not be frightened; we will take care of you, I have a friend . . ."

"Ow," sobbed Mrs. Connor.

". . . A medical man," continued the professor.

However, the effect of this suggestion was not what he had expected. Mrs. Connor dried her eyes, and gave him a look of astonishment. "What are you talking about?" she asked. And going to the mirror, she removed her hat, and rearranged her hair. "How dare you?" she demanded.

There, thought the professor to himself; when it con-

384

cerns a woman, one should listen, and not say anything; because the chances are that what one says is not the right thing at all.

And in his mind he forgave Mr. Gambrino for everything.

Mrs. Connor settled herself in a chair, and sighed deeply. It was clear that she was unhappy; and at the same time that she enjoyed finding herself in a situation which, with costumes, and some music, might easily have been taken from an opera, or a play. As soon as this occurred to her, her eyes filled with tears. "Ah," she exclaimed, "you artists. But it's my own fault; because a woman ought not to let herself be put upon."

True to his decision, Professor Pembauer remained silent, but with a friendly and interested look. Mrs. Connor continued:

"Besides, at my age, a woman has no business making a fool of herself over anybody." And she gave a moist sniff with her nose. "How can I help it if I love him?" she cried; and again burst into tears.

"Love," said Professor Pembauer gently, "ought not to be a cause for grief, Mrs. Connor. Even if it is not returned, or if there are other difficulties, it enriches the whole of life. What is it the poet says? That it is better to have loved and lost, than never to have loved at all. Even I have had a little of it in my youth; it caused me many sleepless nights, but I treasure the experience."

"It did not, however," murmured Mrs. Connor between her sobs, "cost you all your savings."

No, really, thought Professor Pembauer, I was right; he is a thorough scoundrel.

But to Mrs. Connor he merely remarked: "One must pay for one's pleasures in this world, my friend."

The hair-dresser sat up, and directed a look of indignation at the ceiling. "Pleasure?" she cried. "Ho. If there'd been pleasure, I'd have a different story to tell. But all the pleasure I've had has been listening to this high B flat of his. Well, after a while the fun goes out of it. You expect a bit of attention in between. A party now and then . . . dinner and theater, or even the movies . . ."

"The life of an artist," said Professor Pembauer gravely, "is full of toil. I, personally, do not see anything to be gained by high B flats; but that is the point of view of a pianist. I do not doubt that our friend Mr. Gambrino feels that same way about a fugue, or some other form which cannot very well be sung. And perhaps he is right; certainly, if one must make his living as a tenor, nothing is more important than a good loud high B flat, or even a B natural."

"That's what he keeps telling me," said Mrs. Connor. "But look at it from my point of view. A woman has got to have her sleep, nights. And all the more if you've got to get to work in the morning. I like my bit of music now and then; but what about my health?"

Professor Pembauer looked away. "Do you wish me to believe," he asked delicately, "that our friend's voice keeps you awake at night?"

Then it was Mrs. Connor's turn to grow confused. "Excuse me," she exclaimed with energy. "What do you imagine? What I mean is, I'm in a state. So naturally I don't sleep very good. I mean, I'm all of a twitter, like. My heart beats . . . I don't eat right; I'm in love, that's what, and I wanted to get married . . . or something."

And as Professor Pembauer said nothing, she murmured weakly, "I thought naturally a tenor at the opera . . . being so romantic . . ."

She blew her nose. " He has no feeling at all," she concluded.

" And he has taken your savings," said Professor Pembauer thoughtfully, " for his career ? "

" He has," said Mrs. Connor. " In a weak moment."

" That was a very practical thing for him to do," said the professor. " Although, from your point of view, it must seem outstandingly unfortunate. Why did you give them to him ? "

Mrs. Connor made an eloquent gesture with her hands. " How could I help it ? " she asked.

Professor Pembauer nodded his head. Even a business woman, he reflected, is helpless when it comes to love. Only the artist makes money out of his emotions. My poor Mrs. Connor.

Feeling very much moved at the situation of this woman who had worked hard all her life, he adopted a brisk air. " Well, tell me," he said to her: " what does our friend intend to do with the money you have given him? Surely he has not spent it yet."

" He wants to give a concert," said Mrs. Connor. " He says it will start him on his career all over again. In a year, he says, he'll be able to pay me back — with interest. I told him no — no interest."

She blushed; and then she turned pale. " I even told him not to pay me back at all," she whispered.

" Tst," remarked Professor Pembauer. " And what did he say to that ? "

" He said all right, he wouldn't," replied Mrs. Connor.

Professor Pembauer took a deep breath. " So," he said, " with your savings, our friend from Milan is to give himself a concert. No wonder you have heard nothing but high B flats. He is preparing himself for the or-

387

deal. Have courage, Mrs. Connor; when it is over, he
will be more affectionate than ever. He will be devoted
to you, because you have helped him to a career."

Mrs. Connor gave a sigh. "Do you think so?" she
asked.

"I am sure of it," replied the professor. "Those are
things one cannot doubt; otherwise one would be obliged
to doubt all human nature. So do not feel that you have
lost your savings; think, rather, that you have turned
patron of the arts, like the Counts Esterhazy and Lob-
kowitz, the Princess Lichnowsky, the Emperor Rudolf,
and those citizens of Kansas City who assisted Miss Talley
to make her début at the opera."

"Well," said Mrs. Connor uncertainly: "when you put
it that way . . . and if you think so . . ."

"Think so?" cried Professor Pembauer with the utmost enthusiasm; "I am convinced of it. And then, besides, you must remember that Mr. Gambrino is already
well known to hundreds of children and their nurses who
ride each day on the carousel, and who will surely come
to hear his concert, and applaud under any circumstances,
whether he sings well or not.

"Then it will be you, Mrs. Connor, who are the mother
of the occasion, and the patron of his career. Perhaps
you will even have to get up and bow; it would be the
proper thing to do.

"So — get back your good spirits again. And suppose,
to help you, I give you a little glass of Tokay, made for
me by the janitor in the basement. Perhaps it does not
taste exactly like Tokay, but I know that it is harmless,
which is already a great deal in its favor."

Warmed by the Tokay, and encouraged by Professor
Pembauer's simulated enthusiasm, Mrs. Connor pulled
out her powder puff, and did away with the last ravages

of emotion. Then, in front of the glass, she drew on her hat, and gazed at herself with an air of shy pleasure. A patron of the arts, along with princes and an emperor . . . it wasn't so bad, after all. First a helpful friend, and then a wife . . . yes, it was like a play, with a happy ending. And unconsciously she put out her hand to Professor Pembauer, with a gesture she had often seen Miss Grogarty use.

"You have made me very happy," she said.

And she went out with a backward glance, like a soprano.

Left to himself, Professor Pembauer felt gloomier than ever. No, really, he thought to himself; is there no sense in the world? Children who sit in trees like the birds, and hard working women who give their savings to Mr. Gambrino. A concert, indeed. To sing with a steam calliope is one thing, but to sing with a piano which is in tune, is another. He will be laughed off the stage.

The professor went back to his piano, and sat down. And presently the great chords of the Prelude were rolling through the room again. Then he forgot the children, and Mrs. Connor; for he found himself again in a world where everything made sense.

Chapter XII

MRS. CONNOR, on the other hand, went home with a dizzy mind. The sweet smell of the spring night, joined to the odors of the city, met her nose; a few stars, hardly to be seen, shone in the misty sky lost so far overhead; and a barrel-organ in the dusk, in the yellow light of the street lamps, played in the damp spring air. Mrs. Connor stopped to buy herself some flowers, to celebrate a little, and in advance, her share in Mr. Gambrino's concert; and also to take a few to Miss Grogarty in the morning, because it was spring, and because it was so beautiful. Then, having already one bundle, she stopped again, to buy a little sausage, a pickle, some cheese, and a baked apple for her supper. However, that did not seem to her quite gay enough, so she added a tiny pot of goose-liver, and a cruller.

Laden with food and flowers, she approached her house, only to feel her heart stop beating at the sight of a familiar figure in the doorway. It was Mr. Gambrino, patiently awaiting her return. The carousel was closed for the night, and he had some business to discuss.

"What a surprise," cried Mrs. Connor. "How do you do. Come in and have a bite to eat with me. See — I've just been marketing; and there is enough for both of us."

Excitement, and the influence of the season, the slow hum of the city, the fragrance of the evening, and the shine of lights along the avenue, all combined to bring a flush to her face, and a sparkle to her eye. Mr. Gambrino let himself be led inside, and seated in the only chair, while Mrs. Connor went happily about preparing the supper. During this time, he allowed himself one remark, not without portent.

" I have something to say to you," he declared. " Something of an intimate nature."

Mrs. Connor's heart sang. It has come, she thought. And she stood, with the saucepan in her hand, staring dreamily at the little gas stove on which the water was already boiling.

However, Mr. Gambrino made no further statement, until the table was set, and Mrs. Connor had drawn up a stool opposite him. Then he looked around in a dissatisfied manner.

" You have no spaghetti," he remarked.

And taking on to his plate the sausage, the goose-liver, the cheese, and the cruller, he offered her the pickle and the baked apple with a look of forgiveness.

" I didn't know you were coming," said Mrs. Connor.

" It doesn't matter," replied Mr. Gambrino, " because, as a matter of fact, I am not hungry, anyhow. As a business man, I can afford to starve myself a little. The fat is not so necessary to business, as to art."

He spread the goose-liver on his bread. " On the other hand," he added, " for singing, a big dish of spaghetti, with meat, is the best help in the world."

" I'll keep some in the house," said Mrs. Connor meekly.

" It is unnecessary," said Mr. Gambrino, " because I am not a singer any longer."

Mrs. Connor stopped with her pickle half eaten, and stared at him in dismay. What did that mean, not a singer any longer? She felt a mortal chill, and at the same time she was rooted to her seat; she could neither raise her arm holding the pickle, nor lower it. A thousand questions tumbled through her mind, a thousand fears presented themselves to her imagination. The concert? Her savings? She swallowed with difficulty; and slowly lowered the pickle to her plate.

"What do you mean, Gambrino?" she breathed; "not a singer any longer?"

Mr. Gambrino took a large bite of sausage, another of bread, and waved his arm in a reassuring manner. "I will tell you," he said. "I have given this subject my best thought. I approach it as a man of the world, an artist, and a business man. When I had no money, the great thing for me to do was to sing. With my voice, I said, I will get money for myself. Very well: I nearly starved to death."

"Oh, dear," said Mrs. Connor.

"The voice was there," continued Mr. Gambrino, "but the public was not. Still, the only thing to do was to sing, because I had no money. But now that I have some money, it is different. Having money changes the point of view. If I spend it on singing for people, then I will not have it any more. No, I said: one thousand times no. I will keep it; I will invest it, I will put it into a business. Then I will still have it, and I will also have my voice, in case I wish to do a little something."

"But the concert?" cried Mrs. Connor aghast: "the concert that was to start you on your career all over again?"

"Pooh, the concert," replied Mr. Gambrino. "That was when I did not have any money. I see things clearer

now. A singer does not make very much. And then, he
is obliged to work very hard. And finally, in the end, he
dies before he can enjoy himself. No — that is no life
for an artist, my dear friend. A man with a voice like
mine, already has a career; but if he can afford to do anything else, that is much better for him, on the whole.
. . . Come, eat some of this cheese. There is altogether
too much here for me."

He rose, and took several strides about the little room.
Then he sat down again. As for Mrs. Connor, her head
was in a whirl, but she took a bite of cheese, because
he had given it to her.

"You do not say anything," said Mr. Gambrino.
"Here I come to you with this lovely idea, and you say
nothing. You sit there in silence; and you eat. For myself, such a thing would be impossible. At such a moment,
so grave, in the life of a friend, I would make suggestions,
I would offer advice, I would be enthusiastic. But you
northern women — you are like ice."

And he struck himself a blow on the chest.

"But you haven't told me what the business is yet,
Gambrino," said Mrs. Connor feebly.

"You haven't asked me," he replied. "That is what
causes me all this aggravation. So listen now, while I tell
you. What is the business in which there has been no improvement for over fifty years?"

"Tell me," said Mrs. Connor. "Don't sit there asking me."

"I am telling you," declared Mr. Gambrino. "It is
the carousel business. Nowhere else do people do business with the same furniture as their forefathers. Everywhere the world moves forward, but not in the carousel.
One invention follows another; people have automobiles,
running hot water, the telephone; they fly in the air, they

even cross the sea by flying; and still the children ride around on horses, elephants, camels, lions, and a giraffe. Where is the education in that? It does not follow the line of progress, my dear friend. When I see the improvements all around me, I am ashamed for my carousel. One hundred children visit it in an afternoon, and because of me, they still believe in the lion, the camel, and the giraffe."

Like Professor Pembauer, he gave the table a thump. " Here is my opportunity," he exclaimed, " given to me because I have money, and good sense. I will put in some new furniture. I will take out these lions and tigers, I will subtract these animals, and in their places I will put automobiles and flying machines and steam engines. That will be an education for the children, it will be modern, it will be of today. You will see, I will have a big success."

Mrs. Connor rested her head on her hand, and stared dismally at her plate. So this was the end of her savings — to circulate around and around in a carousel. Where was the beauty now? Where was the concert on which — for an hour — she had pinned her hopes, the corsage of flowers, the applause, the bow from the box, the glamour and the glory? She, a patron of the arts an hour ago, was now — what? A hair-dresser with her savings gone.

A tear fell on to the baked apple, and then another. What a weary thing life was, to be sure.

" And you," she said, " an artist . . . what do you know about business? Did I give you all my money to make a business man of you? No, Gambrino, no; with what I had, I could have set up a shop myself, and had people to work for me. But I wanted you to have a career. What sort of career is that — to run a carousel?"

" It is a career of business," replied Mr. Gambrino simply. " And besides, it is too late now; I have already ordered my new furniture. However, if you are thinking of my voice, I will tell you this: I am also having some new music cut for the calliope. No more choruses, my friend; instead, the arias for tenor, such as *Celeste Aïda,* and *Salve Dimora.* And cut just a leetle bit lower, to fit the voice. . . . So, after all, I do not give up my singing."

"The giraffe," moaned Mrs. Connor, "on which we met . . ."

"And finally," concluded Mr. Gambrino, "I have this to say. Since I am now in business, where I expect to make money, it is only right that I should give you, who have made this possible for me, some return for your kindness. So I have made you a partner in the business. Gambrino and Connor is the name, proprietors; it will look well on a sign, I think. In a year you will have your money back. Or at least some interest on it . . . a little something. . . . Do not thank me; it is the least I could do."

With these words he departed, taking with him the remains of the cruller. But Mrs. Connor sat a long time without moving, in silence and despair. Outside, on the Avenue, the barrel organ continued to play, but she did not hear it. The light, bitter voices of children, quarreling in the street below, failed to penetrate to the seclusion in which her spirit rested, lonely and afraid. The dream was ended; it had been short. Never again would she move in the company of princes and a king, and the citizens of Kansas City; instead, she was to have her money back, with interest. She didn't want it; she wanted the dream again.

Alas.

Absent-mindedly at first, and then with determination, she tore to shreds the flowers she had bought to give Miss Grogarty.

Chapter XIII

THAT same evening, Julian Heavenstreet left Miss Grogarty at the stage door of the Embassy Theater, and hurried home to dinner. There he found his wife dressed to go out. " I thought," she said in a breathless voice, " we'd go to a restaurant tonight, Julian; I'm so tired of eating at home."

She had also a new dress which she wanted him to see. But Julian took no notice of it. Polite, but weary, he went upstairs to bathe, while Mrs. Heavenstreet, in the rooms below, looked at herself in the mirror, and hummed a hopeful tune.

" Where shall we go? " she asked, when he appeared again.

" Wherever you please," said Julian.

They dined at the Ritz, because Mrs. Heavenstreet felt that she wanted to be seen.

She had made up her mind to appeal to Julian directly, and by force if necessary; since Miss Arbuthnot was of no help to her, she meant to try her own hand as a woman. It made her feel gay and reckless, to think of what she was about to do. But — how did one go about doing it? To be a woman had always meant to her simply to agree with everyone; and as a result, Julian considered her able and adequate, but no woman. Oh, the contrariety of life. Did being a woman — a noticeable female, that is to say — consist of being disagreeable? Well, she could try, at least.

"What a dreadful soup," she said, and sent it back to the kitchen.

Like the dress, this also made no impression on Julian, who was thinking of Miss Grogarty. It seemed to him that the actress represented reality; and that his being there, in the restaurant with Mrs. Heavenstreet, was only part of a dream. Since it was only a dream, he could afford to be polite about it; and he smiled vaguely across the table.

No, she thought; that isn't it, my dear. She realized that Julian was far away from her: and she wondered what he was thinking about. Is it business, she thought, or is it someone else? She realized that she had failed, at least as far as the soup was concerned, but she had time to be sorry for the waiter, whom she felt she had sacrificed in vain.

So, when he returned with the soup, she gave him a comforting look.

However, the whole thing annoyed him.

Discouraged, Mrs. Heavenstreet allowed herself to droop for a moment, spiritually speaking. But after a while, she remembered that she was a Daughter of the American Revolution; and that the waiter was a foreigner. "There are over five hundred thousand communists," she told her husband, "in the United States." And she looked again, with a startled air, at the waiter, who was of Italian-French parentage and belonged to the Democratic Party.

"Ah," said Julian dreamily.

Mrs. Heavenstreet rested one plump elbow on the table, and leaned intimately forward.

" What are you thinking about, my dear? " she asked.

Julian replied that he had been thinking about the market. " Today," he said, " stocks went up. But they will go down again tomorrow." And he continued his revery, which was as follows: In Venice, at tea time, one goes to the Square, in front of St. Mark's, and orders an ice. But one dines on one's own balcony, above the canal, in order to listen to the singing afterwards.

Mrs. Heavenstreet sighed, and sat back in her chair again. You see, she thought, his mind is far away, in the stock market. If I had been differently brought up, I'd know what to do to get it out again. I would have some wiles.

In her mind she saw herself, with her hair in disorder, and dressed in something odd, making gestures like Delilah, or Scheherazade.

But Julian, from his balcony in Venice, continued to smile dreamily. She is thinking of the communists, he told himself. Tomorrow there will be another letter in the papers.

And feeling, for some unaccountable reason, suddenly sorry for her, he offered her the dish of celery, with a friendly air.

" Julian," she said; " don't let's go home right away. Let's go to a theater. It's so long since we've been."

" By all means," agreed Julian. " What would you like to see? "

Mrs. Heavenstreet looked squarely at her husband. " I'd like," she said, " to see Rose Grogarty . . . in *The Orchid*."

Julian's heart gave a bound; and then fell with a thump. " *The Orchid?* " he asked feebly.

" *The Orchid,*" said Mrs. Heavenstreet firmly.

The face of the President of the Heavenstreet Structural Steel Company remained grave and impassive. But a thousand questions flashed through his mind. Was it mere chance? Or did Alma suspect something? Her own face told him nothing; it was innocent, and hopeful. His pulse was fast; but Mrs. Heavenstreet did not have her finger on it. One does not make a success in the steel business without being able to remain composed in the face of the most dreadful accidents.

"Why not?" he said. " *The Orchid* it shall be. If I can get tickets, at this hour. But you will miss the first act."

"No matter," replied Mrs. Heavenstreet; "I want to see it." She very nearly said, "I want to see *her*" — which was the truth. For she thought that perhaps, in the presence of this young actress whom everyone admired, and with whom her husband was acquainted, she might be able to surprise the secret of at least one wile — enough to bring him to her side with eyes which saw her for once in the way she wanted him to see her.

"It will be such fun," she said; and hurried through her dessert.

They got seats in a box, from which she could examine the stage as closely as she pleased. The play she dismissed at once; it was not important to her. But she followed Miss Grogarty's gestures with her soul; she listened to the actress's voice with the ears of her heart. This, then, was what it meant to be attractive. Was it something one could learn, and imitate? Under cover of the darkness, she draped her body to one side; she waved her arm in a graceful arc. But her corsets held her upright; and her arm hit Mr. Heavenstreet before it had gone very far.

"Yes?" said Julian.

399

" Excuse me," she murmured; " I was reaching for my bag . . ."

He returned to a study of the stage, on which he also saw only Miss Grogarty's copper-colored hair, and sweet, anxious face.

She is tired, he thought; my poor darling. Her work is too heavy for her. Those frail shoulders cannot support the burden of her heart as Alma's can. Alma wants nothing more of life; she is a fine woman; and she will always be able to manage by herself.

But Rose?

And he shuddered to think of what Miss Grogarty's future would be, without him.

Alma, at his side, put down in her mind, one by one, the things she meant to try over to herself, when she got home. I am so glad I came, she thought. And at the same time she felt like weeping, because Miss Grogarty's gestures touched her, and she knew that she could never imitate them.

When the play was over, Mr. Heavenstreet turned to his wife, and begged her to excuse him. " The car will take you home," he said. " As for me, I should like to walk a little. The fresh night air . . . and besides, I have something to think about."

" Julian," exclaimed Mrs. Heavenstreet in tones of entreaty.

" Yes, my dear? " said Julian.

" Nothing," said Mrs. Heavenstreet; and went out to look for her car.

Julian helped her in, and waved an amiable goodbye. Then he stepped back into the crowd; and Mrs. Heavenstreet went off by herself.

But half-way home, she remembered that she had left

her bag in the box. If she waited until morning, would it still be there? That was too risky, altogether.

She told her chauffeur to return to the theater.

It took a long time; for there were motors everywhere, going in all directions. She was sorry she hadn't waited, and telephoned in the morning, or sent down one of the maids. . . . However, there was no help for it; she couldn't very well tell him to turn around again, in all that traffic.

Half an hour later, Mrs. Heavenstreet again drew up before the Embassy Theater, whose lights, by this time, were almost out.

But there was enough light for her to see the figures of her husband and Miss Grogarty emerge from the stage door, and start down the street, arm in arm together.

Chapter XIV

THE ENSUING hours were the strangest in Alma Heavenstreet's whole life. Leaving her bag in the theater, she
had herself driven home, sitting motionless and upright,
her hands crossed in her lap. There was no sensation of
pain; and she thought of nothing. But she was more than
ever aware of things outside herself: of lights along the
avenues, of shadows in the streets, forms, faces, a hundred
tiny sights. Yet these images which flashed by with such
speed, made no sense or pattern; each one was itself, it
had nothing to do with anything else. Life seemed suddenly to have lost its continuity.

And when she reached home, and stood again in her
own room, she still could find no point of meeting between
the numbness inside, and the activity of all her senses.

That she had lost Julian, she never doubted. But what
it meant, to lose a husband, she did not yet know. Did
she, for instance, remain herself — a Daughter of the
American Revolution, and all the other things? Yes, she
supposed she did. Very well; let her proceed from that
point. . . .

To proceed at all, however, was difficult; because her
thoughts went here and there as they pleased. Nothing
within herself presented them with a direction.

I do not want to see him, she thought tentatively, ever

again. And the next moment she denied this, because it was untrue. . . . She longed for his return, to reassure herself, to reproach him, and to satisfy her curiosity.

What would he have to say for himself?

Finding herself near her desk, she pulled out a sheet of paper; it was natural for her to write a letter when she was moved, or indignant. But to whom was she to write, on this occasion? She put the paper back, with a vague smile. Already she was thinking of something else.

I am being punished, she thought, about the soup.

Then she remembered the wiles she had meant to practise; and how she had gone to borrow them from Miss Grogarty herself. This alone struck home; it stirred to shame the numbness inside. She sank down on the bed with a cry.

It is too late, she thought. I have lost him. It is all over.

Her mind, which at the first shock had gone to sleep, was only now beginning to awaken, with the most painful prickles. She found it impossible to sit still; she began to experience a feeling of panic, not unlike nausea. She stood up, and beat her hands feebly together; she pressed her fingers against her mouth, as though to stifle the cries which did not come.

What was she to do?

There seemed to be nothing for her to do.

She might appeal to him, she might throw herself on her knees in front of him, and cry, Do not leave me. But that would hardly be natural to her. And the next moment, stopping in front of her mirror, she addressed herself in these terms: Look at you — what a poor thing you are. Do you wonder that he prefers her? You are already middle-aged; and entirely without charm. While she has copper-colored hair, and the most attractive gestures. So do not feel too sorry for yourself, because this is what happens to women who cannot hold their husbands.

Yet a moment later it seemed to her that she was not entirely without charm. She remembered her youth, when she had been generally admired. Perhaps, if she did her hair a little differently . . .

It was no use; she sank again upon the bed. He was gone, he had left her; probably she would never see him again. Even now he might be hurrying away from her, in a train, or a motor. That was how it happened sometimes — without a farewell. In the morning she would receive a letter.

Her heart turned to water, for she knew that then her life would be over.

But at the same time, she would go on living. Only, how then would she live? Everyone would be sorry for her, and denounce Julian. But this time she would disagree with everybody, for she meant to forgive him. There would be her clubs, her charities, her committees . . . letters to write, meetings to attend . . . she would keep herself very busy.

Under the influence of these thoughts, she grew more calm. She even allowed herself a rueful smile. She wondered how long it had been going on, without her knowing. And how strange that Julian should have lied to her all this time. She should have known, she might have guessed; one did not come home night after night so happy and dreamy from a business meeting.

In fact, she began to feel a little sorry for him. So her Julian had fallen in love — at his age — with an actress. It hurt her — but perhaps it hurt him, too. What a youthful, what a romantic thing for him to have done. What would happen to him now? After all, he was no boy. He

was the president of a steel company. His company made
steel for battle-ships.

She felt a little stronger after that.

To feel pity for Julian — that was something quite
new. Not too much pity — just enough to take the hurt
out of her own heart. As though her child, let her say,
were unhappy — having been foolish. . . .

Children got over being foolish. Perhaps, after all, he
would come back to her again; perhaps he would have
to come back, because she felt so full of pity for him. Yes,
that was the way life arranged itself. And drawing, in
her mind, his errant head to her breast, she experienced
for the first time in her relation to him, a voluptuous and
motherly pleasure.

She gave a hiccup, due to her having kept back so many
tears.

But the sound of his steps entering the hall below, drew
her upright; and she descended to meet him, with a beating
heart.

"Hello," she said; "did you have a good walk?"

It seemed to her that her voice, which she hoped would
be light and airy, was wooden as a board. Julian, however, took no notice of it, nor of her swollen eyelids.

"Why, yes," he said. "But how do you happen to be
up so late, my dear?"

"The play," she explained, "excited me. I was . . .
thinking."

"Yes," said Julian. "It was a good play." He moved,
unsuspecting, toward his own room. "It is a lovely
night," he said. "The stars are very clear; and you can
smell the young pear orchards in the Park. I walked as
far as the lake; and then I came home."

Mrs. Heavenstreet shook her head. Poor soul — how

he lied. And what a dreadful, dreadful pity it was for him to have to lie so. How it must humiliate him; how degraded he must feel. He bent to kiss her cheek.

"Goodnight," he said.

She looked at him with shining eyes. "Goodnight," she echoed. And then, in a low voice, "Poor Julian."

Mr. Heavenstreet went to his room. He did not feel degraded; he was a little puzzled by his wife's last remark, but on the whole, he felt very happy.

BUT MISS GROGARTY
CANNOT DECIDE

Chapter XV

AND Rose, in her little apartment overlooking the park, also paced up and down, and beat her hands together. But in her case it was not so much from despair, as from indecision. As the days lengthened more and more, as the spring drew on, she found herself less and less able to make up her mind. The far-away blue skies, the clouds which traveled over the city, forever coming and going, the warm south wind, with its odors of trees and flowers, all gave her a nostalgia, a longing to be somewhere else. And she was tired — tired of working, of watching, of looking out for herself and her young son, who was at that moment sleeping peacefully in the next room.

"No," she exclaimed; "it is too much responsibility. And the public — who will tear me to pieces in a year — or the next year . . . For what am I sacrificing myself?"

She had no hesitation either on her son's account, or on account of Mrs. Heavenstreet, who was a busy woman, and whom she believed well able to withstand the shock of losing her husband. As for her son, she believed simply that what she did was none of his business. In addition she realized that the social results of a flight such as she planned, were . . . in short, there were no social results. It was only herself, then, that she was obliged to think about — herself, as an actress. For she knew what it would do to her career, to run away with the President of the Heavenstreet Structural Steel Company. That was not the sort of escapade which received no publicity. And the public was no longer attracted to an actress without moral restraint. Those days were over; it was only the virtuous now who succeeded in public life — hard working men and women, or, at least, those about whom nothing was definitely known.

It was too bad; but there it was. She could not have both Mr. Heavenstreet and her career. Besides, he would never allow it. He wanted to take care of her, but not from a position in the wings. She was to be his own orchid, to be looked after. . . . Mrs. Heavenstreet, perhaps, in the end . . .

And standing stock-still in the middle of her pacing, she saw herself doing a revival of Sheridan, or Shakespeare, in a little theater uptown, and for a series of special matinées. But that would be much later — after they were married, and people had forgotten. . . .

He was not unattractive to her. But she was wise not to think too much of it. One did not give up at thirty — or a little more — a career, in order to die of kisses. That was for the young girl, in love with love — or for a business man. No; sun and sea was what she wanted — rest and sleep; security, and peace.

It was hers for the asking; she had only to reach out her hand, only to say Yes to Julian — and within a month they would be in Paris. Next year William could go to a school in Geneva; it would be good for his French. While she and Julian dawdled in Capri.

To dawdle — that was it. For a little while — for a month, for a year, for two years . . . And then? Ah, that was the trouble. Little by little to grow restless again; to read of the new plays, to hear of the latest success, to pine for the theater. And to return, in the end — if he let her — or without him, alone again — to a public grown cold, to critics who had forgotten, to a new generation who had never heard of her. And to a manager grown unfriendly — once bitten, twice shy.

It was not a very attractive picture. She gave a shudder; but she faced it. And facing it, it did not suit her at all.

What was the reverse? She turned it over in her mind. To reign for a few more years as the favorite; then to watch, helpless and afraid, the rise of younger women to take her place. To wage a hopeless struggle against age, to keep her rôles, to keep from growing old, from being forgotten. To tour through the West, and Mid-West, in one-night stands, and stock companies — then to return in older parts, in plays written to give the best to her fading beauty — love tempered with pity, and built on remembrance — the faint perfume of what she once had been. To take part in revivals, benefits in her behalf — charity . . .

It seemed to her equally unattractive.

Nevertheless, such a course had gallantry; it had life. It gave to those who followed it the merit of dying in action.

And then, besides, there was always the chance that the public, her public, would continue to adore her as she grew older. . . .

But even she had to laugh at that.

Wouldn't it be better, then, to take her years of ease? — to lie on the rocks above the sea, while her young body grew brown — to watch the moon, silver and white, high on the snows about Annecy . . . ?

Seizing a pen, she hastily scribbled a note to Julian. It read, simply:

" I give in. When do we sail? "

She had no sooner written these words, than she tore the letter up again, and set herself to write another. It was longer, and it held a note of pleading.

" Very well," she wrote, " I will go. But give me a little time to think, my dear. There is so much to think about, so much to consider.

" I know that we will be very happy. We are young; and we have never had a holiday before. To have one together . . ."

The pen slid from her fingers, and she stared thoughtfully at the page before her. How clearly her inmost mind had betrayed itself. A holiday — yes, that was what it was to be, really. And when it was over? Because holidays were always over, sooner or later . . .

She had been thinking all this time only about herself. Now, for her own sake, she must stop, and think a little about Julian. Would he retire from business? She supposed that he would have to. What would he do, then? Nothing — just as she, also, would do nothing. And in the end he would grow restless, too.

Then he would have to start in all over again, just as she would.

She did not waste any pity on him, on this account. Devoid of sentimentality, her mind concerned itself only with her own problem. If Julian wanted her as much as that, it was his affair. But later — when the holiday was over — would he still want her?

She didn't know; but she thought it unlikely.

And in the train of these thoughts, came still another; what sort of man, after all, was this Julian Heavenstreet, to whom she was about to entrust if not her life, at least her fortune? She knew him only as the lover, the suitor, pleading for what he wanted.

Under such circumstances, all men were alike. It was only when they turned masterly that the real differences became apparent. Was he jealous, for example? She was afraid so.

And sitting, musing in this fashion, at her desk, she idly wrote down his qualifications, in the form of a list, with an answer, or a remark, attached to each.

Jealous — perhaps.
Wealth — yes. This she crossed out again, as being unworthy.
Miserly — no.
Attractive — yes.
Sympathetic — ?
Tolerant — ?
Will he like the sort of people I like? — probably not.
Must I like the sort of people he likes? — I suppose so.
Will he love me when the holiday is over? — who knows?

She made a grimace; and tore it all up. There was, after all, very little that she could say about him. Mrs. Heavenstreet was in a better position to know; she had had him, at least. But then it occurred to her that Mrs. Heavenstreet also would not know, because he was leaving her. And from a man's back, you cannot tell anything: once the back is turned, he is attractive, no matter what.

And then, of course, in the matter of his friends — they were Mrs. Heavenstreet's, too — he had simply accepted what was there for him. If Rose, on the other hand, brought him other, and different friends, he would accept those too, just as easily. Rasselas, for instance, and Stang, the great critic. And Professor Pembauer.

Or would he? That was the question.

It was true that her friends were mostly men. Very well; was she to give up her friends, in order to sit for the rest of her life on a rock?

No — there was too much to learn about him still, before going off. She must have more time — even if they missed the spring altogether. She took up her pen again.

"My dear," she wrote, "I must have a week, in which to think."

And to Professor Pembauer she also wrote a note, on the impulse of the moment.

"I am being so practical that I terrify myself. But how am I to know; or does that also come with art?

"Yesterday Mrs. Connor drenched my hair with her tears. What have you done to her?

"Come to see me.

"Your friend,
"Rose Grogarty."

Chapter XVI

WHEN Professor Pembauer received this letter from Miss Grogarty, he went at once to Mr. Gambrino.

"The time presses," he said. "Is everything in order?"

Mr. Gambrino replied that he was hurrying as much as he could. "Tomorrow," he said, "the carousel will be closed to allow the new furniture to move in. I tell you, it is very handsome furniture, Pembauer. For example, there is an aeroplane which actually goes up and down while the platform revolves. And all the motor-cars have horns, in case you wish to signal to a friend. You will see, we will have a big success, very exciting and exhilarating."

Professor Pembauer drily interrupted these enthusiastic assurances. "It does not sound to me," he observed, "as though the children would find much room on the carousel, hereafter. And meanwhile Mrs. Connor weeps; you have cheated her out of something, Gambrino, because you intend to pay her money back to her. However, this new furniture suits my own plans very well; and it is clear that this is the first truly sensible thing that you have done."

"Exactly," said Mr. Gambrino; "that is what I tell her. Nevertheless, she keeps crying out, 'My giraffe, my giraffe;' so I have kept among the motors and the aero-

413

plane a single giraffe, for her sake. She is so sentimental.
. . . Ah — the women. . . ."

"It is the women," replied Professor Pembauer, like
his great countryman, "who draw us on. Without them,
you would have no capital for your carousel; and I would
have nothing to bother my brains over. Now tell me
quickly: has Miss Grogarty already been invited?"

Mr. Gambrino replied that she had. "And so has all
the list you gave me," he added; "the Misters Rasselas,
Stang, Stoffel, and their friends; the Mr. and Mrs.
Heavenstreet, and many others. The cards of invitation
have just today gone out. Here, in effect, is how they
look."

He held out the invitation, for Professor Pembauer to
see.

"It is as you wished," he said; "or very nearly."

Gambrino (and Connor) Inc.
Invite You To Attend
A Grand Gala Opening
At The Carousel
In Central Park
May the 25
At 9 P. M.

Refreshments! All New Furniture!
Allow Yourself The Thrilling Aeroplane Ride!
Enjoy The Refined Motor Drive!
Appropriate Tenor Solos By Mr. Gambrino,
ch. ten. La Scala, Milan.

"That is to say," said Gambrino, modestly peering over
the professor's shoulder, "that I was a tenor in the chorus.
But as ch. ten., it makes more of an appearance."

414

Satisfied that everything had been done according to his directions Professor Pembauer went home and wrote a letter to Miss Grogarty.

" My dear friend," he wrote:

" By tomorrow you will receive in the mail an invitation to attend the grand gala opening of Mr. Gambrino's newly furnished carousel. It is a venture in which he has associated himself with our friend Mrs. Connor; and one in which I am also interested, but not in a monetary way. I hope that you will make every effort to attend, and also to cause your friends to attend, many of whom have already been invited. Do so, if you like, as a favor to me, to whom you owe no favors; and I venture to say that, if all goes well, you will have these questions which you so kindly address to my ignorance, answered by your own heart, which is, after all, the best teacher.

" With humble regards for your health, and your art,

" Believe me, I am your devoted servant,

" A. Pembauer."

Chapter XVII

DUE to its novelty, and also to Miss Grogarty's efforts, the opening was, as Mr. Gambrino had forseen, a great success. The damp night air, so full of sweet spring smells, the shadowy trees, and the bright lights and gay colors of the carousel, shining like a little jewel in the middle of the dark and quiet park, all served to put the guests in the best of good humor, and to add a richness to the occasion beyond Mrs. Connor's fondest hopes. Arrayed in a ballroom gown which had once belonged to Miss Grogarty, and carrying a bouquet of sweet-peas given her by Mr. Gambrino, she alternately beamed and wept, seated upon her giraffe, whose presence among so many motors touched her heart. It is true that a number of children attempted to storm the platform, but they were beaten off; and remained to marvel at the improvements, and jeer at their elders, whose white shirt-fronts and bare bosoms, high hats and trailing skirts, presented a kaleidoscope of color and of fashion as the platform slowly revolved.

Mrs. Heavenstreet, the wife of the President of Heavenstreet Structural Steel, dressed in a gown of green velvet, with emeralds at her throat and at her wrists, found herself seated upon a motorcycle, next to Mr. Rasselas, who was piloting a small racing car around the

416

circle. She closed her eyes; the motion nauseated her; it seemed to her that the circles grew narrower and narrower, the motion swifter and swifter. Uttering a faint cry, she fell off, into the arms of the publisher, who had been watching her, and was ready to receive her.

"Ever since I first saw you," he exclaimed, "I have been waiting for you to fall off. Divine Creature."

Mrs. Heavenstreet opened her eyes in startled protest, only to find herself already in an embrace from which it was impossible to extricate herself without a struggle.

"No, please," she cried. "And I do not even know you."

"It is the season," he replied; "do not give it another thought. But you look pale, my dear lady, a little seasick. I have an excellent remedy for seasickness."

And drawing a flask from his pocket, he urged Mrs. Heavenstreet to swallow some of its contents.

Oh, well, she thought; I have nothing to live for, anyway. . . .

On the opposite arc of the circle, Miss Grogarty was enjoying a ride in the aeroplane. Dressed in white, with orchids from Mr. Heavenstreet, she rose and fell with little cries of joy, sustained by the admiration of Mr. Stang, the critic, and Mr. Gambrino, who supported her from either side, as well as Mr. Peters of the *News*, Professor Pembauer, and the policeman assigned to that section of the park.

This, thought Mr. Gambrino, as he held her up under the ribs, is the most intimate thing I have ever done.

He was got up in a dress suit especially hired for the occasion. But Mr. Stang had come, as usual, in tweeds. He felt, not unreasonably, that it lent him a certain distinction. He, also, held up Miss Grogarty; and allowed himself to make sure that she was soft, under her dress.

" It is true," he murmured ; and gazed happily upwards.

Miss Grogarty thought that she had never had so good a time. The aeroplane rocked slowly up and down, the music played, and all about her men and women, in their best clothes, laughed and sang and threw her admiring glances. She felt herself to be among friends ; and she leaned down and placed a kiss, like a little pat, on the top of Professor Pembauer's head.

" I have you to thank for this," she said softly.

Mr. Stang gave a groan, and so did Mr. Gambrino. " It is the musician," observed Mr. Stang, " who gets the best in this world. Literature is a dry and lonely art ; and of all forms of writing, criticism receives the fewest embraces."

" Well," said Mr. Gambrino, taking a breath, " if it is to be the musician . . ."

And he held up his face, pale but audacious, for a kiss.

Miss Grogarty laughed, and placed her finger on his mouth. " You're very sweet," she said ; " both of you. Thank you." And with her other hand she waved gaily at Mr. Heavenstreet, who was winding his way around the platform in search of her.

However, when he saw her having her finger kissed, a dismal expression appeared on his face, and he moved away, a little unsteady on his feet, because of the motion.

Miss Grogarty was surprised ; but her spirits soon rose again. Professor Pembauer, on the contrary, allowed himself a thoughtful smile. The kiss on the top of his head pleased him ; he was only sorry that Mr. Heavenstreet had been too late to see it.

" Here," cried Mr. Stang to Mr. Gambrino ; " do you mean to claim for yourself the rewards of music? What impudence. You are a business man, you are in the automobile business. So do not expect anything of an emotional nature."

However, Mr. Gambrino stood his ground. " There is still a giraffe," he replied, " and the steam calliope. As for music, or not music, in a little while you will have the pleasure of hearing me sing; and then you will see something. And if you do not like that, I will take you out and give you a punch in the nose, like any Italian would do."

" Thank you," said Miss Grogarty; " you're both of you very kind. But that's enough. . . ."

Mr. Heavenstreet, winding his way back among the motors, stopped short and leaned dizzily against a post. Was that his wife over there, seated on the rear of a motorcycle, her arms twined about the gentleman in front? It was, it was his wife; it was Alma Heavenstreet.

" Hold me tighter, darling," said Mr. Rasselas: " we're going around a curve."

" Hup," said Alma faintly.

" The flask is in my right-hand pocket," said Mr. Rasselas.

" I have it," said Alma. " Undo it for me. If I let go, I'll fall off again."

Mr. Rasselas unscrewed the flask. " Take a good one this time," he told her. " It will keep off the seasickness."

Alma took a good one.

" Can I see you home?" asked Mr. Rasselas.

" Why not?" said Mrs. Heavenstreet dreamily; and fell off again.

Mr. Heavenstreet picked her up, and put her back on. " Julian," she murmured, " I'm so glad to see you. How are you, my dear? This is my friend, Mr. . . . Mr.? . . . who picked me up when I fell off, and is taking me home."

"Ah," said Julian.

Am I dreaming? he thought to himself.

Mrs. Heavenstreet nestled herself drowsily on the back of the motorcycle, and wrapped her plump arms around Mr. Rasselas. "Go on," she said. "Goodbye, Julian. Get out of the way, dear, or we'll run over you."

And reaching forward, she gave a blast on the horn. "That's in case there's anybody in the way," she explained.

Julian went to the edge of the platform, and jumped. Rose — Alma — what had come over them? He stood in the shadows, and watched as the carnival rolled by, around, and around again. And as he watched, it began to frighten him. The humor of the spring, the sap of life, was too heady; unseen, in the darkness round about, the trees, the bushes, the young green grass, the hidden flowers, sucking up from earth with greedy roots their bit of moisture, crowding each other, pitiless, bursting with life, terrible in the intensity of their will to live. . . . And here, before his eyes, this carnival of desire, this festival of longing . . .

"They had a better time in Rome," said Miss Arbuthnot to the poet Stoffel, as they stood by the lemonade stand. "The Greeks never understood that sort of thing. Rome was the place: I say, they did let go a bit, didn't they?"

Mr. Stoffel gravely emptied the remains of a small bottle of gin into his glass of lemonade. "What did the Greeks," he asked, "or the Romans, know about life? You had to be a Jew, to know about life. I do not believe in the Greeks or the Romans. They are finished. Let us spit on them. I believe in life."

"Do you," asked Miss Arbuthnot, as he led her away in the dark, "believe in the Jews?"

"No," said Mr. Stoffel.

MISS GROGARTY DECIDES

Chapter XVIII

THE MUSIC stopped, the carousel coasted more slowly around its circle, and Mr. Heavenstreet climbed on board again, and went in search of Miss Grogarty. As he passed the motorcycle on which Mrs. Heavenstreet had been seated, Mr. Rasselas called out to him,

"I say, pick your wife up again, will you, like a good fellow?"

Mr. Heavenstreet did not stop, but hurried on until he found Miss Grogarty in her aeroplane. "Come," he said, taking her by the hand; "I want to talk to you."

They walked off into the darkness together, away from the laughter, the little cries, the music, the colored lights. In the still black shadow of a tree, he turned to confront her.

"What sort of party is this, Rose?" he demanded, in unbelieving tones.

"It's a heavenly party," said Miss Grogarty, simply.

Mr. Heavenstreet took hold of her arm, and gave it a shake. "And how," he exclaimed, "are you acting?"

Miss Grogarty's eyes narrowed; and she disengaged her arm. Here already, she thought, is one of the answers. "I'm acting in a natural way, Julian," she assured him. "You may as well know it. I like this sort of thing. It appeals to me."

"And these people," cried Julian; "these unbelievable people?"

"They are my friends," said Miss Grogarty quietly.

She looked at him for a moment; and in the darkness, her eyes grew tender and mournful. He was answering her questions, one by one. What a pity. And that plump, unhappy child — was that the busy Mrs. Heavenstreet?

"Go back, my dear boy," she said, "and pick your wife up from the floor. And do not think too harshly of me."

(*The moon, the full round moon, forever descending . . .*)

"I shall do nothing of the sort," said Julian. He folded his arms. "You are going home now," he declared. "At once. And with me."

But Miss Grogarty only smiled. No — that wasn't the way she wanted to be taken care of. "I'm not going home, Julian," she said; "I'm having too good a time. Take Mrs. Heavenstreet home; and go home yourself, there's a dear. You're spoiling my evening."

Mr. Heavenstreet grew pale. "Rose," he exclaimed; "you cannot mean what you are saying."

"But I do," said Rose.

(*Never to see the sweet white snows above Annecy . . .*)

"Rose," cried Mr. Heavenstreet in anguish; "don't you love me?"

"I never was sure," said Miss Grogarty.

She touched his hand lightly. "I'll let you know in the morning," she said.

Mr. Heavenstreet went back to the carousel, and picked Mrs. Heavenstreet off the motorcycle. Carrying her limp form in his arms, he strode through the crowd, past the urchins who made way for him only to follow joyously in his rear: across the drive to his car; and so, home.

There he put Mrs. Heavenstreet to bed, and tucked her in. And finally, to his own surprise, he bent to kiss her goodnight. Mrs. Heavenstreet had long since given up being surprised at anything.

"Goodnight," she murmured sleepily. But then she thought of something. "Be careful of the curves, darling," she advised him; and fell asleep.

Mr. Heavenstreet gazed at her for a long while. And she seemed to him like a child, so innocent in her sleep — with such a weary droop to her round little mouth, and that one plump little hand curled like a leaf above her head . . .

"You need someone to look after you," said Mr. Heavenstreet. And he sat down, and stared thoughtfully at the tip of his shoe.

Meanwhile, on the carousel, Mrs. Connor hung from her giraffe, and gazed fondly at Professor Pembauer, who was holding on to one of the forelegs. "Well," she said, "what do you think? Would you say it was a great success?"

Professor Pembauer replied that for his own purposes, at least, the evening could not have gone off better.

Mrs. Connor clucked, "Ah," she said, "my Gambrino; what a head for business."

And thrusting her left hand under Professor Pembauer's nose, she exclaimed,

"Look."

There, on the fourth finger, was to be seen a small diamond, framed in gold.

Professor Pembauer congratulated her. "Soon," he said happily, "I will have married friends, to give me home-cooking now and then. In this way the composer, Johannes Brahms, himself a bachelor, enjoyed the friendship of Frau Clara Schumann, at whose home he often ate home-cooked *gänserbraten, knöckerli,* and little tarts, made of cream."

So saying, he gave a voluptuous sigh.

" We are simple business people, my Gambrino and I," replied Mrs. Connor, " and we will live on spaghetti, mutton, and things like custards, or bread puddings. But for a great artist, like you . . . if you would honor us . . ."

And she gave him a starry look, as though to say, because I am to marry a business man does not mean that I am giving up my ideals.

Outside, in the dark, Miss Grogarty stood by herself, in the dew, in the sweet-smelling air. Her back was to the carousel; before her stretched the misty meadows of the park, the budded and silent trees, in whose branches, at dawn, the birds would soon be singing. Far away, out of the darkness, rose the city, the shadowy towers, the golden lights tossed up to heaven like fireworks, the faint roar and hum of the streets . . . all in the old blue fog of night, under the northern sky. She lifted her face to it, she drank it in. . . .

" Oh," she breathed, " it's beautiful."

At the same time she knew that she would never leave it, that she never wanted to go away from it, from the city heavy with life, swollen with life, bursting with the will to live . . . to live, to be itself, to suffer, to aspire, to go on. . . .

" I, too," she said; " I, too."

Back at the carousel, Mr. Gambrino was singing. But nobody heard him. Nevertheless, through the laughter and the cries, Mr. Gambrino sang on. He had closed his eyes; and he was approaching his high B flat, lowered just a little to fit the voice. . . .

There is

Another Heaven

"*Then shall I see, and hear, and know,*
All I desired or wished below;
And every power find sweet employ
In that eternal world of joy.
                              Amen."

HYMN NO. 150

Chapter I

THE STYX lay silent. No oar disturbed the serenity of those bitter waters, on whose dark bosom lilies and weeds floated without movement. Charon's skiff, half drawn up on land, waited in vain; and slowly rotted. Its master slept; and dreams of past glories caused him to smile.

On the other hand, the River Jordan was crowded with barges, skiffs, dingies, and ferries. A clear wind ruffled the waters which bore with joy a never-ending procession of passengers between shore and shore. In formidable numbers men, women, and children gathered on the bank, waiting to be taken over. The Eternal City received them; there was room for them all. White, shining, and august, it rose like a dream beyond the water which flowed about its walls.

George Herman Wutheridge, one-time Professor of Semitic Languages at the University, had not yet arrived at the river; he was still a full day's journey away. He walked without care; his old bones forgot to creak; and a delicious breeze penetrated his beard. Immortal flowers blossomed along the path, from which the bees drew pollen with a faint bumbling hum. One of them, alighting for a moment on his hand, rested its wings while he examined it without fear. " This is not," he said to himself, " a bee of Hymettus, whose honey, allowed to ferment, filled the heads of the ancients with glory, and their bodies with ardor. Rather, this workaday little fellow reminds me of the bees at home, from whose hives came a palatable syrup, proper for spreading on bread, and enjoyed by the children."

"Look out," said a voice at his elbow; "or he'll sting you."

Professor Wutheridge looked gently around. " Do you think so?" he asked the young man whom he now saw walking at his side. And he added in a tone of surprise, "Why should he do such a thing?"

The youth, who appeared to be about eighteen years old, shrugged his thin shoulders. "My mother always taught me to be afraid of bees," he explained.

His pale face seemed drawn in an expression of anxiety. "After all," he said apologetically, "they do have a sting."

Professor Wutheridge regarded him thoughtfully. "Your mother," he remarked, "whoever she may have been, seems to have seen the hindmost part first. My own mother, whom I hope soon to see, was just the reverse, and saw only the good in everything. She died when I was a child, and I do not remember her very well. Perhaps I am wrong in attributing to her the virtues which I used to find in my favorite heroines of antiquity, the mischievous Thetis, the lovely Seti, the great-hearted Naomi, and the wise Bath-sheba, mother of Solomon."

The young man laid his hand on Professor Wutheridge's arm, as though to stop him. "My mother," he declared, and his voice shook with joy, "was a very religious woman. She was the head of our church at home, and of many other things besides. She was known everywhere. Perhaps you have heard of her." And he added

428

simply, as though that explained everything, "Her name was Emma Meiggs."

The professor of Semitic languages gazed long and curiously at this youth whose mother had often figured in the newspapers. "Yes," he said at last, "I have heard of your mother. I did not know that she had a son. She was a great figure: I wish I could say that I had sympathized more fully with her aims. So she, too, is before me . . . that is to say, she is there, where I am going. . . ."

And he heaved a deep sigh.

"Perhaps," he said, "I have lived too much in the past to appreciate the needs of the present. In your mother's voice, uplifted in prophetic utterances, it has often seemed to me that I heard the lamentations of Jeremiah, of Ezekiel, and of all the prophets from Moses to Malachi."

"Yes, that has been said of her," replied young Meiggs with pride.

"I would not like it said of me," declared the professor. "I prefer to speak of joy, like the Greeks. What — has God learned nothing in three thousand years?"

"My mother had many trials," said the young man, without noticing this interruption, "which she met like a saint. Father was one of them. She used to pray for him every night; she prayed that he'd be saved. He went first; then mother; and then me. We'll all meet soon; that is, unless he wasn't saved after all. But I guess he was; I guess he was."

Then it was the young man's turn to sigh. He walked along thoughtfully, his pale face drawn in a puzzled frown. The light of heaven shone on the path, the bees sang, the air seemed perfumed with a thousand blossoms.

"There wasn't much use living when mother went," he said at last. "She always took care of me. She took care of everything."

The professor nodded his head sympathetically. "I know," he said. "I lost my parents when I was a child. And all my life I had to take care of myself. It must be very fine to be taken care of. That is what I look forward to most of all, when I think of meeting my mother again. . . .

"Still," he added a moment later, "I would not like to be told what to do and what not to do. And your mother, as I remember her on earth, spent much of her time telling her neighbors what was right and what was wrong."

"They needed telling," broke in Mr. Meiggs.

"I dare say," agreed the professor, "I dare say. And I imagine most people prefer it, as a matter of fact, to making out for themselves. Still, one cannot study the past without coming to the conclusion that right and wrong have often changed places, depending sometimes upon the climate, sometimes on political necessity, but more often on the simplest rules of self-preservation, in which the diet also plays a large part."

"My mother," said young Mr. Meiggs dreamily, "saved many souls by her work. She took sin away from people; she helped pass laws to make them good. And she's waiting for me now; she knows I'm coming. She'll put out her arms to me, and I'll go into them, and she'll hold me tight."

And his young eyes filled with happy tears.

"You can imagine that I am excited," he said simply.

"Yes," agreed the professor, "that will be fine. I cannot believe that my mother will be waiting for me; for one thing, she has no idea of what I look like. When she left me, I was still very young, and I gave promise then of good looks which the years have failed to confirm. Nor have I anyone else to look forward to meeting, for my life was a simple and lonely one. I found happiness in my work; I was married only to my studies. Perhaps I was fortunate, since in that case, I am taking my wife along with me."

"I too," said the young man, "am as pure as the day I was born."

By this time they had approached the bank of the river and saw before them the great city, over whose domes and towers light seemed to hover like a cloud. The air all about them throbbed with faint music and bells; Mr. Meiggs thought that he could distinguish the tunes of *Old Faithful* and *Rock of Ages;* while the professor listened enraptured to the sound of harps. The flowery meadow air gave way to the cool smell of water, mingled with an unmistakable odor of incense. They stood a moment in silence, reverently gazing; after which the professor exclaimed in tones of awe and delight: "There is the great city, our last and eternal home. Now may sorrow and I be forever parted, at this river into whose moving waters all burdens, however weary, must fall."

Young Mr. Meiggs said nothing. However, at that moment a third voice at the professor's elbow caused him to look around with a friendly smile. A short, stout man was standing beside him, wearing upon his face an expression of concern.

"Is that the city?" asked the man.

"It is," replied the professor.

"I heard you say that here is where all burdens fall," continued the stranger. "Excuse me: I have many."

And he gave a groan.

"My name," he said, "is Lewis, born Levy. It has

been quite a struggle for me to get here. The going was not easy. So there it is, the city. My, my.

"What a sight."

And as neither the professor nor Mr. Meiggs could think of anything to say, he added,

"Well, tell me: will I be welcome there? What do you think?"

Young Mr. Meiggs looked at him critically. "Were you baptized?" he asked.

"I was," said Mr. Lewis.

"Then," said Mr. Meiggs, "I should expect so."

Mr. Lewis nodded his head in agreement. "I have been a good churchman," he said. "I used to loan my pictures to the charities. On Sundays my house was filled with important people, looking at my collection."

"Ah," said the professor.

"Perhaps," Mr. Lewis continued, "they'll keep me out anyway. What do you think?"

And he peered anxiously at the professor, who gazed quietly back at him.

"The city you see before you," said the professor, "is comparatively modern. Younger than Thebes, or even Jerusalem, it is a colony of that mother city which was discovered a little less than two thousand years ago by slaves whose Roman masters, on their way to the Elysian Fields, left them to find whatever home for their troubled souls they could. It is not the paradise of Egypt, shared by the gods and the Pharaohs; it is not Eblis, nor Nirvana; it is not even the Abode of the Blessed of the Rabbi Eliezer. Indeed, I am curious to see just what it is. . . . I imagine we shall find it a not unfamiliar place. As to whether or not you will be welcome there, I cannot say, although I do not see how, if you have been baptized and have led a Christian life, you can very well be kept out."

432

"It's not exactly being kept out that bothers me," said Mr. Lewis, "so much as being let in, and then being made to feel out. When I'm out, I'm out; but when I'm in and at the same time out, it makes me dizzy."

He shook his head gloomily. "It's a long time since I was welcome anywhere," he said.

"I am sure that my mother will welcome you," declared young Mr. Meiggs.

Mr. Lewis looked at him with an expression of hope. "Has she much influence?" he asked.

"My mother is Emma Meiggs," said the young man.

"Ah," said Mr. Lewis despondently; "well . . . I'm glad to have met you."

And as the boat which was to take them over at that moment approached the land, he seized him by the hand, shook it briefly, and hurried to the shore.

A few moments later George Henry Wutheridge, Professor of Semitic Languages at the University, William Wilberforce Meiggs, and Mr. Lewis, born Levy, were on their way across Jordan.

Chapter II

"There's mother," exclaimed William Meiggs as the boat drew near the shore; and he began to wave furiously. "Mother," he cried. But presently his arm dropped to his side, and an expression of embarrassment and uncertainty crossed his face. It was not his mother after all.

Nor was she anywhere to be seen among the crowds of people who were waiting to greet the newcomers. He looked around at the strange faces beaming with welcome, at first eagerly, then anxiously, and at last in a sort of panic. Where was she? What could have happened? Had he made some mistake? Wasn't he expected?

All about him people were embracing with tears of joy and cries of rapture. But William stood silent, gazing around him with a frightened smile, and eyes which saw nothing. It was like one of childhood's agonies over again, to be left out of other folks' welcome. It was like being at a Christmas tree where there was no gift for him; like the Sunday-school picnic when no one wanted to play with him . . . like not being asked to dance at the church sociable, when it was the girls' turn, though he was dressed in his best. . . .

He felt like weeping. On earth or in heaven William Meiggs was lost without his mother.

Perhaps the most unbearable part of it all was its not

being a surprise, really — deep down. How many times as a child had he stood with the same fixed smile, trying not to let others see how miserable he felt? It was always the same, nothing ever turned out as he hoped it would; something always . . . usually . . . went wrong.

His mother would come sooner or later, of course: she always did; but usually . . . never . . . it was never sooner. It was true: never, oh, never sooner. He could say it to himself at last — now that he was there. . . .

He took a deep breath, and turning blindly to the first white-robed figure he saw, "Excuse me, sir," he said, "could you tell me . . . I'm a stranger here, . . . is Mrs. Meiggs? . . . Or perhaps where she lives?"

The stranger replied in a voice full of sweetness: "Mrs. Meiggs lives just down that street, four houses from the second turning, on the left side."

"She's not here," said William apologetically.

"No," agreed the stranger, "she's not."

"I suppose she's home," said William.

But the stranger shook his head. "Mrs. Meiggs is presiding at a meeting," he answered, "to arrange for the observance of Mother's Day."

"Oh," said William. And he added in a small voice, "I'm her son."

The stranger smiled. "How happy she will be to see you again," he remarked.

"Yes," said William. And giving a great swallow, he started up the street to his mother's house.

But as he drew near the second turning to the left, his spirits began to rise, and he found himself smiling. "At least," he thought, "she hasn't changed any." And this reflection comforted him.

He found his mother's house without difficulty. It was

a simple dwelling in no way different from the others all about it: a narrow house in a row of narrow houses, of white material, scrupulously clean, with a bow window and a porch. In the small garden or yard before the door a few flowers of paradise bloomed: lilies, immortelles in pots, and a small pomegranate tree. On either side, as far as he could see, the houses stood exactly alike, an orderly regiment, endless, the same, narrow, white, and respectable.

As he turned in at the gate, he saw that his father was standing in the doorway; and although he had secretly expected it, his heart sank. However, he went up to him, and kissed him dutifully on the cheek, to one side of the long, drooping mustache.

"Well, father," he began, "here I am again."

"So I see," said Mr. Meiggs. And he gazed without enthusiasm at his son.

"I was told you'd be along one of these days," he remarked, "but it didn't seem reasonable, you being so young: I figured we'd be left in peace a while yet." He waved his hand toward the house. "Make yourself to home," he said; "there's not much room, but I expect your mother'll find a place to put you; she always did."

Stepping aside to allow him to pass, Mr. Meiggs followed his son into the house.

"It looks sort of familiar," said William timidly, gazing about him at the horsehair sofa, the worsted mottoes hung on the wall, the one low rocking-chair, the table with its red and white checked cloth.

"Why not?" asked Mr. Meiggs. "It's our home. Our heavenly mansion." And he added,

"Your mother will be back from meeting soon. She said give you her love, and you'll find crackers and milk in the kitchen if you're hungry."

436

" I'm not hungry, thanks," said William.

Mr. Meiggs moved uncomfortably. " Did you have a good crossing ? " he asked after a silence.

" It wasn't so bad," William replied politely. " There were a lot of people coming over, and I came with them."

He ventured nothing further, and the conversation languished. In the silence father and son exchanged uneasy glances. " Now," thought Mr. Meiggs, " I suppose I'll play second fiddle, like I used to."

And pulling out his mustaches with a fierce expression, he cleared his throat. " Herrum," he said.

William cowered unhappily in his chair. But just at that moment he heard a step on the porch, and a second later Emma Meiggs herself came through the door.

" William," she exclaimed.

Crossing the room with deliberate strides as he rose flushing with joy from his chair, she folded him in her stout arms, and kissed him on the cheek. Then she held him out to look at.

" What a big boy you've got to be," she cried.

She smoothed the hair down across his forehead in the way he remembered. " Well, now, tell me," she said: " are you all right ? "

" Never better, mother," replied William.

" I'm glad to hear it," said Mrs. Meiggs. " Well, well, and now you're here. Dearie me. Hm . . . a grown son. Well . . .

" How is everything at home ? "

" Your work is going on, mother," said William proudly. " There's a statue of you in front of the State House."

" No," said Mrs. Meiggs, full of wonder.

" And there's laws called after you," William hurried on, " and a book written about you."

"A statue," said Mrs. Meiggs dreamily: "Well, now
. . . Did you hear that Henry? There's a statue of me
at home." She turned back to her son again. "What's
it like?" she demanded. "Is it a likeness?"

Lifting her chin, she gazed nobly over his head.

William blushed. "It looked like you," he admitted,
"a little. But then some people put paint on it, and broke
off the nose, and . . . and . . ."

"People?" demanded Mrs. Meiggs indignantly. "Do
you call that people?"

"They were sent to jail," mumbled William unhappily;
"that is, some of them."

"They'd ought to be hung," exclaimed Mrs. Meiggs.
"Well, I never . . . Did you hear that, Henry?"

"Yes," said Mr. Meiggs sourly, "I heard it."

"They'd ought to be tarred and feathered," cried Mrs.
Meiggs.

"Spoiling a good statue that way."

"Never mind, Emma," said her husband soothingly.
"That's all gone by for you now."

"That's true," she admitted. She threw him a grateful smile. "I've got higher things to think of," she declared happily.

She continued in tones of enthusiasm, "Just imagine
—everyone is right minded here, working for the truth
and the light. To-day I brought them Mother's Day. I
could be happy here forever."

She went to the cupboard, and took out a stone jar of
milk, a crock of honey, and some bread. "Come," she
said, "let's have a bite together, to welcome my son. This
is simple food, William; we live simply here."

Mr. Meiggs gave his mustache a hopeful pull. "Perhaps, Emma," he said, "seeing as how this is a welcome,
you might say, and what with having William back with

us so early, so much earlier than we had a right to expect, it might not be out of place to celebrate the occasion with a glass or two . . ."

"Henry," said Mrs. Meiggs.

Closing his eyes, Henry took up the beaker of milk. "Ah," he said.

"Yes," murmured Mrs. Meiggs, her mouth full of honey, "I could be happy here forever."

William smiled at her across the table. He had never seen her so peaceful, so noble, so sure and safe, so happy, so uplifted. Except, of course, for that moment about the statue. But that was his fault; he shouldn't have spoken of it. "Mother," he whispered, putting his hand out timidly to touch her, "I'm glad I'm here."

"I'm sure of it, my son," said Emma.

"We're very glad to have you."

"You look much better, mother," said William, "than you used."

Mr. Meiggs winked one eye at him. "Your mother's a good-looking woman," he declared. And leaning over, he pressed a gallant kiss upon her cheek.

"Henry," exclaimed Mrs. Meiggs faintly: "in front of the child."

"'Twas purely meant, my dear," said Henry; "in loving kindness."

"I know," said Emma, patting his hand. Nevertheless, she was obscurely troubled, not so much for the kiss, which was no more than the custom in their new home, as for William, who was, after all, not used to it.

"Finish your milk, William," she said a little sharply, "and let's get on."

William said nothing; he turned back to his honey, from which the sweetness had unaccountably departed.

The rest of the meal was eaten in silence. When the

last crumb was gone, Emma took her son to his room, furnished as it had been at home with a low cot, a motto, and a wooden chair. Seated together on the edge of the cot, she drew him close to her, then held him away and looked at him with tender anxiety.

"William," she said; "tell me: have you been a good boy?"

"Yes, mother," said William.

"All the time?"

"All the time, mother."

She put her arm around him, his head sank against her shoulder. Through the little bedroom window drifted the odors of paradise, the perfume of lilies, the strange scent of myrrh, of cinnamon; the cries of children at play, happy, without envy, cut through the distant sound of music, of voices marvelously sweet mingled in simple glees. William let his head sink lower and lower; an unexpected weariness assailed him, sadness stole through his heart. Why should he be sad? . . . He had thought sorrow ended forever, the heavy sweet sorrow of youth, without reason, without hope; now that he was home again, now that he was here where he had longed with all his heart to be, could he be anything but happy, could he feel anything but joy?

And as the heavenly day wore on, he wept, quietly, without knowing why, while his mother, with her arm around him and an expression of ineffable satisfaction on her face, rocked slowly up and down.

Chapter III

PROFESSOR WUTHERIDGE stepped off the boat in an active manner, and with the liveliest curiosity. "How often," he thought, "have I longed to behold those ancient cities where history began. And here I am in a city stranger than Babylon, though not as old as Rome. Dear me." And making use of a trick taught him by the explorer Beebe, he closed his eyes in order to imagine himself back at his desk in the University. "Now," he thought, " I have only to remember how I used to dream of all this; and when I open my eyes I shall feel the full impact of my situation."

But before he could look about, a pair of soft arms were thrown around him, and he felt himself embraced in a vigorous manner. "George," said a voice; and he opened his eyes upon the very last thing he had expected to see — a young woman. Her face shone with mischief and joy, her auburn hair fell in a curl upon her neck; her brown eyes smiled into his, and her mouth was still framed in a kiss.

" Mother," he exclaimed.

" My son," she replied. At these words her whole being seemed to break into ripples of laughter. " My darling white-headed child."

Professor Wutheridge looked accusingly at this young woman whom he remembered, but only faintly, from his childhood. "You did it to surprise me," he said.

"I did," she admitted. "And really — when you closed your eyes, it was too heavenly altogether. Your face, my darling — so serious. Oh, my stars."

Overcome with mirth, she leaned against him, her cheek close to his coat. Professor Wutheridge cleared his throat; he looked around him with embarrassment. "Mother," he said loudly, in order to explain the situation to some fellow travelers who were passing by.

Mrs. Wutheridge actually giggled. "Yes, my child," she replied.

"Is father here?" asked the professor.

"Your father," declared Mrs. Wutheridge, "is at home, pacing the floor. The arrival of a son has been almost too much for him; he would be here, but diffidence and terror control his actions at the moment. He is being comforted by your uncle Ludwig, who is also in a state."

"My Uncle Ludwig?" asked the professor with surprise. "I was not aware . . ."

"He's not your uncle, goose," exclaimed Mrs. Wutheridge: "but we have to call him something."

"Oh," said the professor. "Um," said he.

"Nonsense," replied Mrs. Wutheridge impatiently; "it's not oh and um at all. Remember where you are."

The professor looked at his mother with an appreciative smile. "I am glad you reminded me," he said. "I confess, I feel an overwhelming curiosity about all this. When you saw me just now with my eyes closed, I was about to give myself a surprise, in a manner of speaking. It is an old trick, to close your eyes, and imagine yourself back where you came from. Then when you open them again, you see everything as though for the first time, with the further advantage of knowing where to look for it. William Beebe, the explorer . . ."

442

"Gracious," said Mrs. Wutheridge; "I thought you were dreaming of your wife. And it was Mr. Beebe. . . ."

"My wife?" said the professor; "I have no wife."

"No wife?" cried his mother in consternation. "No wife at all? Then you are a bachelor."

"I am," said the professor.

"Without experience," continued his mother.

"How else would I be here?" asked the professor simply.

"I have never loved."

Mrs. Wutheridge put her hand to her mouth shaped in a round letter of dismay.

"Oh," she exclaimed.

"Oh, my.

"Oh, my poor boy."

"I see no reason to complain," said the professor gallantly, "of a mode of living which has numbered me among the saved, and also brought me back to you, madam, for the rest of eternity."

She smiled, and reaching out, took hold of his hand. "That was pretty," she said. "Heaven knows where you learnt it.

"But come along: we mustn't prolong your father's anxiety beyond a reasonable limit."

So saying, hand in hand, the white-bearded professor and the young woman with dancing eyes started up the street.

"This is not the sort of city I expected to find," said the professor, as his glance encountered row after row of houses all alike, "although I suppose if I had stopped to think I would have realized that the spiritual sons of Comstock, of Moody, and of William Bryan have always held before their eyes the goal of respectable uniformity.

443

Nor is anything else conceivable to a man of democratic ideals and sound Protestant doctrine. Perhaps I miss a little the spaciousness of the Abode of the Blessed of the medieval rabbis, where the rooms alone were one hundred thousand miles wide; or it is possible that our modern architecture at home had prepared me for the pyramids and cubes of Babylon and Egypt."

" To think," said Mrs. Wutheridge admiringly, " that you are a child of mine. Babylon indeed. You sound like a scholar. Well, are you? Tell me the truth."

" For forty years," said the professor, " I was Lanyarde Professor of Semitic Languages at the University."

" Semitic Languages," exclaimed Mrs. Wutheridge. " My dear — was that necessary? "

" Thirty-nine books of the Old Testament," replied the professor inexorably, " including Genesis, Exodus, and Deuteronomy, were first written in Hebrew."

" No," said Mrs. Wutheridge.

" Fancy that.

" Is it generally known? "

" On the other hand," continued the professor, " a gentleman of Hebraic extraction whom I met on the way assured me that the Jews are not as a rule welcome at home, where they control most of the banks and markets, and contribute largely to the cathedrals."

" I should hope not," said Mrs. Wutheridge; " nor here, neither."

Then it was the professor's turn to be distressed. " In that case," he thought, " how extremely unfortunate for Mr. Lewis."

However, at this moment they came opposite a house like all the others, yet in a way different. For one thing, the windows were of lavender glass, behind which could be seen long curtains of silk; a short pebbled walk, bor-

dered with large sea-shells led to the gate past beds of
sweet-william and marigold, on either side of which stood
an iron stag, staring with unwavering gaze at the street.
There was no porch; at the low steps leading to the door
with its graceful fanlight, stood two small pots filled with
earth from which spouted two apple trees made entirely
of lead.

Mrs. Wutheridge opened the door with a small gold
key: "A foible of mine, my dear," she explained; "for
I do so dislike doors left open, and everyone darting in
and out as they please;" and they passed directly into a
small and tasteful parlor furnished in a period no older
than herself. As they entered two tall young men sprang
to their feet, and stood bashfully at attention. With a
charming smile, Mrs. Wutheridge led them forward by
either hand. "George Herman," she said, "allow me to
present you to your father.

"Darling, here is your son. He has taught Hebrew
for forty years at the University.

"And this is your Uncle Ludwig."

"How do you do," said the professor. And he added
bravely:

"Father and Uncle Ludwig."

The two men bowed stiffly. Mr. Wutheridge senior
cleared his throat, and scraped politely with his foot.
"How do you do, sir," he said. "I trust I find you in
good health?"

"Thank you," said the professor. "And you?"

"Ah," said Mr. Wutheridge simply.

So saying he retired in confusion. Then Uncle Ludwig
stepped forward. "Allow me," he exclaimed, "to bid
you welcome, sir. Your father, as you can see, is a little
upset . . . this reunion . . . the heart is naturally
affected . . . perhaps a dignified tear . . ."

445

"Does he look like oh and um?" asked Mrs. Wutheridge, from under the professor's arm.

"We're very glad you're here," concluded Uncle Ludwig.

"I love him," went on Matilda in what she took to be a whisper, "with a pure passion. Do you blame me, George? His hair is so wavy."

"Matilda," cried Uncle Ludwig, "do behave yourself . . . before your son. . . ."

"Well," said Matilda, "after all those years with the Hebrews, I dare say a bit of pure passion won't hurt him any.

"He never married, Hermann," she explained to her husband. "My poor son. I shall never be a grandmother."

At these words, Mr. Wutheridge senior looked relieved. "What a pity," he said politely.

"Perhaps he'd like a bit of something . . . perhaps a glass . . ."

But Mrs. Wutheridge took her son by the arm. "He's going right up to his room," she announced, "to rest and freshen up. These first precious moments are to be spent with his mother. We have a lot to say to each other, my son and I."

So saying, she marched him out of the parlor, and up the stairs, leaving Mr. Wutheridge and Uncle Ludwig to exchange by themselves their opinions of the new arrival.

Following his mother, the professor found himself in a small, clean room, painted white and apple-green. At first glance the furniture seemed a little undersized; he wondered if the bed, with its dimity of white and green roses would actually hold him, head, feet, and all. As he looked around his new home, the little attic under the eaves, over the garden with its marigold and sweet-william, a strange sadness made of longing and of peace took hold of him, crept through his eyes and nostrils, and knocked at his heart. It seemed to him that he was a boy again, that the long, patient, lonely years between had never been. For an instant the over-sweet, over-grievous feeling of boyhood swept through his memory; he heard the cooing of doves with ears accustomed to their murmur; they spoke of his youth again, faint and almost forgotten.

Then he saw that his mother, who had been hovering about the room, giving it little tidying touches, stood watching him with a strange smile on her face, her hands behind her back. It was a gesture oddly familiar; he could hardly be said to have remembered it; yet it awoke echoes of memories. And he found himself repeating half in a singsong chant.

"What have you got for me, mother?

"What have you got for me?"

But she shook her head; and her smile, from bright, turned watery and uncertain. "Nothing," she said; and drew from behind her back, a china doll dressed like a soldier. "Nothing," she said again, uncertainly, . . . "isn't it silly?"

And with eyes suddenly overflowing with tears, she sank down on the low bed, and laid her head against his coat. "I guess I wanted a little boy," she whispered, as his arm went clumsily around her; "I kept getting ready for a little boy . . . all these years. . . ."

The professor cleared his throat. "I know," he said, "I know. It would have been more fun for you, mother. An old white-bearded scholar . . . how could you have expected anything like that?

"But I," and his voice grew joyous and tender, "I got just what I wanted, mother."

447

Chapter IV

THE REVEREND JOHN CALVIN CRISP left the Museum,
of which he was curator, and stepped out into the fresh
and sparkling air. The light of heaven bathed his forehead, and shone in his eyes, blue as old stones; his sharp
face, proud and severe, and like a saint, moved austerely
down the street, upon his erect, soldierly body, righteous
and beautiful. His voice was musical, and his thoughts
agreeable, dealing as they did with the life everlasting,
and the forthcoming Mother's Day celebration organized by Mrs. Emma Meiggs.

Doctor Crisp had worked long and earnestly on earth;
he had much to his credit, which he liked to remember.
For one thing, it was due to his efforts more than to any
other one person's that the children in the schools of four
states were forbidden the study of biology, history, foreign languages, and the theory of evolution. It was also
due to his efforts that the five-volume work entitled *Sap-
pho, Her Life and Times,* by the aged professor of Greek
at the University, was seized, burned, and its publisher
sent to prison. During the years of his untiring zeal,
fourteen more books were destroyed after their contents
had been noted and largely published in the newspapers.
Among them was the pamphlet on Sex Hygiene in which
Mrs. Mary Howe, the mother of six boys, attempted

to instruct her family in those things which men and women must do, if they wish to have children. At the trial, in ringing tones, Doctor Crisp exclaimed, "There is no word in this book about chastity or continence;" which caused him to receive many congratulations.

During the administration of the reverend doctor as censor of morals, a few young men and women committed suicide: but on the other hand, the Sunday-school was gratifyingly crowded; and after hours of prayer, the children found out what they could, by peeking and feeling.

So Doctor Crisp had many pleasant thoughts to keep him company.

Now, however, he was thinking of Mrs. Meiggs. Her zeal inspirited him; he thought he saw in Mother's Day an opportunity for the instruction of the young. For, he reflected, many children come to us here before they can rightly be said to have learned the difference between virtue and sin. Ignorance alone, although commendable, is not a triumph. Are we to expect an infant, for example, to understand the full horror of adultery? No, indeed. Let us first know, then detest the sin; and end in innocence.

And he murmured to himself the words, "Suffer the little children to come unto me."

But presently his brow grew clouded; and passing the house of Mr. and Mrs. Wutheridge, he frowned slightly. Some people, he thought, enjoy themselves in a very peculiar way. They seem to have a naughty, an irreverent manner more suited to life on earth than to the life everlasting. Joy is to be expected here, after the passage of Jordan; but to spend all eternity in the pursuit of it . . . ? One should have deeper spiritual aims. People like Mrs. Wutheridge impaired, in his humble opinion, the moral tone of the whole. Not that there was

anything wrong, really, with Mrs. Wutheridge: sin, on
that side of Jordan was out of the question; still, for
her to seem so eternally amused . . . And then, those
two men, one of them legal, and one Platonic . . . That
was allowable, of course, although not exactly . . . well
. . . But why couldn't she be sober about it, and a little
bit cast down . . . as one had a right to expect, under
the circumstances . . . ?

His eyes encountering the potted apple tree, he com-
pressed his lips, and looked down, in time to avoid stum-
bling over the figure of a man sitting disconsolately in the
gutter.

"Excuse me, sir," he said hastily, stepping back. But
then, seeing that the man made no effort to rise, he added
more sharply,

"What is the matter, my friend?"

The other looked up wearily. "I'm a stranger here,"
he said.

At this, the Reverend Crisp could not repress a smile.
"So were we all, at one time or another," he said.

But the other shook his head in a discouraged manner.
"You don't understand," he said. "I'm a real stranger,
all by myself. I can't find my people, even."

"That," murmured the Reverend Crisp sympathetically, "is indeed too bad. But perhaps I can help you. I
have a large acquaintance here. . . . Suppose, to begin
with, you tell me your name."

"My name is Lewis," said the man indifferently.

The Reverend Crisp looked more hopeful. "Lewis,"
he reflected: "there is a family by that name just down the
street. The E. Morgan Lewises . . . ?"

Mr. Lewis shook his head with more emphasis than
ever. "That wouldn't be my family," he said. "Not
possibly."

" Well," said the curator, still cheerful, " suppose you tell me your family's name, and then we'll see."

" My father's name," said Mr. Lewis solemnly, " was Levy. My mother was a Weinstein."

And he looked without hope at Doctor Crisp.

" You don't know them ? "

" I ? " asked Doctor Crisp. " Know them ? No, indeed.

" Are they here ? "

" I don't think so," said Mr. Lewis sadly.

" I shouldn't expect so, either," said the Reverend Crisp.

And laying his hand gently on Mr. Lewis' shoulder, he added,

" My poor friend."

" Thank you," said Mr. Lewis gratefully.

" Let us hope that they are not actually in torment," said the Reverend Crisp.

" My God," exclaimed Mr. Lewis, " why should they be in torment ? They never did anybody any harm."

To which the curator replied: " A higher power than you or I, my friend, has decided that for us. They are not here; therefore . . ."

And he shrugged his shoulders as though to say, Where are they?

" Aï," said Mr. Lewis.

And leaning his head on his hand, he allowed a tear to trickle through his fingers. " Not a soul here," he said with a groan, " not a soul to make me welcome, not a grandmother, not a grandfather, not an aunt, or a cousin, or even something distant — nothing, nobody. I might have known it; but I never stopped to think. Naturally, the Levys and the Weinsteins are all together somewhere. And mama says: Where is our Sammy: and papa says: What do you expect, he got himself baptized.

"Mama . . . you should know . . . your Sammy is lonesome. . . .

"I've never been in a place like this before, where I didn't know anybody. There was always some member of the family around, to be given a cigar, or some advice or something. When I needed anything, my cousin Becky would do it for me. Once a year I had her for dinner, with her husband. And every Christmas and Thanksgiving, I ate with the family, at my sister's . . . she set a good table, poor Minna.

"Now I'll never see her again. She's at home with Abraham, Isaac, and Jacob, and great-grandfather Weinstein. And I'm here, and I haven't got so much as a roof over my head."

"We'll soon attend to that, my man," said Doctor Crisp, who did not enjoy this recital.

"My daughters," continued Mr. Lewis, "won't be here for years — never, if they can help it. And when they come, they'll go to their husbands' families. Good girls, but selfish. What a fortune I spent on them.

"Now, I'm here, and nobody knows where I should sleep, even. Not a soul; not a grandmother, not a cousin. . . .

"Nobody."

The Reverend Crisp considered. He was not without sympathy; and he had room at home. In fact he had often thought that a little company between himself and his wife . . . another face, let's say, for his glance to light on . . . another voice . . .

"My friend," he said, "there is room for you at home with me. My wife and I would be glad to have you live with us."

"That's very kind of you," said Mr. Lewis. "Yes, sir; that is really kind."

452

The reverend doctor continued thoughtfully: " Perhaps I could even make use of your services in the Museum, where I am curator."

" Oho," said Mr. Lewis more cheerfully: " a museum."

He rose, not without difficulty. " So, mister," he said; " shall we go home now? I've been sitting here a long while."

As he stepped forward, his foot kicked against a small object, about the size of a stone; he bent over to examine it. " Look," he said; " it's yellow, like gold."

Doctor Crisp smiled coldly. " It is gold," he answered.

" It has no value here?" asked Mr. Lewis incredulously.

" None whatever," replied the curator.

" Well," said Mr. Lewis, " I'll take it along, anyhow. Maybe it has no value, but just the same . . . And it would do me for the start of a collection. Where the heart has nothing to call its own, that's the time to begin a collection.

" It gives you something to come home to."

Clutching his gold pebble, he started off after Doctor Crisp, who was already striding ahead in the direction of the city. After a few steps, he caught up to him, and pulled at his sleeve.

" There's just one person here I'd like to meet, mister," he declared, " if you could arrange it."

" Yes?" relied Doctor Crisp.

Mr. Lewis' voice became low and reverent. " Jesus," he said.

The Reverend Crisp did not reply. Instead, he hastened his steps in the direction of the city. And it seemed to Mr. Lewis that the curator's face expressed irritation and embarrassment.

Chapter V

PROFESSOR WUTHERIDGE and his mother sat together on the mossy floor of a grove of cedars outside the city. The air, made fragrant by the sun-warmed trees and by little flowers among the moss, moved with a slow caress across their cheeks and lay upon their eyes, green and honey-yellow, drowsily sweet. Beneath them the soft and springy moss bent gently toward the river which flowed at their feet, curling coolly about the bodies of Mr. Wutheridge senior and Uncle Ludwig, who swam up and down with one foot on the bottom, or rose suddenly from the shallow stream like dolphins, modestly attired in bathing-suits from elbow to knee.

" Do you think it strange, George Herman," asked Mrs. Wutheridge thoughtfully, pulling with her teeth at the petals of a flower which she held in her hand, " that I should live like this, in love, one might almost say, with two men? Sometimes, I confess, it astonishes me. And yet it is true that I am devoted to them both, it seems to me, equally."

She looked at her son out of the corner of her eye; it was the first intimate discussion she had allowed herself, and she felt a little uncertain of her ground. There he sat, with his white beard; did one speak of such things to people like that? Not so far as she remembered.

"Do I shock you, George Herman?" she asked timidly. Professor Wutheridge replied that his studies had prepared him for such shocks.

"What a joy," thought Mrs. Wutheridge; and she realized that she had always wanted to discuss such things with an old gentleman with a white beard.

"One cannot study the past," the professor was saying, "without coming to the conclusion that women enjoyed the delights of love as much as men; that, in fact, they were interested parties."

"The delights of love?" asked Mrs. Wutheridge.

"The delights of love," said the professor simply.

"What a coarse expression," said Mrs. Wutheridge. The professor looked surprised. "Excuse me," he said. And he added courteously,

"Of what were we speaking?"

"Of love," said his mother.

And pointing to where Mr. Wutheridge and Uncle Ludwig were innocently splashing, she exclaimed,

"There, my son: that is love."

Then, as the professor said nothing, Mrs. Wutheridge continued in a low voice, not looking at him:

"The delights of love, indeed. What are they for a good woman? A sort of struggle in the dark, which leaves her sleepless and irritable. I can discuss these things, because they are finished for me — long, long ago finished. And with my son . . . But when I was young, we never spoke of such things, not even with our parents. When I was married, I knew nothing; I thought my marriage was to be a sort of festival. . . . My own mother — your grandmother — gave me nothing in the way of information except a family recipe for plum pudding. The delights of love . . . I might add that of the two of us, your father and I, I was the one without fear. However,

I soon realized that marriage is not a pleasure, but a sacrifice."

The professor felt his heart contract; he wanted to brandish his fist at his father, who continued to splash merrily about below him. But as he looked at the young and happy face, so innocent and reasonable, his mood changed, and an overwhelming pity for them both moved him. He reached over and took his mother's hand. " My poor child," he said.

Then he remembered Uncle Ludwig; and he dropped it again.

As though divining his thought, she continued:
" Sacrifice makes a mother of a woman. Your father never knew why I grew motherly in his arms. But he enjoyed it. It was what he wanted — a wife and mother all in one."

" Yes," said the professor. " Naturally," he added.

" All men do."

Mrs. Wutheridge shook her head sadly. " Pour souls," she murmured. " Such a mistake. A wife is so much better."

Then before her son could reply, she added,

" The woman who finds herself a mother before her time, will have room in her heart for more than one son."

" Ah," said the professor, joyously: " Uncle Ludwig."
And reaching over, he took her hand again.

" Yes," said Mrs. Wutheridge; " Uncle Ludwig. There they are, the two of them — my two sons, my two children . . . far more than you, whom I left so soon, could ever be. I love them both. But sometimes I ask myself if I have ever been a wife. And it is a long, long time since I was a daughter. . . .

" I wonder . . . if one can grow weary of being a

mother — supposing there is nothing else to be, forever and ever and ever. . . ."

"Just think," said the professor with awe, "if I were still a child. What a nuisance for you, mother. Three of us."

But she shook her head quickly; and it seemed to him that her eyes shone with moisture. "No, my dear," she said; "that would have been entirely different. What comes from the heart — so naturally — "

She broke off in time to welcome the two swimmers, who, having done with splashing, were making their way over the moss in her direction. "Well done," she called out enthusiastically; "I watched you both; you were like two great fish, leaping in the waves."

"Did you notice," cried Mr. Wutheridge senior, approaching with a steady drip; "I had my foot up off the bottom."

"Just once, George," said Uncle Ludwig. "Only once."

"For quite a long time," said Mr. Wutheridge.

"Well," said Uncle Ludwig, "I had my head under. I was swimming with it under. So I didn't see."

"It wasn't your head," said Mr. Wutheridge. "Not your whole head. Only up to your ears."

"That's just as bad," insisted Uncle Ludwig. "If it gets as far as your ears, it feels like your whole head. And that's what counts."

"You both did wonders," said Mrs. Wutheridge comfortably; "you made me actually anxious at times. Now go and dress, and hurry back here; meanwhile George Herman and I will set the luncheon."

When the two men returned from the bushes, they found a snowy cloth spread on the moss, with a repast of milk and honey, dates, cold mutton, and a herring. Mrs.

Wutheridge was already placed; seated on either side of her, they had the professor between them. They were happy; they felt very well; and they gazed at Matilda with adoration. Then they sighed, together.

" What a feast."

" A very good day for this sort of thing," said Uncle Ludwig.

" A very good day indeed," agreed Mr. Wutheridge.

Uncle Ludwig reached for the milk; presently he could be heard smacking his lips over it. " Next time," he said with a gasp, coming up out of it, " I'm going to open my eyes under water."

" No," said Mrs. Wutheridge.

" Ludwig — how wonderful."

" Well," said Mr. Wutheridge, " let him. He keeps one foot on the bottom, anyhow. What I'm going to do, is to dive. Yes — I'm going to leap right in, on my head."

" There," exclaimed Matilda. " How exciting."

" To-morrow," said Mr. Wutheridge bravely. " Or the day after."

And he looked at Uncle Ludwig as though to say, After all, she is prouder of me, naturally.

The professor beamed about him with gentle joy. There he was with his father and mother — and his Uncle Ludwig, whom, it is true, he had not exactly looked for — in short, his family, his own and only people, who were as much himself, almost, as he; and he, too, a part of them — all except Uncle Ludwig, and all so good looking, so happy and attractive. . . . The warm and sunny air caressed his nose with the perfume of cedars; the flowers and moss upheld the luncheon-cloth with small and springy arms. The drowse of eternity, like a balm, lay upon his heart. He had been so much alone; and now he was to have company, forever and ever.

Raising the milk pitcher above his head, he exclaimed.
" I am happy; my children. Indeed, I feel that I
am young again, but at the same time, I am full
of hope and courage. What could be better than that?
To-morrow I shall go swimming with you. You will see;
you will be astonished."

And making a swimming motion with the arm which
held the milk pitcher, he exclaimed,

" Yup."

Mr. Wutheridge senior and Uncle Ludwig moved uncomfortably in their places; they regarded each other
with sober looks. To tell the truth, they had forgotten
him; now their happiness was dimmed because this old
gentleman with a beard wished to share it. Their anxious
glances sought Matilda, heavy with dismay.

" There," she said quickly coming to the rescue, and
patting the professor's hand, " you must go a little slowly,
my dear. The water here is cold, and very swift; there is
a terrible undertow. Besides, we've no extra bathing-
suit; and in the second place . . . in the second place,
I'd be all alone."

" Then," said the professor, after a moment's thought,
" I'll go fishing."

" Yes," said Mr. Wutheridge senior; " that's it."

" That's just the thing," exclaimed Uncle Ludwig.
" Fishing. Yes, indeed. Down a ways, where we won't
disturb you."

" And you can sit," the professor said happily to his
mother, " and talk to me while I fish."

But Mr. Wutheridge's face grew longer than ever.
" Matilda," he cried; " do you mean that you would leave
us to swim all alone?"

" Do you mean," asked Uncle Ludwig anxiously, " that
you'd go off, out of sight, while we were swimming?

"Supposing something happened?

"And you not there to see it.

"The current . . . the undertow . . .

"No, no. No, no.

"Matilda, I cannot allow it."

Mrs. Wutheridge sighed — and laughed — and sighed again. "You see, George Herman," she said, "I can't leave them. You'll simply have to do your fishing by yourself, my dear, while I watch the — gentlemen."

The professor felt his lower lip tremble. "Yes, mother," he said; and looked sadly at his father. "I could fish here," he said meekly: "I wouldn't be much trouble. And it doesn't matter if I don't catch anything."

But Mr. Wutheridge shook his head. "Just think," he said, "if I got caught on a hook."

"Or I," said Uncle Ludwig, "with my head under water. . . ."

The professor took a deep breath. "Well, well," he said, "we won't think about it any more. I'll just sit here with mother, and watch you swim. It's not important, really; it's not important at all."

Chapter VI

WILLIAM WILBERFORCE MEIGGS followed his mother down the street in the direction of the Museum. He would have preferred to walk beside her, with her hand in his arm, but that was too much like his father: it would have made him feel uncomfortable, as though he were pretending to something. It would have been glory — glory he often dreamed of, but never deserved: to stand up in front of everybody with his mother on his arm, like a man. But that was unlikely; he knew he'd never get to it. And besides, it wasn't just glory; there was some wish of his heart about it that made him feel queer inside. Well, why should he give himself airs? If he did, his father would attend to it, anyway; he'd make him feel small again, smaller than ever. He'd do it just by being there, so large and easy, where he belonged; and he wouldn't have any doubts about it. Whereas William Wilberforce belonged a little in the rear, in a modest position, and not too much noticed.

That's where he'd always been at home, after all; and what chance had he ever had to better it? The most a man could be, until he was somebody's husband, was his mother's son. Even after she'd gone, there was so much to keep him down — all the thoughts people helped him to think, all the feelings people made it easy for him to

461

feel. There were the songs people wrote; and the sermons in church; and books about great men's mothers — the way they said the word, even — mother — it sounded so sweet and lawful. A man's best friend was his mother. Other people made trouble sometimes, but not a mother. No — no trouble, ever; just taking care of things, keeping trouble away. Probably if she'd been there, he never would have had that last fatal illness. But then, where would he be now? Still at home, all alone, with no one to take care of him; haunted by what she'd want him to do, and not to do — and feeling, all the time, so unable to do anything at all, so lost and lonely, so young and unable. . . .

Mrs. Meiggs sailed down the street ahead of him. Her thoughts, concerned with good works, reflected the order and peace about her, and ignored her son, whose education she meant presently to undertake at the Museum. What peace, she thought, what goodness all about. No need, any longer, to be afraid of joy, for the battle was over, and the victory won. Nothing could be wrong again, ever; nothing here was a sin. Mrs. Wutheridge's apple tree was a little out of taste; and her two men seemed a good deal, but not, oh, not a sin. And if having two men weren't a sin, why surely there was nothing wrong in having one — and being happy about it. And Mrs. Meiggs was happy; for the truth was that she loved Mr. Meiggs. She had always loved him, even on earth, where he made so much trouble for her. Only then she had often felt dark and full of shame. Now the shame was gone; they had both been saved, and there they were. Saved.

It made her feel very dreamy, almost girlish, she thought. Well, nobody minded, that was a blessing. The women all about seemed to feel just as girlish as she did; and the men twirled their mustaches, and looked pleased

and manly. They could afford to, naturally — being in
bliss.

Man and woman created He them. What was simpler,
really? The blessing of earth, the peace of heaven . . .
now she could enjoy them. Love, and being happy, and
no chance to sin any more. . . .

There was William, of course : his meek presence a little
in the rear demanded to be remembered. She loved him,
too; but not in the same way. He wasn't, as Mr. Meiggs
was, a person outside herself, a stranger, all shining with
beauty. Yes, beauty; it didn't look like beauty, perhaps,
but it felt like it. William was just herself, something
she'd borne and suckled and nursed and tidied and cared
for; she couldn't feel girlish about William. Not that she
wanted to; no, when she looked at him she felt her heart
flooded with motherly feelings. They were precious; but
they didn't make her feel new and dewy.

"Come along, William; why do you hang back so,
treading on my heels? Walk here, with me."

Not new and dewy. On the contrary, it made her feel
full of cares, though strong to see to them: it was a
triumph-feeling-with-tenderness. But there was always
someone at her heels — "Do come along, William" —
and no real gaiety, like being with Mr. Meiggs and feeling
shy and breathless. At home she'd always felt ashamed
of feeling breathless; and that had left her with nothing
but the triumph-feeling-with-tenderness. But here, where
there was nothing to be ashamed of . . .

New and dewy she felt, and meant to, what was more,
for the rest of eternity.

They'd put up a statue to her at home; but did they
know what she looked like, really? The Mother's Day
leader, the church-woman militant . . . yes, she'd done
her best, she had nothing to feel ashamed of. And they'd

no call to spoil her statue that way, either . . . ah, well, that was over for her now. And casting up her eyes, she murmured: " Forgive them, Father, for they knew not what they did."

She was a little vague as to what might still be above her; but her eyes went up, none the less.

Supposing — only supposing, of course — they were to put up a statue to her here, too. What would it be like, she wondered. Probably they'd place it at the door of the Museum, next to the replica of Moses: a fine, noble, tender-looking woman. But then, at the same time, she had another picture: it would be a statue of herself and Mr. Meiggs, hand in hand — well, perhaps she might be just a little bit in front, seeing that it was she, really, who had saved them — both of them looking up, with such a happy pure expression . . . a dewy look . . .

She sighed. Would there ever be such a statue? Not without a lot of striving first, she knew, and good works done. She set her lips.

And with a determined face, she entered the Museum, with William at her heels.

They found themselves in a large, square room, lighted from the ceiling. Ranged about the walls were solid-looking cases of oak and glass; and in the center, a very fair facsimile of the Ark of the Covenant, the original of which — as was the case with most of the treasures of this Museum — was elsewhere, in other hands. The tablets of the law, cut in granite from the quarries of Vermont, and set like a screen before the Ark itself, were printed in English, thereby avoiding the troublesome Hebrew vowel-points and noun-endings, or the implication that the Ten Commandments had not been handed directly to King James I from the fiery cloud on Sinai.

In the first glass case, marked " Fundamentals," was

to be seen a small wooden ark, painted brown; Noah and
the animals, all cleverly carved, paraded its decks; and
the whole was encased in some miraculous manner in a
sealed glass bottle. Beside it was coiled a snake made all
of brass; a bit of petrified fungus marked " manna, B.C.
1700 " and a matzoth.

William gazed at these relics with awe-struck curiosity.
Then, moving to another case, his gaze was arrested by
a huge tooth, sharp and pointed like that of some great
animal. It lay there without a tag; and it was while he
was wondering about it that he became aware that his
mother was no longer beside him, and that her place had
been taken by someone else. He turned to see who it was.

" Why," he exclaimed, " it's you, again." And he held
out his hand to Mr. Lewis, born Levy.

" Yes," said Mr. Lewis, " it's me."

He shook hands with William.

" This is where I am," he said. And he added, half
proudly, half doubtfully,

" I'm in the Museum."

William smiled happily. " Then," he said, " you're all
right, aren't you? I'm so glad. I was going to speak to
my mother about you. But . . ."

" But . . . ? " echoed Mr. Lewis.

" But," said William hurriedly, " she's so busy — with
Mother's Day and all . . . busier here, even than . . .
She never has time for anything. . . .

" I mean . . . we haven't really had a talk ourselves,
yet. . . ."

Mr. Lewis looked at the boy thoughtfully. " So," he
said.

" Anyhow," said William more comfortably, " it's all
right now, isn't it; because you were welcome after all."

Mr. Lewis shrugged his shoulders. " Welcome? " he

said slowly; "yes — perhaps. But what does welcome
mean? It means that I wasn't thrown out; it means that I
have a bed to lie down on, and something to eat. And
when I walk along the street, people give me bows, but if
I weren't here, whom would it hurt?

"Nobody says to me, Sammy — or even Samuel —
where have you been? And what I mean is, if nobody
wants to know where you've been, is that a welcome?"

William nodded his head; he remembered his first long
evening in his mother's arms, and all the things he had
wanted to say — for which he had no words — and how
she hadn't asked him . . .

"I guess you're right," he said.

Mr. Lewis seemed satisfied. "We shouldn't talk too
much in a Museum," he said. "Come along, and let me
show you the collection."

Waving his hand in the direction of the four walls, he
declared, "It's just what you see."

And leaning close to William, and lowering his voice
to a whisper, he added,

"It's not much of a Museum."

"No?" asked William, startled.

"No," said Mr. Lewis gloomily. "Look at that matzoth. And the ark. There is not an original piece among
them.

"Have we no primitives?"

Chapter VII

He looked around him disconsolately. "I'm used to a Museum with pictures," he said; "pictures of the Apostles, panels of the Mother of God, or ladies dressed like saints. Then I know what I'm doing. And statues, by Michael Angelo or Donatello, or those fine old Germans who used to carve angels out of wood. You see, I know a good deal about Museums; and something about art. But here it don't do me any good; because nothing is real, anyhow, before Luther."

He pointed to a case standing against the opposite wall. "Over there," he said, "are the real treasures. Do you want to see them? There's the very hammer used by Luther's father in the copper mines of the Counts of Mansfeld. I know it's real, because, for one thing, you couldn't make a hammer like that to-day. And Anne Boleyn's garter. A bloody cloth from St. Bartholomew's Day: a witch's finger, loaned us by Cotton Mather: the manuscript of a book called *Elsie Dinsmore;* and a fine painting of Bishop Brougham's new cathedral at home."

"Such a collection is interesting, and even valuable. But is it art?"

"Art?" asked William in surprise. "Why should it be art?"

"Well, then," said Mr. Lewis, "all right; is it history?"

467

"I think," replied William, peering at the cases, "that the things you've mentioned, like Cotton Mather's ring, are very historical."

"There aren't enough of them," said Mr. Lewis, "to make a history."

"And anyhow," William continued, "this isn't history; it's religion."

"Religion," said Mr. Lewis.

"And what is that?"

William stared at him in amazement. "Look here," he burst out finally, "isn't all this enough for you? Here you are; you've been saved from hell-fire; you can taste bliss forever and ever; and you ask what is religion. That seems very ungrateful, to me. Only a few days ago you were wondering if you'd even be welcome here."

"My people," said Mr. Lewis thoughtfully, "have always been like that. You must excuse me." He shot a quick glance at William from under his lashes. "And you," he said, "you are tasting bliss?"

William's eyes flew around the room in search of his mother, who, however, was not to be seen. "Yes, I am," he said stoutly.

Mr. Lewis nodded. "I'm glad to hear it. Perhaps I have more to ask of heaven than you have. After all, you were born to come here. But with me it was different: I had to make a choice."

"Well," said William, suddenly feeling a little irritable, "you made it, didn't you?"

Mr. Lewis smiled at him sadly. "Yes," he said, "I made it. And so now I ask myself, where is everything I expected."

William shrugged his shoulders. Whatever had he expected then? Heaven had always been for William the place his mother was going to be; that was religion, as it

468

applied to him, personally. And what other way should it apply to him? To be saved was the important thing, not to die any more, to be home forever and ever with Mrs. Meiggs, and to keep out of the flames. Whether he found himself, then, in God's presence, or in a Museum, seemed singularly unimportant. What had the Jew expected? He had received what they all had — life everlasting, and the opportunity to enjoy himself without sinning any more. It wasn't William's fault if he wasn't satisfied.

"Oh, come on," he exclaimed, "let's go look at the witch's finger."

But he felt irritated at Mr. Lewis, and annoyed about something — what was it? — and a little vexed with himself — but why? — and altogether aware that something had happened — somewhere — to trouble him, just a little, just a very little . . .

Nothing had happened to trouble Mrs. Meiggs, however. She sat in the curator's office with Doctor Crisp, and discussed good works. Her face was pink and fresh-looking, her eyes shone, and she allowed herself to cross one knee over the other, under her dress, which was mostly of lace.

"Early in the morning," she was saying, "the children, dressed all in white, will go out to pick flowers for their parents in the woods and fields outside the city. Then, each carrying a bouquet, they will gather in front of the Museum, for speeches; and after that there'll be a parade, with a band, and ice cream and lemonade on somebody's lawn. That's the way I see it. We must have a king and a queen, to wear paper crowns; and someone to be the spirit of motherhood."

"Who," said Doctor Crisp gallantly, "could better express the spirit of motherhood than you, dear Mrs. Meiggs?"

She blushed with joy. " Oh, no," she murmured, " I am not worthy. Perhaps Mrs. Stowe . . . or Queen Victoria . . ."

"Mrs. Stowe is too old," said Doctor Crisp, " and Queen Victoria might feel a little disinclined, seeing that her own son . . . you understand . . ."

"Ah, yes," said Mrs. Meiggs with a sigh; "poor woman.

"Well, then . . . if it must be me . . ."

She uncrossed her knees. "One must do one's duty," she declared.

"As for the children," said the Reverend Crisp, "shall we let them choose their own king and queen?"

But Mrs. Meiggs looked doubtful. "I think not," she said. "It would make them feel too important. And besides, they'd be chosen for such stupid reasons, and not at all for the things we want — piety, and devotion, and modesty . . . don't you think?"

"I dare say you're right," the doctor agreed. "Well, then — whom shall we have? Let's say for queen . . . there are many pretty girls to choose from."

And his eyes shone happily.

"Indeed there are," said Mrs. Meiggs graciously. "A pretty face under a golden crown. How sweet that is."

"Exactly," said Doctor Crisp. "That is just what I meant. And the king," he added thoughtfully: "I was wondering, if perhaps your son — that is, if you do not think him too old . . ."

"Too old?" cried Mrs. Meiggs. "Of course not; what an idea. Why, he'd like nothing better."

And she sat more erect than ever.

"Then it is decided," said Doctor Crisp. "The mother — the son: very beautiful. As for the queen, if we are to have a pretty face, as you say, we might have Lucy

470

Tompkins. She is very pretty. Or Amy Coulter, with her blue eyes. Or dark-haired Emily . . ."

"Exactly," said Mrs. Meiggs; "yes, indeed. But suppose we leave the queen for later, Doctor. Perhaps we'll find someone who will really fit the part; someone who will bring something spiritual to it. We don't want just a pretty face, do we? No."

"No?" said Doctor Crisp faintly. "No."

"Perhaps," continued Mrs. Meiggs, "if we even took the little Johnson girl — from down the street . . . you know, the homely one . . . to show how spirit rises triumphant over everything . . ."

"Very beautiful," croaked the Reverend Crisp. "Still . . ."

"Yes," cried Mrs. Meiggs, full of fire. "That's it; it has just been shown me. We mustn't have a pretty face, Doctor; we must stick to spirit."

"Ah," said the doctor gloomily; "spirit. Well . . ."

"Then that's decided," said Mrs. Meiggs. "And now about the speeches . . ."

Then it was the doctor's turn to sit up.

"I thought," she said, "we'd ask Mr. Bryan to speak."

"Mr. Bryan," said Doctor Crisp without enthusiasm; "yes; a very good idea. But to tell you the truth, Mrs. Meiggs, very few people here seem anxious to speak. Doctor Beecher spends his time in the library among the romances; and Bishop Wilberforce prefers to visit the zoo. That, Mrs. Meiggs, is the truth of the matter."

Mrs. Meiggs gazed at him unhappily. "Whatever shall we do?" she murmured. "For we cannot have Mother's Day without speeches."

The Reverend Crisp paused. "It is true," he observed, "that I was not considered an orator at home. But I was always ready — and I might say able — to speak. There

471

were many things I would have liked to have said. In fact, I have here a little speech . . ."

And he drew it carelessly out of his pocket.

"Then," cried Mrs. Meiggs happily, "you will speak?"

"I will speak," declared Doctor Crisp.

Mrs. Meiggs clapped her hands. "How marvelous," she breathed. "Why, we're all organized. Only the ice cream to attend to."

"And the band," said Doctor Crisp.

"We'll get the city band," said Mrs. Meiggs.

"And the parents," added Doctor Crisp, "will supply the ice cream."

"In return for the flowers," concluded Mrs. Meiggs, joyously.

Chapter VIII

MR. LEWIS came back from the Museum carrying a small piece of gold to add to his collection which by this time included about a dozen pieces of varying sizes. Without value, but hidden carefully in a drawer, they gave him, as he had said, something to come home to. He counted them, described them, weighed them, and arranged them in order; and wrote it all down. That gave him a catalogue, of which he was proud.

And he needed something to be proud of, he thought. His home with Doctor and Mrs. Crisp was not an unhappy one: the eminent divine and his pale, patient wife did what they could to make him welcome. Mrs. Crisp dryly admitted that she was ready to take the place of his mother; and Doctor Crisp also seemed glad to have him there. But did he feel at home? Or was he glad in turn?

No, there was something wrong with it. He felt it at once, always, as soon as he put his foot in the door. It wasn't the sort of home he was used to; for one thing, it didn't feel like a home. It was just a roof and some walls, without love in it, with people never really talking to each other, not out of their hearts, never really seeing and feeling each other. . . . He thought of his own childhood home, of his mother and father, of the Friday night

473

suppers, the warm light over the table — did it come from the candles? or from the way they all looked at one another, slow and searching and loving? he couldn't be sure. But there it was, or rather there it had been, something warm and his own, something that he could understand, not this strange, sweet-and-sour politeness. . . .

That light of love; where would he find it again?

But they were all like that, he thought, all the people of the city, everyone he met. He got bows on the street; and all about him he saw uplifted faces, shining with a sort of happiness, a cold righteous lonely happiness, not the warm thing he remembered, not the way his mother used to look, beaming around the table on Friday nights — or even later, when he was Mr. Lewis, with a picture gallery, and big cigars to smoke. . . .

Another happiness, a different joy . . . far away, far away, home.

He sat at table, at the evening meal which consisted only of bread and milk, gazing thoughtfully at his companions. No honey had ever entered the Reverend Crisp's house. Mrs. Crisp kept from her table the sweetness she had never had in life, denying her husband, in one thin simple gesture, the gratification of his senses, and punishing herself for having longed, on earth, for something sweeter than she'd got.

"What a stranger she is to me," thought Mr. Lewis. "How far away she looks, sitting there. Is she part of this, any more than I?" But then he thought:

"It is I who am the stranger here."

He was both right and wrong. He was a stranger; but so was Mrs. Crisp. Forty years of loving no one had made everyone seem strange to her. Forty years across the table from her husband, whom she disliked, and bore with pious fortitude, had left her unable to love anything. She had been a faithful helpmeet year in, year out, performing without ardor but with a sense of adequacy the duties of a wife from the hour of getting out of bed to that of getting into it again. She had looked for a reward of angels and thrones of glory; but all she got was her husband, forever and ever.

She no longer disliked him. Still, she was obliged to admit that she felt less enthusiasm for life eternal than she had looked for. It seemed to her very much like life at home, without the odd chance of sinning by mistake; and without — she set her lips in a thin line — the honey, if she had anything to say about it.

Thank God, she still had her principles. Forty years without a separation, except for that one extraordinary time when she went to visit her sister — that strange sister of hers who so incredibly divorced her husband, not because of adultery — oh, sinful word — and not in anger, which one could understand, but because — imagine admitting such a thing — he hurt her . . . and so was lost to Mrs. Crisp for all eternity. Mrs. Crisp who had not divorced her husband although she disliked him, and so sat face to face with him across the bread and milk forever and ever and ever.

Well, he was a good man, she guessed; he'd got them both safely past the flames, and over Jordan: she'd have to do with that. But he needn't expect, for the dryness he'd given her all her life, to revel in the heavenly meadows like a bee.

She glanced at Mr. Lewis. What would life have been like with him, she wondered. So much money, so many pictures, such big cigars. She gave a slight shudder; but not of revulsion. There was nothing dry about Mr. Lewis.

Without meaning to, she put her hand up to tidy her

hair. Nothing dry about him; and nothing sinful either, seeing that he sat there, at her own supper table, saved and healthy. Supposing she'd had the thrones of glory at home, the way he'd had, and now could rest, and feel sweetness — drowsy peace, and joy at remembering . . .

She sighed; it was too late for the thrones of glory. But there was still time for sweetness, perhaps. Nothing sinful, or wrong; that would be impossible, fortunately — but something warm and friendly, something she'd always missed, except for those two weeks with her sister — something like a picnic in the woods, with young folks whispering, and far-off music, and sweet smells; and flutters of laughter — giggles, even — in her heart.

Well — why not? There was Mrs. Wutheridge, with two; and she'd even loved one of them first. Surely, oh surely, if Mrs. Crisp, who had never loved anybody, were to have a friend, would anyone wonder?

Or, if they wondered, did she — should she — care?

"I suppose," she said tentatively, "you're very busy at the Museum these days, Mr. Lewis?"

"Eh," said Mr. Lewis, roused from his reverie, "what? The Museum? Oh — yes. Busy. Yes. Not very."

"I used to go there very often," she said. "Doctor Crisp used to take me. I loved the Noah's Ark. To think of all that, inside a bottle. I don't know how they do it."

"Exactly," said Mr. Lewis.

"A Museum," said Mrs. Crisp, "is a very inspiring place."

Mr. Lewis leaned closer, and dropped his voice.

"Have you ever seen an angel, Mrs. Crisp?" he asked.

Mrs. Crisp sat bolt upright; she looked at her husband, and he looked at her.

"I never go to the Museum any more," she said in a small far-away voice; "and I used to go so often."

"I mean a real angel," said Mr. Lewis doggedly; "with wings."

"Bother," said Doctor Crisp. And he frowned into his milk. What was the man after? Wasn't he content with life eternal, and work in the Museum? Why couldn't he settle down quietly, and accept what there was? These foreigners, he thought, . . . these Jews. Well, that was it, of course: at heart Mr. Lewis was a Jew. These Jews then, with their restless questions. An angel with wings: —what good would that do?

No good at all. Not with wings, he thought, looking across the table at Mrs. Crisp; no—but say an angel like Mrs. Meiggs, with a firm happy look in her face, and organization in her hands; a woman full of love, and good works, a pure but juicy woman, the right companion for a busy man. A woman—an angel—whose every other word was honey. . . .

He gave a dry swallow.

Well, then, simply a loving woman. What had Meiggs done to deserve such a thing? And why not himself? The lusts of the flesh had never bothered him; at least, they'd never got the better of him. He'd risen above them; and now he had bread and milk without honey; whereas Meiggs, who had lived such a disgusting life, and had only been saved by the skin of his teeth, had the sweetness, now and forever.

And here was this Jew, with his talk about angels, and other theological phenomena; as though that could make any difference. Wasn't it enough to be saved, to be in a state of bliss; to be comfortable, and at peace? But Jews were like that—they always made a nuisance. Mr.

Meiggs had settled down; Doctor Crisp had settled down.
. . . It did no good to ask questions. Otherwise one
might want to know why Mr. Meiggs, for instance . . .

Not that Doctor Crisp would rather have been Mr.
Meiggs; or anything, in fact, but Doctor Crisp. But if a
reward for right-doing were really to be a reward,
oughtn't it, perhaps, be something more than an endless
opportunity for that self-same right-doing?

These theological problems . . .

He sighed deeply.

"Yes," Mrs. Crisp was saying, "it's a good long time
since I was there. I always felt that I mustn't disturb
Doctor Crisp at his work. But now that he has an assistant — perhaps — that is, if it wouldn't be too much
trouble —

"There must be so many new things to see," she murmured.

Mr. Lewis closed his eyes wearily. Things to see —
statues, pictures, Noah's Ark — dead things in a Museum. Was that theology? Where was the living word,
the veritable presence, the wonder and the glory? Was
it for this he had foresworn Abraham and Isaac, the
hard religion of his exiled fathers, his brown-eyed
mothers? In order to eat the bread and milk of paradise,
and work in a Museum?

He replied, sighing; "You must come visit me now, instead of Doctor Crisp."

Mrs. Crisp smiled; and looked coyly down at her plate.
"I'll come very soon," she declared.

"Do," said Mr. Lewis, and lost himself in the milk.

Chapter IX

MR. LEWIS got up, and went outside. In front of the house he met Professor Wutheridge, carrying a fishing-pole, and wearing a large straw hat. "Well, well," he exclaimed joyously, "I am glad to see you."

"And I," replied the professor, "am glad, in turn, to see you. I was afraid that perhaps you might not have been welcome here, after all."

Mr. Lewis shrugged his shoulders. "Worse things have happened to me in my life," he said, "than that I shouldn't have been welcome here. What are you doing? Fishing?"

And without hesitation, he also turned in the direction of the river.

"I'll go along with you," he said, "if you don't mind."

"I shall be more than happy to have your company," the professor answered.

The two men walked soberly down the street together. Over them the cloudless sky beamed with eternal light. Sweet odors conspired together in the air, the kiss of cinnamon, the perfume of lilies. Children played in the little gardens, seesaw, house, red rover red rover: their light, shrill voices competed with the low cooing of doves. They were in bliss, no one could ever again take their games away from them. It did not keep them from quarreling, but they never wept. The knowledge that they were saved stilled their fears.

At the river the professor looked up and down. Then he chose a sloping bank of grass on which to seat himself. "Come," he said; "you have nothing to do; sit here with me a while; do not leave me all alone."

Mr. Lewis sank gratefully down beside him. "What have you got for bait?" he asked, with practical interest.

"Bait?" said the professor. He pulled out a piece of bread. "I shall tie this on the line," he declared; "and that will tempt them."

So saying, he tied the bread on to the line, and threw it into the water, where it presently dissolved. Then placing the fishing-pole against a tree, and drawing his hat over his eyes, he extended himself on his back and gazed peacefully above him.

"I should like to take home a fine carp to my mother," he said, "or a great herring, such as swim in the blue waters of the Sea of Cinnereth."

Mr. Lewis gave a sigh. "Cinnareth," he said; "Cinnereth. That is in Galilee, where Jesus was."

Professor Wutheridge nodded underneath his hat. "Yes," he said simply; "Jesus walked above its waters; and His disciples fished for herring in its depths. Jesus also taught in the vineyards and villages upon its slopes."

Mr. Lewis looked about him uneasily. Then he leaned down until his mouth was level with the professor's hat. "Tell me," he whispered; "tell me something. Where is He now? Where is Jesus, I mean."

The professor's eyes were closed; he opened them with surprise. "Jesus?" he exclaimed. "Why — I don't know. Isn't He here?"

"I don't think so," said Mr. Lewis.

"I haven't seen Him, either," said the professor, looking around. "Well, tell me: did you expect to find Him here?"

"Didn't you?" asked Mr. Lewis.

"Did I?" murmured the professor. He shook his head. "I'm not at all sure," he said; "in fact, I'm inclined to think not. I know that I expected to see my mother again. But Jesus? No — I think not. At least, not after I got here."

At these words Mr. Lewis let out a low wail. "But why not?" he cried. "What's the matter? When I speak of Him to Doctor Crisp, he doesn't say anything, and I get a look. If I mention angels to Mrs. Crisp, she changes the subject, or I get another look. What is it? Where are they? And if they're not here, then what did I come here for? Answer me that."

The professor sat up with a thoughtful air; he pushed his hat back on his head, and took hold of his beard in both hands. "How can I answer you that?" he replied. "I came to join my father and mother; but I do not know what you came for. Angels? Here? My friend, you know nothing about angels. They were beings of another world, which perished long before this city was ever dreamed of. There were no angels in Greece, or in Rome. But in Assyria there were bull-headed Kerubs, lion-faced and winged Seraphs, lesser gods, the baalim of conquered cities, the djinns and demons of the waterholes. Vindictive and august, they ruled the ignorant tribes and nations of the desert. What have we to do with such beings here? Or with the valkyries of the Norse Wotan; or the houries of Mohammed? I do not remember that an angel ever appeared before Luther. The Devil came to tempt him; and received an ink-pot flung at his head for his pains. We have some hairs of his tail in the Museum. So much for angels.

"And as for Jesus — after all, we know little about Him, less than we know of Bel, or Mammon, or Mars, or the Phœnician Aphrodite. We know that He was at least half a Jew; and that the Jews crucified Him. Since they did not want him at that time, it is unlikely that they have Him now. But on the other hand did you expect to find Him lolling here among the lilies? Or fishing in the river?"

So saying, he felt his line gingerly, to see if there was a fish on it.

"No, my friend," he remarked, sinking back again, "this is a city made to receive in beatitude those who have gone regularly to church, and have not sinned too much. Its citizenry numbers many important people, but not the great archangels of the Thebaid, the Kerubs of Safed, or the saints of Rome; and not, so far as I know, that most mystic of all figures, Jesus, the Son of Man.

"However, I do not see why it should trouble you."

"Trouble me," groaned Mr. Lewis.

"Unless," continued the professor, "you care for theology in other than a practical sense."

And he looked earnestly and sympathetically at Mr. Lewis, who nodded his head sadly.

"I guess that's it," he said. "I was born to it."

"Of course," agreed the professor enthusiastically: "I had forgotten that you belong to the race of the psalmists, of the prophets, of Hillel of Jerusalem, of Philo of Alexandria, of Loria of Safed, of Jochai, of Akiba, of Eliezer of Worms. Now you find yourself among such men as Oliver Cromwell and W. J. Bryan. Well, that is sad for you."

And placing his hand on Mr. Lewis' knee, he inquired anxiously,

"Why did you do it?"

Mr. Lewis gazed darkly at the river whose blacker water, icy cold, passed under him with a steady movement, and without sound. "Do I know?" he murmured at length. "I was unhappy because nobody wanted me. Nobody, that is, except my family. But who wanted my family? Nobody. So I grew up to understand that there were two lots of people; one, like myself, whom nobody wanted; and the other lot, who did the wanting and not wanting.

"I was ashamed of not being wanted. I thought to myself, what is the good of being a Jew? I get nothing out of it. Those others, they look happier than I feel; they go to church on Sunday, and their religion gives them pleasure; while mine only keeps me out of things. When they die they have angels, and Jesus; and while they're alive, they enjoy themselves. So I said to myself, Sammy, if you stay a Jew, you're more of a fool than I think."

"Tut," said the professor, shaking his head.

"So there I was," said Mr. Lewis.

"And were you any happier?" asked the professor.

Mr. Lewis looked thoughtful. "On earth," he said, "I was a little happier. For one thing, I didn't have to be ashamed of being a Jew any more. I had no friends; but I was too busy to know it. Here is where I know it. The Jews I grew up with — they would have been my friends. In church I had only acquaintances; but I made so much money all the time that nobody noticed it."

He was silent, biting the sweet end of a blade of grass. "What I really wanted," he said at last, "was a religion for my heart. Try to understand me. The God we worshiped in the Temple at home, never loved me. He was just a big eye behind a lamp, looking to see if I behaved myself, or if He could do to me what He did to Job.

Maybe He loved Israel — but not Samuel Levy. In church I had Jesus. Everybody loves Jesus, even a Jew. How can you help it, when He loves you back?

" And there He was, this Friend, Jesus, in the church. Did He love me? Why not? Did He want me? Sure.

" So I came over. I thought maybe I won't be welcome everywhere, but He'll be there, and He'll be glad to see me. Well — it's not like what I expected. I can't find Him anywhere! nobody even speaks of Him. My mother, where is she? Somewhere with her ancestors. The angels, you say, are all dead in Assyria, or else in heaven with the popes. Maybe that's where Jesus is. What do you think? Did I make a mistake? "

The professor did not reply at once. Instead, he arose, and taking up his fishing-pole, carefully drew in the line. The bread had disappeared.

" There are fish in this river," he observed: " they ate my bread."

So saying, he took out another small piece, and tied it tightly to the line. Then he placed it gently in the water. The current caught it and lodged it under a stone, where an eel ate it, with exclamations of pleasure.

But the professor returned to his seat with a thoughtful air. " My friend," he said, " I can see that you love Jesus; but I wonder if you understand Him. You seem to me like those early disciples, also Jews, who followed Him in grief rather than in joy. He spoke to their inmost ears; but only their ignorant hopes and fears replied."

He looked around him, at the sunny, peaceful river bank, the flowers growing in the moss, the cedars bending dark and green above them. He looked back at the city, from whose narrow white houses a low and happy murmur arose and mingled with the river-silence.

"Look," he said, "at this city of houses, this home of reunion, this heaven of repose; here its inhabitants see, and hear, and know only what they desired or wished on earth; here the few powers they developed in life, and only those, find eternal employment. Here is no want, no change, no hope, no pain, no fear — only peace, only rest from the battle, only shelter from the storm."

He put his hand once more on Mr. Lewis' knee. "But the Son of Man," he said gently, "hath not where to lay His head."

Chapter X

PROFESSOR WUTHERIDGE went home without his carp, and without a herring to bring his mother. Nevertheless, his mind was peaceful; as he walked back through the streets, he thought to himself, How fortunate it is that there are no angels here, in whose glorious company I should feel abashed and uncomfortable. What place is there for glory in heaven? The heart of a free man longs for a democracy, where all will be neighbors. From his mother he expects love; and from his father wisdom and benevolence. And from those around him, friendship and good company.

Glory is for earth, whose troubled dreams still deal with day and night, with light and dark, with life and death.

Musing in this fashion, he passed through the gate of his garden; and saw his father seated on the steps of his house, with his knees drawn up under his chin. As the professor walked up the pebbled path neatly bordered with shells, Mr. Wutheridge gazed at him politely. "Well, sir," he inquired, "did you have an agreeable fishing?"

The professor sank down on the steps beside him. "Yes, father," he replied; and taking off his hat to cool his forehead, he added modestly, "Several fish were attracted to my line, but nothing serious came of it.

486

"I had also," he remarked, after a pause, "an enjoyable talk with Mr. Lewis of the Museum."

"Splendid," said Mr. Wutheridge, without enthusiasm.

And he relapsed into silence, from which he presently burst out with:

"Your mother has gone for a walk with your Uncle Ludwig."

"That will be nice for them both," said the professor happily.

"But what about me?" asked his father. "What is there for me to do? Am I simply to sit here, all by myself?"

"I will sit here with you," said the professor.

Mr. Wutheridge gave him a vague look. "Yes," he said; "thank you. But whom am I to talk to?"

("To play with?" thought the professor, startled. "Is that what he means?")

He replied:

"Shall I tell you what Mr. Lewis had to say?"

"Where do you think they are?" demanded Mr. Wutheridge.

"Who are?" asked the professor.

"Matilda, of course," replied Mr. Wutheridge. "And Ludwig."

"They are not by the river," said the professor, "because I just came from there."

"That's something," said his father.

"Perhaps they're in the Museum," suggested the professor.

But that only made Mr. Wutheridge feel worse than ever. "Learning things," he said bitterly.

He hugged his knees. "They could have waited for me," he said.

"But they never consider my feelings.

"Anyhow," he burst out finally, "it's me she's married to, not him, and I won't stand for it."

"What," asked the professor apprehensively, "will you do?"

"You'll see," said his father darkly; "I'll do something."

And he mumbled between his knees,

"She'll be sorry.

"I'll get sick," he declared. "I'll get an illness. I'll go to bed and groan."

"Do you want an illness?" asked the professor, surprised.

"I want her to be sorry," replied Mr. Wutheridge stubbornly.

"Well," said the professor thoughtfully, "I don't think you can get an illness here."

"I know it," said his father gloomily; "I've tried.

"Just the same," he concluded, "I won't have her not paying attention to me. I won't have her going to the Museum with Ludwig, and learning about things, while I stay home. That's not what marriage ought to be, at all. It didn't use to be like that at home. She wouldn't have dared.

"For one thing, I caught colds very easily."

He peered anxiously into his son's face. "You don't think she likes him better than she does me?" he asked.

The professor smiled. "I think she likes you both very much," he replied. "But perhaps — Perhaps, my dear father —

"She would like you even better without a cold."

"No," said Mr. Wutheridge firmly, "no. She was always happiest with me when there was something to take care of. I am sure of it, because I was happiest then, too. Merely having her there, so sweet and capable, looking after me. . . . It was a great temptation to become an invalid. However, I remained healthy, on the whole. A woman feels motherly toward a man, or nothing. I mean, of course, a good woman. It is called the maternal instinct.

"Besides, she ought to like me best, anyhow."

"So?" said the professor. "I was not aware . . ." And he added simply, "You don't think that perhaps a woman would rather feel something a little less motherly . . . ?"

Mr. Wutheridge looked at him in scorn. "You never married," he remarked.

"That is true," replied the professor. "But I have read the poets."

"So have I," said his father; "I have read Longfellow, Emerson, Tennyson, Whittier, Mrs. Browning, the Rossettis, Bulwer-Lytton, and a young man named Stevenson. Well, what of it? A good woman is a good woman still."

And he quoted nobly.

"'Build thee more stately mansions, O my soul.'"

"Yes," said the professor. "Still —

"You don't think that mother — that a woman would rather have children out of her own body . . . ?"

"I am the one," continued Mr. Wutheridge inexorably, "with whom she ought to go to places like the Museum. Because, after all, I am her husband, and she has certain responsibilities toward me. It was I with whom she lay in bed; it was me she consoled in the dark."

"Excuse me," said the professor hastily, and he got up to go.

"Here," exclaimed his father, "where are you going? Sit down; what do you want to leave me for? You are just like your mother. All right — go; and leave me all alone."

The professor sat down again. "Very well," he said politely; "but let us talk about impersonal things for a while. Did you ever hear of the buried cities of Sumeria, of Lagash, of Akad, and Gish?"

"What a day for a picnic," murmured Mr. Wutheridge, gazing gloomily about him.

"The legend of the flood," continued the professor, "was handed down to the Sumerians, a non-Semitic people, from the Semitic tribes they conquered when they invaded Mesopotamia from the north. The Sumerians, in turn, handed on the legend to the Babylonians who conquered them; and from the Babylonians, the Jews gave it to the world. The Sumerian name for Noah was Uta-Napishtim; and he lived in the city of Shurippah, by the Euphrates."

"Fine," said Mr. Wutheridge. "Splendid. The thing is, one is always being made a fool of by a woman." He let go of his knees, and sat up. "I'll tell you what we'll do," he exclaimed; "we'll go fishing. When she gets home, we'll both be down by the river, enjoying ourselves, and not here at all."

"But father," expostulated the professor; "I have already been fishing."

"Then," said Mr. Wutheridge enthusiastically, "We'll go to the Museum. Just you and I. I'll show you Noah's Ark in a bottle. A very interesting thing. Come along."

And leaping to his feet, he attempted to pull the professor up after him.

"Hurry," he cried, "or they'll be home again before we get there."

But it was already too late. For at that moment Mrs. Wutheridge and Uncle Ludwig themselves turned in at the gate, and started up the pathway to the house. The lady was in the best of spirits; but the professor thought that Uncle Ludwig looked a little anxious.

"George Herman," cried Mrs. Wutheridge as soon as she caught sight of her son, "did you catch me a fish?"

The professor did not answer; instead, he turned to look at his father, who had drawn himself up, cold and noble, in the doorway.

"Ah," said Mr. Wutheridge; "so you are home again. Well. Ho."

And he gave them both a frigid bow.

Mrs. Wutheridge regarded her husband with a smile half amused, and half weary. "We had a lovely walk," she said gently; "and Ludwig plucked these anemones for the house."

She held out a little bunch of flowers, the color of the sky. "But I thought," she added, "that they would do better in our room, my love, next to your bed."

Mr. Wutheridge regarded her distantly. "Then you weren't at the Museum?" he asked.

No, they'd simply been walking. . . .

"Walking," he exclaimed with an indignant snort; "and what was I to do, Matilda, while you were walking? Sit here, by myself all day, with no one to talk to? Walking . . . how do I know you were walking?"

"George," exclaimed Matilda dangerously.

"Oh," cried Uncle Ludwig, "I say . . . remember where you are."

"Well, anyway," mumbled Mr. Wutheridge; "I've had a dashed unpleasant day. I don't feel very well."

"My poor darling," cried Mrs. Wutheridge; "again?"

"Yes," said her husband loftily, "again. But just the same . . ."

"Ludwig," commanded Mrs. Wutheridge, "take these flowers, and put them in water. I'm going to see to it that George lies down. My poor boy. Come, we'll go inside together; and while you rest, I'll tell you of what I was thinking all the time we were walking. Can you guess?"

So saying she smiled at him archly.

Mr. Wutheridge blushed a deep pink. "No," he said; "I cannot." And he followed her into the house.

But on the threshold Mrs. Wutheridge stopped long enough to smile, and to make a little face — was it a wink or a pout — at the professor. Whatever it was, he thought, with a sudden ache in his heart, it was charming — and exactly like a naughty little girl.

But the ache, as he sat quietly by himself on the steps, went on aching, in a small, lonely way. What was it he had said: what was it one looked for in one's mother, from one's father? And from all about . . . friendly company. . . . Where was his father, then, the father everyone had a right to have, no matter how old or how young? The father to look up to, to bring one's troubles to — not the same troubles one brought to one's mother, of course, but graver, manlier troubles, such as only a father would understand. Lagash, and Thebes . . . Those weren't troubles — but they were things one would want to talk about, naturally . . . Not, oh not one's father's troubles; and such troubles, besides . . .

He sat there for a long time, without moving, listening to the doves, his eyes veiled, his hands in his lap. At last, with a sigh he got up to go in. But just then a little girl with a wide, blue hair ribbon went running down the street, weeping bitterly. "What," he exclaimed, "tears in heaven?" And he ran after her, to console her.

She gazed at him dimly through waters of woe. "I

came too soon," she explained. "Next week I'd have been five." Sniffle. "And now I'll never be; I'll only be four-going-on-five forever and ever."

And she made a wet sound with her nose.

The professor nodded his head. "Yes," he said; "I, too, will never be five. And wouldn't I like to be; because then . . ."

"Then," broke in the little girl eagerly, "you're just grown up enough."

"That's it," agreed the professor: "you're just grown up enough."

Hand in hand, and much more cheerful, they walked down the street together, to see the Noah's Ark.

493

Chapter XI

WILLIAM WILBERFORCE MEIGGS sat in his tiny room
and stared at the motto over his bed: "A Man's Best
Friend Is His Mother." He could hear Emma's voice
down-stairs in the parlor, and his father's deeper replies;
they were laughing together, making happy remarks. He
supposed he was glad that his mother was happy — after
all the sadness and trouble she'd had in her life. Still, it
didn't feel like being glad — not the way he felt it.
"What's the matter with me, anyway?" he thought.

Was he lonely? Well, perhaps. But why, my goodness? Wasn't he used to being alone most of his eighteen
years? He had no friends to speak of — except his
mother. Yes, he'd had her then — far more, now that
he thought of it, during those last few lonely years, when
she'd gone, than he'd had her since. That was it: he'd
had her once; and now where was she?

She was there, of course — but it wasn't the same any
more. She didn't seem to feel like looking after him the
way she had once; he knew that, he could tell. It was as
though she'd turned away somewhere, and in turning had
forgotten something. Only he, William, hadn't turned
away; and he hadn't forgotten anything. All he'd been
aiming at those eighteen years was to be a good son, and
to love the mother who looked after him. If she didn't
want to look after him any longer, where was he?

And who would look after him? He couldn't very well do it himself; he never had, he wouldn't know how to begin. It wasn't just deciding where to go and what to say; it was a spiritual thing, being looked after. He wouldn't know how to do it all by himself. She still told him what to do; but her heart wasn't in it. That was what hurt; and that was how he knew she'd stopped looking after him.

There oughtn't to be mothers, if they were going to stop. You needed something that wasn't going to change, ever. Otherwise, better take care of yourself — if you could. He supposed you could, if you learned. Only, you wouldn't be likely to learn a thing like that up there, where they had Queen Victoria and Mother's Day and all the rules they had on earth, besides.

Look — there was the professor going by down the street, hand in hand with a little girl in a blue hair ribbon. Well, that was a funny one. Hey, Professor — Professor Wutheridge.

He thought he'd go after them; he could take the little girl with the hair ribbon's other hand, and walk with them, two grown up people and one little girl. . . .

Hey, Professor — wait a minute.

But when he got down-stairs, and looked in the parlor to make sure his mother wouldn't stop him, what he saw made him forget all about the little girl with the hair ribbon.

His father was kissing his mother.

Why should it make him feel so queer in his stomach? He stood there in the doorway with his mouth open; and his knees felt watery. Little girls on a Sunday-school picnic — brothels of shame — little boys' stories told in a whisper . . .

"Excuse me," he breathed and hung his head. He tried

495

to tiptoe backward, to creep out unnoticed. And not to look — not to have to look any more. . . .

But Emma had seen him. Flushed and confused, she pushed Mr. Meiggs away, and stared at her son. "William," she said, "come here."

He shuffled across the room to her, not looking up, seeing only a sort of haze in front of his own feet. "Yes, mother," he mumbled.

Frowning, she smoothed the hair away from his forehead. Then she tipped his face back, to look at him. But what she saw in his eyes, made her drop it again. "Well," she said. "Well —"

And finding herself blushing, she bit her lip.

"Bother," she exclaimed impatiently.

"We were just talking about you, William."

Something inside the boy let out a silent, derisive croak.

"Were you, mother?" he said dully.

Mr. Meiggs stepped back and pulled his mustaches. He felt embarrassed, but he was also enjoying a feeling of satisfaction. At home, among his friends — largely of the barroom — he liked to be seen kissing a good-looking woman; not that it had come his way very often. All in a spirit of gallantry, however. . . . But a friend was a friend: he wouldn't have wanted his son to stand there looking at it. On the other hand, to embrace his wife, although a pleasure — which was a surprise to him in the first place — was a pure and proper sort of thing to do; and it was time that William saw it that way.

Yes, he thought appreciatively, it was a pleasure to kiss Emma now. The dryness had gone from her embrace; she yielded herself with tender joy, she seemed to like it. That was doubtless because there was nothing sinful in it any longer. He, too, felt tender and happy. The mustaches remained to be pulled in a manly way, but his thoughts were young and innocent. He might have been a boy again.

All the more reason, then, for William to see it, and to find his place which was not — as Mr. Meiggs realized with a swoop of joy — in the first fiddler's seat, but in the second. No more second fiddle for Mr. Meiggs; not he; he had come into his own, he had come into his proper place as Emma's spouse, her love, and her life. And the younger and more joyous she seemed to feel, the more she seemed to want William to stand on his own two feet, and not bother her. Oh, very nice, very nice.

Probably it would be a little hard on William, but what of that? Sons who took a man's lawful wife away from him and made her over into their own mother, couldn't expect the man to feel sorry for them later, when they'd lost her.

And, if she turned back to him now, wasn't it natural? A husband and wife were the right thing for people to be, the only even thing. Fatherhood, motherhood . . . one went into them, and one came out of them again. Lovers . . . and then a father and mother . . . and in the end, lovers again.

In the end, peacefully . . .

"Yes, sir," he informed William, " you've been elected King of the May."

Well pleased with himself, he took his stand beside his wife, without, however, quite daring to put his arm through hers.

William faced his parents, his head and spirits equally drooping. King of the May . . . what new and horrid thing was that? From under his trembling lashes he cast a glance full of dislike at his father. You leave my mother alone, he thought; go on, leave her alone.

"What does he mean, mother?"

497

Mrs. Meiggs was vexed; her son's gloomy face troubled her, and she wanted so much not to be troubled. She wanted to be gay, and all-of-a-piece, as she had been before he came. Why did he always look so miserable; why did he remind her only of her duty toward him? Oh — duty. She disliked him for it. It made her feel irritable. So —

"Do you have to stand right on top of me?" she asked her husband.

That's right, thought William passionately; do you have to stand right on top of her?

"William," she exclaimed, "stop mumbling. Stop looking at your feet. Whatever is the matter with you? It's more than a body can bear."

William looked up obediently. "What do I have to be king for, mother?" he asked.

Mrs. Meiggs told him. "You're to have a crown," she said, " and walk in the parade. All the children will be in it. Mabel Johnson is the queen. You and she can walk together."

"But she's only eleven," cried William in consternation.

"What," said Mrs. Meiggs, " has that got to do with it? She's a sweet, well-behaved girl. You ought to be ashamed of yourself, making it so hard for your mother. You ought to be grateful, instead of doing nothing but make objections."

"I haven't made any," said William in a panic. "Only, couldn't somebody else be king, mother? I don't want to be. Please let somebody else be — please, mother."

Mrs. Meiggs was exasperated. "Why don't you want to be?" she asked. "What's the matter with you? To walk in a parade, with a nice gold crown . . . Can't you do something for your mother, for once, when she asks you? Or do you want me to get down on my knees and beg?"

"I know what it is," said Mr. Meiggs: "he's too good to walk in a parade, that's what. He fancies himself too high. Wants to be carried in a roll-chair, that's what."

"Be still, Meiggs," said Emma. "When I want your advice, I'll ask for it."

"I was just joking," said Mr. Meiggs.

"I'm too old for a children's parade," cried William.

"Too old," exclaimed his mother, "too old . . . and how old is that, pray? You're not too old to expect your father and me to take care of you. You're not too old to come tagging after me like a sheep wherever I go — till I vow I can't call my soul my own. You're not too old . . ."

"I'm sorry," mumbled William. "I won't any more. "But not King of the May, mother — please don't make me. . . ."

Mrs. Meiggs stamped her foot. "And I tell you," she cried, "that you're going to be king, and there's an end to it. You're going to the armory with me to-morrow, and be fitted for a crown. I've worked hard enough for this, and I won't have you spoiling it for me. If you don't want to do it for your own sake, then you'll do it for mine, whether you like it or not."

And pushing past Mr. Meiggs, she stamped out of the house to cool her face in the heavenly air.

"Well," said Mr. Meiggs, looking slyly at William, "you've done it this time, young man. Too old, hey?" And he burst out laughing.

But William crawled up-stairs to his attic room again. His eyes were blurred with tears; something hot and dreadful, like a storm, was getting all ready to burst inside him. It felt like hate and misery; and he couldn't bear it. How dared he feel such a thing? It frightened him. Think where he was. His glance fell on the motto over his bed; it swam about on the wall.

Mabel Johnson — that little child . . .

" I'm not going to do it," he cried defiantly. " I'm not going to walk with a lot of children."

And suddenly the storm inside him burst. He rushed to the bed, and gave it a kick. " I'm not going to stay here," he cried. " I'm not going to stay here any more, not any more at all. . . .

" You wait and see."

Chapter XII

THE LITTLE girl's name was Elizabeth; and she had longed all her life to be five. But pneumonia took her at four-and-a-half. Well, there was nothing to do but make the best of it.

She trotted along, holding on to the professor's hand, and discussing life's up and downs. "I came here all alone," she said. "My mama and papa aren't here yet." They'd be along soon, she guessed; she could wait. In the meantime she had a doll called Mrs. Og Beezle, because she looked naughty, although she didn't do anything. "She just looks," said Elizabeth. "But she'd be naughty if I let her.

"We could go home to my house," she suggested, "and play. You could be the papa and I could be the mama, and Mrs. Og Beezle could be our child."

"I wonder," said the professor, "if I would care for such a child, who looked naughty, and didn't do anything."

"Well," said Elizabeth thoughtfully, "we could say she did something. We could say . . ."

And reaching up on tiptoe, she whispered in the professor's ear.

"Bzz bzz bzz."

Professor Wutheridge looked shocked. "No," he exclaimed.

"She wouldn't really do it," Elizabeth explained. "It's only make-believe."

"Never," said the professor firmly.

"All right," said Elizabeth.

"What else shall we play?"

"We could play twenty questions," suggested the professor.

"I'll ask first," said Elizabeth quickly, "What's black and white and red all over?"

When the professor had guessed, it was his turn to ask.

"What king of Erech," he asked, "waged a successful war against King Khumbaba?"

"Oh," said Elizabeth, and looked around.

"You don't know," cried the professor accusingly.

"I do too," replied Elizabeth. "Only I don't care to answer."

"Gilgamish," cried the professor.

She gave a skip. "Don't let's play that any more," she said. "Let's play house. I'll be the mama, and you can be my little boy."

The professor looked down at the diminutive figure trotting along at his side. "All right," he said: "let's."

But when he made no further move, she gave a pout. "Why don't you begin?" she asked.

Yes, he thought, why don't I? But how did one begin to be someone's little boy? William would know, because William had been: all his life he'd been Emma Meigg's William. To belong to someone: how enchanting that was. To be told, George Herman, hadn't you better . . . and wrap yourself warmly . . . and here's a fine eggnog with nutmeg in it, because you look a little thin. . . .

That was only the least part of belonging, he knew. He could guess the rest, the heavenly feelings. Belonging:

that meant, first of all, not being alone. It meant more than arms to run to when things went wrong; because not being alone meant being together when things went right, too. It meant sharing things, the good as well as the bad. It meant looking at people with a gentle, whole look, because one wasn't alone — two people, really, were looking out of one face. There are two of us to like you, or to be liked by you: together we make a family.

Was it wrong to want to be a family? Perhaps it was — but everyone did. It meant not having to be proud all by oneself. Look, mother, I've been made a Fellow of the Royal Society of Archæologists. Well, my son, how marvelous of you.

So she was proud of him. And he could go quietly on with his work, while she took care of the medals.

Would you like a trip to Egypt, mother? I could show you where the frogs came up for the Israelites. Of course, my dear son, I'd love it. Leave the trunks to me.

But perhaps a mother wouldn't be interested in frogs, really . . .

Ah, well, that was it, she'd have to be, if she was a mother.

"I think," he said to Elizabeth, "that you'd better begin, just at first."

Elizabeth gave a hop. "Let's play," she said, "making up names. I'll begin. You're an old beard-in-the-face."

"You," replied the professor, "are a little bow-in-the-hair."

"You're a long white beard-in-the-face," she said earnestly. "You're seventeen and eleven lions and tigers."

And she burst out laughing. "You're nothing but an old dried-up apple skin," she cried.

"Am I really?" thought the professor.

"Perhaps she doesn't like me."

He was unable to make up his mind, because, looking back at the moment, he saw his mother hurrying after them. She arrived with her chin up, and her eyes stormy. "George Herman," she demanded, "where are you going?"

"This is Elizabeth," replied the professor, "and we are going to see the Noah's Ark.

"There is also a dried frog," he added, "which I would like to see."

Mrs. Wutheridge put her arm through his. Then she peeked across his stomach at Elizabeth, walking soberly, with long steps, at his knee.

"Ah," she said. "So you're Elizabeth.

"Well, oughtn't you be going home now, Elizabeth?"

"No, ma'am," said Elizabeth. "I oughtn't."

"Dear me," said Mrs. Wutheridge.

"Elizabeth's mother and father," explained the professor, "haven't come yet."

"Poor Elizabeth," said Mrs. Wutheridge promptly; "then she's all alone."

And she made a pleased sound with her lips, like a smack.

The professor looked at his mother with surprise. Was he mistaken, or did she seem to relish her remark?

"Yes, I am," said Elizabeth. Seeing that no one was looking, she stuck her tongue out at Mrs. Wutheridge.

Then she turned to the professor. "Let's play some more," she said in a wheedling way. "Do you know what you are? You're a . . ."

She had no chance to finish.

"You're a little girl with a dirty face," said Mrs. Wutheridge calmly.

Elizabeth gave a gasp. "I am not," she cried. And she added in tones of mortal enmity,

"You're a dreadful old worm in a bonnet."

"Really," exclaimed the professor, "Elizabeth . . . my dear mother . . . is this quite . . . I mean to say . . ."

"Anyhow," chanted Mrs. Wutheridge, "I haven't got a dirty face!"

Hanging on the professor's arm, she also gave a hop.

"Guess where I was to-day," she said to him.

"But I know where you were," he replied, thoroughly confused; "you were out with Uncle Ludwig. And then you put father to bed. And now . . ."

"Now I want to go down to the river," said Mrs. Wutheridge.

"I can't go down to the river," declared Elizabeth. "They won't let me."

Mrs. Wutheridge made a face. "All right," she said cheerfully. "You can go home, then."

"We were going," said the professor, "to see the Noah's Ark. And there's a dried frog which came up out of the water . . ."

"I don't want to see a frog," insisted Mrs. Wutheridge; "I want to go down to the river."

Elizabeth gave a stamp, lively but small. "I want to see the Noah's Ark," she exclaimed.

"Just the same," declared Mrs. Wutheridge, "we're going down to the river. So you may as well make up your mind to it."

She held the professor's arm tighter than ever. "Wasn't it funny," she said, "when I came home? There you sat, both of you, so solemn and gloomy. And poor Uncle Ludwig; he was all of a twitter. I love doing things like that."

She looked across at Elizabeth. "You wouldn't know what we were talking about," she said languidly. "We're discussing family affairs."

"I want to see the Noah's Ark," said Elizabeth.

"And anyway," she added, "we were playing together. you didn't have to come along and spoil everything."

At the same time she winked away a tear.

Mrs. Wutheridge looked at her coldly, across the professor's stomach. "You can't play with him," she said, "if I don't want you to, because he belongs to me. You're just a little-nothing-at-all, and if you had any sense, you'd run away home, and not bother us any more."

"Oh," breathed Elizabeth. "Ow," said she.

And with a howl she burst into tears.

The professor gazed after her retreating figure in dismay. Then he glanced at his mother; she was smiling.

"Oh, my," he said.

Shaking his head, he gave her a look full of reproach. "You hurt the child's feelings," he said.

Mrs. Wutheridge nodded gaily. "Yes," she admitted; "why not? There's only room for me. I don't want other little children playing with you."

Other little children, thought the professor . . . ?

All at once her mood changed. "Now come," she said gravely; "tell me: what am I to do with those two at home? They're so jealous of each other; and it's all so silly."

With that, she gave the sky an arch look.

But the professor gazed at her gloomily. "Tell me the truth," he said; "admit that you like it."

"I suppose I do," she replied. "But it's only in fun. Anyone can see that. After all, I am a wife and a mother."

"Are you?" asked the professor doubtfully.

"You do not seem like a mother to me."

"Don't be tiresome, George Herman," said Mrs. Wutheridge coldly. "I asked you to tell me what to do, not to insult me."

"But that," said the professor drawing himself up, "is just the trouble: I'm not sure that I know what to tell you. And what is more, I'm not at all sure that I care. At the moment, it seems to me that I am more interested in the dried frog at the Museum. I was going to show it to Elizabeth."

He added thoughtfully,

"She would have enjoyed seeing it, I think."

Mrs. Wutheridge let go his arm, and stood still. "Oh," she exclaimed, "you are tiresome, after all. You're like your father all over again; always wanting to do things I don't want to do. . . .

"Well . . . go to your dried frog, then."

And with a toss of her head, she turned back to the house.

The professor looked after her sadly. "Now," he thought, "I've vexed my mother."

But even as he spoke, his face assumed a doubtful expression.

"My mother?" he thought. "Why do I say that?"

"I have no mother or father here. I am an old man with a beard; and they would all like to be my children. How lonely that is for me.

"Why do I stay here, I wonder?"

And with slow steps, and in a thoughtful way, he turned in the direction of the river, to stand for a long time looking out across its moving waters.

Chapter XIII

MRS. CRISP had great hopes of Mr. Lewis. She could not exactly express them; and she did not intend to love him. Nevertheless, she felt giddy when she thought about him.

In the first place, there he was, right under her nose, forever and ever. Like her husband, of course — but she knew her husband by heart. There wasn't very much to know, when you came right down to it; and as for what there was, all she could do was to sit still, and look at it. Mr. Lewis, on the other hand, would take a bit of finding out; she thought that she might move a little, in the finding. She felt a sweet stir at the thought.

To move — to live, to grow, to put out branches like a tree, leaves, even, maybe . . . Not to be winter-locked any more, with nothing moving, nothing even stirring ever so faintly, anywhere. . . .

To grow . . . ? What a thought — at her age.

Still, there it was. It didn't feel like growing, exactly; it felt like curiosity. Finding out . . . what she'd missed, perhaps, for one thing . . . that is, supposing she'd missed anything, actually.

Well, she'd ask, now, and find out.

They went together on Mother's Day to admire the parade. As they walked down the street, among other couples also moving in that direction, she said to him:

"I wonder that you don't miss your wife more, Mr. Lewis."

"No, ma'am," replied Mr. Lewis, "I can't say I do. Seeing," he added, "that she died before me, and in the arms, you might say, of another man — which is one reason, I suppose, why she isn't here; one, that is."

"Oh, dear," said Mrs. Crisp. "Oh, dearie me."

"No," said Mr. Lewis firmly, "I don't miss her. What I miss is Jesus and the angels."

"Yes," said Mrs. Crisp; "that's a queer one."

"And I mean," continued Mr. Lewis, "to find them, before I'm done."

"In another man's arms," murmured Mrs. Crisp dreamily. "I suppose people are like that, after all.

"Not that it matters to me, of course," she added.

"What a time of it you've had, by and large." And she took hold of his elbow through the crowd.

Mr. Lewis did not notice her.

"If He isn't here," he said, "where is He?"

Mrs. Crisp shook his arm. "Dear me," she said; "are you always thinking about religious things?"

"What else should I think about?" demanded Mr. Lewis with some asperity.

"You could think about your wife," suggested Mrs. Crisp.

Mr. Lewis demanded to know if that was what he had come to heaven for.

"You came," said Mrs. Crisp, "to get out of roasting in hell-fire, that's what. And for the glory of His Kingdom," she added, a little irrelevantly.

"So then," said Mr. Lewis, "I should think of what goes on between husbands and wives? Don't be foolish."

She gazed up at him innocently. "Isn't it all the same?" she asked. "What's marriage for, but the glory of God? And what's the Church for, but to get you into heaven?"

"Is it?" said Mr. Lewis.

"Well, you're here, aren't you?" asked Mrs. Crisp.
"And so am I," she added.

"Hum," said Mr. Lewis.

"If you didn't want to come," said Mrs. Crisp coldly, "why didn't you stay Jewish?"

"I wanted love," said Mr. Lewis. "And Jews don't get it."

Mrs. Crisp nestled closer to his arm. "There," she said; "didn't I tell you? Love."

"No," said Mr. Lewis firmly, "not love, not like that — not like what goes on between men and women. What I mean is love — that's something else again. Like what you'd feel inside your soul for something beautiful you couldn't quite get hold of. Like what you'd feel for goodness.

"Like what you'd feel for God."

"It's all the same," said Mrs. Crisp.

Mr. Lewis looked at her sternly. "Do you believe that?" he asked.

"I was taught it," she answered; and her face took on a stubborn expression.

"Well," said Mr. Lewis, "I wasn't. I was taught that God's goodness was far away, like something you couldn't reach to; but if He felt like it, He'd forgive you. Does it matter if you're happy? Not so long as you behave yourself. There's no way out of that for a Jew, because God never promised them anything. Does he say to a Jew, come to me, all ye weary laden, and I will give you rest? For forty years the Jews lived in the desert, looking for a home. When they found it, He took it away again. And what does your church do? It makes a home up here, for dead people. Well — heaven or Jerusalem, what's the difference? It's all the same; God's love is still far away, like something you couldn't reach to. God's love — it should make you feel new, and ready to split with happiness. It should be for the living; because they are the ones that need it. It should be close at hand, where you could touch it; in your heart, where you could feel it."

"Well, just the same," Mrs. Crisp insisted, "it's peaceful here." And she quoted: "' Jerusalem the golden, with milk and honey blest. Beneath thy contemplation, sink heart and mind oppressed.'"

"And that's heaven enough for you?" asked Mr. Lewis.

"It's heaven, anyway," replied Mrs. Crisp. "And whether it's enough or not, don't hardly signify."

Chapter XIV

By this time they had come to the square, where a crowd of people was already gathered, composed of the mothers and fathers, aunts, uncles, and ancestors of the children chosen to march in the parade. Worming their way to the front, Mr. Lewis and Mrs. Crisp found themselves facing the Museum, on whose porch, garlanded with flowers, sat the committee, headed by the curator. Doctor Crisp's glance was sober, but tender, fitting to the occasion, which everyone recognized to be of the first importance.

Soon the talk among the parents ceased, and all necks were craned in the direction of the river, from which the steady thumping of a band began to make itself heard. The committee on the porch stood up to look; the crowd rustled, exclamations were heard, and several ladies, standing on their toes, or bending forward, bumped against their neighbors, who received the bump with good nature.

"Here they come," said Mrs. Crisp.

As she spoke, two elderly gentlemen, dressed in white, appeared on the street, marching soberly forward, and pushing in front of them long-handled brooms. They were followed by the parade itself, led by the band, composed entirely of orphans. Elizabeth marched in the band; she held a harp, which she plucked from time to

512

time, but seeing that she walked between a trumpet and a drum, her contribution to the music was almost inaudible. Nevertheless she kept glancing from side to side, to see if the professor was there, as she wished to be noticed.

Behind the band, when the parade started, was William Wilberforce Meiggs, wearing a gold crown, and beside him Mabel Johnson, also with a crown. The king and queen were stationed beneath a sort of canopy, covered with roses, and upheld by pages.

The progress of this unit was necessarily slow; and since the children were all of them anxious to arrive at the Museum well up in the parade, so as to see their parents and be seen by them in turn, the older ones, who had been placed in the rear, soon forged to the front, jostling and upsetting the very small ones, whose prostrate bodies remained sunk in dejection along the march, while giving voice to their grief. These hardier children, once under way, had no intention of stopping for the royal canopy, but pushed on regardless; with the result that the band arrived first, the older children second, and the royal pair in the rear, followed by the babies, many of whom preferred, however, to sit down on the curb and gaze at the spectators, or to try to eat the flowers they carried.

As soon as the parade had come to a halt in front of the Museum, the Reverend Crisp arose from his seat. " My friends," he intoned in a deep voice, " my brethren: This is indeed a happy, happy day. For it is the day on which the son remembers and reveres his mother. Who amongst us has not sat at the knee of a good and gentle woman, and gazing up into that loving face, shining with tenderness, learnt the first articles of faith? Who amongst us, I say, has not gone to that comforting and

513

comfortable lap, there to weep out his childish sorrows. And later, in manhood's busy season, who has never turned back to that remembered haven, for forgiveness and understanding?"

" I have a friend here," said Elizabeth to the drummer. " Do you see somebody with a long white beard anywhere?"

" Everywhere," said the drummer.

" Oh," said Elizabeth, " you're so provoking."

" You're no great beauty yourself," replied the drummer.

" But," boomed Doctor Crisp, " a mother's love is not a selfish love. No, my friends, no, my brethren: there is no element of selfishness in a mother's pure love for her child. The word I think of more than any other in this connection, is the great word, the mystic word, sacrifice. I am reminded of a story told of one of our missionaries — a father, this time, but nonetheless, a parent. This devout man, hemmed in during an uprising in China, is said to have exclaimed just before he was killed: ' When you take the news back to America of my death, tell them that my final message was that when my boy is twenty-five years old, I want him to come here to China as a missionary.' How great a spirit to give birth to so great a vision. And what a consoling message for the young man. When Mrs. Adoniram Judson was about to bid her children farewell upon the ship in Burma, as they were leaving her in order to return to America to be educated, she took them in her arms one after the other, covered them with kisses, and raising her tear-laden eyes, exclaimed, ' I do this for the sake of Burma and Jesus Christ my Savior.' Oh, that we too may feel the greatness of that vision today."

" Eh," said Mr. Lewis, " what's that about Jesus?"

"Nothing," said Mrs. Crisp. "It was about Mrs. Adoniram Judson."

Under the canopy covered with roses, and held at a rakish tilt by the four weary canopy-bearers, the queen shyly took the king's hand. "Isn't that beautiful," she breathed. "Don't you love it?"

King William withdrew his hand. "Love it?" he said; "what would I love it for? She got rid of them, didn't she? They went home, and she stayed in Burma. All that about mothers and fathers; it makes me sick. People do what they want; it hurts them sometimes, but they do it, and the groans don't count.

"I'm going to get out of this. You wait and see."

"Let us now," cried Doctor Crisp, "rise and pay tribute to our own Mrs. Emma Meiggs, who is here to-day as the representative of all of us, and as the symbol of that eternal good, that endless joy, that priceless boon — motherhood."

At this he stepped aside, the door of the Museum opened, and a number of ladies appeared, representing the different reformed countries. These took their places, making way for Mrs. Meiggs, who came hurrying through the doorway while the band played, wearing a large gold crown, and carrying a bouquet of roses and lilies-of-the-valley in her arm.

"Ho," said Mrs. Crisp; "so that's it. Well, she don't look so handsome as all that, to my way of thinking, if you want to know."

And she added, under her breath,

"Anyway, whatever comes, I'm saved."

Mr. Meiggs in the forefront of the crowd, raised a mild cheer; the spectators sang "Rock of Ages, cleft for me"; and Mrs. Meiggs posed in the doorway.

"Go on," said Elizabeth to the drummer; "don't be

515

so mean. You're bigger than I am. Look around a little. He has a long white beard."

" Stop bothering me, will you? " cried the drummer. " Can't a person have any peace around here? "

Mr. Lewis stood in the clear light of paradise. Before him were grouped the children; beyond them, on the porch, stood the committee of the righteous, Doctor Crisp, the ladies representing the reformed countries, and Mrs. Meiggs with her arms full of flowers. A little in front of him was William, his eyes smarting with bitter and childish tears; and all about him the parents nodded their heads, gazed at their own children, whispered, and blew their noses.

The little darlings.

Bless their innocent little hearts.

A fine looking woman, that.

Yes, sir, a real mother.

So, reflected Mr. Lewis: whatever comes, she's saved. Well, now — what does that mean, saved? What did she gain; or what did she lose?

What she gained is right here under our noses: peace, and her own righteousness forever and ever. No more pain, no more terror, no more growing old, and dying; bread and milk, and honey if she wants it; Doctor Crisp, the Museum, the company of the blessed, without sin — or anyhow without much sin. . . .

What did she lose? Well, for one thing, she lost her life: you don't need eyes to see that. Fifty years without joy — that's what I mean. Fifty years of bearing with something she didn't like, so that she could come here. Fifty years of starving herself, her heart and her mind.

So now I look for Jesus here, with this starved woman. Was he interested in starving? Go away. Then why did He feed the multitudes on the shores of Galilee?

516

Why did He say, I am the Bread of Life?

I am not come to destroy, He said, but to fulfil. Let the dead bury their dead, for God is not God of the dead, but of the living.

All the same, life is not easy to find — not even on earth. Death is easy — everyone finds death. But life? Strait is the gate and narrow is the way which leadeth unto life, and few there be that find it.

And if you don't find it — what does He say? Ye are the salt of the earth, but if the salt have lost its savor, wherewith shall it be salted? Have salt in yourselves, and have peace.

Have salt in yourselves.

Doctor Crisp raised his hands. "Let us pray," he said.

Why, that's a way to live, thought Mr. Lewis, to have salt in yourself. What has that to do with death?

His heart beat; he looked at Mrs. Crisp with wide-open, shocked eyes. "Mrs. Crisp," he exclaimed, "Mrs. Crisp — I know where He is."

"Eh?" said Mrs. Crisp. "Where who is?"

Mr. Lewis did not answer her. "He's home," he cried. "He's home, where I came from — down there — on earth. He's been there all the time.

"Then what am I doing here?"

And turning on his heel he pushed his way wildly through the crowd, in the direction of the city.

Once clear of the crowd, Mr. Lewis moved with more deliberation. He was in a hurry, but there was time, still, for what he had to do. He went home. There he gathered together his collection of gold pieces.

There's no use taking them, he thought. Sooner shall a camel go through the eye of a needle than a rich man shall enter the kingdom of heaven.

I shall leave them to the poor.

517

And seizing a pen, he wrote out a last will and testament: I hereby bequeath my collection of gold pieces to the Museum, to be known forever as the Samuel Lewis Collection.

The will did not entirely please him; but he did not know why.

He left the house, and walked rapidly to the river. There he stood for a moment on the bank, admiring the warm light, breathing in the air perfumed with cinnamon and lilies. Behind him he heard the singing in the square, the faint thump of the drum, the light tuneless voices of the children. His heart contracted with sudden anguish; all at once a desperate fear took hold of him. The river stretched dark and broad before him; was that a mist on the opposite bank? He could not see very clearly. What if there were no other shore? What if terrible sea-monsters waited in those somber depths? What if dreadful whirlpools sang in those bitter currents?

He looked behind him; for the last time the light shone on the narrow houses, the orderly gardens gave up the incense of flowers. He took a last deep breath. "Yes," he said, " it's pretty here."

Faint with terror, he flung himself into the water.

Chapter XV

AT once a mortal chill bit through his bones, and his heart melted. It seemed to him that he no longer breathed; yet he struggled. He wished to turn back, but there was no longer any direction; there was only forward. In the icy darkness, strange creatures without form floated at his side; they spoke to him. "Samuel," they said, "do you remember your childhood? Think back a little. What was it you wanted? Love?"

"I have forgotten," said Mr. Lewis. "But perhaps it was love."

"Why, then," asked the voices, "did you run away from those who loved you? Were you ashamed of them, Samuel? They were hurt so easily. They fought with no one; when they were offended, they simply sat and wept."

But Mr. Lewis had forgotten.

"You were afraid," said the voices sadly. "You were afraid that you would be like them."

"Aï," said Mr. Lewis.

"You were afraid of such terrible meekness," the voices said. "Think back, Samuel: you are a child again. Who is that standing there with the pale face, and the dark eyes full of pain? That is your father, Isaac Levy. He has just been insulted; and those he loves have been insulted with him. What does he do? Nothing. He wrings his hands."

"I have forgotten," said Mr. Lewis.

The grave voices went on: "Your young heart breaks with sadness and with anger. You will not let people insult you, or those you love.

"What will you do? You will run away, you will be different, you will be strong and terrible. But you do not run away — not then — not yet."

"Forgotten," moaned Mr. Lewis. "All forgotten."

"Love is what you want," said the voices. "Your heart cries out for love. And he loves you, your pale sad father; but he makes you ashamed. No, you will not love him, it is too painful for you. You will have nothing to do with him."

"I have forgotten," whispered Mr. Lewis.

He was lost, there was neither heaven nor earth, he was naked and cold, without love, without hope, without father or mother. "I had forgotten," he said. The voices went on inexorably,

"I am the Bread of Life; I am not come to destroy, but to fulfil. For unto everyone that hath shall be given, and he shall have abundance; but from him that hath not shall be taken even that which he hath.

"What has a man more than his life?

"Sammy, you were ashamed of those who loved you. And love was taken away from you . . . even the little that you had."

Mr. Lewis struggled on through the icy waters, drowned in darkness. This is death, he thought; this is annihilation. There is no other shore. The voices of his strange companions grew closer and more urgent. They reminded him of something — something far away, something he remembered.

"Sammy," they said, "see, now, why were you afraid?

Were you afraid that people would hurt you, too; and that you would only sit and weep?"

"Yes," said Mr. Lewis. "I was afraid.

"I was afraid to be a Jew, like my father."

How sweetly, then, the voices replied:

"Ah, Sammy, you did not have to weep because your father wept.

"You had your own salt, even then. Didn't you know that, Sammy?

"You had your own savor."

The dark waters seemed to grow lighter; he could feel his body again, he could feel his limbs and muscles, he breathed, he took in breath. "Look," said the voices: "there is your home again, as it used to be. Now it is Friday evening, and the candles are lighted. Who is that sitting there in the corner, all by himself? That is you, Sammy. Look at yourself: should you be ashamed of what you see? You were a child, like anybody. You were a little tree growing, your roots were in good dust, in rich and noble dust. But all the time you were you, you were not the dust, you were the tree. You could have been a hero, even. Do you remember the little boy you played with one summer in the country — what was his name? Isidore. He was killed in the war; he was a hero, Sammy. And the little girl who kissed you so sweetly, in the old garden, behind her house . . . those eyes were the eyes of a Jewess, Sammy. Like your mother's."

"I remember," whispered Mr. Lewis.

A single current of hope seemed to warm the bitter waters. Perhaps . . . perhaps there was another shore. . . .

He swam more strongly; he could no longer see his pale companions, the deep blue water hid them, but their voices floated about him, strong and sweet, reviving, re-assuring:

Remember . . . remember . . .

Why were you ashamed?

Why were you afraid?

Oh, I remember . . .

Why was I afraid?

Why ashamed?

See, father, I am not afraid any more. I can even pity you, now; I am sorry for you, that is all. You were you, and I was I; but I was afraid I would be you all over again. Well, I am simply myself now. A man, a Jew — what does it matter? What did it ever matter? To live, that is what matters; to be myself again. I did not have to weep because you wept. I did not have to be afraid of you. I did not have to run away from you. I could have loved you.

I can love you now.

I have my own salt. I have my own savor.

I have always had it.

The water grew shallow; his legs touched bottom; and with all his strength he waded ashore. It was still dark, but there was enough light to make out the road. How new he felt, how young and light and free; joy seemed ready to burst in his heart. He set off swiftly, without a single glance behind. He was in such a hurry. . . .

In the dim light two figures appeared on the road before him, also walking in his direction. One of them was a young man, wearing a paper crown; and the other was an old man with a long white beard. But he hurried by.

"Who are you?" they cried after him.

"Hey — wait a minute."

He shouted back to them: "My name is Levy. I am on my way home, to meet a Friend."

Their voices followed him faintly. " What do you want so much," they cried, " that you rush by in this manner?

" What has He got for you? "

" The Bread of Life," answered Mr. Lewis joyously. " The Bread of Life."

*" For there is nothing hid, which shall not be mani-
fested; neither was anything kept secret, but that it should
come abroad.*

" If any man have ears to hear, let him hear."